The Devil's Wind

ALSO BY RICHARD RAYNER

The Cloud Sketcher

Murder Book

The Blue Suit

The Elephant

Los Angeles Without a Map

The Devil's Wind

A NOVEL

Richard Rayner

 HarperCollins*Publishers*

HarperCollins books may be purchased for educational, business, or sales promotional use. For information, please write: Special Markets Department, HarperCollins Publishers Inc., 10 East 53rd Street, New York, NY 10022.

Grateful acknowledgment is made for permission to reprint the following photographs: "064 DOG" by Michael Light from *100 Suns* reprinted with the permission of Michael Light. "Premiere at Carthay Circle" by Max Yavno reprinted with the permission of the Center for Creative Photography at the University of Arizona.

FIRST EDITION
Designed by Joseph Rutt
Printed on acid-free paper

Library of Congress Cataloging-in-Publication Data

Rayner, Richard.
    The devil's wind : a novel / Richard Rayner.—1st ed.
        p.   cm.
    ISBN 0-06-621292-8
    1. Organized crime—Fiction.   2. Las Vegas (Nev.)—Fiction.   3. Atomic bomb—Testing—Fiction.   4. Anti-communist movements—Fiction.   I. Title.

PS3568.A94D48 2005
813'.54—dc22   2004047570

05 06 07 08 09 WB/RRD 10 9 8 7 6 5 4 3 2 1

For Päivi, and Harry and Charlie.

A woman always has her revenge ready.

—MOLIERE

PART 1

California

1

SEPTEMBER 2, 1956 / LOS FELIZ, CALIFORNIA

I first met Mallory Walker high in the hills above Silverlake, at one of those parties where Luis Barragan announced his continued existence to the world. It was during the Labor Day weekend, and Luis, such a figure, almost a legend in architecture, was pretty much at his wit's end, in danger of sliding off the map. He was in his late fifties by then, maybe sixty, and it was years since he'd designed a building. He still lived large, considering he was a man for whom so much had gone wrong. But, then, in life, as in architecture, Luis had a reckless disregard for convention and the niceties. And luck never quite left him.

"Good of you to show your face," he said, reeking of gin and sweat and about half a gallon of lemony eau de cologne. He was rumpled, with hair flowing like milk out of his ears and from the open neck of his blue silk shirt. "Come in here," he said, dragging me into the kitchen, where it was quiet and a tray of filled martini glasses stood on the counter, waiting for the help to take them out. Beer dripped from a chubby keg on the breakfast-nook table and a fly buzzed, drowning in the dregs of a tequila sunrise. "I dreamed about you last night, Maurice. You were lying dead in the desert."

"I'm touched, really I am," I said. "But you should worry about yourself."

"Don't I know it," Luis said with a deadpan, almost dazed expression. He was big, a belligerent man with multiple chins, eyes set far apart, and scars on his forehead, and his face puckered as he reached for a glass and saw the fly dying there. He thrust this glass aside and took instead one of the martinis, draining it in three long, slow gulps. He shut his eyes and swayed like a tree about to topple. "Oh, God!" he announced with drama.

"How much do you need? Five grand, ten?"

His eyes popped open again. "Jesus, Maurice! How long is it since we've seen each other?"

"It's been a while."

"More than four years."

"Really? I'd no idea it was so long."

"After all we've been through together . . ."

Sometimes Luis had a voice like a phone ringing. He could give you the idea that once he got going he'd never stop. This was one of those times. Righteous indignation warmed him to his task.

"After all the trouble we've known, all the ups and downs, all the water under the bridge, and I finally decide to call you, and you offer me . . . *money.*"

With me he couldn't pretend. He was almost beaten and he was afraid. Sure, he'd swallowed his pride and invited me to the party. That meant something, but I enjoyed seeing him on the hook. "I thought you liked money, Luis," I said. "I do."

"I need work," he said. "There—I've said it. I'll design a fucking toilet if I have to. Anything."

Luis had mentored me in our chosen profession. He'd been my partner, my friend, and, later, the rival I left behind, at least in terms of wealth and the acclaim of the wider world, and I knew no other terms. My wife had turned up her nose when she heard about the party, and my solo attendance more than hinted at condescension. But I liked Luis, and not only because he reminded me of struggles I'd overcome. He was exuberant, alive, and he had a childlike enthusiasm in spite of everything. Though often angry, he was never jaded. Besides, he and I understood one another. People don't know much about the private lives of architects. We're not like actors or politicians, but we have our feuds, our traumas. Believe me. We're in the tough position of trying to be artists and practical men at the same time. This particular juggling act had left Luis with his balls all over the floor. Practical was something he knew about but couldn't quite bring himself to achieve. Once, years before, when I'd started working for him, I'd asked for the single most important advice he thought he could give a young architect. "Marry money," he'd said, maybe meaning it, maybe not. I'd gone ahead, allying myself with several millions of dollars and the daughter of a U.S. senator.

"Where's Jennifer?" I asked, referring to his wife, the third of his wives that I knew about. She was a designer herself, a good one, and the daughter of impoverished New York bohemians, folks with an eye for the good art they couldn't afford.

"Out of town."

He caught the question in my raised eyebrow.

"Back tomorrow," he said. "Or the day after. Soon, anyway."

"And the kids?" Luis hailed from Peru, originally. His children tended to be dotted throughout the Americas, like features on a map.

"With her."

"How convenient," I said, wondering what Luis had going on, already guessing at the answer.

We walked through the high, narrow hallway into the living room, a wide and airy sunken space that flowed through sliding doors onto a patio of dazzling tile. The room was filled with Luis's nice things, his pictures and his sculptures, but the atmosphere was of neglect and I wondered how long his wife had been out of the picture. One leg was gone from the chrome-and-black-leather sofa; a couple of Luis's guests perched there nonetheless, whispering as they sipped their cocktails, like determined revelers on a ship going down. Another fellow, dressed in black, with a beret cocked to one side, stood at the fireplace, eyeing Luis's family photos in their frames of ornate and tarnished silver. Perhaps he was thinking of stealing them. And through the sliding doors I heard the hubbub of jazz and saw the rest of the revelers, the shadowy figures gathered around the pool's late-afternoon dazzle, the losers and beatniks and hangers-on swilling the liquor that Luis must have gotten on credit from some merchant who never guessed that he was being stiffed. Luis, when he wanted, had fine manners.

"Who are *they*, Luis?" Some clown had started up on the bongos.

"Not your kind of people."

"I guess not."

"Artists."

"Oh, sure," I said. I hadn't come to the party to gloat, although I was happy enough to let him know who was calling the shots now. "I bet their art keeps them very busy. And laughing all the way to the bank, too."

"What about you, Maurice?"

Here it comes, I thought; soon he'll be down on his knees.

"What are you working on?"

"Oh, you know how it is."

"No, I don't," Luis said, stepping toward me, looming at my side like a shaggy bear. "Tell me."

"The people behind the building I've just done in Nevada. They want five more hotels. Three in Las Vegas, maybe a couple in Cuba."

"That's a lot of work."

"Yeah, I guess it is."

"Can you handle it?" he said, angling now, not even bothering to be crafty about it.

"Luis—are you asking me for a job?"

"Would you give me one?" He kept his voice buoyant but his shoulders were tense, hunched a little, struggling with the anger and humiliation. Here he was, the great Barragan, seeking employment from his former disciple. And there I was, Maurice Valentine, the man of the moment, realizing I might actually need and want him on board.

"Maybe," I said.

"We'd get to go to Havana—with someone else picking up the tab?"

"Frequently."

"Sounds like my kind of project," he said, expansive now, but still nervous, sweat falling from the creases on his forehead and splashing onto the black velvet of his monogrammed slippers.

"Get in line, pal," I said, toying with him, and we went through slid-ing glass doors, out of the room into the blaze of the setting sun and the beat of those crazy bongos. Luis's house was long, low, flat-roofed, pro-jecting straight out of the hill, held in place as if by architectural alchemy—that is to say, by steel struts that were invisible beneath the structure. He'd built the place soon after the war, when he'd been at the top of his game and in full command of his career, ranked along-side Wright, Corb, Saarinen, and Mies, the greats. The shimmering pool seemed suspended in midair and had thus far defied both termites and earthquakes. A metaphor, in a way, for Luis himself, who snatched an-other brimming martini from a waiter's tray but neglected to offer me one. This was another part of Luis—self-obsessed, oblivious. Or maybe this was how we always were with each other—jostling and jousting. And I did remind myself that he was in the process of digesting a hefty slice of humble pie.

"There's someone I need you to meet."

"Don't tell me," I said with an inward groan. "A girl."

"A young architect."

"Who happens to be female."

"How did you guess?" Luis said. His smile was wicked.

"I know you, Luis," I said. "Is this why Jennifer's out of town with the kids?"

"She's different."

"Aren't they always?"

Luis had confessed to me once his belief in the superior force of certain women, partners who would inspire him in work and to whom he could devote himself in worship, preferably of the sort that went on between the sheets. This figure of the muse—conveniently for Luis, or maybe not—presented herself to him in the shape of someone new every couple of years or so, and when he was around such women his stubborn dreaminess exploded into production. He took from them the black magic of their will; in return, he offered devotion, dedication, sub-mission. Sometimes they swallowed him in marriage. On other occa-sions they would abandon him and he would languish. What can I say?

Luis was a romantic, a character type I didn't completely understand and wholly despised.

"She's *saving* me," Luis said, hugging me tight so that I felt his sweat, and the reek of gin and eau de cologne rocketed up my nostrils. "She's been asking about you. In a way that almost makes me jealous."

And so, before I could protest, he introduced me to Mallory Walker.

2

$\mathcal{I}$ was a big-time architect, a man of the world, a cynic, adept at maneuver and compromise. Ideals and grand plans had no place in my life. I was scrambling always to get ahead, working always to make the process look *smooth*. I fancied that I knew about people, what made them tick and the noises they made. In my experience, money and power made things go, caused the squeals of delight and fear, the squawks, the base grunts of satisfied desire. In a more elegant way, or so I liked to think, I was driven by ambition. Maybe I was blinded by it, too. I'd risen high fast, and in my professional and social lives I tended to meet only people as jaded and unimpressable as myself. I was unprepared for an encounter with a woman whose motives were so pure she might have been a saint—or a devil. And so, for a long time, I got Mallory Walker all wrong. I should have been terrified. Instead, I scarcely paid attention as she strode toward us from the other side of the pool.

My first impressions were of a cool hand and a firm, bony handshake. A slender figure in blue linen and flat heels. A lean face with hair cropped short and bleached blond, almost silvery in color. Full lips, nose slightly upturned. An impression of impudence, of life. Her eyes were a pale gray-green, and powerful, of startling clarity; she looked at me as though she knew my every secret.

"Pleased to meet you," she said, as simply as that. Her voice was clear and clipped, with no identifiable accent.

A studied voice, now that I think about it.

"Isn't she glorious?" said Luis, barely able to restrain himself from bouncing up and down as he whispered in my ear. He was absurdly pleased with himself, and this, I remembered, was how things tended to go when he was around. Complications ensued, simple missions transformed themselves into unwanted drama, imbroglios. Once, when invited to design a bungalow, he offered a mansion, something more like a castle, really, complete with turrets and crenellations, and then fled to Mexico with the wife of the man who'd given him the commission. Of course, it had been a very *beautiful* castle. But I wanted no part of Luis's romantic shenanigans. Not that I was straitlaced or a Puritan, far from it. I liked to get laid. But my own infidelities were clear-cut, calculated. I believed in damage control. Better yet: no damage at all. I liked to think my indiscretions were discreet and discrete, without risk. The white suits I wore were always immaculate.

"There's a building of yours I adore," Mallory Walker was saying. Her voice did have an inflection, I now realized. She spoke like a patrician, a daughter of the elite. "It gives me goose bumps, actually."

"Is that a fact?" I said, anxious to be out of there, her refinement adding only a slight interest to what struck me as routine flattery. She's read something about the El Sheik, the hotel I'd built in Las Vegas, I thought. Or seen one of the newsreels.

"The Slominsky house," she said, and something sly and wicked flashed in those gray-green eyes. Evidently she thought she'd surprise me. She was right.

"How the heck do you even know about it?"

I'd built the Slominsky house in the desert about six years before—a throwaway, almost, a favor for friends. The Slominskys were Russians, émigrés, a family of vast and unknowable proportions. Different nieces and nephews and second cousins arrived on the scene week by week. They were like one of those families in Chekhov, always in crisis, and Konstantin Slominsky, the patriarch of the clan, was a musician, some sort of composer.

"There was never any press," I said. "Not even in the architectural papers."

"I've been there," she said, and her gray-green eyes seemed to drift and go misty before coming back to my face, full beam. It was as if, for a moment, she'd gone swimming somewhere. In some memory long ago.

"You know the Slominskys?"

"Not really."

Luis was already squirming. His chins jiggled. His slippered foot tapped. He made an ineffectual attempt to stop himself spilling his drink. "Damn!" he said, smiling between gritted teeth. Hearing praise for someone else's building didn't rank high on his list of pleasurable activities, especially when the building in question was mine, and most especially when the praise came from the lips of his savior, or mistress, or whatever Mallory Walker was to him. But Luis was returning to form, and he knew how to play the game.

"Mallory knows everybody," he said. "And she's seen every building in California. She's like you, Maurice. She's got *pull*."

"Luis, that's the most outrageous slander," she said, her hand touching the sleeve of his shirt. Her fingers were long, slender, supple, and strong-looking. She said to me in a smoky whisper: "Luis exaggerates."

I whispered back: "I know."

A waiter floated by, and Luis swiped a fresh martini in one paw, while his other, a massive square hand matted with thick hair, closed around the bare skin of Mallory's shoulder. She didn't react to the clumsy gesture, keeping her eyes on me all the while.

"Want this?" Luis said, offering her the glass.

"No," she said, turning to him with something cold in her voice and eyes. Whereupon Luis gave one of his silly grins and drained the glass while she watched, expressionless. A chilling moment: somehow she was egging him on, certain that her refusal of several ounces of high-octane liquor guaranteed his immediate consumption of the same. She's interested in control, I thought, and she knows how to achieve it.

Her scrutiny came back to me, and a faint smile played on her lips.

"Maurice has asked for my help on a couple of big projects," said Luis. From his pocket he fished a handkerchief of yellow polka-dotted silk and mopped at the sweat that ran in rivers between the scars on his forehead.

"That's great," Mallory said. "The old crew back together."

She beamed a smile aimed only at me.

"Nothing definite yet," I said. Over by the pool, that fool of a kid was making with the bongos again. "I'd better go."

"Stay!" Luis roared in protest, threatening to engulf me in his gorilla arms. "We'll go someplace. Get some dinner. The three of us."

"I'd like that," said Mallory.

"It's no good," I said. "I have to stop by the office."

"See?" Luis said, delight and amusement all over his face. Presumably I'd endorsed, proven, some observation he'd made about me earlier. Bully for the prescience of Luis Barragan. "He doesn't stop. Always planning the next move."

His voice once again shifted from its customary burr. It wasn't a ringing phone this time, but the boom of a circus barker. "Life's a ladder to this guy. Always moving up."

"Miss Walker—it was a pleasure to meet you," I said, ignoring him. "Luis, we'll talk."

He caught me by the door. His hands were gummy and the gin was in my face again. "Thanks, Maurice. I mean it. And I'm glad you met Mallory."

"How long have you known her?"

"A week. Maybe more."

"A *week*," I said. "And Jennifer's out of here already?"

"I know, I know," he said. He looked forlorn, placing a hand to his chest with a sad and almost exhausted sigh, the gesture surprising in this extravagant and theatrical man. "She's not like the others. I don't know what it is. She makes me ache."

3

*O*ur house, or, rather, one of our houses, the biggest of our houses (we had a few), was a palace in the Moorish style, built in Beverly Hills in the 1920s by a silent movie star who hanged himself in the five-car garage. Eight bedrooms, ten bathrooms, a billiards room, a gym, a pool tiled in green and gilt mosaic, a kitchen big enough for a one-ring circus, several baronial fireplaces, and a library with sets of leather-bound great literature that I dipped into sometimes; these volumes had been on the shelves when we moved in, and appeared to pass from owner to owner, as if enshrined.

A grand affair then, this house, with a vulgar swank I could be ironic about while not so secretly enjoying. "The architecture's a mess," I'd announce in an offhand way, "but the old place has got something. Maybe I'll knock it down someday, put up something of my own." I knew I never would. I'd married an American princess and it was only fair that our main residence should be complete with minarets and a baroque history, defended by electric steel gates with spikes on them. Luis Barragan, actually, had found the house for us; he said it reminded him of Barcelona. But then, Los Angeles, although no city of its own, had pieces of so many other cities in it.

In the living room I kicked off my shoes, flicked on a lamp, and padded across the glazed red tile to the bar, where I poured Johnnie Walker Black over ice cubes dropped into crystal. I made my way up the broad, open stairway that curved from the marbled hall, pausing for a moment at the top while I decided which way to go. Then I stepped into the bedroom of our sons, Chester and Bobby.

Checking on the children wasn't a habit of mine. I did my job as a father but didn't dote. I was the semi-distant figure who made jokes and sanctioned fun, was too busy to show up for their softball games, guarded the money and the tickets when we made our annual pilgrimages to Manhattan and Hawaii, and was called upon, only when all other avenues of diplomacy had failed, to settle arguments. Surprisingly, there weren't many of those. The boys were easy with each other. I saw them most mornings at breakfast; sometimes, if I'd been away on a job for a few weeks, I returned to find them transformed, grown inches at a time, abuzz with news of UFO sightings, *I Love Lucy*, or Mickey Mantle's latest exploits at bat. Only after a few minutes did I realize that these strange and individual creatures, already so much themselves, were in fact still mine.

The door, ajar, swung without a creak and opened wide at my touch, admitting me to darkness and the smell of warm, sleeping boys, a mixture of freshly laundered linen, filthy socks, sweat, and the sweet linseed compound with which they oiled their baseball gloves. They could each have had their own room—Lord knows, we had enough—but chose instead to share.

Ches was ten, born in 1946, four months after my marriage to Jackie, and Bobby came along a year later. They'd always been close and fought rarely—strange, given that they were half brothers. Or maybe it was because of that: Jackie and I had kept this secret about Ches's birth to ourselves, never so much as hinting at it or referring to it; perhaps the boys sensed the truth, and warded off threats to their brotherhood with a fervor full-blood siblings don't feel or need to worry about. I'm sure they knew more than we thought about all sorts of issues; at the same time, we were never going to find out *what* they knew—nobody keeps a secret as well as a child.

Gently, I reached out, brushing away the damp hair that was glued to Bobby's cheek. Maybe he'd had a nightmare; like me, he was prone. I touched Ches's head next, finding it, as I'd expected, cool and smooth, unruffled by dreams.

I smiled, standing amid their odors and warmth. I felt calm, centered, sure that I loved the boys equally, even though Ches wasn't mine.

I left them in bed the way I'd found them and pulled the door softly shut. I collected my whiskey from the table outside their room and walked along to our bedroom to find Jackie still awake, enthroned among pillows in a black silk nightgown that showed well against her pale, freckled skin. She was smoking and reading *The New Yorker*. A snifter of cognac threw its wavering shadow across a white button of sedative, her sleeping pill, on the nightstand.

"I looked in on the kids," I said. Jackie had been pregnant with Ches when we met, as she'd told me soon enough; she'd informed me, too, that she didn't know the identity of the father, and I can say in all honesty that I wasn't bothered. Do I protest too much? Did the subject nag at me secretly? I really don't think so, though I am no expert at mapping the hidden sources of my moods and feelings. I'd tried to shut all that out, even before I met Jackie. We were the product of the war and its promiscuous, liberated mood, all those years when a lot of guys in the military couldn't, or wouldn't, allow themselves to think they'd survive, and women, too, had joined in a sport whose name was getting laid as quickly, and as often, as possible. Besides, I said to myself, a senator's daughter inevitably came with a price tag, even for a rising young architect who'd won medals in the war. So I kept my counsel, making the marriage without regret. "They're sleeping in the same bed."

"They often do that," Jackie said, still reading the magazine, flapping a hand until she found her cognac. Her hair was ginger, her hazel eyes ornamented by plucked eyebrows, perfect arcs. Those eyebrows were theater in themselves. She cocked one now, looking at me at last, and put her glass aside. "How was the party?"

"Dull. I didn't stay long."

Shrugging off my sports coat, I slid back the door that led to my walk-in closet, my favorite place in the house, designed by me. Fifty slim drawers of polished oak held the shirts that were sent from Jermyn Street. Sumptuous suits, racked on a device that whirred from the wall at the push of a button, filled the space with the odor of soft, rich fabric. Scores of ties, hand-woven in silk in Florence, or in bright, vertically striped wool by a woman in the Orkneys, hung to the side of the wall-length mirror like festive streamers. My shoes were arrayed on the floor like soldiers on parade. Cuff links, bright with gold and enamel, lay in velvet-lined boxes. I must have had two hundred pairs.

I liked *things*, stuff, clothes, cars, always the best. And why not? They were the symbols of the taste I'd always known I had and had worked hard to afford. But I should say that my dream wasn't only about the rich wife, the big house, the shiny things; it was about being at the center of it all, close to the ticking heart of the mechanism where decisions were made, where the game was worked out—where magic happened.

"I'm thinking of asking Luis to come in with me on the hotels," I said, slipping into a silk kimono and shutting the closet behind me.

"I guessed," Jackie said with a quiet smile as I sat down on the edge of the bed. She always seemed to know what I was going to do before I did it. Which was strange, because I didn't consider myself predictable. But then she was much smarter than she liked to let on, smarter than me. She was tough, intuitive, exact.

"Is it the right thing?"

She laid aside the magazine and gave the question her full attention. "He's gifted, and he's the devil you know. You can always fire him."

"I'll probably need to."

"Probably."

"There was a new girl tonight. An architect. A rich kid *playing* at being an architect, more likely."

"Same old Luis. Pretty?"

"I didn't notice."

This made her laugh. "Sure she is. Especially if you tell me you didn't notice."

"She gave the impression that she wanted to go places."

"With *Luis*?" she said, looking at me archly before picking up *The New Yorker* again.

Thus, my wife: the senator's daughter, the realist, the transplanted Manhattanite whose gleeful cynicism had been tempered in the hot-house atmospheres of El Morocco and the Stork Club, the woman who disliked the sun and had seen the Grand Canyon and pronounced it "corny."

"Was she the savior type?"

"Luis wants to think so," I said, but then I remembered Mallory Walker's unyielding gaze. "Probably she's going to bleed him dry of every idea he's got."

"Daddy called," she said, bored with this subject already, flicking the pages of her magazine.

"And?"

I guess I sounded eager, and she stifled a yawn—pure theater. "He wants to have lunch with you tomorrow."

"What's that about?"

"I've no idea." Another yawn. "He never tells me anything."

"Oh sure," I said. Jackie was her father's most trusted confidante, and I waited for the scoop. But she wasn't going to give any more. Her face was a mask.

"Now come to bed, honey," she said, reaching for her cognac, making with the eyebrows and tapping the pillow beside her. "I'll make you forget Luis's girl."

4

*T*his is it, Beth!" says Dick Dyer, throwing an arm around his daughter's shoulders.

Beth, snuggling close to her father, looks up at the new sign, a brave red horse prancing against a white background above the gas station. She stares at the sign for a while, feeling the cozy heat of her father's body, and then her gaze moves toward the diner, a small concrete structure in the shape of a hot dog that was loaded off a truck and assembled within five hours two days ago. In the door of the diner, Bendix, the Negro chef, raises his hand in a slow wave, and Beth's face splits, grinning.

"Remember this day," Dick Dyer says. "Because here's what I know. If you put your mind to it, you can do anything."

Beth lifts her eyes to the adored face of her father, a big man, broad in the shoulder, with dark eyes and a witty mouth. His clothes are shabby, his pants are too short and flap like flags around his ankles, but he marches with a confident stride and carries with him the air of better, greater, things. He is, in his own way, a dreamer, a poet. He suffers from headaches, too, and sometimes Beth glimpses him sitting alone in the dark in the bedroom he shares with her mother, eyes screwed shut, hands clamped to the sides of his head. At such moments she imagines that his pain is a dragon and she is a warrior, a Joan of Arc, heaven-sent to slay it. She knows that she would do anything for him; aged eight, she is passionate and determined, qualities that never leave her, even in the worst times.

"Things have been tough, and I won't say they haven't," her father goes on. "But we didn't quit. And now we're pulling together and pulling through. Look at this place."

"It's great, Daddy," Beth says, surveying once again the splendors of the new forecourt, knowing that this is an important day for her father, and another big one for her, too, only five days after her birthday, when he'd put his face close to hers and his whiskers tickled her skin while, together, they blew out the candles on her cake. Today is the day when the refurbished gas station opens for business, complete with its shiny sign, new pumps, and hot-dog diner.

"Uh-oh, here comes Mommy. Better look sharp, youngster," he says in a conspiratorial whisper, and Beth sees her mother approaching, a slim, small-breasted woman with gray streaks in her wavy hair and an expression that seems perpetually haunted. Years later, when she thinks of her mother, Beth will be reminded of the Dorothea Lange photographs of sharecropper women, faces with a quality both stoic and haunted, not knowing when the next blow will fall, only that it will. Beth is close to her mother, but their intimacy never achieves the troubled glamour of her attachment to a father who can turn everything into a grand adventure.

"Why isn't Beth at school already?" Karen Dyer asks.

"Oh, come on, honey," says Dick in his quick, nervous way, grinning like he owns the sun. "Let the kid stay, at least until things get rolling."

"Any customers yet?" says Karen, who has brought with her the sweet, almost overpowering smell of fried onions. Beth can see the damp stains beneath the arms of her mother's cheap print dress.

"No luck yet," Dick says, narrowing his eyes as if the very act of squinting might summon traffic. "But it's early, babe, it's . . ."

"Only ten," agrees Karen, glancing instinctively at the pale band of skin that still stands out against the tan of her wrist; but her watch was hocked last week. "Or something like that. Did you put out those things?"

"Sure we did," says Dick, turning to Beth for support. "We put out fifteen of 'em."

"Sixteen," corrects Beth.

"All the way up and down Victory Boulevard," says Dick, referring to signs that read: GAS—EATS—NEW STATION—FREE COFFEE & GIFT.

"Good," says Karen, but now she brings other news. "Mr. Bendix says we need sugar."

"We bought sugar yesterday," says Dick Dyer, his handsome face creased in a frown.

"He can't find it anywhere."

"Goddammit," he says softly, hands moving toward the sides of his head, clutching at his thick, dark hair. With a sudden pang in her chest Beth sees the strain her father is under, starting to crack.

"I'm tired of this, plumb worn out by having to take care of every detail," he says, flat, weary, and Beth sees something awful pass between her parents—her father's aching need, and her mother's momentary dread of it.

"Don't worry, Daddy," she says, squeezing his hand. "I'll go get the sugar."

"Beth—would you, please?" her mother says. "Go to the Sherman Market. They give two bags for a quarter."

Moments later Beth has the coin in her jeans pocket and is on her bike, gliding through the shimmering heat on Oxnard Street, bumping up onto the sidewalk to avoid a thundering fruit truck, and then swooping down into the concrete gully of the flood-control channel that snakes all the way through the Valley. The channel, dry for months because of drought, gives Beth a clear run, and she stands up from the saddle on her father's old bicycle, feet pumping the pedals, jerking from side to side while she gathers momentum, then spinning dizzily along.

At the end of the journey, back on the surface streets, she leans the bike against a wall. The dim insides of the Sherman Market beckon like a grotto. At the door Beth stops in the cool air that pulses from the groaning refrigerators. She finds the shelf with the sugar, hoists two bags under her right arm, and reaches in her pocket for the quarter. Switching the sugar to her left arm, she tries the other pocket. Unwilling to believe the dread that has announced itself, she puts the sugar bags back on the shelf, and checks all her pockets until she is sure: the coin her mother gave her is gone, and, with the descent of this certainty, an image forms in her mind: the quarter jiggling, rising above the rim of the frayed denim pocket, tumbling through space, chinking against the hardness of ground, bouncing, rolling along the concrete gully. Oh God, I'll never find it, Beth thinks with despair, not in a million years. She considers, for a moment, the possibility of cycling back to the gas station and explaining what has happened. She knows how her mother will react, with a brief look of disappointment and an almost indiscernible sigh; it's the idea of her father that stops her, the black melancholy that will follow his explosion of rage.

Beth knows then that she will steal the sugar, and, though she has never stolen anything in her life before, understands intuitively that this step must be undertaken with confidence and resolve. While the storekeeper is busy with another customer, she walks back out into the blazing sunlight, not running, but not dawdling either, as though she has every right to be doing this. For a moment she convinces herself that she actually *has* paid for the sugar. But then she hears a voice:

"Child!"

Beth's heart almost jumps out of her mouth. In order to escape, she realizes, she must clutch the bags tight under her arms and run. Instead, hypnotized by the command in that voice, she turns, seeing, with a wave of relief that almost makes her knees buckle, not the shopkeeper but a white-suited man, much older. In his hand he holds a thin malacca cane, which he points at her with an admonishing waggle. The brim of a white fedora with a black band is snapped down over one eye. His air, Beth thinks, is rather grand, even though he has a mottled, blotchy face and an ugly nose like a beak.

"Do you like sugar, child?" he says, lowering the cane and leaning toward her. His voice is leisurely, gentlemanly.

"Not really."

"Are you *dreadfully* poor?" he says, moving even closer.

Beth stands up straight. "We don't have much, but we get by," she says, echoing the catechism she's heard a hundred times from her mother.

"Well," says the man, except that it comes out: *wuh-hale*. "My own autobiography would be entitled *Me and the Wolf.* The aforementioned beast being poverty, prone to be at the door, even for the best of us."

"You talk like a book, mister."

"Maybe I do," he says, his shaggy head snapping back. "But I've earned the right now that I'm so terrible old and decrepit. And what else do you do, excepting that you steal sugar?"

Beth glances up and down the boulevard, wondering whether it's too late to try to make a run for it. A truck goes by, rattling and heaving, the sun flashing off its windshield like lightning bolts.

"Any skills—mmm?"

Alarm hits her now, and she wonders whether this is the sort of man her mother has warned her about. The man's sharp gray eyes, peering out from beneath the fedora, seem to read her mind.

"Oh Lord, child, I don't mean anything like that. Look, I'll show you a trick!"

From a pocket in his vest he plucks a silver dollar. In a flash the coin is joined by another, and a third, all of them rippling up and down, in and out between his long fingers like a school of porpoises. Tossing the coins so that they soar and glint in the air, he waits, watching, and then, with a single snap of the wrist magically collects all three.

Beth's mouth is wide with astonishment. "How did you do that?"

"No, no, child," he says, waving a modest hand. "I refuse to divulge a secret of the trade."

"Are you a magician?"

"In a way, certainly," the man says, thinking about this, not unpleased. "It's your turn now."

Beth, realizing she's being called upon to perform, feels at a loss.

"Delight me! Enthrall me! *Astonish* me with your talents!"

"Don't have any," says Beth, digging with her toe at the ground.

"Come now," he says, soft and coaxing, purring almost like a big old cat. "Can you dance?"

"No."

"Can you *sing*?"

"No."

He stands up straight, legs akimbo, and growls, yanking the fedora even further down his face. "A poem, then?"

"I do know some poems. At least I *think* I do," she says, her brief enthusiasm replaced by a frown. "Daddy reads me poems. He has a book."

"*Wuh-hale*, that's excellent."

"I'm not sure I can remember any."

"Try."

He waits, expectant, while Beth screws shut her eyes, calling up the picture of her father and a book, incandescent beneath the lamp on the table in front of him, his face intent and his voice quivering. The words issue from her mouth like an echo:

> *But our love it was stronger by far than the love*
> *Of those who were older than we,*
> *Of many far wiser than we.*
> *And neither the angels in heaven above*
> *Nor the demons down under the sea,*
> *Can ever dissever my soul from the soul*
> *Of the beautiful Annabel Lee.*

The old man in the white suit, the wizard, as Beth now thinks of him, pushes his hat back from his forehead. "That's a beautiful poem, child, and very sad. Do you know what it means?"

"No, sir, I don't. I learned it from my father, that's all. It sounds kinda old."

"Poe."

"Excuse me?"

"That's the name of the man who wrote it. Edgar Allan Poe. His parents were actors. He was a drunk, a drug addict. He fell in love only once and he never got over it. He died young. He died obscure. Life didn't seem like life to him anymore. He wrote another poem, about a raven. Do you know that one, too?"

Beth's shoulders rise and fall in a swift, dismissive shrug. "My daddy doesn't like ravens. He says they're evil birds. Unlucky."

"Superstitious twaddle!" the man says. "Are you *entirely* ignorant, child? Are you a mere street urchin? Do you know anything *at all*?"

Beth answers with a defiant glare. "I know 'Annabel Lee.'"

"So you do," he intones in his musical way. "So indeed you do. Now! Do you know the next verse?"

"I think so."

"*Good.*" He seized the sugar bags and dropped them on the ground. With a strong grip he takes her face and turns it, so that, even as she looks the other way, down the street, her nostrils catch the whiff of tobacco on his fingers. "Try the next verse," he says. "Don't move your eyes. Don't move your face. Don't move a muscle. Let yourself go quiet and sad."

Taking a deep breath, Beth looks for the peaceful spot inside, the place known to her when she sits alone with her father, watching him while he looks over the newspaper or listens to a ball game on the radio.

For the moon never beams without bringing me dreams
Of the beautiful Annabel Lee;
And the stars never rise but I see the bright eyes
Of the beautiful Annabel Lee;
And so, all the night-tide, I lie down by the side
Of my darling, my darling, my life and my bride,
In her sepulchre there by the sea—
In her tomb by the side of the sea.

Finished, Beth feels light, free—exhilarated—and she sees the old man pushing the hat so far back on his head it seems certain to tumble from his head, the way the coin fell from her pocket. But, just in time, his fingers find the brim and pull it back down over his eyes.

"I'll be damned," he says slowly, fingering the dimple beneath his beaky nose. "The child has a gift, a considerable gift."

Reaching in the pocket of his white vest, he flourishes a business card. "You've heard of me, of course," he says, leaning on his cane.

Though the name on the card means nothing to her, Beth knows how she is required to respond and nods vigorously.

The man slaps his thigh. "You steal, and you act beautifully, child," he says. "Now you must learn to lie."

Beth, bemused, wants to ask what he means by this, but he's not through yet. Taking her roughly by the shoulders, he turns her again so that she faces north, toward the low green trees of the orange groves. "What's there? Just a few blocks away?"

"The railroad," she says, remembering the long lines of freight cars with hobos hanging off them, thinking of how she and her mother and father had arrived in the Valley three years before.

"You may not even need that train. But remember this, child. In this world we can always get to where we want to go, if we want to get there. *Always*, do you hear me?"

"Yes, sir," she says brightly, having heard the same hopeful, and dangerous, message from her father.

"What's you name, child?"

"Beth. Beth Dyer."

"*Wuh-hale*, Beth Dyer. I expect to hear big things of you one day. Great things! Mind you don't forget—magnificent things!" He raises his cane, as if threatening to strike. "Now take your sugar and git!"

5

SEPTEMBER 3, 1956 / BEVERLY HILLS

*J*oe Nelson snapped a breadstick and smiled with spiteful glee. "The old bastard has cancer of the colon," he said, almost purring with pleasure, describing the imminent demise of the senator from Nevada. "It's advanced. It's painful. He's finished." Joe's mouth opened like a cavern, a portion of breadstick disappeared inside, and he chomped mercilessly; his teeth were long, strong, yellow, snaggled; he had a punitive face. "He's fighting it. But he'll be dead in a year. Tops."

Joe slapped his hands together, brushing away the crumbs, the grin replaced now by something pained. He tried a laugh, but what came out was more like a gloating yap. "It just goes to show," he said. "Sometimes justice will be done."

Who could say what Joe had against the man, really? They were both Democrats, after all, but Joe was bipartisan in his ability to hate. I had only a general idea of what he'd pulled to achieve such high office. Jackie had never volunteered the details, if she knew them. Joe wasn't a leader through charisma but by virtue of his connections and clout.

"What's good here?" he said, taking a bored glance at the menu. He had dark eyes that were rarely interested, dulled by incessant calculation. We were at Romanoff's, in a privileged corner booth, and from where I sat I saw Romanoff himself, smile wider than the pinstripe on his gaudy suit, stepping forward to the restaurant door to greet a couple who were rich and famous or doing a convincing impersonation. Romanoff himself was a crook from New York who about twenty years before had decided to pass himself off as a member of the Russian imperial family. He was a fake, but Los Angeles was crazy for fakes if they got away from it. I knew from personal experience.

"Everything's good, Joe," I said. "But you'll have what you always do—the beef, rare."

Food was only fuel to Joe. He had no taste for wine or liquor or clothes or cars. Showgirls left him cold and he never gambled. He had a long, strong body and arms like a chimpanzee's. He had stiff, wiry, gingery red hair cut *en brosse* and a sour face that seemed always to be restraining rage. Often the attempts were unsuccessful. He was a merciless man who manipulated other men and got fun out of it. I think this was the only fun he ever did get.

"Find the waiter, will you?" he said, and I raised my hand, snapping my fingers. "Yeah, the guy's dying in agony and my only regret is I didn't have more to do with it," he went on, blowing on the shamrock that decorated his lapel, buffing the green enamel with his napkin. Joe was a professional Irishman. He spoke at St. Patrick's Day parades, made conspicuous donations to Holy Mother charities, and had put his name to a revisionist history of Cromwell; in fact this was largely the work of a Harvard Ph.D. to whom he'd given $3,000. Money could buy anything, so why not a name on the spine of a book? That was the tough part, the money part. So, yes, Joe was also interested in acclaim and public regard of a certain sort. Not that he was vain in the conventional way, but he expected his due, and on terms he refused to compromise. He was stubborn, obdurate, addicted to politics, the staircase, the whirring machine.

His restless hands attacked another breadstick. His terrible teeth tried a smile but his eyes remained sub-polar. He said:

"Wanna be a senator for Nevada?"

I managed not to sputter into my martini.

"Well—*do* you?"

It came like that, abruptly, with a disdain that bordered on the casual. Except with Joe nothing was ever casual. He was more calculating than anybody I'd ever met, and I knew some people who played a mean game of poker—his daughter, for example.

"You know I'm serious."

That was true; I did know. Over the years Jackie and I had plotted for the moment when her father would draw me deeper into this world. I'd nudged and schemed, but in the end it was Joe's deck of cards we were playing with. And he relished the power to shock and slap.

"You're ready, son. It's time."

Part of Joe's myth about himself was that he'd been an infantryman in WW I. He said that he'd sighted in on a German captain, allowing him to take a piss and button up his fly before dispatching him with a bullet through the neck. I didn't know whether the story was accurate or not. Joe was fifty-seven, born a year before the turn of the century, so he'd have been only a teenager if he made the trip to France in 1917, 1918. Maybe it was a lie, but so what? It was back in the long-ago and unknowable past, a fiction, perhaps, but adding a more colorful layer of reality to those chill, careful eyes that certainly looked like a sniper's.

His father had been a saloon keeper, his mother a seamstress, but they were dead now, forgotten. In the 1920s, Joe studied for the Illinois State Bar, qualified, and set up practices in Chicago and, later, New York, specializing in labor law. But he made his real dough by investing in trucking firms and real estate parcels throughout several major cities, holdings he disguised with subtle Chinese boxes of corporations when he became a congressman in the Depression. He served two terms, went back to business, held a position under Roosevelt during WW II, supervising the mass manufacture of trucks and arms, and ascended to the Senate when Truman unexpectedly beat Dewey in '48. I'd heard that he lost a lot of money once but he never spoke of that. His fortunes, when revived, were never allowed to sag again. Money, as far as he was concerned, was the heart of every matter. He hated, for instance, to hand over ready cash to so dubious a cause as a restaurant, and always expected me to pick up the tab. Joe was *nouveau*, but politically embedded, which, in this great land of ours, allowed his Radcliffe-educated daughter to pretend it had been Nelson silver spoons almost all the way back to the *Mayflower*.

"There's plenty of juice in your war record and those medals you won. I've always thought so." He risked another of those wintry smiles. "They'll lap you up."

"How would this work?"

"You don't need to worry about that," he said, breadstick churning as if his mouth were a cement mixer.

"I *will* worry about it."

"Look." He began moving forks, spoons, and salt and pepper shakers about as though organizing his battalions. "Ike will get the second term, that's a given. Adlai already looks like a guy on the way to the electric chair," he said. "The old bastard in Nevada will last long enough to get reelected. Then, when he dies, we'll be ready. You'll get the nomination, I'll see to that. You'll probably have to shake about two hundred and fifty hands."

"It's that simple?"

"We're talking about Nevada," he said with scorn. "A million square miles of scrub. A couple of thousand slot machines, a few roulette wheels, some poker tables, and two nice, warm seats in the U.S. Senate—all in the hands of juice guys who don't give a damn what happens so long as they go on making piles of dough."

"I like Nevada."

"I know. That's what makes this perfect."

If Joe said he'd secure me the nomination, I'd no doubt he'd deliver. He made no claim lightly, and I remembered the times I'd visited him in Washington. His performance was very different there; he was calmer, seemingly kinder, a dispenser of elaborate courtesy. I thought of the polished tops of the ninety-six desks in the Senate Chamber, the doors of polished mahogany, the marble floors reflecting the ceiling lights; I pictured Joe's office—high-ceilinged, spacious, smelling warmly of leather and cigars, the fireplace flanked by filigreed columns, the high windows looking out toward manicured verdure and the Washington Monument. On Joe's desk were photographs that had been taken of him with Roosevelt, Truman, Churchill, Eisenhower. The one with Stalin was hidden, a no longer convenient, and therefore obliterated, part of the back story.

"Is there anything you want to tell me?" Joe said, jerking me back to the present.

"Like what?" I said, a tingle running down my spine. I was used to thinking on my feet and I didn't like the look of Joe's thrusting, almost gloating expression, as if, having handed me a carrot, he proposed to kick me in the balls.

"Something you never told Jackie maybe?"

I gave him my best Maurice Valentine smile, the modest, charming one I used on clients. Meanwhile my mind was racing. What did the old bastard know? About my affairs? No, not that, I thought—I'd always been careful. Besides, the notion that adultery should be punished was peddled by Hollywood and Washington while being openly scorned in both those cities, where men fucked around and expected to get away with it. Let the suburbs with their postwar tract houses flounder in their angst and marital melodrama. We of the elite were beyond such petit-bourgeois soft soap. We did what we wanted and paid the bill only if we had to. No, there was something else. My name, I thought. He knows I changed my name.

"You think I'd let you marry my daughter without checking you out?"

Joe looked pleased with himself, putting me on the spot.

"J. Edgar Hoover owed me a favor," he went on, hand-brushing the top of his wiry hair. "He still owes me plenty."

I shouldn't have been surprised. But I didn't want to give Joe the satisfaction of knowing that inside I was sweating. "Does Jackie know?" I said in a cool tone.

"What's to tell?" Joe said, leaning forward, attacking another breadstick.

"Not much." Really, when I thought about it, I had nothing to be ashamed of.

"So, spill," he said.

I told him the story. I'd changed my name neither casually nor from the need to cover up any secret. I'd wished to erase my previous self, that's all, discard it like an unwanted suit. I'd needed a fresh start, a blank page, a whole new design. And so, on December 15, 1945, before the Honorable Rufus H. Smith, one obese and spectacularly bored judge sitting in Court C of the Santa Monica department of the Superior Court of California, Maurizio Viglioni became Maurice Valentine, a smoother, slicker name for the life I intended to create. I paid a lawyer $175 to complete the paperwork and the deal was done. My new personality began to take flight. It was Maurizio Viglioni whose father was a failed Philadelphia engineer, Maurizio Viglioni whose mother had run away with a stockbroker, Maurizio Viglioni who, in spite of his glib facility with the pencil, had struggled in his studies at the Philadelphia School of Art & Design, Maurizio Viglioni who, like tens of thousands of others, had enlisted in the Air Force the day after Pearl Harbor and won medals he didn't feel he deserved—Maurizio Viglioni whose nerves had been torn to shreds. Maurice Valentine determined never to let himself look back. He was a different customer altogether: calm, with an eye for the main chance. It was like schizophrenia, except the money was better.

"I kept the hooey about the architecture degree and the medals," I told Joe. "That was smart, I think. And I was lucky. Within a couple of months I met Barragan and Jackie. The rest you know."

Joe gave me a frank, cold look of assessment. A look not without arrogance, and maybe not without a grudging admiration for the seeming ease with which I'd shed a former skin. Memory loss was something he understood; in his line of work it was a survival tool. The first time I'd met Joe had been back toward the beginning of 1946. Jackie took me to a party, down at the beach in Malibu, mentioning that her father was in town and might drop by. When we arrived Joe was already holding court, his black footwear, long and shiny as coffins, planted beside the swimming pool almost like a challenge, an assertion of mastery far from home. Movie stars sunned themselves, producers chewed cigars and eyed buttocks and brayed about their deals, but somehow Joe had made himself the center of gravity. With his hands stuffed in his pockets and his flinty eyes squinting against the glare, he surveyed me. "You're screwing my daughter and you're an architect. Any money in it?" He'd heard of Luis Barragan but he was in no way intrigued by craft, by the ability to sit at a drafting table with nothing but a pencil and call into existence a world of delineated space. He quizzed me about the practical end of it, all the while, no doubt, wondering whether I might be the solution to the problem of Jackie's pregnancy. What impressed him was my drive. He saw it in me; he sniffed it, as we spoke of politics and power and money. "How far do you want to go?" he asked, unsmiling, and I felt happy, warmed by privilege, like Octavian sitting at the feet of Julius Caesar, knowing that implicit in his question was the deeper one—what will you do to get there? I assured him, and myself, that there would be no limits, and soon Jackie and I were married and Joe and I were family. During the last ten years the pretending to like each other had turned into the real thing. Almost. I admired Joe and liked to watch him at work. At the same time I knew of what he was capable, having seen him rig committees and squash other architects to send work my way. He was formidable, a lanky Sherman tank in Florsheim shoes and socks that had yet more Irish regalia on them.

"We'll need another angle for the press," he said, tapping his teeth with a breadstick. "Best to give it to them ourselves. Find a tame reporter, a guy from *Life* maybe, or the *Post*. Better yet, a woman. You've got that charm," he said, not gloating, not chiding, a blunt recognition of a usable fact.

I'd passed the test, I knew, and Joe had already moved on; he was in another of his elements, putting in the fix.

"You wanted a career as an architect, but didn't want to ride on the tails of being a war hero. How does that sound?" he said, musing out loud, plotting. "You needed to be your own guy. So you concentrated on your career for ten years, made a success of yourself, and now you want to give something back by way of public service. And we'll bring up those medals every chance we get."

"Will they swallow that?"

"They will if I say so. They'd better," he said. "All I need to know is this—are you in, Maurice? Can I count on you?"

6

*A*ll of our lives we go along, guessing that power is a secret conspiracy, that even in a vast country the most important decisions are made by a few men who might not be good and might sometimes be elected. But not necessarily so. They are, for us, shadowy presences, and we wonder what it might be like, being in a room with them while the pie is sliced. What would the smell in that room be like? How small or large or light or dark would that room be? Would the clock strike? Would those looming men of power talk about how hungry they were and make capricious demands of the waiters?

Now I knew: Joe had sent back his beef, asking that the horseradish first be warmed to room temperature, not because it tasted better that way, but because otherwise it left a further stain on his already jaundiced teeth.

The whim of a senator.

I'm not complaining about this. That would be pissing in the wind. Besides, I'd dreamed all my life of being in such a room, and now I, too, had been granted admission. I was on the inside, and I left Romanoff's with a funny, buzzy feeling inside my head. The world looked different. The sun glittered harder. The palm trees swayed and shook their fronds in applause. I felt all of a sudden like a visitor from another planet. Displaced, deliciously.

I wanted to be by myself, and so I drove around, not seeing where

I went, aiming myself at the ocean while I adjusted to my new position in the world. Maurice Valentine, senator at forty! How good did that sound?

Back at the office I called Jackie. She wasn't at home but I tried the country club and waited while the phone was taken to her. In the background I heard footsteps, chatter, shouts and splashes from the pool, the sizzle and *thwock* of tennis balls, the melodies of wealth at leisure.

By now my mind had snapped back and I was thinking in practical terms, planning, making strategies. I wondered whether Jackie knew what I was about to tell her? Was she already party to the specifics of my future? She was Daddy's girl and to some extent I was the invention of the two of them. Did I resent this? You bet. Was I about to let the promptings of wounded pride upset the triumph of my progress? Never. Besides, beneath my smooth manners and smooth exterior, I had my own cunning, a furtive capacity to take and hold what I wanted. Maurice Valentine was more than a match for anybody, I reckoned.

Jackie's first words were: "The kids—are they okay?"

So, I thought, he hasn't told you. And a moment passed while I savored the subtle shift implied in the relationship between her and Joe and me. I wasn't just Jackie's husband anymore. I was on the way up in more ways than one.

"I just got through with lunch with your father."

I left a pause.

"And?" she said.

"He wants me to be a senator for Nevada."

"For *Nevada*?"

I knew that she hated Nevada: too hot, too dry, the air conditioning wreaked havoc with her hair, and she only liked to bet on the sure thing.

"It's the Senate, Jackie. And who knows where we might go from there."

Still, she paused, making some mental calibration before she whooped. "I knew Daddy would do this for us."

I didn't say anything, knowing that whatever Jackie might think, Joe was doing this for one person only—himself. Joe worshiped his daughter, and had a certain ironic regard for me, but he wasn't about to install anybody as the senator for anywhere out of philanthropic instinct. He'd be expecting plenty and no doubt had his own agenda, as always. The trick would be to establish mine. But all that was for later.

"Tonight we'll crack a bottle of champagne," I said. "A good one. Or maybe we'll go out. Really celebrate. This is great news, kiddo."

I hung up, tidied my desk, leafed through my messages. I glanced at a sketch I'd made on the back of an airline ticket, turning the ticket this way and that, trying to figure out what I'd had in mind. I spoke with each of my draftsmen, checking progress, reviewing possibilities. I'd learned to enjoy the teamwork of architecture, the part whereby other people did most of the work: finding contractors who got the job done instead of trying to rob me blind; listening to the client and turning him into a collaborator instead of an enemy; gathering and harnessing the talents of my employees. I had more than twenty people on the payroll, now that a rush of commissions had followed the success of the El Sheik.

I called Jackie again but she'd already left the club. Restless, I took a pencil, fed it into the mechanical sharpener, balanced it on the edge of my desk. I'd told Joe about why I'd changed the name, but we hadn't discussed the circumstances. The FBI report would have had some of it, most likely, but not the whole story. Again, I had no need to be ashamed, though shame, of course, had been a part of what drove me, shame giving birth to something that never allowed itself to look back.

I'd been a patient at a clinic in Minnesota, a 1930s functionalist structure, built in a high, windy place, designed for TB patients but given over, in those months toward the end of the war, to victims of shell shock and terror, men with hollowed faces and eyes that were dead to memory, or else crazy, wild with electricity. Lots of us. Hundreds of us. The reasons for my presence in that place are simple to tell. I won't tell them now. That comes later. But while I was at the Menninger Clinic, my home on the funny farm for several months after I was officially, honorably, discharged and pensioned out early in 1945, I was taken in hand by one of the nurses. Alice was twenty, the daughter of a farmer with a small holding on the high plains. She was tall, slim, angular, almost gawky; she was strong in body and in mind, with clear skin and hair the color of burning straw. She sat with me for hours, holding my hand while I stared into space and said nothing. She read to me from the newspaper and books. She told me stories about her family and where she grew up. She was obsessed by a man in her town who had apparently gotten away with murder; she was sure he'd be brought to justice one day; she was naïve that way. Many days she'd bring flowers to my room and arrange them in a vase by the window. She worked hard to awake my interest in life again, riding with me on the bus to St. Paul and the movies. We saw that old warhorse *Mrs. Miniver* together, and *Dark Victory*, and it was during *The Big Sleep* that she rested her head against my shoulder and I saw that her goals with regard to me might extend beyond healing. I saw a possibility stretching ahead of me as clear as the image of Bogart cupping Lauren Bacall's chin. I would marry Alice, set up a small architectural practice in Minnesota, have children with a woman who loved me despite my being broken inside. I was situated at a crossroads—one way would probably lead to a stable and happy life. But the other?

It's no easy matter to look back and make sense of your life and choices. Three days later I left the Menninger Clinic without goodbyes or a backward glance. I never spoke to Alice again. Maybe I'd feared that if I stayed the knowledge of my failure would wake up with me over the cornflakes and go to bed with me, too. Wanting something else, something more, I submerged myself and my ghosts, hopping a train to San Francisco, and then to L.A., beginning life anew as a nothing. But a nothing with talent, I told myself, a nothing who might go far. Ambition substituted for identity. Ambition cauterized the pain and guilt of the past. Ambition was the arrow that summoned Maurice Valentine and aimed him at the target.

After that, everything was easy. I couldn't blame myself for anything, because I didn't exist. My progress down the chosen road was swift and smooth.

With the flat of my hand I rolled the pencil to and fro. I had no wish to turn back the clock. Ten years of hard work and self-invention had brought complications but paid off. Things I'd dreamed of were coming within reach. Senator Valentine. Maybe even President Valentine. Did I dare to think of that? I'm afraid I did. In America, the greatest of democracies, such things happened, or were arranged. The country seemed to stretch before me like a woman wanting to be taken. I saw no limits to what I might accomplish.

Then Mallory Walker strolled in.

7

*S*he wore a narrow silk dress that was the rich, delicate color of a plum. Her bare arms were white, almost luminously pale, scarcely tanned, and her hands were gloved in supple leather that matched the dress. The long gloves reached above the wrist, and sunglasses glistened over her eyes like lustrous shells. Thrown by this elegance and her offhand, almost arrogant manner, I took a moment to recognize her. The halo of silver hair was the giveaway.

"Luis's friend," I said, and found myself wishing to be punctilious, polite, impressive. "How may I help you?"

Without invitation she sat on one of my Alvar Aalto chairs, the blond springy wood bending to her shape as she crossed her legs. She reached in her plum-colored leather satchel and fetched out a cigarette case and lighter. The case, I noted, was platinum, embossed on one corner with gems that spelled out her initials: MW. The lighter was made to match, and she leaned forward, putting the thing on the edge of my desk. She waited for me to get up and light her Camel. I did.

"I want you to build me a house," she said. "I have the site and I have the money. I'm very, very rich."

She drew on her cigarette, the words spoken in an offhand way that was familiar yet strangely thrilling.

"I guess Luis didn't mention that."

"It must have slipped his mind," I said, already enjoying the banter.

"What *did* he tell you about me?"

"He worships you," I told her. "He thinks you're his muse. I'm afraid to say that you're the latest in a line. But maybe the most impressive to date."

She laughed, neither offended nor surprised.

"Where's your money from?"

"You're very direct," she said, tapping ash from the Camel. "I like that."

She kept on her gloves but the sunglasses were off now, balanced on the edge of the chair, and her gray-green eyes scanned my office, checking the framed designs on the walls, the desk I'd built myself, the pencils jutting like spears from the jar.

"My father's Brent Walker."

"As in Walker Shipping?"

"Well, yes, Daddy owns ships. Among other things."

Sure, I thought—like a hotel chain, a steelworks, a newspaper, an airplane or five. I didn't bother to restrain my appreciative whistle. "You *are* rich."

"Does that worry you, Mr. Valentine?"

"Call me Maurice," I said. "On the contrary—I like rich women."

"That's what I heard. You're interested, then?"

"In what?" I said, thrown for a moment.

"In building my house," she said innocently.

"Why not get Luis for the job?"

"I want you," she said. Nothing in her face signaled the true meaning behind the casual double entendre. I rocked back in my chair with my arms clasped behind my head.

"I'm flattered. But why me?"

"The Slominsky house."

There it was again: the least sung of my projects held up for praise.

"Also, you're clearly not afraid of other people's ideas."

"Ah," I said. "You see this as a collaboration?"

"I want to have my say."

"Design the house yourself."

"I'm not ready."

I began to see how she was thinking. Architecture is no easy career for a woman. Even today a female architect will be on site with the contractor and find herself being treated as an onlooker, a guest—worse yet, a decorator. Back in the 1950s the situation was ten times more difficult, and when I'd met Mallory at Luis's party I'd assumed that she was ambitious and in for a bumpy ride, if she was serious about the career. Now I gathered that she was indeed in earnest, and had a game plan: to work alongside me and gain experience, move into the house we built, and, slowly, in conversations and in meetings, take more and more of the credit for herself. Questions of who did what on a co-authored project tend to get lost in time and out of this obscurity arise career-boosting opportunities, commissions. Frank Lloyd Wright had pulled stunts like this, and Aalto, too. It's a rarely discussed and almost accepted way of getting ahead in the architectural world, especially when you're starting out. I'd done much the same with Luis Barragan. I looked at her with a new admiration.

"Where did you study?"

"At Yale."

"Good school."

"The best," she said, and there was a hint, surprising, barely perceptible, of something hard in her voice, a steeliness that belied her wealthy upbringing—or suggested qualities beyond that.

"And what has the best enabled you to build?"

"Nothing," she said, accepting the rebuke with a wry smile.

"Well—plenty of time yet."

"Actually there's one building. A small bank, up in northern Cal. But they were pretty much forced to give me the commission."

I fell into her trap, asking: "Why was that?"

Her delivery of the punchline was perfect: "Daddy bought the bank."

I laughed, starting to find her likeable and not only alluring. "Do you have a picture?"

She had that challenging, impudent look on her face again. "Of my father?"

"Of the bank."

She reached again into the plum satchel, this time for an eight-by-ten glossy. The structure in the picture was routine, boxy concrete modernism, just the sort of sub-Mies stuff they were peddling at the Yale School of Architecture, circa 1954. Clean lines, unpretentious, elegant in its way. Maybe I was harsh. After all, if she was already a fully developed talent, not to mention being as rich as Vanderbilt and beautiful enough to give a monk the night sweats, then why would she need Maurice Valentine? And Maurice Valentine was starting to like the idea of being needed by this young woman.

"You probably think I'm sleeping with Luis. I'm not."

"It's none of my business."

"I thought you might be curious."

She was right, of course. I was curious.

"He follows me. He calls me in the middle of the night. The other day he tried to break into my apartment," she said, for the first time not meeting my eye. She looked past my shoulder and out the window, with something faraway in her eyes. "I went to the party to tell him I couldn't see him anymore. I didn't like to have to do that. He went crazy. Started shouting and smashing things. This was after you'd left."

I'd seen Luis in his ugly rages. "He hit you?"

"I can look after myself," she said coolly, and I didn't doubt her. Whatever else, Mallory struck me as tough and capable. She wasn't looking for me to solve her problems with Luis. Or not in a simple way.

"You want me to build a house with you," I said. "But I've known Luis for a long time and he's a great architect. No question about that, and I'm thinking of asking him to come back and work for me." I spread my hands compassionately. "So you see—there's a conflict."

She didn't blink. She tapped against her sunglasses with a manicured nail and ran her fingers over the smooth platinum surface of the monogrammed cigarette case. Having held out another cigarette for me to light, she exhaled smoke, smiling at the ceiling.

"I've been thinking—Luis isn't exactly a team player, is he?"

Now what was she up to?

"Maybe you should find yourself another partner. A junior partner, naturally. Someone steadier than Luis. Someone younger than Luis. Someone with financial resources."

Calmly she rested her chin on her fist, the cigarette trailing its plume of smoke from her other hand.

"Someone like—"

"Yes, exactly. Someone like me," she said, tilting her head with an inviting smile.

Wow, you're even more ambitious than I thought, I said to myself.

And what she didn't know, couldn't know, was how my situation had changed and blossomed since the last time we met. A career in politics—a term in the Senate, maybe two, and then who knew?—would mean goodbye to architecture for a while. The firm, Maurice Valentine & Associates, would continue and flourish, with the help I'd shove its way from Washington, and perhaps I did need to leave the venture in steadier hands than Luis's. Which didn't mean that I at once contemplated handing over my entire caravan to a young woman in her twenties, however clever and proud and ruthless, and beautiful, she might appear, and whoever her father might be. But I was intrigued by the move. She was playing a game of power, the sort of game I liked. She was something of a bitch, this Mallory Walker, with cool bitch eyes and a magnetism I felt increasing by the moment.

She was on her feet now, walking across my office. But not toward me: instead she was inspecting a photograph that I'd had framed and put up on the wall; it had been taken at the opening of the El Sheik in Vegas.

"These other men in the picture," she said, standing with her back to me, so I saw where her cropped hair stopped in a razored line across her neck above the top of her dress. "Are they friends of yours?"

"A couple of them." I came from behind my desk, standing beside her. "The guy standing next to me—that's Paul Mantilini. He put up the money for the hotel. And for the new ones, too."

She looked at me. "What's he like?"

"He knows architecture. He knows what he wants. And he's easy to deal with," I said. "He's tough, too. I like him."

"That's good, isn't it?" she said, crinkling her eyes in a smile. I got a sense of something different, then, but I read it wrong. She was beautiful, in certain lights, but fleetingly, almost hauntingly. Standing that close, I caught a whiff of her scent, a witchy and intoxicating perfume I didn't recognize.

"At least come look at where I want to build—the site I've bought for my house."

She looked up at me with some promise of an offer shining in her face. I knew from my schedule that in twenty minutes I was due to meet with some worthy charitable personage who'd flown in from New York to talk about building an art gallery. The commission would be important. But, standing there, gazing into those startling gray-green eyes, I reminded myself that the function of worthy charitable personages was to dance attendance upon men of skill and talent, men of power—men like me.

"Sure," I said. "I'll come."

8

*C*ars from Europe were rare in those days, a real extravagance, and hers was a beauty, sleek and silver, low and quick and small, all Marilyn Monroe curves and Nazi engineering, a Porsche, which she drove fast and with no fuss, working the shift smoothly, handling the machine like an expert, like an extension of herself as we headed through Brentwood and up the hill toward Pacific Palisades, the hot wind in our faces.

"I was a regular little grease monkey when I was a kid," she said. "Always in a car or under one with my hands covered in oil."

I smiled, my hand tapping on my knee, trying to connect this picture with the young sophisticate beside me, gorgeous in her silk dress, sunglasses nestling over her eyes. "How did your father like that?"

"He was fine about it. He made his first bucks in scrap metal and says he still doesn't trust a guy who's too clean. He expects people to make something of themselves."

"You're close to him?"

"Sure. Not that we speak every day. My mom died when I was a kid, so me and my dad were pretty much forced to get along."

"Did he ever marry again?"

"Oh, God. Only about fifty times," she said, laughing. "He switches wives like shirts. The current specimen is just about the worst ever. She specializes in amateur theatricals and nervous breakdowns."

"That must make things tricky."

"Not really. She knows never to come between my father and me."

She said this with pride but with wistfulness too, almost a pang of regret, then changed the subject. "What about *your* father?"

"I haven't seen him in years."

"You don't get along?"

"Something like that."

Guiding the car, her gloved hand neat and quick on the shift, she asked about my wife, my kids, how my firm worked. She more or less interrogated me, and I gave the answers readily enough. She seemed to want to get to know me in a hurry and she was good at it. Besides, what man doesn't like being quizzed by an attractive woman?

"Your sons," she said. "Do they take after you?"

"They live in their own world. Jackie sees more of them than I do," I said. "They're durable, adaptable. Maybe they get that from me."

"You're tough?"

"I see which way the wind is blowing. I *bend*."

"I probably don't know you well enough to say this. I'm going to anyway because I think you're being falsely modest," she said. "I admire the heck out of the way you stood up in front of HUAC."

For a moment I glimpsed my face in the side mirror on the passenger door, teeth showing through the trademark Maurice Valentine smile, the smile that reassured strangers and drew them in. In 1949, when Luis Barragan and I had still been partners, he'd been summoned before HUAC and invited to prove his loyalty, to name the names of those of his friends who'd been Communist Party members or sympathizers in the 1930s and during the war, when Stalin's Russia had been our ally, not our enemy, and the reds had dared to raise their voices against what Hitler was doing to the Jews in Germany. Luis, stubborn, the natural contrarian, took his seat in front of the microphone and told the congressional suits and their bloodhounds to go hang themselves, a satisfying moment for him, no doubt. He was famous only within his field and this virtuous stand merited no more than three paragraphs in the *Los Angeles Times*. But word went around, you'd be amazed how quickly. Within days the movie producer whose house we were to build in Malibu decided to employ different architects. The judges reversed their decision in an architectural competition Luis had supposedly already won. An insurance company that had commissioned a new office building canceled the contract. The plan for an apartment complex in Brentwood was deemed inadequate. And so on. The world simply turned its back; within six months Luis's firm was bankrupt and he was encouraging me to go it alone, a move I'd decided was inevitable. With Luis (and other left-leaning architects) unemployable, the firm I started quickly flourished, and when, not long after, my own turn came to face the inquisition, I went to Joe Nelson for help and cut a secret deal. Lots of people, smart people, not evil people, did this. I didn't try to convince myself it was the *correct* thing to do; in almost any situation, I reckoned, morality was a makeshift, that side of things a mess so tangled you could never get the hang of what was right or wrong. It was a question of survival. I saw what was happening and refused to become a victim. I met members of the committee over a quiet dinner in a private room in a hotel and told them a little of what I knew. It was a game we played—Joe had fixed it so that I would name names that had already been named and nobody would ever know. I was off the hook, out of the danger zone, provided with safe haven in that swelling storm of self-righteousness. An announcement was made to the press that, given my war record, my proven history as hero and patriot, I was being spared the need to testify. I came out smelling like roses, admired by all, and it was a lie. The Valentine chariot rolled on. The dust I left behind was dust I didn't look at.

The Porsche approached a red light and Mallory's foot went on the brake, and I saw the muscles in her thigh grow taut beneath the plum-colored silk. "I know from my father—plenty of his friends wriggled and wormed but in the end they sang the song and sent their friends down the river," she said.

"It was a tough time," I said. "Not easy for anybody."

"You took a stand," she said, eyes inscrutable behind those shell-like dark glasses as the light changed and she gunned the Porsche away, its engine high-pitched and whiny, a thoroughbred. "It says a lot about you."

Pacific Palisades was barely a village then, more like an outpost, for German writers, émigré composers and musicians, for movie people who wanted to breathe in the ocean views and forget Hollywood for a while. The English were especially fond of the place, and Union Jacks hung outside tea shops that dotted the generous broadness of the main street. In between the post office and the fire department was a slim, reddish building I didn't know, that had gone up since I'd last been in the neighborhood. Mallory slowed, bringing the Porsche once more to a standstill so that a girl on her bicycle could cross in front of us, and then we picked up speed again, heading for the uplands, climbing and winding along a series of roads that had only recently been built and paved. In Los Angeles, architecture was in a restless state of evolution and reinvention. Few buildings had a suggestion of permanence—it was something I liked about the place.

The Porsche passed between two stone markers that stood on either side of a rough dirt track, bouncing down into a valley and back up a curving slope before Mallory stopped the car and killed the engine. The sudden quiet was ripped by the shriek of crickets, and we climbed out of the car.

In the distance, beyond the browned slopes and parched ravines, the brush that was scorched tinder-dry, I saw the promontory of Point Dume, its rounded snout thrust into an ocean gleaming like puddled steel. Thin wisps of cloud trailed through a sky of exhausted blue. Rocks sparkled, paining the eyes, and a breeze gusted in from the desert, scalding the skin and setting the teeth on edge. A hot, dry wind without odor and with more static electricity than the Department of Water and Power. My scalp began to itch. The wind lifted Mallory's hair so that it seemed almost to float and she opened her lips and breathed deeply in. I imagined the desert heat, inside her throat, scouring her lungs, and felt thirsty all of a sudden, on the verge of a headache. She smiled, even while the wind rubbed my eyes like sandpaper and caused me to regret the two martinis I'd drunk at lunch. The Devil's Wind, the Indians used to call it, a wind that set fires and made people think nasty thoughts about carving knives.

"I want my house right here," said Mallory, marching to the top of the hill with a bounce in her step. The heat, or the wind, or maybe it was both, seemed to have infused her with energy. I guess it works on some people that way. "Facing the ocean. Don't laugh at me."

"Believe me, I won't," I said, trudging in pursuit, forcing my brain to make calculations. The track could be widened into a road, utilities brought in. The hilly terrain eliminated the drainage problem. The rock beneath the topsoil could be blasted away for the laying of foundations. "Not on top of the hill. It's too exposed."

"It'll be wild—I'll love that," she said with her arms outstretched, spinning around.

"Too much sun, too many storms, too much wind on days like to-day," I said. I sounded like I was with Ches and Bobby, delivering a lecture. "Wild weather is beautiful to think about and not so easy to live in. A house needs shelter."

Walking straight past her, I headed down the slope on the other side, feet scratching and sliding until I found the spot. There's one on every site, the secret place that unlocks the heart of the landscape. Here it lay in the shade of a tree, an ancient California oak, its leaves gray with dust. That tree was a whole lot older than L.A. itself. "We cut into the slope here," I said, brushing away the sweat that prickled in my eyebrows. "Twist the house so it faces northwest."

I enumerated the virtues of this idea. "You've got the ocean view from most of the windows. But you've got protection, too. The house will be cooler in summer, warmer in winter. And there'll be more privacy—in case somebody else decides to build around here."

"Let me see," she said, and came bounding to join me, a tomboy despite the silken dress. She stumbled, caught herself, and crashed into me, laughing. Her skin was hot, and I smelled the sweat beneath that perfume on her body. Her eyes darkened, and she had a different smile, a whole other aura, something troubled and erotic.

She pushed herself away from me, ran a hand through her cropped hair, walked a few steps, and then back again. She scratched the top of her head, took off her sunglasses, and looked about, eyes narrowed, making a circle, a full three-sixty. An expression of surprise and pleasure spread across her face.

"It's darned clever of you, Maurice," she said, the first time that she'd used my first name. She looked at me for a long time before touching my hand, a gesture of thanks and acknowledgment. "This is so much better."

We cooled off at a soda fountain in the Palisades, sitting on stools at a long, clean counter, while, with a notebook in my hand, I jotted down some details about the kind of house she wanted. Routine stuff: the number of rooms and fireplaces, the height of the ceilings, the type of heating, whether there'd be a swimming pool, a library, and so on. I asked how much she was prepared to spend.

"How much do you need?" she said.

"You want to make a splash?"

"A big one."

"A hundred grand should cover it," I said, naming, for 1956, an exorbitant sum.

"Not a problem."

"Your father will cover it?"

"More, if I ask him," she said, sucking on her strawberry shake. "Once you meet, he'll probably want to throw a few more commissions your way."

She was doing her best to make the proposition irresistible; she was succeeding, but I knew I mustn't seem too eager. The Valentine way was to play things cool.

"What does your father think about this? About your being an architect?" I said. "Shouldn't you be married to the son of Pennsylvania Steel by now? Or someone?"

"I tried that. It didn't work out."

"How come?"

"He seemed like a nice guy. But then I realized he divided all women into three categories. Tramps, near tramps, and pushovers. Secretly he hated me because I was smarter than him."

"You're divorced now?"

"Years ago, already," she said. "Went into it with a full heart and came out bleeding. Then I was ambushed by architecture."

"You make that sound dangerous."

"No, it saved me. I was on the road with a friend and I happened to sleep in a house by Frank Lloyd Wright. I woke up in a room that felt like a church," she said. "Not that I believe in God. How can anybody?"

"Lots of people manage it."

"They're fools. This world's brutal. And God quit a long time ago. Who can blame him?"

"You're a pessimist."

"I'm talking too much."

She looked down: despite all her polish, she seemed, in that moment, genuinely shy. But when she glanced up again her eyes were hard as marbles, flashing.

Thinking now, I don't know whether she'd just shown me a part of her real self or whether this was another part of the act, designed to ensnare me. Sometimes the two got mixed up. I thought her ambitious, determinedly self-sufficient but not wholly self-possessed. I thought I understood her. I was wrong.

She talked about Yale, how strange it had been to arrive there having already experienced marriage and divorce. "Those other kids. They made me feel like a granny," she said.

Sure, I thought, and every professor on campus was trying to get into your pants.

"I met Luis when he came to give a lecture. He cut quite the figure, this big shaggy bear of a guy in his black suit. He told me that if I ever came to Los Angeles I should look him up."

"I wish you'd come straight to me."

"I know. I guess I was intimidated."

"I find that hard to believe," I said, grinning. "You waltz into my office and you want to build a house with me. Next thing you're suggesting I ditch my old pal and hire you instead."

"That's not what I said."

"It's what you meant. At least I hope so. I wish I'd had half your guts and drive when I was your age."

She toyed with the straw in her milk shake. The jukebox was playing jazz, a wistful saxophone melody, a cool sound of beach and the ocean, a tune of summer seduction.

"Not much surprises you, does it?"

Her tone was frankly admiring, her demeanor suggesting that the two of us were alike—people of the world, on top of our feelings and desires.

"I've seen a lot. I'm an old man."

"Not so old."

She took the straw from her glass and passed it along my lips. My mouth tingled with the sweet taste of ice cream and strawberry. Anything seemed possible.

"I'd love to see the hotel you built in Las Vegas."

"The El Sheik? I thought you liked the Slominsky house."

"I do. I love it," she said.

I told her about some of the upcoming projects—the other Vegas hotels, the ones in Cuba. "And something's going on that I can't talk about. I'll be out of the office for a while."

"A sabbatical?"

"Kind of. It'll mean plenty of work for the firm. But I'll have to restructure things."

"I'd like to be a part of that," she said. "And I'm sure my father would like to invest."

She smiled, her gray-green eyes aglitter with suggestion and invitation, and by the end of the afternoon, when we emerged from the soda fountain into the dazzling glare, our hair lifted from our scalps by the gusting wind, I was seriously considering bringing her into the firm. Might be fun, I thought, to help this young woman, shape her, maybe fuck her, too.

9

JUNE 1, 1944 / SAN FERNANDO VALLEY

*T*he whole of the San Fernando Valley cooks like a great big oven with nothing in it. Her chair positioned in the shade, Beth fans herself with *Theater Guild News*. Age thirteen, gangly, coltish, with ankles sprouting beyond the faded cuffs of her peg-leg jeans and breasts budding beneath her T-shirt, she hears Bendix, the chef, puttering about in the hot-dog diner. The long, round, concrete walls of the diner are stained and cracked, tormented by months of heat.

Beth waits for her mother. And waits, flipping through the magazine, sniffing the food that Bendix is frying, though he knows, pretty much for sure, that today, as on every other day, no hot dogs will be sold. Nor any gas, either. In Europe, the Allies are poised to invade northern France; in the Pacific, U.S. Marines fight the Japs hand-to-hand in the caves on Biak Island; in Hollywood, *Double Indemnity* packs in the crowds at Sid Grauman's Chinese; but here in Van Nuys, Dick Dyer's grand vision of a gas station continues its death by inches.

"It's geography," Dick Dyer had said about six months back, glum, grim, angry at this, the latest evidence of the world's injustice. "Just plain bad luck." The war, the speed of growth in the San Fernando Valley, the widening of certain boulevards only a few blocks away, have left the once busy corner of Whitsett and Takongo in a backwater. The people from the oil company wanted to shut the station down. Dick Dyer loaded his family into the car and drove down to El Segundo to argue against the plan. He offered to put his own savings, his wife's savings, actually, into the business. "We need more time. That's all there is to it," he told them. Beth remembers, will always remember, the smile of happiness and triumph on her father's face when he marched out of that building. He'd won a reprieve.

The afternoon crawls along like torture, the heat begins to dip a little, 105, 102, 100, not that you'd notice. The heat is dry, punishing, a whiff of the desert. No cars appear, no customers for gas or the diner. Nor is there any sign of her mother. Beth shifts her chair, making sure to stay in the shade. A book has replaced *Theater Guild News* in her hand, the light blue Yale University Press edition of *Romeo and Juliet*, purchased at Pickwick's in Hollywood. But it's too hot to study, and, besides, Beth knows much of the play already. A drop of sweat falls from her forehead, splashing down into the end of Act 2, right where Romeo visits Friar Laurence in his cell; the moisture is sucked up by the paper and quickly evaporates, leaving a tiny round wrinkle on the page. In the diner, Bendix switches on his radio, tuned to a local station that relays Leopold Stokowski and the Symphony of the Air, direct from New York.

The gas station will close before long, Beth knows, and another reminder of her father will vanish. Beth believes that, somehow, this is all her fault. She senses further disasters looming for the Dyer family. But these are in the future and must be prevented. They *will* be prevented, she says to herself, and to that end she watches, listens, is attentive to everything, determined to overcome all obstacles, outwit any enemy. In the drawer of her bedside table she still keeps the business card given her by the old man with the malacca cane; she believes in his prophecies and the possibilities of her own magic. Clarence Logue, the English and drama teacher at Van Nuys High, calls her "a child of dangerous will." Beth views this as a compliment. She's decided to be unconquerable.

"Where *is* she?" Beth says, hauling herself out of the chair, tucking her book under her arm, and bounding up the steps in the diner, where Bendix leans against the counter, reading. A ceiling fan chops the air. A smaller one whirs away on the counter, inches from Bendix's face. There are three more going on the booths, making sheafs of unread menus flutter. But still the heat is too much.

"Hot dog, lady?" says Bendix, smiling, a big, balding man whose wide-spaced eyes have a gentleness in them.

"Coke, please."

"Play you at chess?"

"Sure," Beth says, laying out the pieces at one of the booth tables while Bendix opens the Frigidaire.

She presses the glass to the side of her neck, runs the cool curve of the bottle across her brow and cheek.

Bendix, playing white, stares at the pieces for a long time before selecting a pawn and nudging it forward. In this first game he fights Beth to a draw, but in the second she beats him in fifteen moves.

"You're too good," Bendix says, letting out his breath slowly.

"Lucky."

"That ain't so."

"I need to practice," Beth says, staring at the face of the red clock behind the counter. "My mother's late."

"She'll be here," Bendix says.

"She's always late."

"She don't let you down, though, does she?"

"Bet she's with her new boyfriend," she says. Her mother's seeing someone—a wooden lunk who thinks he looks like Clark Gable.

"She be workin'. You *know* she be workin'."

Beth snorts with mirthless laughter, and the clock on the wall shows fifteen after five, when, at last, she hears a car pull into the gas station, bears the old Ford's engine tapping loudly. She and Bendix look at each other, knowing this is no customer, and Beth smiles, almost light-headed with relief.

"See?" Bendix says

"I'll need to fly," says Beth, turning to see her mother at the diner doorway. Karen Dyer wears blue overalls and a red scarf tied around her head like a turban. The shoulders of her overalls glitter with steel shavings but the lipstick on her mouth is freshly applied, and Beth knows she took a moment in the car, fixing herself. Things like that are important to her mother, who looks pretty but hard these days, with her peroxide hair. A little like Betty Grable, and that's the idea, Beth supposes. For the last two years Karen Dyer has been working on the assembly line at Douglas Aircraft in Culver City. The drive is a marathon, the hours are long, but the job pays well.

"Mom, you're *late*," Beth says.

"Hello, sweetheart. Are you ready?" Karen says, laying down two packages on the counter. Beth eyes these suspiciously.

"I've been ready for *hours*."

"I know, I know. I stopped off at Bullocks. Spoke to such a nice guy," Karen says. "Why, Beth dear. You look hot. Your face is *pink*."

"Mom, it *is* hot. It's been over a hundred degrees."

"You look like a mess. You can't go looking like that."

"It's an audition," says Beth with mounting exasperation, "not a birthday party."

"It's important, you know," Karen says. "It will be watched, this play, maybe by important people. If you get the part."

"I'll get the part," Beth says.

"Not looking like that you won't," Karen says, crossing her arms in triumph. "Look what I brought you," she says, opening one of the packages. "I bought you this. It's so pretty and that nice man in Bullocks gave me such a great deal. Put it on."

"Mom, it's a *dress*."

"So? Dresses are good. Men like dresses. Mr. Logue is a man, isn't he?"

"I won't wear it."

"Then you don't go to the audition, honey," Karen says, legs akimbo, hands on her hips. "It's as simple as that."

Her mother's tough, resilient, and she won't quit, Beth knows. It's Greece and Troy between these two, Grant and Lee. With Beth and her mother, every engagement escalates to war almost immediately. One or the other of them is always trying to take Bataan.

Beth, studying the clock, sees there's no time to waste.

"Fine. Good. You win."

"I'm *right*, Beth, sweetheart," Karen says, enveloping Beth in a scatter of steel shavings. "You'll see."

Beth glances at Bendix, cocking her head to one side, and he answers with a faint nod, showing his back while Beth rips off her T-shirt, tugs down her jeans, and slips on the red and blue cotton print dress, turning so her mother can do the buttons at the back.

"Now," Karen says, opening the other package. "Shoes."

"Oh *Mom*!" says Beth, recoiling. "Not loafers."

But her feet are soon tucked into them.

"You look beautiful," Karen says, and Beth itches to be away, speeding on her bike to the audition. But she knows her mother isn't about to let this happen, not in a million years, not after having spent precious money on the dress and shoes.

A car ride is endured.

"Don't come in," Beth says, staring across the concrete desert of the playground while her mother parks the Ford outside the school gates. "Let me do this by myself."

"Just win, sweetie," Karen says.

"It's not a race, Mom."

"Be your best," Karen says, reaching as if to touch her daughter's cheek, but Beth already has her hand on the door handle.

Feet skidding, squeaking on the waxed linoleum of the empty corridors, Beth dashes toward the gym, pausing to calm herself and take a breath before flinging open the doors. She's greeted by a pleasant, chalky smell, and the sight of Clarence Logue, bristly about the chin, bristly on top of his head, and bristly, most of all, in his temper and his dealing with the recalcitrant pupils of Van Nuys High, packing up his things into a satchel of worn brown leather.

"Ah. Beth Dyer. Late. Very late." Mr. Logue is thin and wears a short-sleeve shirt with a striped woollen tie. His voice is dismal as a metronome. "The twenty-fifth would-be Juliet of what has been an extremely long and discouraging afternoon. An *exhausting* afternoon. Thankfully, as it happens, you're *too* late. I already assigned the part."

"Who got it?" says Beth, heart plunging in the direction of her scuffed canvas toes.

"Cynthia Koscwicki," says Mr. Logue, his face pinched by an unpleasant smile.

"Cynthia *Koscwicki*!" says Beth, appalled, her voice rising with outrage at the injustice, the tone her father might have used. "You're kidding me?"

"Beth," says Mr. Logue, buckling the strap on his satchel. "You weren't here."

"It's fine," Beth says, knowing she must think and work fast. "I didn't want that part."

"Oh. Sure," says Mr. Logue. "The nurse, decrepit and aging. That's the part for you. Well, you got your wish. And I'm going home."

"Romeo," Beth blurts out.

"Beth Dyer. So capable. So ambitious." Mr. Logue smirks. "I'm not auditioning for Romeo today."

"It's a better role," Beth says, determined to be quick, bright, flashing, like Romeo himself. "He grows. In his emotions. In his language. At the start he speaks like a poem. But by the end, when he thinks Juliet is dead and in her grave, he talks straight, from the heart. 'Well, Juliet, I will lie with thee tonight.' He's learned tragedy."

"How old are you, Dyer?" Mr. Logue asks, with the bored, embittered air of a smart, pedantic, passionate, solitary thirty-year-old stuck teaching kids when he knows he should be fighting for his country, *would* be fighting, were it not for his absurd feet with their fallen arches.

"Thirteen."

"What can you conceivably know of tragedy?" Mr. Logue's unshaven cheeks turn red. "Oh yes, I forgot, your father. The *suicide*," he says with disdain. "He hanged himself, didn't he?"

Beth swallows, one of her legs kicking, shooting out, just like that, an unprompted spasm, while she tries to fight back the tears that burn in her eyes. Her father hadn't meant to kill himself, not really. In those last weeks he'd been sick and sad, that was all, broken, like a machine that had suddenly run down.

Mr. Logue waits for her to fold, to crumple, to run away.

"Come hither, man," she says, ignoring the tears that stream down her cheeks. "I see that thou are poor. Hold, there is forty ducats. Let me have a dram of poison, such soon-speeding gear as will disperse itself through all the veins. That the life-weary taker may fall down dead."

Mr. Logue screws up a fist, and then that fist slaps into a palm.

Beth gets the part.

10

*L*uis Barragan came by the office, flopping down, drained by the heat, and, as it turned out, other matters. His bulky frame sagged over the edges of the springy Aalto chair. His wide eyes were bloodshot and dulled. He sat with shoulders hunched, sweat running down the lines of his face, brooding like an owl. At last he announced: "I don't know where she is."

"Who?" I said, feigning ignorance, though of course I knew exactly what he was talking about. She'd been on my mind, like a property of which I was about to assume ownership. I was already planning our affair; planning it to start very soon.

"Mallory—she's vanished."

My face mimed shock and sympathy. "When did you last see her?"

He scratched at his chin. "At the party, on Sunday night."

"That was only two days ago. Give the girl a break."

"I've been by her apartment. The door's locked. The mail's still in the box. I'm worried that something's happened to her."

"Maybe she doesn't want to see you."

"Why?" His voice caught and broke; his hands clutched at his forehead. Luis was gripped by a fever.

"Maybe you scared her off with that famous temper of yours," I said, remembering what Mallory had told me.

"I swear to you, Maurice, I never even raised my voice."

"No fists through walls?" I'd seen Luis do that once, when a movie producer canceled the contract for a house in Malibu.

"Nothing like that," he said, his voice trembling. "We had some words—I wanted her to stay. She wouldn't listen."

I could picture the scene: Luis pleading, maybe down on his knees, with his arms thrown out like some guy in opera, Mallory watching him with cool eyes.

"I've done nothing *wrong*," Luis said with renewed fire, feeding on his ability to believe that, somehow, he was always in the right: Luis, HUAC martyr; Luis, architectural Don Quixote; Luis, unjustly spurned servant of his muse. "I've held her hand, kissed her once or twice. It's gone no further."

He sounded pathetic, and I'm afraid I was starting to enjoy this interview. "Gee, I thought you said you were sleeping with her."

"No," he said, blinking, dolefully watching me from his perch on the chair.

"It's what you wanted me to think."

"Did I?" His expression was mournful. "I guess I did."

I shook my head, wondering how anybody could get himself into such a mess over a woman he'd only known a couple of weeks.

"I know, I know, I'm an idiot," Luis said, catching my thought. "But I need her."

"No, you don't. You *think* you need her."

"I need her like I've never needed any woman before."

"Horseshit."

"She's my good luck charm."

"And Jennifer? I thought she was your good luck charm too."

"It fades," he said, defiant, petulant. "The glory fades."

"For you, it fades," I said. "Because you make the mistake of believing in it."

"You're hard, Maurice."

"I'm a realist."

"How did this happen to me?" He stamped his foot like a child. "How?"

This was an animal cry, the confusion and panic of the ill-fated man, and I thought he was about to burst into tears. But he gathered himself, mopping at his face with a handkerchief, issuing a sigh that would have been heard at the back of Carnegie Hall. He was a campaigner, and, if no wiser at dealing with these storms, at least accustomed to them. I don't know how old Luis was then. Maybe sixty. His exact age, like much else about him, was a matter of conjecture. He was from Peru, and claimed that his father had been among the first explorers of the lost mountain city of Machu Picchu. I was as inclined to believe that as I was to participate in some street huckster's game of three-card monte. He claimed that before arriving in America he'd designed a house for Trotsky in Mexico. This, whether true or not, had been brought back to haunt him by Senator Joe McCarthy. Luis claimed plenty of things, although his achievements in California were beyond dispute or question: a house for the movie actor and art collector Edward G. Robinson, an airplane factory for the Hughes Corporation, a church of wood and glass high on the cliffs of Palos Verdes. Architecture and eating and drinking were almost mystical experiences for him. And love, naturally. He went overboard about everything.

"Remind me of the name of this woman," I said.

"Mallory Walker."

"Where did you meet her, anyway?"

Thinking I might as well get the story from both sides, I watched the happy look that came over Luis's face. An expression of pure joy that swept aside the mood of the previous moments. I almost envied him his innocence.

"It was outside a movie theater in Westwood," he said. "It was one of those science-fiction pictures—giant ants running around in the sewers of Los Angeles."

I'd heard about the film; I hadn't seen it, but for a week or so Ches and Bobby ran about the house, playing atom-mutated bugs. I remembered, too, Luis's fondness for the exotic, the fantastic, the lurid; tales of horror and spirits and ghosts, or science run amok. He believed in unreal stories. As a young man, he told me once, he'd done the art for movie posters that had adorned the streets of Lima and Buenos Aires. *The Hands of Orlac* was one of his favorites, the movie where a pianist loses his hands in an accident and is given those of a murderer instead. Luis had a poetic eccentricity I saw as self-destructive.

"She came up to me outside the theater. She said we'd met when I lectured once at Yale. I didn't remember. It seems incredible to me now, that I could have forgotten her. Even if I'd seen her for only a second that first time."

I thought of my own first meeting with Luis, soon after I arrived in Los Angeles in the winter of 1945. I'd asked around and discovered that he was the hot architect in town. So I contrived an introduction at a party. I flattered him, said I'd come and work in his office for nothing if he'd take me on as an apprentice. Already I had my plan in place. I wasn't an apprentice for long.

"As soon as I saw her again, I knew it. I *knew* I was in love," he said, his face all mushy and radiant with the memory. "How can you explain it, Maurice? You never can. That moment—the encounter with the goddess."

I bounced an eraser on the desk in front of me, already impatient with Luis's nonsense.

"She changed things right away. She told me to get in touch with you again."

"Wait a minute," I said, alert again. "That was *her* idea?"

"Absolutely. She said you owed me. And therefore you'd help."

"She said that?"

"She gave me the courage to throw the party. To call you. I've been in a mess, Maurice. I don't mind admitting it."

I thrilled at this new evidence of Mallory's deviousness; she was something, a female Machiavelli. She fixed all this to meet me. I felt my dick go hard under the table.

"That's why I need so bad to find her," he said, wringing his hands, then tugging at the hair that gushed from his ear.

"Luis, you'll survive. You always do."

"I wonder. Maybe not this time," he said. His eyes went crafty. "When will we talk about the other thing—Las Vegas and Cuba?"

"Soon enough."

"When?"

"Don't push me," I said, not uncivil. "There are a lot of things to figure."

"Like what?"

I shrugged, and he backed off, seeing that I would say no more. So he returned to the other subject, his hobbyhorse, his muse.

"I feel like working. I *am* working," he said. "Like never before. I'm making so many drawings I don't even know where they are. I've mislaid a whole portfolio full of stuff. Don't know where it is. *Pfft!*"

He waved a hand above his head, as if to say there were plenty more ideas circling up there, waiting for him to pluck them down. I'd seen him when he was inspired—his hand struck across the page with speed, with flourish, never needing to make a correction.

"That doesn't matter, the portfolio. *She* matters. I must find her."

I raised my hands: How was I supposed to help?

"You'll let me know if she calls you."

"Why would she do that?"

"She's interested in you. You'll let me know?"

Lying came easily, almost naturally, to me by then. "Sure," I said.

"As *soon* as she calls. Please, Maurice. I don't know if I can live without her."

11

I'd built our Malibu beach house in 1950, soon after my partnership with Luis ended, right around the same time I did the Slominsky house. I'd built it quickly, with Jackie's money and a feeling of liberation, the idea being to create an advertisement for my gifts and not just a living space on the sand. I'd persuaded a famous photographer to take pictures of the house for free, and then, pecking away at a typewriter, I'd sent copies of these to journals in Germany, Japan, France, Sweden, and Britain. I reckoned the pictures were more likely to be published if they featured, along with the building, an attractive woman standing about the place; Jackie served as model. You didn't have to be Einstein to figure this stuff out, but I think I was the first architect who did it. I was good at the image thing. And when a magazine called *California Style & Architecture* started up in 1952, Jackie encouraged me to get friendly with the editor. "He's queer and you're cute," Jackie had said, and another useful alliance was formed.

The house comprised two boxy structures in concrete and wood, standing only fify yards back from the ocean, raised above the sand by a fretwork of stilts, and connected by a narrow redwood bridge than ran over the swimming pool. The idea, originally, had been that one side of the house would be for the kids, the other for Jackie and me. It hadn't worked—soon the kids' mess was all over. At either end, angled like a wing, was the roof of a car port. When Mallory guided her Porsche beneath one of these, turning the ignition so that the whiny engine died and our ears filled with the busy racket of the surf, I realized that I'd never previously brought any of my mistresses or one-night stands here. In the annals of my infidelity this was a first, and I wondered why. What was special about her? Was I so entranced by my feelings of superiority over Luis and my upcoming career in politics that I felt myself invulnerable and deserving of whatever the hell I wanted? Or was I secretly trying to destroy everything and obliterate myself?

I've often wondered.

"I love the ocean at night when the moon's on it," Mallory said. "Let's walk on the beach awhile."

But I was impatient to get inside.

The house smelled pleasantly of heat and salt. Moonlight carved the tall, open-beamed area of the living room, making stark patterns on the walls. The floorboards shone like they were floodlit, and Mallory's eyes glowed, looking over our family clutter: the surfboards, the fishing tackle, the diving gear, the magazines on the floor, the books that were already salt-damaged and sagging in the built-in bookcases.

I walked up and slid my arms about her waist. "Sorry about the mess," I said. "The maid comes in Fridays."

"Don't worry. It's a charming space," she said, smiling and pushing me away, gently, but firmly.

She was expecting to be wooed. I could do that.

"Drink?"

"You bet," she said, and I went into the kitchen, making busy with a bottle of scotch, some ginger ale that opened with a frothing fizz, and ice from the enormous, and largely empty, refrigerator. While I was fixing the highballs, I called out, asking about her day, giving her the latest about Luis.

"Did you tell him anything?"

"What? And spoil our fun."

Walking back into the living room, a glass tumbler chinking in either hand, I saw that she was standing beneath the fireplace, above which was a 342-pound marlin. An entire marlin, stuffed and mounted, its glazed eyes looking down. That thing was longer than a torpedo.

"Here," I said, handing her a glass. "My wife caught that. Last year in Hawaii."

"She's a fighter, then."

"I'll say."

"And her father's a senator. Is that why you married her?" The acid words came with a tough smile, as if she was taking up her stance prior to a duel. "Or was it just the money?"

"Is that what Luis said?"

"Something like that."

I stood close to her again, raising my glass in a toast. "Actually I married Jackie for her money and contacts. Joe only became a senator later. Though I guess it was in the cards. Then Jackie and I started to like each other. Who could have predicted that?" I said. "We make a good team."

"Like the USC Trojans?"

I laughed, pleased by the comeback.

"Are you unbreakable?"

"Am I a target?"

"Could I make a mark on you, Maurice? Or do you only fall for rich and powerful people?"

"That would include you, wouldn't it?"

"Yes, it would."

"You think I'm weak?"

"I think you're predictable."

"Do you mind?"

"Not at all."

She'd responded to my sexual impatience with a note of challenge and now we were fencing, cut and thrust. She was smooth and tough at the game, never showing the same face for very long. Keeping me on my toes. She'd agreed to spend these days with me and I began to see that I was in for an exciting time. At least I got that part right.

She wore scruffy jeans and a white T-shirt that seemed to shine in the moonlight. Kicking off her shoes, she settled herself on the sofa in front of the fireplace; her feet were bare and long and her toenails glowed like pearls. "Tell me about Las Vegas," she said, tucking her legs under her.

"You've never been there?"

She shook her head.

"It's a boom town. Growing like crazy," I said. "It's restless, kind of shrill. The way any place is when it's in the throes of acute prosperity."

"There's money—I guess that appeals to you."

I smiled. She was going to have to do better than that to get a rise out of me. "I told my people we're coming. They'll lay out a red carpet."

And can be relied upon to be discreet, I said to myself.

"What did you say about me?"

"That you're a young architect I want to work with."

"Lucky I brought my portfolio."

"I mentioned that you're a woman. They were . . . *surprised*."

"I bet."

Was she being ironic? I couldn't tell, but wondered what else Luis had told her about me.

She put aside her drink. "Are we going to talk all night?" she said, and lay back, arms crossed behind her head. Her eyes invited my kiss but when I put down my own drink and moved toward her she quickly planted her bare foot on my chest, holding me at bay.

"Suppose I give you want you want," she said. "What's to stop you throwing me out on the street?"

"That's a risk you take." Lifting her foot to my mouth, I kissed the pearled toes one by one. I pressed my lips against the high arch of her instep and licked away the salt. "Besides, don't you want it too?"

"I want this chance."

"You really want me to screw Luis?"

"I'm not interested in him. Just in myself, and you."

"Then I guess this is the perfect arrangement. Isn't it?"

She pondered, watching me in the moonlight. At last she said: "Take off my pants."

To which command I replied: "My pleasure."

I reached for the buckle of her belt, undid the top button of her jeans, unzipped the zipper, peeled the denim off her narrow hips. Snaking to the floor, the belt and its buckle hit with a clang. She wore no underwear and her skin was sleek as satin on either side of the darkness between her legs. Her lips parted a little. Her smiling eyes met mine.

"Now what?" I said.

"I think you know the answer to that."

It was a game of control and submission, a game of pleasure and expectation with the thrill of danger attached. Again, a game I thought I understood. And if you know you're in the game, I said to myself, then you're going to win.

Someone clever once said: Never sleep with anyone who has more problems than yourself. What he should have said was: Never become a part of those problems and never forget the location of the exit.

I thought I was in command, kneeling in front of her, brushing my lips down her leg to the thigh. I thought I was on top, kissing the firm, warm tautness of her belly, gently taking her nipples between my lips and teasing them until they were erect and she began to sigh. I thought I was running the show, slipping my tongue inside her, scarcely moving until her desire mounted and her hips began to rock, dictating their own rhythm. Then I plunged my tongue in deep, like a sword. She arched, shuddered, and my face streamed with her juice. In her abandonment she cried out, a sound that was strange, lost, almost angry.

She was panting and her fingers gripped my hair, raising my face from between her thighs.

"Take me to bed," she said. "I want to fuck you."

12

*A*fterwards I made us another drink and fell into the deepest sleep. In my dream I was diving down to a wreck, an airplane that lay in shallow water, sleek and gray and looking about as long as Manhattan, covered only with a fuzz of moss that didn't hide the freshness of her paint. The dream was soundless: I didn't hear my breathing, or the hiss of used air leaving the compressor and bubbling to the surface. All was silent. I swam inside, entering the nose, where the architecture changed, grew infinite, as if this weren't an airplane at all. I dropped down through narrow corridors and steel stairways. Garbage drifted in the water: a sheet of newspaper, its headline still visible—ADRIFT!; a boot that was floating. I was carrying a flashlight and in its beam I saw the snout and trailing fin of a shark. My heartbeat quickened, but the shark showed no interest in me and passed out of the light with a swift flick of its tail. My feeling of unease remained, however. I was lost but still couldn't stop myself going further down into the wreck, deeper and deeper, along corridors that twisted and grew more narrow while the pressure of the water increased. I was searching—but I didn't know what for. The airplane groaned, its struts and skeletons shifting, as if it had been perched on a ledge and was starting to fall. Now I knew I had to get out. I turned, trying to swim, and the flailing beam of my flashlight lit up a corpse. Then a second. Then one more. Bloated corpses, bursting from their uniforms, moving gently as they hung there, faceless corpses dancing in the underwater currents.

I woke with a jolt, heaving myself upright, sweating in the darkness with my heart going like a hammer. Only on hearing the rumble of the surf outside did I remember that I was at the beach house, with Mallory.

She wasn't in bed. She sat on a chair in the corner of the room, dressed only in her white T-shirt, naked legs crossed, toes shining, her skin like marble in the moonlight that angled through the windows. Her face was in shadow. Smoke rose from the burning point of her cigarette. She'd been watching me, observing me.

"Bad dream?" she said.

"I guess." My mouth felt parched and my skin was clammy.

Taking her time, she stubbed out her cigarette and came toward me, lazily padding across the floor.

"Still frightened?" she said, and handed me a glass of water.

I took long, thirsty gulps; my eyes never left her. "No, it was a weird dream, that's all."

"About the war?"

"I don't want to talk about it."

"Maybe you should."

"It doesn't matter," I said, finishing the water. "It's not me anymore."

She gave me an odd look then, a mixture of sympathy and regret.

"Poor baby. I'll put you to sleep."

She climbed in with me between the covers. Her body was warm, hotter than mine, even though she'd been sitting in the chair. In that strange, half-dreaming, half-waking state, I felt her lips on my neck, my nipples, my belly. She passed her tongue all over me, licking my fingers, my toes, my thighs, my balls. When I was erect, she straddled me. Leaned over me so that her fine hair stroked my face and our lips met at last. Her tongue pushed deeper and deeper into my throat, almost choking me, deliciously, as if what she felt at my prick had communicated itself to her mouth and her tongue had become *her* penis.

Maybe it was my dream, or the brilliance of that hot moonlit night with the wind starting to gust outside. I'd slept with many women in my life but never felt such abandonment before. I wanted to give myself to her entirely. I wanted her to unleash all her appetites on me, to leave me drained, possessed, wrecked.

My second sleep was dreamless.

13

*B*y this time my relationship with the desert was complicated. I no longer saw it the way many people did, as fit only for snakes, hermits, and military maneuvers, as the wasteland you drove through to get from Los Angeles to Las Vegas. Right from the beginning I'd had an eye for the wind-haunted emptiness, the twisted trees, the white sky so immense it swallowed the landscape, the shrubs that flowered only for a day before the heat killed them, the evidence of his own striving that man left at the side of the road in the form of ramshackle huts, defunct diners and fruit stands, or makeshift wooden crosses marking the fatal car crash. The desert, in some way, had made its call to me. I'd understood that the real nature of the place wasn't in the quiet and ghostly beauty that photographs sometimes showed. The real desert was what happened if you took a wrong turn in the shape-contorting heat and ran out of water; then you sent up your prayers, hoping to find your way out again before you began to dream of drinking the blood of a lizard and your brain fried in its pan. In its heart the desert was majestically cruel and indifferent, but not, as I'd discovered when I started doing some work out there, unchangeable, not, in the short term, *unusable*. The sand could be made to gush with money; the building of the Hoover Dam and the subsequent growth of Las Vegas had shown that.

We left the beach house after breakfast and hit the desert before noon, by which time the sun was huge and merciless and the wind buffeted the sides of the Porsche so hard it seemed the car might fly away. Outside Barstow a truck had tipped over, littering the highway with splintered crates and crushed peaches. An ambulance sped past us, siren screaming, bearing away the casualty, or maybe there was more than one.

We talked a little about architecture, about Richard Neutra's Lovell House, on which Mallory had written a paper, but most of the time we were quiet. A not quite comfortable silence. My body felt bruised and I needed a cooler moment to gather myself. Only hours ago I'd taken pleasure and excitement in the idea that she was obliterating me—a crazy notion. Maybe I'd dreamed the whole thing. I couldn't, of course, *entirely* deny the extravagance of my feelings, nor of her allure during the night. I wasn't nuts. But I wasn't about to let those feelings take over. I was clear about what was going on, and if some of the play was on the rough side, that was fine, too.

I checked the real estate signs at the side of the highway: out here in the arid nothingness, in the most forbidding and forlorn part of Nevada, people dreamed of turning a deal, making a buck.

"People are trading land here? They must be crazy," Mallory said.

"Maybe. Maybe not."

"Deserts resist history," she said.

"We're Americans," I said with a smile. "Don't you know that we *make* history?"

"You can't beat the desert. Ask the Egyptians. The Assyrians. The Babylonians. That's why great ideas come from the desert. Great religions, great passions. It's what the sand's good for."

"I'll show you something," I said.

"What?" she said, turning her head with sudden glee and excitement, a child promised a gift.

"You'll see."

Following my instructions, she swung the Porsche off the interstate and we turned left, heading for Indian Springs. The road went arrow-straight, raised slightly above the bleak, brown scrub with a ditch on either side. Mountains loomed in the distance. An early snowfall crowned the lofty peak of Mount Charleston, yet down here in the dust bowl we had the top up and the windows shut tight against the heat. You got the idea that all weather systems were acting simultaneously, that the desert could encompass everything. We saw no other vehicle for more than thirty minutes. The emptiness, though I'd seen it plenty of times, spooked me. Then a chocolate-colored bus rumbled by, jerking us in its slipstream. The hills seemed to close in. A Joshua tree flung its arms out like a drunken hitchhiker. In the foothills steam from the hot springs clung to the ground. Dumped on the road's loose gravel shoulder was a dead dog.

We passed through Indian Springs, the only place to buy gas or a drink between Vegas and Beatty, then seventeen more miles of nothing before a turn in the road and a sign forbidding us to proceed.

"Don't worry," I said to her. "Go on."

After two more miles there were more signs, dire with warnings. In the center of the road was a checkpoint, a sentry box, and a candy-striped barrier. A soldier emerged from the sentry box, walking with deliberate slowness in the heat. He had his carbine at the ready and his boots squeaked on the newly paved road. I flashed him the ID pass that was in my wallet and he raised the barrier, sending us on our way.

Now Mallory was curious, but with a smile I refused to answer her questions. "You'll see," I said, enjoying this. "Don't be impatient."

We drove about ten more minutes in the cooking heat. An army truck swept by, green and flashing in the desert light, like some enormous, rattling bug. We passed along another road, this one smooth and new, courtesy of the Corps of Engineers.

And then we came to the houses: six of them, neatly arranged in a semicircle, as if a suburban neighborhood had sprung up in the desert.

I told her to stop the car and we climbed out while she drank in the strangeness of the scene. A car stood in each driveway. Garbage cans were at the side of each house. Grass had been planted out front, and sprinklers, rigged up from a nearby water truck, were weaving their cool vertigo.

"You want to take a look inside?"

I opened the front door and our feet sank into a beige shag carpet. Off to the right was a kitchen. In front of the sink a female mannequin had on a red checkered apron. The cupboards were amply stocked with cans and ketchup bottles. The fridge was loaded with milk, cheese, vegetables. An open box of cornflakes was on the table. In the living room, seated in front of the enormous TV set with his pipe in his hand, was the male mannequin. On a table to this guy's side was a Seagram's whiskey bottle and a copy of *Life*, the current issue, with the youthful Elizabeth Taylor on the cover. The window at the back had a lace curtain, through which could be seen a gazebo and the desert, patches of sagebrush here and there, the cruel white wilderness.

Mallory still hadn't figured it out. She took the Seagram's bottle, twisted off the cap, and sniffed at the nut-brown liquid. "Fake," she said.

"Tea, most likely. Some stuff even the army doesn't care to throw away."

"The army?"

Her eye was caught by a column of ants, marching across the fireplace toward a crack in the white plaster of the chimney, proof that the desert had not been conquered entirely, or maybe not at all.

She said: "These are accommodations for the troops, right?"

"Guess again."

"I don't get it," she said, frowning, puzzlement in those cool graygreen eyes.

"We're in the middle of the Nevada proving ground."

"Where they explode the bombs?"

"The *atom* bombs. Every month, sometimes two a month, sometimes every week. The biggest bitches of all."

"I still don't get it," she said, frowning at my manner, and so I was serious for a moment or two while I explained what was going on. After the big bang at Bikini Atoll (that bomb had been called "Gilda," with a picture of Rita Hayworth painted on it), the government decided to bring the nuclear program closer to home, where, in theory, it could be better controlled and more easily observed. It made the whole process cheaper, too. The Nevada desert was chosen from among various possible sites, and, once the tests got underway, it was decided to gauge the effect on a variety of urban and suburban environments, to see what stood up and what didn't, and what was simply vaporized, and to get some idea of what troops might encounter entering a town after an attack.

"Each time there's a test we put up some structures," I said. "It's all gotten more and more elaborate. Next time we're putting up a hospital. They need to know how a hospital might stand up. I guess I can understand that."

Mallory was staring at me like I was insane. "Where do you come in?"

"I'm the architect."

"You *design* this?"

"As architecture, the work couldn't be simpler." I rubbed my fingers together. "Lucrative, too. It's government business."

The contract had been pushed my way by Joe Nelson, who sat on the Senate Atomic Energy Sub-Committee. He'd spoken to someone, who spoke to someone, who lifted a phone and called me. I had clearance to go anywhere I wanted on the test site, any time. I'd climbed the tower where one of the bombs had been let off. I'd hunkered in a trench with some of the troops.

"You build this so it can be destroyed?"

"It's absurd, isn't it? Sometimes they use pigs."

"Pigs? For what?"

"They dress them in army uniforms," I said. "You think I'm kidding?"

"It's sick."

A look came over her face that I'd seen only once before, the first time I met her, at Luis's party, when the Slominsky house had been mentioned and something dark had come into her eyes. I got a longer view of the whirlpool this time. Suddenly she looked younger, much more raw, bewildered somehow. And angry.

"You think the Russians are going to attack us? That we'll look up one day and the sky will be filled with parachutes?"

"Probably not," I said. "I don't think about it, to be honest. I do my work, I take my money, and I go home."

She went on another tack. "You won medals in the war, didn't you?"

"Luis told you that?"

"It's not true?"

"Sure, I won medals. Now I look out for myself."

She walked up to the mannequin like she wanted to slap it. Her powerful, collected stare was nowhere to be seen. "Who are you, Maurice? Really?"

I smiled, happy to have cracked her mask of cool. She liked to play games in bed and now she knew I could surprise her, too. It's always like this between men and women, isn't it? A form of combat, a constant attempt to seize the initiative. A game. I'd made her show her hand a little, and she'd revealed a different version of herself, a sense of outrage, a vulnerability. I began to wonder whether appearing in my office had been an act of prickly bravery, not merely arrogance and ambition. You're in turmoil, I thought, somewhere deep down, and why is that? I liked her more. Beneath the smoothness and the money she was afraid of something but she fought back with guts.

"Right now I'd settle for a Coke," I said. "I'm parched."

PART 2

Las Vegas

14

SEPTEMBER 5, 1956 / LAS VEGAS

*W*e entered the El Sheik at dusk, not that you could ever tell the difference, the casinos of course being the same at every hour even in those days, clockless and air-conditioned, a never-changing rhythm of whirring slots, cards shuffling on the green felt, and ivory balls clicking in the grooves of the spinning wheels. The population of Las Vegas was less than 75,000 back then, and acres of untouched desert stood between the buildings on the Strip. The whole place had the atmosphere of a small town indulging in an endless spree. You could play roulette, craps, faro, blackjack, poker, or any other game you might care to dream up and explain to a dealer. You could bet one buck or a thousand on the big fight, the big game, or, if you wanted, on two cockroaches crossing the floor. The atmosphere was looser, though one thing was unchanged. An everlasting law was at play, a law that was true in 1956 and still holds fast: you don't beat the house. You do not, under any circumstances, ever, beat the house. That is, was, the immutable; the house won, always, meaning the money gushed into the drop boxes beneath the tables and was transported into the counting room, where a skim was immediately taken off the top and delivered in a bag or leather satchel to some faceless, slow-moving man who sat in the back room of a nondescript restaurant in Chicago or Detroit. In 1956 J. Edgar Hoover still denied the existence of organized crime in America. I'd seen what went on. It was organized, certainly, and it looked criminal. Politics didn't prevent it, went hand in hand with it. Las Vegas was a place where crooked money could legitimize itself, as much a part of the system as the zero on a roulette wheel. Not that I cared, or had a judgment on any of that. I liked the city. It had a madhouse energy all of its own and I didn't have to live there. I didn't even gamble. I was just the architect.

I kept a suite permanently at the El Sheik, a cabana situated at the far end of the swimming pool. All I had to do was collect the key from reception. That was my plan, but while we were in the lobby I was spotted by Nick Mantilini, Paul Mantilini's son. He was standing in the pit, in between a couple of the roulette tables, and smiled, signaling that we should come over.

"The heir to the king," I said to Mallory. "We'd better say hello."

"Fine by me," Mallory said with a cool smile. "I like heirs."

Nick was talking with a tall, spindly, dark-haired guy—Will Rothschild, the owner and editor of the *Las Vegas Press*, one of the local rags. "I'm not saying anything more. I'll have news for you later," Nick was saying to him, already turning to greet me. "Maurice, a pleasure as always. Who's your friend?"

I made the introductions. "This is the new architect?" Nick said. "Maurice, you old dog, you didn't mention that she was a woman. A *beauty*."

Nick had a cocky arrogance, played golf like a pro, and was a demon with a racquet in his hand. He was athletic and smart and women were usually impressed; now that Mallory gave no sign of being so, he was piqued, inevitably, and tossed out his charm like it was a ball he was planning to hammer over the net. He asked where she was from, filled her in on the various shows that were in town. He was craggy, well-groomed, self-assured, with startling, restless blue eyes that weren't his father's. He always looked like a race car stuck in traffic—too big and powerful for his expensive suits, too impatient to listen to most conversations. Sure, he could be smooth when he wanted, but I have to admit I felt challenged by him. Nick was aggressively competitive and thought he had my number. Maybe he did. He wanted to be loved by his father but respected and feared by everybody else. He had good looks and didn't bother to hide his vanity, which was colossal. His nose crooked at the tip where he'd broken it in a football game.

"I'd like to show you around," Nick said to Mallory, "if Maurice will allow it."

"I'm a big girl now," Mallory said. "I don't need anybody's permission. And that would include his."

"Great—I'll get things rolling," said Nick, reminding me, and letting Mallory know, lest she fail to appreciate, that we were on his turf now, in his realm. He both revered and resented his all-powerful father. That had been my first impression, when I first met Nick a few years back. He'd worked on himself since then and most of the rough edges had disappeared. Like Mr. Crosby sang: "Ac-*cent*-uate the positive, ee-*lim*-inate the negative." He played cards with impatient flair and looked to the future.

"Do you like to gamble?" he said, sliding an arm around Mallory's waist, guiding her toward the nearest roulette table. He signaled to the croupier, who slid over a pile of chips that he pressed into Mallory's hand. "It's easy."

"I bet on black," she said, pushing the chips across the baize.

"All of it?" Nick asked.

"Everything," she said.

"She's rather lovely," said Will Rothschild to me, smiling with his mean, ferrety teeth. Rothschild was English, a fact he never failed to advertise, and he had the limpest handshake this side of the Rocky Mountains. Yet he cut a dapper figure: a Jew, he'd run guns to Jewish Palestine after the war, had left England under dubious circumstances, and had failed in Los Angeles before arriving in Vegas in 1950, or thereabouts, picking up a job as publicist for one of the hotels. He'd been on the lam, like lots of people who came to town. Now he part-owned the Desert Inn and had various real estate ventures, as well as the *Press*, which he'd purchased for a couple of thousand dollars. He brought some English race car driver to the Nevada salt flats to stage a bid on the world speed record. He wasn't quite the tame reporter and trod on toes sometimes, never too hard, but hard enough to establish, usually, the true story. Which, usually, he didn't publish, choosing to concentrate instead on the comings and goings of Sammy Davis Jr. and Peggy Lee. Probably this was wise. He was grabby for power and saw himself as a publisher of the type supposed to have gone out with derringer pistols and the Comstock Lode, a stylishly *corrupt* publisher. He claimed relationship to the famous banking family. "Remote branch. Bit of a black sheep, dear heart." He was another gambler who'd rolled in from somewhere but had ended up in Vegas.

"Where did you find her?"

"She found me," I said.

"That's usually the way, isn't it?" he said. "I say, your girl's winning."

This was true; black having come up three times in succession, Mallory found herself a center of attention, and in command of a growing heap of chips. She let them ride, much to the delight of the crowd that, murmuring, nudging, surrounded her and Nick.

"I heard something rather intriguing about you today, Maurice," Rothschild went on. "A little bird whispered in my ear. Words about Washington and Nevada, the Senate."

"Who told you that?"

"It's true, then," Rothschild said, light twinkling in his small, raisin-colored eyes. "I'll be super-nice to you from now on." He scratched his chin. "What about the incumbent?"

"Come on, Will. I can't talk about that."

"Strictly off the record, old chap."

I was saved by the cry of the croupier: "Black!"

"Maurice, take her away, please. I insist, before she breaks the bank," said Nick, laughing. I got the idea, watching the croupier load Mallory's chips into a flat wooden box, that for some reason I didn't yet understand, this whole little show had been staged for my benefit. The house had allowed Mallory to win, for now. No doubt something would be demanded from me in return.

"I'll have a guy go cash these in for her," Nick said, his strong arm about my shoulder. "But Dad wants to talk in the morning—and breakfast's on you. Deal?"

"Deal," I said.

Midnight approached by the time Mallory and I circled the steaming, floodlit pool and I unlocked the door into the cabana, finding further offerings—roses, fruit baskets, bottles of champagne cooling in ice buckets with green foil around their necks.

"These guys like you," Mallory said, sitting on the corner of the king-size bed with her hands splayed on the silk cover. The check, which was for a sum of over ten thousand dollars, was still in her hand, and she glanced at it, blinking. Her eyes, for a moment, looked surprised, enormous.

"I build their hotels," I said.

"And I heard something about the Senate," she said, tilting her head to one side. "What's that all about?"

She was quick and sharp and she didn't miss a trick. "You've got good ears."

She shrugged. "Mr. Valentine goes to Washington. Is that the story?"

"Maybe."

"And that's why you need help with your firm?"

"I'm still trying to figure things out. It's all happened pretty fast."

"It's exciting."

"I guess."

"Who was the tall English guy?"

"He owns one of the local papers."

"And we're meeting your boss for breakfast? Is that right?"

"You're gonna put it in your date book?"

"No," she said, her fingers playing on the silk coverlet, though I gained a sense, behind the neutral expression, of her mind ticking away, storing something, calculating how it might be used. Then she smiled with quick brightness and said: "Let's go for a swim."

We changed, and swam a few laps through vapors that rose from the surface, fogging the heat of the desert night. We were alone in the pool, though one of the attendants had forgotten to remove the craps table at which gamblers could play while taking a dip. The thing was floating about like a barge, an obstruction Mallory negotiated by diving beneath it and popping up on the other side before continuing with her smooth, powerful stroke. She was sleek, like an arrow in the water.

Afterwards, in the cabana, we cracked the champagne, drank a bottle quickly, and fell, half-drunk, onto the bed, where Mallory started to fuck me with the same fierce, dominating, hypnotizing concentration as the night before. My eyes were shut but my hands touched the smooth skin of her thighs, traveling up her back, where they found a long and bumping ridge on the skin.

I opened my eyes. "Where did you get the scar?"

She stopped moving and looked down at me, hands pressed against my chest. "What scar?"

When I remember her at that moment I seem to see a challenge flashing in her eyes, and I wonder whether she was daring me to interrogate her, to dig at the truth, to compel her to tell the story of that scar. But maybe this is my imagination, memory playing me false, creating a moment in which our story might have changed. Because I questioned her no further. Okay, I thought, if you want to go on playing these games, that's fine.

"My mistake," I said, raising my lips toward her small, high breasts. "Don't stop fucking me."

15

*I*n the morning I lay back in bed, lounging at my ease while she showered, dried, and slipped into her underwear.

"Like the show?" she said, standing by the bed with her hand on her hip, not saucy, watching me watching her.

"Trying to figure out what kind of show it actually is."

"Not enjoying it?"

"Oh, I'm enjoying it all right." I tapped the mattress beside me. "Maybe you should come back to bed."

A well-aimed piece of fruit smote me on the forehead. Not thrown hard, but not softly either.

"Ouch!"

"Come on, mister—get your ass out of there. I want my breakfast."

She was all business. I took my own shower, made a couple of calls, and we hurried past the swimming pool toward the lobby, where, at nine A.M., the crap-shooters already split the air with their cries. Or maybe they hadn't stopped from the night before. Nick Mantilini appeared to greet us. He must have been waiting.

"I'll take you in to my father," he said.

Paul Mantilini sat at his usual table, looking out the window at the eighteenth hole of the golf course. He sat perfectly still, not moving his head, but knowing of our presence. Maybe he saw our reflections in the glass. Sometimes I wondered whether he had some hidden sense that most of us don't possess, or maybe we once did and lost it long ago, a primitive awareness, a knowledge of who was where in a room and what was moving, an instinct that had survived in him from man's distant past, or had been awoken by the dangerous edges of his own life. For at the moment we arrived within a yard of his table, he turned his face, an impressive, perhaps studied, effect. And what a face it was: tanned, lined, rumpled, and smiling, yet the most divided face I ever saw. The left side of it was cold and watchful, the cheek hard, the eye almost dead-looking; the right side, the side he showed us now, was bright and alive, alert and intelligent, almost friendly. "Tell me about yourself and the world," the right side of his face seemed to say. "I'll kill you if I want," warned the left. A squarish face, with a strong nose, and hair mounting above it in waves of careful, pompadoured gray. A suave face that never quite let you forget its potential for menace.

"Greetings, Maurice," he said, speaking so softly I instinctively leaned forward to catch the words. I never knew what Mantilini was thinking because he gave the impression he was thinking of everything at once. "Who's your friend?"

"Dad, this is Mallory Walker," said Nick, stepping up, eager as ever to please his father. "She's the architect Maurice called us about."

"A lady architect?" he said, curiosity briefly flashing in the right side of his face. "I don't care if she's Cleopatra and Maria Callas rolled into one. I hope she'll sit down and join us in a cup of coffee. How do you like it, my dear?"

"Black, very strong," Mallory said, slipping into the chair opposite Mantilini by the window. I saw that she'd brought her damned portfolio with her.

"The only way to drink it," Mantilini said, his eyes resting on her, assessing, not possessing. Then he returned to his grapefruit, slicing into the pink flesh, and spoke to me without looking up. "There's some problem with the wiring in the show room."

"I'll talk to Entenza," I said. Del Entenza, who'd been the main contractor on the hotel, was based all the way down in Phoenix, because in southern Nevada there was nothing—only the desert and what we were creating. "It'll get fixed today."

"Will it?" he said, laying aside his curved grapefruit gadget with a look of genuine surprise and pleasure on the lively side of his face. The left was as grave and inscrutable as ever. "Will it really?"

"Sure." I'd known Mantilini to relax when he was talking about music or pictures, about which he'd striven to educate himself, but never about his buildings, never about the matter at hand. A part of him secretly expected, perhaps wished, to have to do everything himself, the way he'd built his life, brick by brick, though he had hundreds of guys to whom he gave orders. Entenza had told me the stories: the bootlegging days, the assassinations, the men hurled down elevator shafts in New York *pour encourager les autres.* I remembered myself how Mantilini had dismissed the attentions of Senator Joe Kefauver and his committee to investigate organized crime in America; he'd swatted them away, lazily, like flies. And then it was back to business as usual in the city that he ruled like a Medici prince. All this was legend, and bore no recognizable relation to the man I worked with and made deals with, who was watchful and almost studious, a predator no doubt, but with a passion and a nose for architecture. His house in Palm Springs had been designed by Neutra, and I had a relationship with him that I thought I understood. I saw my father-in-law, Joe Nelson, as a guy who'd fuck you up the ass while loudly explaining to the world, and to you yourself, the absolute necessity of the procedure. Joe was vain about his power and needed to be seen to win, whereas Mantilini's power would simply swallow you up, obliterate you without a trace. With him you'd just be found dead in the desert with your throat cut. Metaphorically speaking. Maybe even literally. Mantilini made no show of secrecy; nor, on the other hand, did he disclose his motives. I didn't know why he hired me in the first place. He never said. I suspected, and appreciated, Joe Nelson's hand. But Mantilini was practical and unsentimental, and my continued relationship was about my competence, my ability to think about what he wanted and give it to him. I'd completed the El Sheik on time and under budget. At one moment, early in the construction, a bomb went off, killing a worker and damaging the foundations. My calm impressed Mantilini; I left him to sort out the underlying problem (I really didn't want to

know about it) while fixing the damage and making no fuss about getting on with my end of things. I asked questions—I wanted to be sure
about my own safety and that of my various crews—but I didn't press. I
showed I could work in his room and keep my mouth shut. We didn't
get drunk or party or vacation with our families together. But we ate
dinner from time to time, and talked architecture. He had the knowledge of the enthusiast who could afford to buy, to collect buildings like
so many baseball cards, and he understood the business well enough to
know exactly how he'd helped my reputation. He didn't ram the issue
down my throat. And various of my peers came to envy my handle on
Las Vegas as an architectural playground.

Mantilini fingered his neck beneath the turtleneck of the black
sweater that rose almost to his chin; the fabric was silk, the best, hand-
woven by a guy whose name and address he refused to give me. "More
than my life's worth, Maurice," he'd said. A part of Mantilini was very,
very peacock. "Do you understand this game?" he said to Mallory, his
eyes inviting hers to look out the window, where the merciless sun already beat down on the pampered green of the golf course and where a
man in plaid pants, having missed his short putt, as if at Mantilini's psychic bidding, hurled aside his putter in a tantrum. "Cow-pasture pool. I
don't get it. I wish I did. Lots of my associates golf. I know several sena-
tors and they all seem to golf. Maurice," he said, looking across at me
suddenly. "Tell me this. Joe Nelson—does he golf?"

"He hacks around," I said.

"And you golf, too, right?"

"I hit a few."

"See. Everybody's at it. But I grew up in Brooklyn. We don't golf in
Brooklyn."

"What *do* you do there?" Mallory said. She leaned across the table a
little, her gray-green eyes wide with interest, her face cupped in her
hands. Already flirting, and I thought: You *bitch*. But I thought it, at that
point, with a smile.

"We knife each other. Shoot each other. If no other weapon comes
to hand we whack each other over the heads with baseball bats."

"Just the usual, then?"

"She's *funny*," he said to me, and his laughter would indeed have seemed unrestrained, were it not for that uncanny almost-lifeless left eye, still watching her. "What do you think, Maurice. Are you going to hire this young lady?"

"Maybe. I'm giving the matter full consideration."

"Then maybe she'd better show us what she can do."

"I don't think that's necessary, is it?"

"Give the girl a chance, Maurice. She brought her portfolio. She went to a lot of trouble." And then to her: "Come on, my dear. Show me what you've got."

He signaled to Nick, who hastily cleared a space on the table so that Mallory had room to unzip her portfolio and show her wares, while I fumed.

The work was exceptional. Better than that—brilliant. Rendered in charcoal, yet light, dazzling, inspired. There were twenty drawings in all, roughs for five hotels, seen from four different perspectives, each of them much finer than anything I could do myself, each from the unmistakable hand of Luis Barragan.

I was flabbergasted, but Mallory avoided my eye. Thus was the mystery of Luis's missing portfolio explained, and I gained a further insight into the extent of this young woman's deviousness and daring. Her signature had been added to the bottom of every drawing.

Mantilini had donned a pair of reading glasses and he leafed slowly through the drawings, pondering each one for a long while before licking his finger and turning to the next. "These are something," he said, pushing himself back in his chair. Taking off the glasses, he folded them, placed them on the table, and looked at Mallory afresh. "You'd better watch out, Maurice. I might not need you at all," he said, flashing a smile. "This young lady is gifted. *Very* gifted."

Just then a man bustled up to the table, Albert Kluphager, a pit boss at the El Sheik, an aggressive, dogged type with a perpetually harried expression and a shameless toupee that in moments of stress or anger he'd been known to whip off his head and stomp. His job was to watch the tables and catch the cheats, those who worked against the house and those who were supposedly working for it. He was good at his job, I'd gathered, though he had lots of traffic to deal with and demanding masters to please, not to mention the ulcers. A little leather box dangled from around his neck, and I wondered why he needed a camera at this hour of the morning.

"What's up, Albert?" said Nick Mantilini, who'd been silent, watchful while his father inspected Mallory's drawings.

"Caught one stealing, boss," he said, and snapped his fingers, summoning a woman who strutted across the restaurant without fear. A mink stole was draped around her shoulders. Beneath that, a black satin gown, cut to the thigh, and a long expanse of leg. Roxie: I couldn't remember her last name, if I ever knew it, though I'd spent a weekend with her a couple of years back. She was a skinny brunette, and in heels she towered over Kluphager, was so much taller than him that it seemed she could take hold of the camera strap and hang him up by it. But she looked too bored and exhausted to bother. Chewing gum, her wide, generous mouth working constantly, she awaited whatever punishment the lords of the El Sheik decided to mete out.

Mantilini's eyes had already drifted away, to elsewhere, to the golf course. He had no patience to deal with this.

"Stealing? Who from?" said Nick, shrugging his shoulders inside his suit jacket, taking on the job.

"Steve Greene."

"The actor?" Nick, pleased and happy, looked at Mallory. See?—his expression said—stars grace the El Sheik.

"He dropped fifty grand."

"How much did she take?"

"Two," said Kluphager, seizing the mink stole from Roxie's shoulders. His stubby fingers showed where little pockets were stitched into the lining, each the perfect size for a couple of casino chips.

"That's new," said Mantilini, showing interest for the first time, inspecting the stole. "That's neat, Roxie, that's really very ingenious."

He smiled at her, with understanding, it seemed, and not without a suggestion of warmth. He'd made a deal once with a movie actress who came from Los Angeles with the heir to a New York department-store fortune in tow. Her take was to be twenty percent of whatever the house got from the guy, and she stood at his side, egging him on while he shed $150,000 at craps and roulette. The sucker never knew he'd been had. Roxie wasn't at that level, but attractive women like her were a part of Mantilini's operation. Like the rest of us, however, they had to know their boundaries.

"I knew you'd want to see it," said Kluphager, beaming, proud.

"At breakfast," said Mantilini, his entire face stony for a moment. Then the smile was back. "Say, Albert. What's that box around your neck for, anyway?"

Nick smiled and looked alert, knowing, like I did, that Kluphager was about to be called to account for not merely doing his job and keeping quiet about it.

"This? Oh, gee!" Kluphager fondled the box tenderly. "This here is the real McCoy. This is one beautiful gadget. Cost me five hundred bucks. It's a Scintillator."

Mantilini's lips moved fractionally but he suppressed the smile. His hooded left eye, turned toward Mallory, closed in a slow wink.

Kluphager, oblivious to these signals of warning, took the box from around his neck and plopped it down on the table. "Look, boss. Here. I'll show you." He fiddled with the clasps. "See?" Extracted from its box, and switched on, the Scintillator emitted an ominous buzz and crackle. "It's a Geiger counter, see? No beeps. No high-pitched whiny noise. That means we're in the clear."

"Good to know, Albert," Mantilini said. "Especially since the test's not until tonight."

"Better safe than sorry," Kluphager said.

"Albert needs it to tell him when his dick's getting hard," said Roxie, chipping in, popping her gum with a spritely and wicked smile. "Otherwise he ain't got a fucking clue."

We all laughed, Mantilini himself the loudest of the four of us who were sitting at the table, and Kluphager mournfully assumed the air of a kicked dog. Maybe he was starting to worry that he wouldn't get his Scintillator back. Certainly he knew he'd become a comical figure. He scratched at his rug, and I wondered if he was about to hurl it to the floor. He restrained himself. "What should I do with her, boss?"

"Maybe this is none of my business," Mallory said. "But I've met Steve Greene. I know he'd give her the money if she asked for it."

"That's not the point, Mallory," Nick Mantilini said. His smile was easy, lordly, tolerant. He brushed his hand across the tip of his nose and he leaned his big head close to hers. "If she hadn't taken the two grand, Steve Greene would have lost it at the table. That money belongs to the casino."

"Maybe he wouldn't have gambled at all without Roxie at his side," said Mallory, not letting go. Something determined was in her face, with a hint of that anger I'd seen before. "Maybe that two grand would have broken the bank."

"Look . . ." Nick said, becoming impatient.

"Maybe she did you a favor."

"This is our business, and I should think that we know how best to run it, wouldn't you?"

Paul Mantilini said: "Stop it, Nick. That's enough." His face was hard, but not, this time, without emotion. He was impatient, testy with his son, treading on him, gently, but putting him in his place. "You take Kluphager and Roxie and tell Roxie what she needs to be told. Talk to the dealers, too. I'm sure some of the other girls will be trying this trick with the mink stole."

"Sure thing, Dad," Nick said, but his smile looked like it was held in place with fishhooks. "I'll take care of it."

"Go do it," said Mantilini. We watched while Nick gathered himself up, and, saying nothing further, marched out of the restaurant with Kluphager and Roxie following, each of them, I assumed, about to feel the full weight of his transferred anger. Which may have been Mantilini's idea all along. He knew how to push Nick's buttons, and I reflected that it can never be easy, being the son of the king.

Mantilini's eyes crinkled at the edges. "Kids," he said to Mallory. "Do you have any?"

"None," she said.

"The best thing you can ever do. Despite the heartaches. It changes you like nothing else," Mantilini said. "Believe me."

"I'm sure," she said, showing no interest in his family pride and the tussles it led to. "What will happen to her?"

"Who?" said Mantilini, with something cold in his voice again, warning her not to go on, but she was undaunted.

"To Roxie."

"What will happen to her? Nothing. Not a thing," said Mantilini, and I knew he hated to be pressed, about decisions, about architecture, about his business. "She'll give back the money."

"And then what? A whack with a Brooklyn baseball bat?"

They stared at each other, neither flinching. Here we go, I thought, waiting for Mantilini's anger to explode. Trying to find out who owned what in Las Vegas was the ultimate shell game, everything being hidden behind a myriad of fake names and dummy corporations. But I'd figured out that Mantilini had big holdings in the Sands, the Desert Inn, the Riviera; he had the controlling interest in the El Sheik, and no doubt some plump share of the hotels we were about to build. He had the mansion in Tahoe, the estate in Napa, the yachts, the airplanes. Behind his position as a titan lay control of the law in Las Vegas and much of the political clout; and, behind all that, the foundation of the pyramid, was a threat of violence so final and unanswerable that it need rarely be invoked and was never referred to. Not by him, and never in his company. Mallory, in ignorance, or arrogance, had flouted a taboo, casually broken a primary rule of his court. She'd passed, certainly, the point at which I might protect her. Or care to.

I waited for the storm, which she, too, seemed to anticipate, her eyes asparkle. But then something extraordinary happened. Mantilini narrowed his gaze, studying her hard before sudden delight lit his face.

"Beth?" He sounded uncertain, younger somehow, full of animation, enthusiasm. "Beth Dyer?"

"Will she be hurt?" said Mallory, ignoring this strange current that was rippling around the table.

"Of course not." A frown crinkled the edges of Mantilini's eyes. "You're not Beth?"

"Who's Beth?" said Mallory, her face a blank.

"It was something you said," Mantilini began. "Or the way you said it, the way you got angry. You reminded me of someone I knew." His voice fell away, but he didn't stop looking at her. "You do look like her, in the eyes. But she wore glasses. And her hair was a different color. And longer. And her cheeks were fuller. And she had more of a figure."

Her eyebrows were raised. "Otherwise we're exactly alike?"

"I know, I know," Mantilini said, joining in her laughter, mocking himself, fingers flicking lightly at his coiffed gray hair. "Going cuckoo in my old age."

16

MARCH 1, 1951 / LOS ANGELES

$\mathcal{B}$eth Dyer pushes through the revolving doors and enters the store, an art deco temple of bronze and swirling copper located on Wilshire Boulevard, a major thoroughfare named after an oil millionaire who was also a Marxist. Beth's mother, Karen Dyer, works in the store, in charge of men's shirts, ties, and gloves, and Karen's second husband, Bill Cotterez, is manager of the entire men's department. He's an impresario, in a small but successful way, vain and punctilious, prone to flashes of doubt and temper. Short and high-strung.

Beth's brisk walk is determined rather than graceful. Head held high, her dark shoulder-length hair flying behind her, she seems possessed by energy and will. At nineteen she is meticulous, practical: she can mend fuses, fix stage lights, repair recalcitrant bits of machinery. Yet she is also mischievous, bold, and carries with her always the air of being unstoppable. For this visit to her mother she has dressed up, a little, wearing capri pants, a black blouse, and a short tan raincoat that she takes off and throws over her arm.

On the second floor she waits, her mother having run downstairs to talk to one of the buyers. Beth runs her finger along the cool steel that rims the glass counter of the glove-and-tie case, her eyes lingering on the silk and leather treasures inside. She loves the store, with its transporting smells of perfume and new cloth, its movie-set luxury that resembles an ocean liner. When her mother got her first job here, the year after the war ended, just when Cotterez came into their lives, when they were struggling and hunting for a new apartment, he let them sleep in the store for a few nights, in a roomy broom closet, bundled up in sleeping bags amid the zinc buckets and tubs of sweet-smelling wax. While her mother slumbered, Beth would sneak out of the closet and roam around. At night the store was the most thrilling place she knew, a ghost ship awaiting its passengers.

Beth espies a man approaching the unguarded glove-and-tie counter. He's of late middle age, medium height, olive-skinned. A coat of dark cashmere is slung over his shoulders, the rich and supple fabric sparkling as if with diamonds, and Beth guesses, correctly, that outside it has begun to rain. The man is suavely handsome, with a groomed mane of slick gray hair, and a studied casualness of movement that belies the flicker of command in his liquid brown eyes. One of those eyes, she notices, is oddly inert, almost sinister.

"I need some gloves," he says, peering offhandedly into the case with the manner of a man accustomed to having his needs and whims instantly gratified. "Maybe a few pairs."

Her nerve doesn't falter. Never has life seemed to her so simple and clear. Mistaken for a salesgirl, she neither protests nor laughs. Instead she throws herself into the role. Here is a chance to act.

"Certainly, sir," she says, holding the handsome older man's gaze for just a moment. Beth has studied the texts of her craft, spent long nights with a pack of cigarettes, a bottle of red wine, and Stanislavsky, Boleslavsky, and Michael Chekhov for company. She has been transported by one of the essences of acting: namely, that it can be exciting, even easy, to make anybody believe that you are somebody else—if your craft is unsurpassed. She knows that, instantaneously, she must enter the character she is about to become. She sees herself as a salesgirl who is studying to become an actress. That's easy, a mere inversion of the actual situation. She imagines that such a girl might ask herself who each customer wants her to become in order to sell him (or her) gloves and ties. In effect, such a girl would *always* be acting, pursuing a multitude of roles throughout the day. So, in the spirit of her imaginary creation,

Beth surveys this rich and powerful man in his fabulous cashmere coat, considering the roles to which he might respond, the possible moods. Flirtatious? Not all men enjoy that. Demure, flustered? No, she thinks, and then recalls a scene from a movie she enjoyed, with a brainy girl in glasses in a bookstore. In a flash she whips from the pocket of her capris a pair of spectacles in their case. Dark frames, plain glass instead of lenses. She dons them.

"Now let me see," she says, bending down to examine the wooden trays beneath the counter. "What sort of gloves do you have in mind? Winter gloves? Woollen gloves? Dress gloves for the evening?"

Her voice is soft and husky, almost academic, but enthused, almost quivering with passion for . . . *gloves.*

"Gloves are gloves, aren't they?" says the man in the cashmere coat, barely disguising his impatience.

Her gaze holds his, her smile pained, but tolerant. "Really, sir," she says. "I assure you there's much more to gloves than that."

"Something to keep my hands warm. It's getting stormy out there."

"I understand," she says, lifting one of the trays on which the gloves are arrayed, quickly deciding on the pair she'll make him buy. These are silk-lined and of robust, rust-dark leather; they look both comfortable and luxurious. "Try these," she says. "They're hand-stitched. Imported from Italy."

"Who makes them?"

"A man. An Italian, naturally. I think he works out of a loft in Milan. Feel how soft these are. He puts a lot of love into these gloves. Look at the stitching. He's got incredible craft and taste," Beth says, noting that her customer is interested now. He seems to be lapping this up, so she goes on. "I like to think, when he's done for the day he warms his stiff fingers around a coffee cup. He has no family, so he can take his time, maybe ordering a cognac while he watches the world go by. Perhaps he reads the newspaper, or some poetry."

"I want this guy's life, not just his gloves," the man says, and Beth feels his smile, subtle and powerful, lingering on her face without apology. He has a soft, pattering way of talking. Maybe he's of Italian blood himself, Beth speculates, though he has no trace of an accent anymore. He says, "Can I try these on?"

"Sure. Absolutely."

"Help me, will you?"

She opens the end of the gloves, fitting the supple leather onto his square, strong palm, and over each of his fingers, one by one. "How does that feel?" she says.

"Good," he says, his eyes still on her face. "Have you been in Milan?"

"Only in books," says Beth gaily, in the voice of her character, who might think: Aren't books better?

"You should go. You'd like it," the man says simply, as though he expects her to drop everything and fly there immediately. He splays his hand, admiring the glove. "I'll take a dozen pair," he says.

Beth, gratified, surprised at the ease and extent of her success, checks quickly beneath the counter. "I'm afraid we've only got six," she says.

"That'll have to do," he says, glancing quickly at his watch, an elegant disc of gold on a wrist matted with hair. A workman's wrist, Beth thinks, a wrist that once knew hard times. He twirls the coat off his shoulders like a matador's cape, landing it with a thump on the counter beside the pile of gloves in their boxes. "Now. What about some ties?" He puts his elbows on the counter, staring at her with his strange brown eyes, his oiled gray hair shining in the store's bright overhead lights. "You have ties, I take it."

"Excellent ties," says Beth, still in character, aware that she's being teased, allowing herself to go a little red in the face.

"Do the ties have stories too?"

"Some of them."

"I want a tie with a story. What about this one?" he says, pointing to a silk tie in gaudy yellow.

"That's a tragedy," Beth says.

"Won't do, then," the man responds. "No tie should be a tragedy, *or* a comedy."

"A romance?"

"Certainly. Show me this," he says, his finger picking another.

"One of my favorites," says Beth. "It's silk, of course, woven in a style they call *jacquard*. This one's from"—she quickly checks the label—"Denmark. Copenhagen."

"The Vikings make ties these days?"

She keeps her face deadpan. "Designed by a man who fell in love with a mermaid. Hopelessly."

His laughter is gleeful, infectious, and she starts to giggle, too. "No, this won't do," she says.

"No? I haven't had so much fun in weeks. I'll take the mermaid-lover. Now show me some more."

Some minutes later Karen Dyer returns from her meeting, plump Bill Cotterez prancing at her side in his elevated heels. By then eight silk shirts and a dozen silk ties make a festive heap on the counter along with the gloves and the cashmere coat.

"Mr. Mantilini! What a pleasure to see you, sir! What a wonderful surprise!" says Cotterez, bubbly and nervous with enthusiasm, his flattery guns popping wildly, face shining with an eager reverence that Beth hasn't quite seen before, and so she understands at once that the man in the cashmere coat, this Mantilini, is even richer and more powerful than she thought. "How may I assist?"

Mantilini's eyes crinkle around the edges, frowning. A self-conscious gesture, Beth thinks, and guesses that he's about to start playing a game with Cotterez. She knows she shouldn't, that it's unfair to the man who keeps her mother in relative luxury these days, but she finds herself looking forward to this, Cotterez being put in his place.

"It's . . ." Mantilini begins, scratching his head.

"Cotterez, sir!"

"Sure, I knew that," Mantilini says, his glib smile advertising the lie. "But your first name."

"Bill, Mr. Mantilini."

"Right. Bill. *Bill.*"

"I'm amazed you remember. That's wonderful, Mr. Mantilini. The last time you were here you bought—"

"Sure," says Mantilini, cutting him off. Cotterez manages to stop short of wringing his hands but his laugh is a nervous explosion, a mannerism that has long grated on Beth's nerves. She considered it such darned uncontrolled acting. With alarm flaring in his eyes Cotterez surveys the heap of silk and boxes on the counter. He's very afraid, Beth sees, of losing this sale, this customer.

"I'll take over now. Thanks, Beth," Cotterez says with a gracious nod. Cotterez has charm, sure enough, when he wants to use it, but Beth can't look at him without thinking of a reptile. A toad, specifically. She shivers, remembering the times when her mother's not been there and he's tried to touch her. "Enjoy your lunch," Cotterez says, his smile telling her to buzz off.

"Have this stuff boxed and sent to my hotel, will you, Cotterez?" says Mantilini, his tone refusing to allow the possibility of argument. "I'm going to ask Beth here to show me a few suits."

Cotterez, on the rack, maintains his fixed grin. A situation in which a favored customer demands the services of a particular sales assistant, attractive in some way or another, is familiar and useful to him, a tool of his trade. But Beth is his determined and willful stepdaughter, no employee, and he glances her way with a questioning twitch of the lips, wondering whether she has created this scene for the purpose of causing him exquisite embarrassment, or whether, perhaps, she is prepared to continue with the lucrative imposture.

"Certainly, Mr. Mantilini," Beth says, ignoring her mother's look of doom and daggers. "Would you care to step this way?"

"Call me Paul," Mantilini says, taking her arm. "I'm guessing that some of these suits might be worth a whole goddamn book."

17

I'd held myself in check all through that breakfast, not knowing whether to spit or laugh at Mallory's antics. I felt rage and amusement about equally, I think. Maybe the anger was winning out, though I always admired anybody with moves. And she had a few. Steering her out of the El Sheik after we'd said our goodbyes to Paul Mantilini, summoning the Porsche from the valet guy, I told her to drive us downtown, and we headed for a bar I knew, a sad and dim place on Fremont Street, somewhere right off the Mantilinis' map. The barman was tall, with a square, sunburned face; his chest was massive and ruddy under his open shirt. He gave us our coffees, returned to his spot at the counter, and eased himself onto a stool. He pulled a paperback out of his shirt pocket. The spine opened with a crack. A jukebox glowed in the corner. At the back was a tiny stage for a stripper, but, thankfully, no stripper. Slot machines stood like sentinels.

I sat facing Mallory over two steaming cups of coffee. She was tearing open tiny bags of sugar and spilling them into hers. Bag after bag.

"Sweet tooth?"

She said nothing; she watched me, though.

"Maybe you can tell me what the hell's going on?"

Another bag of sugar spilled its guts. "I don't know what you're talking about," she said.

"Are you crazy?"

Her mouth worked nervously, and she glanced toward the door. Then she picked up a spoon, wiped it on a paper napkin, and began to stir.

"Did you really think you could get away with it?"

"With what?" she said.

"That little stunt you pulled."

"I don't know what you mean."

"You know damn well what I mean," I said. "They're not your drawings. You stole them from Luis."

Her eyes were bold. "So? You took his ideas too. That's what he told me."

"Maybe I did and maybe I didn't. That's not the point here," I said. "Your game—that's the point here. I want to know what it is."

Her look was defiant. She flicked at her silvery hair.

You're a clever young woman, I told her, far too clever to suppose that you can meet Mantilini once, impress the hell out of him, and persuade him to ditch a guy like me, someone he's been in business with for years. If this *was* her plan, then to defeat it was easy, I said. "I go to Mantilini, tell him that Luis did the drawings. I think I know how he'll respond. He'll be amused, but he'll see you're not serious. End of story."

"I'm very serious," she said.

"So tell me what it is you want."

She tapped coffee off her spoon on the edge of the cup. "Got a cigarette?"

"No."

She sank into a long silence, and I noticed the dark lines that appeared beneath her eyes. "I wish you weren't in the pockets of those people," she said.

"I'm not."

"Really?" Her expression was doubting, scornful.

"I built a fine hotel for a man I like. It's the world I live in. I have power over only little pieces of it. That's what life is, for most of us. In case you hadn't noticed."

"You think I'm spoiled?"

"You tell me."

"I'm not," she said. "Not in the way you think."

She smiled, but it was an awkward smile, and her elfin face seemed ravished by strain all of a sudden. I found myself looking at her with an unexpected sympathy. How old was she? Twenty-four? Twenty-five? She was young, yet seemed to be driven by some dreadful force, some burden or ambition beyond her years. Perhaps this was down to her father, her *rich* father, the shipping magnate, pushing her, expecting too much from her. I remembered myself at her age, at the beginning of the war, when my life had been formless, without shape. A relationship had finished, one of a number that failed in those years, and the architecture career of Maurizio Viglioni was going nowhere. I'd been an idealist back then, still based in Philadelphia, with big Le Corbusier–like ideas for civic projects and new housing for the underprivileged and the poor. Nothing had come of them. I'd been my father's son, a dreamer, a washout.

"Maybe coming to Las Vegas wasn't such a smart idea," I said. "Let's get out of here."

"We only just arrived," she said, her coffee cup paused halfway to her mouth.

"I think we'd better head back to L.A."

The cup rattled down into its saucer. "Look," she said. "I was anxious, way too eager. Nervous about meeting Paul. I mean, who wouldn't be? He more or less runs this town, right? I wanted to make an impression and I made a mess of things. I didn't mean to piss you off." She reached for my hand across the table. "I'll behave from now on. Promise!"

"You won't try and get me kicked off my own projects?"

"No, and I know I shouldn't have tried the thing with Luis's drawings. That was dumb," she said. "I guess I was hoping I might get to see Mr. Mantilini alone. Something like that."

A hint of impudence was back in her face.

"You're bad," I said. "What was all that about, anyway?"

"What?"

"When he thought he knew you."

"I've no idea." She glanced quickly at her watch, a narrow and elegant platinum band. "I *wish* I knew him. Then maybe I *could* get you thrown off your own projects. God knows, it's tough enough being a woman in this business."

"Even with Brent Walker to help?"

"Yeah, that's me. Poor little rich girl."

"Listen—I'll fix for you and Paul to meet, if that's what you want."

Her face was intent. "When?"

"I thought tonight we'd have some dinner, take in a show, relax in the cabana," I said. "Maybe tomorrow. I'll see. Or maybe when we next come back to town."

She studied me, smiling at the barman, who came with a coffee pot to refill our cups. "Is there a phone in here?" she asked, and followed his directions past the glowing jukebox to the back. Two minutes later she was back, sitting down with a smile.

"Don't tell me you called him," I said.

"Who?"

"Mantilini."

"Of course not, silly." But not saying who she *had* called. The girl has secrets, I thought, but she looked at me in that way of hers, winning and direct, changing the subject, asking me about politics, Nevada politics specifically, quizzing me about my plans and ambitions.

The senior senator for the state, I told her, was a guy named Walton C. Booth, known as "Boss" Booth, now serving his fourth term, a man in his seventies, bitter and vindictive, an old bull of the red-baiting school. "My father-in-law says he's a twisted SOB who expects people to kiss both the cheeks on his ass and the hole between," I said. "But Boss Booth is sick and dying. Which is where I come in."

"It's that simple?"

"I've been on the outside too," I told her. "Trust me, the inside is better. But you know that."

"Yes, I do."

A man with a buzz cut and sunglasses strode into the bar, wearing a mohair suit and a narrow tie knotted to a small, perfect triangle at the top of his white-on-white shirt. An organization man, I thought, a believer in Eisenhower, Coca-Cola, the possibility of an enduring marriage between Marilyn and Joe, and an endless stream of Norman Rockwell covers on the *Saturday Evening Post*. He asked for directions to the proving grounds, and I changed my mind a little, figuring he was maybe a TV reporter, in from L.A. to cover the test the next morning. The barman told him the way and he left, but no sooner had the door shut than it opened again, this time admitting a tall black with a scruffy beard who walked to the bar and demanded a glass of water. The barman blinked, and with no expression on his square, sunburned face, poured the glass. The man, who had bulging, bloodshot eyes, drank the water thirstily before glancing about the place. Then he, too, left, and the barman wiped the counter and rinsed the glass in scalding water, muttering, "Get back to where the niggers live."

"Excuse me, Maurice," Mallory said. "I left something in the car. I'll be right back."

Her lips pecked me swiftly on the cheek, her eyes held mine briefly, and she was gone.

The barman picked up his paperback. Scratching his sunburned chest with a lazy finger, he said, "Quite a lady."

That's all I need to top off the morning, I thought, a barman with a gooey, romantic streak. I grinned, not happily, sipping my coffee and running my finger across the table, its surface roughened and scarred. Suddenly I realized: the guy thinks she's not coming back.

At the door the sunlight dazzled my eyes after the dimness. Looking up and down Fremont Street, busy even at that hour, with the cascading neon holding its own against the desert glare, I saw no sign of the Porsche. Mallory was gone.

"Bitch," I said under my breath.

Back in the bar a fresh cup of coffee was waiting for me, and, alongside it, a shot glass filled with whiskey. This guy really thought I was a sap. I pushed the whiskey away, but with a gleam in his eye he started talking about love and the girl he'd just met. Love was real, love was contagious, love was a fever, love renewed and changed you. All the usual baloney.

"You read too much," I said. He blinked at that, but didn't ram it down my throat that I was the fool who'd just been stood up in a bar. Instead he called me a cab.

"Good luck," the barman said, as though he thought I needed it.

18

$\mathcal{I}$'d been back at the cabana at the El Sheik for about two hours when Nick Mantilini showed up, rapping at the door. He wore a sharp sportscoat over a black silk shirt, and his dark hair was still mussed from the shower. Maybe he'd been playing golf or tennis, out there in the Nevada heat. He leaned against the doorjamb with a negligent air. "Busy?" he said, and I shook my head, inviting him to come on in.

If Nick had been bothered by the incident at breakfast, he gave no sign of it. Probably he was used to his father putting him in his place. After all, he'd had a lifetime's experience, and maybe he understood that you have to inherit a world before you can rule it. And inheritance, inevitably, comes at a price. Like a senator's daughter.

He made himself at home, nosing about, poking at this and that. He picked up a book that Mallory had left behind, *Peyton Place*, noted her underwear lying where it had been tossed, on the floor, and the *haute couture* black dress on its hanger in the closet. Tossing the book aside, he inspected her platinum cigarette case, which she'd left on the bedside table, the lamp picking out the gems that encrusted one corner with her initials.

"Nice," Nick said. "From Tiffany's, I bet."

When we first started building the El Sheik I'd seen Nick as a young man in a hurry, always running, impatient and hot-tempered. He'd shown up on site, and, seeing work unfinished, or failing to measure up to some standard he didn't tell anyone else about, launched into vicious tirades. "What kind of pissant job is this?" he'd say, fixing the workman with a terrible glare. He'd fired a couple of guys without telling me and opened someone else's head with a brick. He'd been a pest, and I went to Del Entenza, the Phoenix contractor, for advice. What could I do? We decided not to bother Mantilini with the problem, assuming that he'd hear about it, deal with it. Which is what happened. All part of Nick's growing-up process, I guess. Since then he'd learned the value of a gracious smile, gracious words. He started to study men rather than lash out at them. He was becoming his father's son, the son of the father I knew; but then maybe the first Nick I knew, crude Nick, *ur*-Nick, had been a reflection of Paul Mantilini's past, the version I never met.

"Where's Mallory?" he said, his voice soft, politely inquiring, not interrogating.

"I haven't the foggiest idea."

"Really?" he said, returning the cigarette case to the table, looking back at me with a cheesy smile. "She's walked out on you already?"

"Something like that."

"Women. What can you say?"

Nick had never been married, not so far as I knew. And he didn't compete for the younger, glamorous women, the fashion models, the actresses, the heiresses, the babes (but always with something special or different), with whom his father tended to have short-lived, uncomplicated affairs. A couple of women were in the picture, both of them older, stylish, and worldly, one a singer, the other the bored wife of some rich, fat movie producer back in L.A. I'm not sure how sex featured in Nick's scheme of things. He wanted power.

"She'll be back," he said with a certainty he assumed I'd find comforting. "How long have you known her, anyway?"

"Just a few days. It's a casual thing."

"Sure it is," he said. "She's lovely. Where did you meet her?"

It occurred to me then that his father had sent him, wanting to check Mallory out. "I met her at a party," I said. "Then she sort of barreled into my life."

"She's rich, right?"

"How'd you know that?"

"She's got that air. To the manner born. Isn't that the phrase?"

"If you read Shakespeare."

"Sure, I've read him. Sons are always fighting their fathers, revenging their fathers, *killing* their fathers," he said, touching the crooked tip of his nose. "I didn't just play football in college. I read all that stuff."

Smiling, he got down on his haunches, peering into the trash basket. "Where's the money from?" he said.

"Her father's Walker Shipping."

"Never heard of it."

"It's big."

"Yeah, well, I love the ocean but I wouldn't want to get involved." Nick smiled, showing his teeth, and sprang to his feet with two crumpled pieces of paper in his hand. "She must be rich, if she can throw money away," he said, nudging aside the cigarette case, examining the first beneath the lamp on the bedside table. It was the check for the $10,000 that she'd won at roulette the previous night. Then he smoothed out the second piece. "You'd better read this," he said. "It's a love letter. Maybe she wrote it to you, Maurice."

"I sincerely doubt that."

"Still. It smells of perfume," he said, handing me the paper. "Expensive."

I raised the crinkled paper to my nostrils and started to read aloud:

I'm thinking about you, but then I'm always thinking about you. I'm never not thinking about you. But right now I'm thinking of one time in particular.

I stopped, realizing I didn't want Nick to hear this, and continued silently while he observed me.

I'm thinking of when I first saw you, the time the bomb went off in my heart. God, I thought I was going to die. My knees buckled, sweat broke out all over my hands and my body, my head swam—I had all the symptoms.

Thought I was going to pass out on the spot. And then afterwards it turned out you scarcely noticed me at all! You scarcely realized I was there! How was that possible? Oh, but I got my revenge later, didn't I, my sweet, my angel, my lover? I made you love me good.

The writing didn't sound like the Mallory I knew, but then who *was* the Mallory I knew? The schemer, the manipulator, the Mallory who'd used Luis Barragan and had stolen his ideas to get to me and had then started thinking about using me, too? The Mallory who'd ditched me in the bar? Or the Mallory who hated the bomb and stood up for pit-girls, the reckless Mallory who burst through the cracks, hell-bent on trouble, the Mallory whose eyes blazed with anger, and, sometimes, unspoken hurt?

I put the paper aside. "She didn't write this to me," I said. "I don't know if it's her writing at all."

"She's a good architect," Nick said. "That's what my father says."

I picked my words carefully. "She shows promise."

"I guess. He knows his stuff, my father."

"He certainly does."

This seemed to satisfy him. He moved softly to the door, padding on his big quarterback's feet. "It was nice to chat," he said, leaning against the frame for a moment. "Maybe you'll give me a call when she comes back?"

"*If* she comes back."

He said: "I'll see you."

19

SEPTEMBER 7, 1956—4:00 A.M.

I'd planned the entire top floor of the El Sheik as a private gaming room for the high-rollers—the Thousand Sun Lounge—and it was here that Mantilini tended to hold his parties and do his more lavish entertaining. I'd gone for something extravagant and flashy in the design, a king's court as conceived by a Hollywood set designer on an enormous budget. Chairs were thick with gilt and cushioned sumptuously in red plush. Floodlights picked out decent copies of masterpieces by Renoir and Monet on the walls. Jeweled mirrors glinted behind the kidney-shaped curve of the bar, and a staircase took an elegant turn up to the balcony, so that gamblers could walk up and down, watching themselves in the mirrors, flaunting their luck or their loserly sangfroid. All was artifice, a stage set where real money could be lost and won. A single sheet of plate glass, the largest in western America, comprised the room's outer wall. By day, the window gave a clear view across the desert; at night, as now, there was a sense of infinite, dark, distance; come the dawn, it would offer the best seats in town.

I arrived after midnight, when the party was already in full swing, the room a smoky circus jammed with people gambling, shouting, drinking themselves into oblivion. It was the night of a testing, and more than two hundred of Mantilini's friends and associates were gathered for the spectacle. Lana Turner was there, clad in a tight-fitting dress of burning white, clinging to the arm of a tall, courtly man with a long face that made him look oddly like a monkey—John Huston. Dick Powell was there, so was Gloria Grahame, and someone said Sinatra was about to arrive. A few guests had cameras slung about their necks, to catch a picture of the explosion, or maybe they were Geiger counters, Scintillators, like Kluphager's. A table was set up, as usual, for side bets on the big event. How many windows would break, in the El Sheik, in the city as a whole? How many seconds between the flash and the impact of the blast? Over in the corner of the room the pianist was on his feet. "And now I'd like to play a number of my own," he said, red in the face, high as a kite probably. "It's called 'Atom Bomb Boogie.'" Sitting down again, bouncing on his stool, he raised his hands and struck a couple of doomy chords; then he grinned, the tune settling into a bouncy, raunchy rhythm.

I'd eaten dinner with a couple of guys I knew over at the Desert Inn; it had been thick steaks and a decent burgundy. I was wearing a fresh shirt and one of my Jermyn Street suits. I was well-groomed, well-fed, everything the fashionable architect should be. I had no idea that my life was about to snap in two.

From the balcony I watched Paul Mantilini work the crowd. He moved slowly, giving full attention to whoever pressed his hand, his shining gray hair slick and raked back, his white tuxedo jacket snug across his shoulders, immaculate. He dropped a word here, shook a hand there; he laughed, or leaned forward to listen; he saw Nick, his son, and whispered in his ear, instructions, most likely, orders, given by Mantilini with the blend of seductiveness and iron that defined him. His air of command was lazy, yet absolute; he conveyed the impression that everything—the splendor of the hotel, the quality of the liquor and champagne, the clear weather, even the atomic firecracker that was about to light up the pre-dawn sky—had been put in place according to his wishes. This was his realm.

It had been in December 1950, when the Russians exploded their first atomic bomb, when Mao Tse Tung's Communists had taken power in China, when North Korea had invaded South Korea, when it seemed the Communists might engulf half the world and not stop there, that Harry Truman decided a permanent nuclear test site was required in the continental United States. Our nuclear people, the AEC, the Atomic Energy Commission, looked at Utah and North Carolina; they looked at northern Nevada; but they decided, in the end, on southern Nevada. And everything changed.

A-bombs on the doorstep: the idea scared some of the Las Vegas casino owners; they foresaw tourists shunning the place, a chain reaction that might raze the whole fledgling city. But Mantilini, at heart an optimist, or a realist who recognized that certain types of change were inevitable and must therefore be embraced before they could be controlled, chose instead to look for the possibilities. Every month or so, just fifty miles away, across the sand and scrub, would be a live replay of the awesome power that had flattened Hiroshima and Nagasaki. What an opportunity! Who wouldn't want to see that? He set his publicist to work, dreaming up photo shoots where luscious girls sported mushrooms covering their privates like fig leaves, or atop their heads—the Atomic Hairdo. He had his barman dream up a new concoction, a lethal mix of brandy, vodka, whiskey, gin, and juices—the Atomic Cocktail. He embraced the crazy glamour. He threw a shindig every time the desert air cracked. The sky's blinding brilliance, the shaking walls, the tumbling window shades, the whacking blasts, the dice that were jolted over when they had already stopped moving across the baize—these became part of a show that helped him put Las Vegas on the map as never before. Mantilini, always gratified by the many and wondrous ways the world found to give him money, proved to himself that he had vision.

"You made it," he said, joining me on the balcony, his voice soft and gentle, almost musical. His face creased in a smile. "Where's your friend?"

"She left me. We were in a bar and she walked out." I laughed, not bitterly, almost fondly, helping myself to a glass of champagne from a passing waiter's tray. Mantilini himself neither smoked nor drank, and he never gambled. "Can you believe it?"

"You know what? I *can* believe it. She's something, that one, a real pistol," he said. "Her work was great, though."

"Not hers. She stole it from Luis Barragan."

"Really?" He seemed amused. "Your former partner?"

"The same."

"That's beautiful," he said, shaking his head in appreciation.

"Mallory's bold all right, no doubt about it," I said. By then I'd pretty much written her off, figuring that she must have driven back to L.A., or San Francisco, back into Daddy's arms, or wherever. Good riddance, I thought, but not without a pang, remembering the intoxicating, witchy smell of her, the cool flash of her eyes.

Mantilini moved closer toward me. Down below I saw a woman blow on a pair of dice, springing forward, shouting as she threw them. But the noise of her shout faded away as Mantilini spoke, his voice still soft, but clearer now, almost seductive, each word traveling distinctly down the passage of my ear. "You're taking a crack at the Senate."

He had his hand on my arm and his entire face was a smile, and suddenly I saw Joe Nelson's proposition in a new light.

"You're behind it?"

"This is my state, remember. Let's say this—you have my blessing."

I guess I shouldn't have been surprised; all the same, my worldview rocked a little, shifted. I'd always assumed that Joe Nelson and Mantilini barely knew one another and that, insofar as they did, Joe called the shots. He was the senator, after all. Sure, I'd understood that Mantilini was powerful, *all*-powerful within the city he controlled, and I'd been taught that even in American democracy elections can be fixed. But I hadn't grasped that he'd been the man to do it. That job, I'd believed, was more in Joe's line. The idea that the two of them were acting together, colluding, with Joe as junior partner, was the beginning of an education for me. I was still naïve. I didn't see the full picture yet. But I was starting to grasp that the world I thought to be real wasn't the real world at all. That for those who truly control and rule, power doesn't separate itself into separate entities—money, business, family, crime, politics. It's all one, a juggernaut.

"This could be a sweet deal, kid," Mantilini said. His smile was casual, benign, his strong, manicured fingers resting on the rail in front of him. I liked the sound of that—the sweet ones were my kind of deal.

"You tell the world you're going into politics and you're going to step aside from your business for a while." He was like a parent, patiently explaining the ABCs. "That's a crock, of course. Everybody knows you'll be feathering your own nest. Making money for yourself. That's the way this works. Why be a patriot, why be involved at all, unless it can make you rich?"

I felt a rush of energy and gratification. I relaxed, as if a suit, some new armor of prestige, had been cloaked around my body. I understood that Joe Nelson owed Mantilini, or needed Mantilini, and Mantilini in turn needed me. It felt good, this power.

"What's in this for you?" I said. It was much easier to ask Mantilini this right up front than Joe Nelson. Mantilini was the more confident, the more secure, and I felt at ease with him. But he wasn't about to tell me, not yet, not here.

"We'll talk about it, Maurice. You have my word," he said, laying his hand on my arm. "Tomorrow."

Just then a cork flew past his ear and a woman exclaimed: "Happy birthday!"

She came toward us bearing a champagne bottle—a regal blonde dressed in black, escorted by the English reporter, Will Rothschild, and, on the other side, Nick Mantilini, who, like his father, sported a tuxedo of spotless white.

"Well, hello! Look who's here," Mantilini said sportively. "Maurice, this is my friend Katherine. Kate, for short."

"The architect. I've heard about you," she said, breezy, confident, her smile an advertisement for American dentistry. Her long fingers squeezed Mantilini's arm and she planted a kiss on his cheek. "Nick sent a plane. He wanted you to get your birthday present."

"But it's not my birthday," Mantilini said, imperturbable, nonchalant, only a little puzzled.

Nick burst out laughing, and Kate got it—she'd been tricked. "Oh, Nick, you terror!" she said. "Okay, I'm a *late* birthday present. An *advance* birthday present. Take your pick!"

"I will," Mantilini said. She was young, vibrant, like all of his women, and I'd met a few. They tended to be sparky, witty, with some quality he didn't try to tame. He saw himself as a Svengali, I guess, and certainly more came into it than the simple deal of an older guy of substance expecting to get laid in exchange for the crumbs he let fall from his table. He was casual but definitive with his introductions to producers, agents, movie stars, the Hollywood types who fluttered around him. If he took someone under his wing, he expected results on their behalf. He was loyal that way.

"It's a pleasure to see you any time," Mantilini said. And to his son: "Nick, this is grand."

"That's okay, Pops," Nick said, beaming, although I knew that all his life there'd been women like this. "Any time."

I took this chance and signaled to Rothschild that we should move away from the others, and strolled across the balcony toward the window with the darkness of the night beyond. "Will, you've been holding out on me," I said.

"How so, dear heart?" Rothschild had a quick smile along with his languid manner and small, sharp, crooked teeth. He always seemed to know more and be smarter than he was prepared to let on.

"I know who told you about my Senate run," I said. "It was Nick, wasn't it?"

"Perhaps," he said, looking back across the room to where Paul and his friend Kate were laughing, while Nick stood apart from them a little, fingering his glass with a watchful smile. "My God, I just realized," Rothschild went on. "Paul's behind the whole thing, isn't he?"

"Perhaps," I said, and Rothschild smiled, accepting the rebuff.

"Of course, he absolutely *loathes* Boss Booth. As I do myself," he said.

I remembered that Rothschild had once, in print, called the aging senator "that sadistic old bum from Tonopah." Apologies for the language, dear heart. There'd been a lawsuit, and an attempt, failed, to ban Rothschild from the Nevada State Assembly. "Anything else?"

"Boss Booth's a witch-hunter. Paul hates that."

"Sure he does," I said. "But he's no bleeding heart, either."

"Boss has the State Tax Commission in his pocket," Rothschild said, his back to the window while his sunken brown eyes roved the room, darting from one group to the next, hungry for incident or the whiff of a story. This was a habit of his, always on the lookout for the usable indiscretion. "I hear they plan to cut up rough about gambling. It could be that. You ride in on your white horse and make the problem go away. But, of course, the Boss is still with us."

"He's sick."

Rothschild flicked an eyebrow. "Hadn't heard that," he said.

"Can Paul pull this off?"

"Naturally, if you get the nomination. The whole population of Nevada is less than that of New Haven. Then again, everything could be swayed by the girl blackjack dealer vote. You'd better get to work, old boy," he said, smiling, his gaze fixed on one of the tables. "Where's your lovely, by the way? The girl I met last night."

I shrugged. "Easy come, easy go."

"You've got rare qualities, Maurice, I always thought so." His look was sharp and ferrety. "You've got charm and nothing sticks to you. It may just be that in politics you'll find your *métier*, dear heart."

The party went on. I got a little drunk, and, when Mantilini slipped away, leaving Kate in my charge, I spoke and danced with her, because she was young and smart and gorgeous and because this behavior felt like my due. I was careful not to take the flirtation too far, and to shower Mantilini with compliments, guessing that she'd report them back. I had moves to make, an adjusted future to plan. A golden time, if I played this right. Standing close to that young woman, laughing at her jokes, flattering her, but thinking about what I'd heard from Mantilini and Will Rothschild, I felt close to the heat, really on the inside now, moving close to the source of power.

From outside, through the stretch of the plate glass, came the first signs of dawn, a barely perceptible lightening of the sky, and I remembered nights during the war, nights when I wasn't flying and would wait at the airfield for the planes coming back. Staring into the blackness, listening for the engines, searching for a glimmer. You tend to tell yourself the light is there before it really is, your brain sensing the light, poised, waiting to flood over the edge of the horizon. So it was now in the

El Sheik. The room filled with a tense expectation as we waited for a different sort of dawn.

With his arms thrust in the air, his strong hands and hairy wrists shooting from the sleeves of that white tuxedo jacket, Mantilini summoned us all to silence and made a speech from where he stood on the balcony. "I guess we should all raise our glasses in a toast to our friends in the federal government—a big thanks for giving us the greatest show on earth, and for giving me the chance to make a few honest bucks out of it." He left a pause before his calm face split into a grin. "A few *more* honest bucks."

I joined Kate, leading the applause, and then it was Kluphager, bothered and beleaguered as always, ratty wig askew, Scintillator dangling at his chest, sweating heavily, yanking a white handkerchief from his pocket, yelling: "HEY, EVERYBODY, LISTEN UP. IF I WAS YOU I'D PUT ON YOUR DARK GLASSES."

This was greeted with jeers, boos, cries of "Shame!" and "Coward!"

"Suit yourself," Kluphager rejoined, "see if I care." A big stopwatch replaced the handkerchief in his hand, and, in a high-pitched, nervous, almost squeaking voice, he began the countdown: "Ten . . . nine . . . eight . . . seven . . ."

At that time the U.S. had about 4,600 A-bombs stockpiled, and I'd seen, I don't know exactly, maybe eleven or twelve nuclear blasts. As a onetime flyer, I'd been allowed to go with guys from the USAF photographic group, flying out of Lookout Mountain Air Force Station in Hollywood, while they photographed one of these babies, which had been called "Grable." I knew what was coming, in other words, something both beautiful and terrifying, huge and unthinkable, an act of brilliant human savagery. I was something of an expert about all this, being attached to the nuclear program in a crazy peripheral way that made me money. Yet still my stomach was tense, my mouth dry.

"Five . . . four . . . three . . ."

Sweating, shrill, as if he himself were about to have an orgasm, Kluphager brought us to a peak of expectation while the numbers crept down toward . . .

"Zero!"

Whereupon nothing happened. A pile of chips spilled across the green baize at one of the roulette tables. A woman giggled, clapping a gloved hand across her mouth. Roxie, the brunette Kluphager had busted and tried to humiliate, burst out with: "Shit, Albert. Your timing's way off. As usual."

Laughter; then a piercing flash of light transformed the gloomy dawn into a noon more dazzling than any desert had ever known. For an instant, for the fraction of an instant, the body of Kate beside me became a skeleton, seen in X-ray. Her body came back, but her face was like beet, slapped with glow. The glass in her hand shone bright with mysterious life. Outside, the desert shimmered and wavered, shaken by a godlike fist. A bubble of boiling red appeared on the horizon and grew into a mushroom and slowly rose from the ground to which it remained connected by a lengthening stem of swirling dust. The mushroom sped upward, seething, swelling, the red fire still burning in the middle of it. The red soon mingled with grays, browns, and beiges, the churning earth and the smashed rock that had been lifted from the desert floor. The mushroom turned itself inside out, blurring at the edges, forming other shapes in the cloud—funnels of smoke, arches that formed and disappeared within an instant, long strips that wisped away. Lesser flashes of light cut and ripped the sky like lightning bolts, and black dots began to appear, as if the air had been scattered with the full stops from a thousand exploded typewriters.

All this happened in silence, in a blink. What was it Oppenheimer had said at Los Alamos? He'd quoted the Bhagavad-Gita. "I am become death, the shatterer of worlds." That had always struck me as a stagey response, the rehearsed one-liner of a self-dramatizing man who, despite his words, was only beginning to grasp the enormity of what he'd helped make. But, when faced with this, it was tough to know what to do or say. The aftermath of the explosions was each time so awesome, so vast and unpredictable. In that moment you could indeed believe that the world was about to end.

People around me were gasping, cheering, hollering. Kate wolf-whistled with her fingers in the corners of her mouth. Rothschild smiled in his weary, nothing-surprises-me way. Nick pumped his hands together, slowly, clapping as if he'd seen a guy on a football field making a play he wished he'd made himself. Mantilini, expressionless, gazed out of the window, toward where, I knew, soldiers in masks and asbestos gear marched through the glowing dust into the fake, and now no longer existent, suburb I'd designed and helped build. The AEC kept saying how they required personnel to remain seven miles back from the blast; the military kept ignoring this, bent on creating troops hardened for the atomic battlefield. In 1956 the question was not if this would happen, but when. We all lived with the fact of our imminent destruction; I feared and secretly loved it—it meant I could behave however the heck I pleased.

Someone pushed a martini glass into my hand. Sipping at the gin, I eyed the mushroom out there in the desert; it had risen 16,000 feet in the air by now and was edged in the blue glow of ionized air. I concentrated hard on this, not noticing at first the reflection that appeared in the window.

A dark figure stood behind me, but when I turned I scarcely recognized her. "Mallory?" At first I thought she must have rushed inside, somehow escaping from the blast. But I realized this wasn't right—only seconds had passed since the bomb went off, sixty miles distant. So her appearance was the result of something else, something planned; and her appearance was bizarre.

Dried sand caked her face. Dirt daubed and smeared her slacks and T-shirt, too. Her gray-green eyes glittered within dark circles of kohl, makeup that had been carefully applied. A disguise, then, or a re-creation of something. She looked fierce, furious, ready for a fight, and she shook off my hand when I reached for her.

"Mallory," I said. "Are you all right?"

Remember: this was all happening quickly while the sky outside flickered and blazed. I still can't put together all the details. But I know the shock of the explosion, the sound of it, hadn't arrived yet when she showed up. She timed her entrance with precision, for she'd been standing in front of me only for a second or two when it did arrive, a whacking thump, a long, shaking thunder, like a hundred trucks rumbling through a tunnel. The El Sheik shook and shivered, swaying—as designed—on its foundations. The shock sucked out no windows. No cracks zigzagged the plaster. The structure was sound; a reproduction Picasso tilted on the wall; a couple of glasses fell from a table, failing to smash. Nothing else, then words:

"She's got a gun."

This came, calmly, from Kate, the regal blonde, and I was aware of Mantilini starting to turn, the left side of his face, with that strange, lifeless eye, turning toward us.

A nickel-plated revolver pointed stubbily from the end of Mallory's outstretched arm.

"Mallory," I said, taking a step toward her.

"Cocksucker," she said. Beneath the mud and dirt that caked her face, her eyes smoldered. "Say goodnight," she said, and instantaneous with her voice came another flash, another explosion. But this one seared closer. A rush like the roaring of water filled my ears. My feet seemed to lift from the ground and float in front of my face. That's odd, I thought, and memories flashed, crowding in. Bobby, smacking a baseball. Ches, in his diving gear. Jackie, smoking a cigarette in bed, reading. And Mallory herself, smiling her cool smile. A lighthouse, a flashing bright light, was inside my skull and my eyes seemed to fizz and crackle before the light failed and I fell into the depths.

20

*O*nly Mantilini's fingers move, flipping the matchbook between them. Otherwise he could be a statue, sitting at a table on the balcony of the now deserted Thousand Sun Lounge, surrounded by discarded newspapers. His white tuxedo jacket hangs from the back of a chair. The ends of his silk bow tie dangle loose around his neck. He's put on dark glasses to face the sun. The guests and gamblers have gone; likewise the dealers and the cocktail waitresses; all the gaming tables stand empty. The barman remains, however, ready to bring Mantilini more coffee when he needs it. Outside the day is clear, the desert peaceful, with no sign of the explosion that blistered the sky three hours before; the distant mountains stand out clear. The matchbook makes another slow turn between Mantilini's fingers.

Nick Mantilini comes from the elevators, bounds up the sweeping curve of the staircase to the balcony. Approaching, Nick wonders how often in his life he's seen his father like this, still and reflective; many times, he thinks, but only at times of crisis.

Mantilini hears his son's familiar footstep, does not turn, asks:

"How is he? How's the architect."

"The bullet grazed him."

"He'll be fine?"

Nick wishes the news were completely good; but it isn't. "They're worried about his eyes."

"He'll be blind?"

"They think he'll be okay. They don't know yet."

"I'll call Joe Nelson, give him the heads-up," Mantilini says calmly enough, but Nick knows what he's thinking: a blind senator won't wash, even in Nevada. "Were you in touch with Jackie yet?"

"She's on her way, with the kids."

Mantilini nods, facing Nick now but with the sunglasses still over his eyes. "Make sure a car's at the airport. Comp them everything. And tickets for the shows, if they want to do that."

"I'll take care of it," Nick says, thinking that his father has been up all night and still appears fresh. Trouble acts on him like a drug, Nick knows. The old man's energy becomes boundless, but it's a watchful and restrained energy, waiting to uncoil and strike. He might go for days without sleeping. Nick came with his father to Las Vegas in 1942. They climbed down off the train and took a cab, his father eyeing the grizzled prospectors and the prairie dogs lying dead in the street. He'd said, "Where the hell's the town?" and had kicked the car door when they got out, pretty much the last careless gesture he can remember his father making.

"What about the girl," Mantilini asks. "Where is she?"

"The guys are still out looking for her."

"Call Tony in L.A. That's probably where she'll head."

"I've done that."

Mantilini pulls on the loose ends of his tie in a way that makes Nick think of a garotte. *Learn to read men*, Nick remembers his father saying, *study their eyes, study their hands*. His father's hands are big, like shovels, Nick used to think when he was a kid. Thick with hair, seamed with scars across the palms. One time Nick had complained about having to go back east to college; he'd wanted to stay in Vegas and learn the casino business quicker. "When I was your age I worked five hundred feet in the air handling freezing-cold steel and I watched my brothers die," his father had said, one of a bare handful of occasions when he spoke about his earlier life. "You're *going* to college."

"When were you at the hospital?" Mantilini asks.

"An hour ago."

"Call them again."

Nick signals to the barman who brings a phone up the stairs and plugs it into a wall socket. He dials, talks to a doctor, restrains the smile that tries to crack his face when he knows he can give his father good news.

"It was just the gun flash," he says. "His eyes are going to be fine."

"Are they sure?"

"He's calling for pencils and a sketchbook. He's pissed as hell. He'll be back on his feet in no time."

Mantilini smiles, dusting his hands together as if brushing away dirt, sipping at his coffee, relaxing a little as he leans back in his chair.

"That's good, isn't it, Pops?" says Nick. "Pops" is the code they adopt now that Nick is an adult and occupying an important place in his father's business. "Dad" is childhood; "Dad" is the older and envied half-brother who was killed in the war; "Dad" is the barb in the entrails beneath the skin of the Ivy League.

"We got lucky," Mantilini says. "She remind you of anybody?"

"Who?"

"Valentine's girl. The one who shot him. I thought she looked like Beth Dyer."

"Your old friend? She's dead. I heard it from Sandy Berman. I thought you knew."

"Yeah, maybe I did," says Mantilini, flipping the matchbook. "Sandy always liked her."

"Is that right?"

The phone that Nick put down starts to ring.

"Pops, it's Senator Booth," Nick says, whispering, his hand over the mouthpiece.

Mantilini gives a slight smile. He discards the matchbook, sips at his coffee, wipes his hands on a napkin, takes the receiver. "Morning, Boss," he says, waving Nick away. "Thanks for getting back to me. What's cooking, you old scoundrel?"

21

SEPTEMBER 7–8, 1956 / LAS VEGAS, ST. JOHN'S HOSPITAL

I woke up with my head pounding as though fifty sledgehammers were slamming it. My tongue was swollen, my throat was parched, and when I tried to open my eyes I couldn't see. I screamed, thinking I'd gone blind. I gagged, starting to vomit, and was aware of a presence, a figure smelling of starch, cupping something cold under my chin. A steel dish, I thought, held by a nurse. Clever me. I'd dealt with nurses before. I realized I was in a hospital, but I had no idea why. I could remember my name: Maurizio Viglioni. No, that wasn't quite right, was it? Not anymore. I was Maurice Valentine, acclaimed architect, man of ambition, the slick senator-to-be with the golden future mapped out. And with the retrieval of these seemingly vital pieces of information, I drifted back to sleep. I dreamed I was underwater.

The next time I woke my head wasn't hurting so bad and I felt someone propping me up, gently, and sliding a pillow behind my back. This same someone unwound the bandage that swathed my head and the world came back to me in a blur. I dimly perceived the outline of a figure. A human being, I realized. Did this mean I was one? A tall man, ghoulishly gaunt, a doctor, held a mirror in front of my face and asked what I could see; I told him I saw my face and didn't like the look of it. I muttered something about wanting to get back to work. He told me I was a lucky guy and needed to sleep.

Hours later I woke again. I heard a rustling, paper, as though the pages of a magazine were being flicked. My vision was clearer this time but the room seemed dark, no light except a lamp shining on the reddish head of a woman sitting in a chair, reading a magazine. Her hand tossed the magazine aside.

"You've been in the wars, honey, and you look like hell."

My wife, naturally.

"Hey, Jackie, how are you?"

"I'm fine." Her voice had softened and her cool fingers touched my forehead. "What about you?"

"I've been better. Where am I?"

"In Las Vegas."

"What happened?"

Her intake of breath was sharp. "You don't remember?"

I shook my head, a mistake. The room spun like a carousel, and when I'd finished heaving into the steel dish, Jackie said: "She shot you."

"Who?"

"Mallory Walker."

A face swam into my memory, a pair of gray-green eyes and a cool, commanding look. Nothing more, not then. But I threw back the sheets and with a herculean effort raised my feet and swung them over the side of the bed, my toes touching the linoleum floor. The metal frame holding tubes and bags that fed into my arm clattered and danced, threatening to topple. I put out a hand to steady it.

"What the hell do you think you're doing?"

"I'm going to find her," I said, but my voice sounded weird and foreign.

"You won't make it as far as the goddamned door."

Clearly no help was coming from Jackie's quarter. I couldn't say I blamed her.

"The hell I won't," I said. My clothes, I guessed, were in the closet with the sliding door. Go on, Valentine, I said to myself, you fought in the war, you got medals, now do something really tough and walk across the room and reclaim your pants. I fell toward the white iron rail at the end of the bed, tearing the tubes from my arm and dragging the iron frame down with me so that it fell on the floor, summoning an army of nurses and a couple of doctors.

"That was smart," said Jackie, when they'd put me back to bed. She lit a cigarette and drew on it, angling the smoke upward out of the side of her mouth, away from my face. Smoking was permitted in this private room, evidently, or maybe Jackie didn't care at that point. "Maurice, why did you have to do this?"

I looked at the ceiling.

"No answer? That's fine," she said.

I noticed, between her fingers, shining circles of bead—a rosary. Jackie had been born a Catholic, and was a Catholic still, a certain sort of Catholic. She didn't abase herself before God, or anybody. She liked the ceremony, the comfort of the ritual. She was practical, in this as in everything, and took only the bits of the religion that were useful to her. She believed in confession, absolution, the washing away of sins. She believed in the power of the Church, different back then. She'd taken the boys to Ireland, to visit relatives, and to Rome, where she had an audience with the pope. Joe fixed that. Her lips had brushed the ring of the pontiff. I missed the trip, having business elsewhere, down in San Diego, I seem to remember, with some business guy who wanted a new house and whose wife, a stunning brunette, had a roving eye.

"Maybe it's best you don't say anything. Because we're going to forget the whole episode. Just move on," Jackie said, stabbing out her cigarette in an ashtray on the bedside table.

Forget the whole episode, just move on: summing up, I knew, her brisk, no-nonsense way of handling the juggernaut, ignoring the juggernaut, keeping the juggernaut at bay.

"The kids have arrived," she said, her smile bright and brittle, a quick slash in the pallor of her face above the black silk of her dress. "I'm going to bring them in."

I felt nervous, afraid all of a sudden. I didn't want the boys to see me like this. "What have you told them?"

Her eyebrow went up. "I told them that you were shot. What other option did I have? I didn't tell them all of it, of course. I told them you were shot by some crazy woman you didn't even know."

Oh God, I thought, but when Ches and Bobby shuffled in, bickering (in itself unusual, a sign of tension), each trying to push the other ahead, I was glad. My heart was lighter seeing them. I forced myself to sit up and make light of the situation. "What do you know? Here are my troops. Come here, guys."

They submitted to my weakened hug. "How are you, Dad?" said Ches. He seemed to have grown about two inches since I saw him last, less than a week ago. His dark eyes were sleepless and bloodshot, rimmed with black, and I realized with shame how worried he'd been.

"Someone took a potshot at me," I said, going along with Jackie's version. I made a gun of my thumb and forefinger. "Bang! Like I was a rabbit or something. Or a guy in a movie."

Ches looked pained, though Bobby tried to laugh. He dipped his blond head close and kissed me. He hadn't done this in years. "Did it hurt?"

"I don't remember. I guess so. It hurts now."

"Last night we drove out into the desert," Bobby said, restless as usual, bubbly and excited. "We looked for UFOs."

"See any?"

"I don't know," Bobby said. "Maybe. I think so. Didn't I, Mom?"

Jackie smiled, shrugged, and I tried to picture the scene: the three of them together in a car, out beneath the stars in the stillness of the night. Jackie would have been smoking, thinking, figuring out how best to handle the situation, how best to handle me, get me back in line. She was a plotter, a thinker—had been even when I met her, back when she was barely out of her teens.

"Maybe you did see one, Bobs," I said. "Strange things going on in the desert."

"Don't encourage him, he's bad enough," Jackie said, herding the two of them together and forcing Bobby to stand still while she pushed the hair out of his eyes. "Come on, you two. Your father's tired. We'll see him later."

"Bye, Dad," said Bobby, and Ches surprised me by darting forward, leaving me with a kiss. He was a quiet and studious kid with his world suddenly shaken, and I found myself thinking of my own childhood, of a long-ago incident, of the day my mother walked out on my father. A fine, clear, winter morning with blue skies, and snow on the ground. I was ten and somehow I'd known it was going to happen. From the silences between my parents, the mood in the house. A tense and wispy mood, as if the structure itself were changing, mutating, filling with cobwebs. Kids pick up on these things. My father never got over that day, I guess, though he wouldn't talk about it, or anything to do with his family. His father, the grandfather I never met, I later found out, had been a lumber tycoon, with mills up in northern New York State, near Ithaca. The mills failed and he went off and tried to sell furniture throughout the Midwest. Lost his shirt to a con man, became a con man himself, went to jail: a colorful character, my grandfather, a wild one, but my father never discussed him. It was forgotten history, deepest shame. My mother's leaving became another chapter. For years he maintained the pretense that she was only on vacation and would soon be back.

Jackie and the kids had been gone only a couple of minutes and my eyes were still open when the door opened briskly and Paul Mantilini came in, alone, wearing a dark suit and a warm smile. "Hey, architect," he said, squeezing my hand. "How are you feeling? How are the eyes?"

"Still in my head. Just about."

Mantilini pulled up a chair, flipped it around, straddled it with his chin resting on his hands over the back. "Jackie says you don't remember what happened."

"Not too much."

"It's a miracle you're still alive," he said. "That gun was right in your face when she pulled the trigger."

My mind strained, trying to call up the picture.

"We were at the top of the hotel. It was after the flash, right after the blast hit."

Those words—*flash*, *blast*—triggered a rush of memory. Dizzying images pressed in: I saw a mushroom of boiling cloud, I saw the sky on fire; I saw Mallory's reflection, dark in a window, her face caked with blood and dirt. I remembered the gun in her hand, the flash springing from its muzzle. I recalled my shock—the pain, the bewilderment. The blackness that had crashed over me.

"Why would she shoot you?"

"I've no idea."

"You had a fight?"

"Not exactly. Nothing to merit this."

He moved his head, only a fraction, but I understood the gesture: in his experience, he was saying, the consequence of the mildest argument might be very violent indeed. He smiled reassuringly.

"And you met her at a party, is that right? Your friend Luis introduced her to you."

Mantilini looked at me, but he seemed to be talking to himself, musing out loud, and I wondered how he knew this. Then I remembered the conversation I'd had with Nick, when he came to the cabana. Mantilini had been piecing the story together.

"It doesn't matter, I guess," he went on. He sighed but his eyes remained steady. "Listen, I'm sorry, but I've got some bad news. She's dead."

"What?" I said, uncomprehending, closing my eyes while nausea swept over me. I felt like I'd been kicked in the gut.

"They found her car in Lake Mead this morning. She ran off the road the other night when she was trying to get away. They've found her body too, all banged up. I'm sorry."

He touched my shoulder and let his hand linger there. "The best thing you can do? Forget this ever happened. Throw yourself into the Senate run. Do it for your wife, your kids. And for me, too, Maurice. I need you."

He signaled to the nurse who had just come in. She stepped forward with a loaded syringe.

I tried to rise, but it was no good. Firm hands pressed me back.

I sighed as the needle pierced my arm.

22

SEPTEMBER 10, 1956 / THE DESERT

*Y*ou thought you could get away with it. You reckoned you deserved a pat on the back, a dip in the honey pot," said Joe Nelson, banging his big left hand on the outside of the car door. "I've got no quarrel with that. But take it as a lesson, Maurice. Who the fuck *was* this girl?"

"Does it matter now?" I said, my eyes blinking against the harshness of the light.

"Sure it matters. Shit, yeah, it *matters*." Freed from the Senate floor, Joe gave rein to his barroom, barnyard language. He went on slapping at the door, while his other hand fiddled with the radio, tuning in to a news station. Which meant that the car, briefly, had no hands on the steering wheel; but fortunately it was a Cadillac, like riding on cushions, on air, like floating, courtesy of Paul Mantilini, and the desert road that stretched ahead of us was straight and empty. "Always know what you're getting yourself into. Otherwise people like me are gonna wonder whether you're the kind of guy who couldn't pour piss out of a boot if the instructions were printed on the heel. You're smart, Maurice, so don't act like a jerk. How's Jackie?"

"She's mad as hell."

"She's like her mother. She'll get over it," Joe said, giving me a sideways look, his face sour, though he showed his long, fearsome teeth in a smile. Both his hands were back on the wheel, but, hearing something he didn't like on the radio, he scratched his wiry, red hair and shouted suddenly: "You fucking louse!"

I didn't *think* he was referring to me, though I shut my eyes for a moment and leaned against the cool glass of the window. I'd gotten out of hospital only that morning. I felt dizzy, light-headed. My throat was dry. Pain stabbed my head and the light burned my eyes. I'd have been hard-pressed to name the day of the week. And here I was with Joe and his plans and his mean, snaggletoothed grins.

"You hear about Boss Booth?" Joe said, his long arm reaching for the radio again. "His health took a turn for the better. Sometimes there's no justice, goddammit."

I felt sick, nauseous.

"Doesn't change a thing," Joe said. "Boss is a mean old buzzard, but he's sick and he'll die sooner or later. Maybe it'll be sooner. Who can say? Anything can happen in this world. Meanwhile we're gonna get you ready, prepare the ground. Put our flag in the sand. Let Boss know we know he's done."

I wondered, then, about the purpose of our morning drive. Clearly it wasn't just so Joe could enjoy the pleasure of my company.

"Paul wants to bring you up to speed on the deal," he said. "Let you know what's at stake."

I looked out into the desert. The road stretched ahead, mounting slowly with salt flats glistening among the parched monotonous wastes. A dust devil, a miniature whirlwind, swirled and subsided again. Here and there at the side of the road jutted the sharp, stark branches of Spanish bayonet and the tortured arms of Joshua trees. A diesel truck rumbled along, laden with boxes of fruit, bound for Vegas. What *could* be at stake, out here in this wilderness?

Joe sped the Cadillac through Indian Springs and on toward Beatty, now and then banging on the door, or railing at something said on the radio, hitting the gas with his narrow, coffin-like shoe. On either side of the highway broken bottles glittered in the scrub, alongside the occasional burned-out car, shot-out road sign, and derelict building. About ten miles short of Beatty we took a right turn and I assumed we must be heading toward Camp Mercury and the test site. But Joe steered off-road, and we bounced softly along a track leading to the crest of a hill where another car, another Cadillac, was already waiting. The doors of this car were open and four men were gathered, turning toward us when they heard the motor: Paul and Nick Mantilini, a man I didn't recognize, and, to my surprise, Luis Barragan, who wore a white suit, silk cravat, and a new white panama hat that probably had been bought for the occasion. On seeing me, Luis doffed the hat with an ironic sweep, then returned to the matter at hand.

Joe cut the engine and through his open window I heard Luis's voice, confident, booming, bringing in references to Mies van der Rohe, Lewis Mumford, and the "unique opportunities of the site." He was putting on a show, and Mantilini *père* was listening, giving him his entire attention. Nick looked bored. The man I didn't know stood with one hand on his hip and the other holding a jacket that was slung over his shoulder. He was a short, solid man, almost square in shape, with graying hair stiff like a porcupine's and an acne-pitted face.

The group broke up as Joe Nelson and I got out of the car and Mantilini came toward me, wearing slacks and a blue silk sports shirt. He stood beside me with his hands in his pockets, relaxed, smiling, jingling the coins in his pocket, but surveying the desert as though he owned it. Which, as he was about to reveal, he did. All that lay in front of us, about fifty square miles. "It's like Frank Lloyd Wright said. 'The desert is where God is and man is not,'" he said. "But not for long."

I asked him to elaborate.

"The other night you asked what I hoped to get out of making you senator for Nevada," he said. "The answer is this—a whole new city."

Mantilini spoke with pride, with determination, with a pleasure I'd never heard in his voice before. "A few months ago Ike gave a speech. The gist was that he wanted to take some of the nuclear business out of the hands of the military. Give a part of it to people who know how to adapt it for peace. Warm the cold, feed the hungry. You get the idea—the usual political baloney."

I remembered the speech. Afterwards the press had gone crazy with stories about atomic locomotives, atomic devices for cutting lumber, atomic rays to fight cancer. A new atomic everything to solve any problem and cure any ill.

"I'm not interested in any of that crap," Mantilini said. "I'm going to build."

Mantilini turned his eyes away from me to the scene in front of us, the desert that was covered with tough thistle, tumbleweed, and straggling sparse creosote bushes, the thousands of acres of flatland that stretched ahead before a range of hills rose out of the shimmering haze to close off the view, their jagged peaks stark in the cutting light.

"Right here," he said. "This is where it'll be. A whole new city."

"You mean . . ."

"Double the size of Vegas."

"See, Maurice, I'm tight with some of those guys at the AEC," Joe Nelson said, chipping in. He had his place on the Senate Atomic Energy Sub-Committee, I now recalled, and Boss Booth was the *chairman* of that committee. I was beginning to realize what this was all about. "Soon they're gonna stop the above-ground tests," Joe went on. "Take them deep below. And they want to build a power plant in Indian Springs."

"With all that cheap juice it'll be the Hoover Dam all over again," Mantilini said. "But bigger, better."

The idea was audacious, almost inconceivable, but then who was to say? For it was, also, an extension of the vision he'd shown when the A-bomb tests first started. Though Las Vegas was still essentially a small town, Mantilini had put the place on the map. Now he was thinking in even bigger terms. He wanted to leave a mark; in some interesting way he was grandiose; it was his strength, maybe his weakness, too.

"Don't tell me," I said. "Boss Booth hates the idea."

"The Boss is a northern Nevada guy. He gets his support from the miners, the oil barons," Mantilini said, his tone calm and imperturbable. "That's the past of the state. The future is here in Vegas. With me."

"It sure is," Joe Nelson said, his manner subtly adjusting itself now that he was in Mantilini's presence. He was flattering, almost fawning. Joe was bully and bootlicker both, and I wondered how big a slice of this desert pie he was cutting for himself. "And the sooner Boss Booth is dead in his grave and Maurice here is safely in the Senate and sitting on *my* committee, the better things will be. Why, we'll all be happy as clams. But much, much richer."

"A whole new city," Mantilini said.

And more millions than either he or Joe could count, I thought, and I didn't doubt that they could count a few.

"This land is already worth ten times what Dad paid for it," said Nick Mantilini, who'd been standing to one side, listening to all this. "So even if we don't build, we'll make a pile of dough."

"But we will build," Mantilini said, firm, frowning at his son. "High and handsome and very big. Think about this, Maurice. Consider the possibilities. Not just one hotel, but twenty. Fifty. A city hall, a civil center, schools, roads, a hospital. Luis here"—he included the grinning Barragan as his arm made a regal sweep—"Luis thinks there should be an opera house. It's not a bad idea. We'll build this together."

Only now did the short, solid man, the man I didn't know, step forward and seize my hand in a fierce grip. His white shirt clung to his chest. He had a strong face, a pug's ears, and a huge gap-toothed smile. His name, he told me, was Jimmy Hoffa. "Pleased to meet you, Senator," he said.

"Not yet."

"Only a matter of time," Hoffa said, his grin so wide now it looked like he could swallow a cactus. His belly was no doubt tough enough to digest one. He was a union man, a leader of the Teamsters. He and Mantilini had known each other for a long time. "I knew him when he was running booze in trucks across the Canadian border," Hoffa said in a whisper. "I was just a kid then. But I could see he was equipped for authority. He says to people, 'It's got to be like this, and no other way.' And they listen to him. It's a gift that only leaders have."

23

*J*ackie had gone back to L.A. with the kids. I called her that night from the cabana at the El Sheik. "It's a land grab," I told her. "It's like Miami in the 1920s except Paul has this big idea about building a city. And Joe wants me to be the rubber-stamp guy on his committee."

"You got a problem with any of this?" Jackie said, calling my bluff as she usually did. And she was right, I shouldn't have had a problem with it, not really. But I'd been through something. I'd been briefly blinded. I'd nearly died and I didn't know why. I was grateful that Jackie and Joe and Mantilini had elected not to cast me out for my potentially embarrassing indiscretion, but what the heck had happened? Sure, I'd been a bastard, trying to use Mallory like that, but she'd had her own agenda, it now seemed. What, exactly, had it been? And, at the back of everything, was another question. Had I been in love with her? I told myself not. But I was in a tangle.

"*Il faut payer*, darling, you know that," Jackie said. "*Il faut payer.*"

Could I tell Jackie how I felt? No, I thought, she'd only tell me to get over it. "They're planning some shindig in a couple of days. To introduce Maurice Valentine to his public," I said. "I guess you should be there. The kids, too."

"I spoke to Dad about it already."

"You did?"

"Before he flew back to Washington."

"What's he saying about me?"

"He's on your side, darling. He's saying that I have to support you. And be seen to support you. So we'll be there, on the steps of city hall, waving your flag," she said, with subdued and subtly barbed irony. She was prepared, in the interest of our shared goal, if not exactly to forget this, the most blatant of my infidelities, at least to glide over it. Like a shark.

Briskly she gave me news about some work that needed doing on the house, and about a couple of people she'd met at the country club who were already eager to donate to my political bandwagon, once it got rolling.

"They see you in the part." she said. "They think you'll be good at this. And I'm telling them how strongly I agree."

"The rubber-stamp guy."

"You know there'll be more to it."

"Should I be worried?" I said. "By the way, Luis is here."

This was news to her.

"You were thinking of involving him anyway," she said. "It's for the best, isn't it?"

In our marriage we'd survived without too much tumult, priding ourselves on our realism. Jackie had a cradle-bred knowledge of the mechanism whose inner whirrings I was just beginning to discern. She was soothing me, in her diplomatic way, telling me to hold my nerve and think clearly. Another thought fumed through my mind.

"I never realized your father and Mantilini were so tight," I said.

"Only because of you, darling," Jackie said. "They formed an alliance to make you senator of Nevada."

"How'd they meet each other?"

"I've no idea. Years ago, I think."

"I'd wondered. So Joe was behind my getting the commission for the El Sheik?"

"Ask him."

"I did," I said. "He said he wasn't."

"Maybe he doesn't want you to know."

"Maybe," I said. "Why?"

"You're asking me to explain my father to you," she said. I could almost hear her eyebrow raising on the other end of the line. "I can't do that—not even for myself. I've given up trying."

Her voice hinted at something, almost reproach, and I wanted to inquire further. But she said: "Don't worry, Maurice. You must be tired. Get some sleep. Goodnight, darling. I'll kiss the boys for you."

I was sitting on the edge of the bed. The only light in the cabana came from a lamp on the desk but in its beam I saw something glinting, encrusted with gems. With a sinking heart I realized it was Mallory's cigarette case. Looking around the room, I saw her book, and, hanging in the closet, her dress, along with her underwear, laundered now and in a bag. Not much evidence of this dead woman about whom I'd actually known so little. Mallory had died. Who was missing her? Wondering about her? I thought of the letter that Nick had fished out of the trash can.

My knees buckled, sweat broke out all over my hands and my body, my head swam—I had all the symptoms.

To whom had she written these words? Not to me—I was certain of that. I was a good-enough-looking guy, clever, ambitious, of course; but I'd never inspired the fever. Nor felt it, either—not with Jackie, or anybody else, thank God: that sort of recklessness could upset your calculations.

A knock came at the door. For a moment, sitting in the dimness, I had the idea that if I opened the door it would be her, back from the dead. But it was Luis Barragan, bringing with him a gust of warm night air, the sound of laughter from the floodlit pool, and the smell of gin. "I believe you have something of mine," he said, barging in. He was drunk. "My drawings."

Luis had lost some weight. The lines on his brow were deeper and his pale jowls sagged. He was drawn and tired, yet still he seemed smug, aggressively buoyant. He peeked under the bed and made a show of ripping back the covers. "Where are they?"

I remembered the portfolio had been in Mallory's hand when we left the hotel after that memorable breakfast with Mantilini. Which meant she'd taken it with her in the Porsche.

"At the bottom of Lake Mead, probably," I said.

"Ah—with herself, then, eh?"

"She's in the morgue."

"Did you go see the body?"

I'd spent an hour down at the Las Vegas police precinct house, where a detective showed me the salvaged wreck of the Porsche. He was balding, skinny, with dark bags under his eyes so that he resembled a tremendous racoon. He'd seemed bored and slightly resentful, but then the average Vegas cop's idea of a good day's work was breaking into an appliance store and stealing a few TV sets. I was welcome to view the corpse if I wanted, he said, not that there was much left to look at. "She got pretty banged up," the cop had said, and I declined his offer.

"No," I told Luis. "I didn't."

Luis responded with a grunt. His skin was greasy. He sucked at his teeth. "You stole her from me, Maurice, like she stole my drawings, and I wanted to hurt you for it." He sagged, flopping down in an armchair, crossing his stocky legs. "Then I realized I never had her in the first place. It was you, Maurice. Always you. Only you."

"How do you figure that?"

"You lied to me. You lied through your teeth when I came to see you." He thumped the arm of the chair and I wondered if I was in for a dose of Luis's operatic anger. But he restrained himself. "Did she have a secret of some kind?" he said, almost to himself.

"Doesn't everyone?"

His mood changed yet again and he regarded me with a malevolent grin. "Her secret was you, Maurice. She was obsessed with you."

"That's ridiculous."

"Isn't it?"

"I meant," I said, holding on to my patience, "that it wasn't true."

Luis shook his head. He told me that he'd been distraught during those days after his party. That had been the last time he'd seen her. She'd promised to meet him the next day but didn't show up. Then he came to see me and I gave him the brush-off. "I was desperate," he said. "I broke into her apartment. It was easy. I smashed through the lock with my shoulder. And do you know what I found?"

"You think I'm psychic?"

"Nothing. I found nothing."

"That's not surprising. What did you expect?"

He told me I didn't understand, as usual. "I mean there was *nothing*. The apartment was small and it was clean and it was empty. No clothes, no papers, no books. No mail. Like a shell after the hermit crab was gone."

"Are you sure the place was hers?"

"Of course I'm sure. She gave me the address. I spoke with the land-lady. Before she refused to give me a key and I broke the door down."

"Landlady? I'd have thought Mallory would own a place."

He shrugged. "Me too. But who can say? In the end she was a very unpredictable girl."

I was thinking of when she collected me from my office, before we drove down to the beach house; she'd said she had everything she needed, in a single small suitcase, in the trunk of the Porsche, ready to go. Most of that stuff was here in the cabana now, waiting to be packed up and thrown away. Taken to the dump. Although you remember the dead, in a way it's as though they never existed.

"So I went through the trash," Luis said. "And in the trash I did find something. I found you. Photographs of Maurice Valentine. Newspaper and magazine articles about Maurice Valentine. A character analysis, in her handwriting, of the great and illustrious Maurice Valentine. And, I tell you, she had your number."

"What did she say about me?"

"Oh, it was sharp, it was mean, it was good, but it's *my* secret," Luis said, and his voice had that insistent, nagging quality, his ringing-phone voice; his multiple chins giggled with mirth.

"Did you keep the material?"

"Why would I? It was trash and in the trash it stayed. Where it belonged. Then you were gone from your office and I started to put two and two together. My disappointment with her turned into rage against you. But I didn't know where you were until Mantilini called me and gave me the lurid details of your little melodrama. And then he asked how I'd feel about working with you again."

Luis's smile was resigned, wringing what pleasure he could from this particular irony. "An entire city! He's nuts, of course."

"I wouldn't say that to his face if I were you," I said. "And I wouldn't bet against him pulling it off. He's no fantasist, whatever else he may be."

"He has the money?"

"He's a rich man."

"Not rich enough for this."

"There are other sources."

"The Teamsters?"

"He's played those guys like a dream," I said. "They wanted to come in with him on the Havana hotels. But then he realized he didn't want all that money to be so far away beneath the palm trees. And under a foreign government. So he's sold them on this idea instead."

Luis rose to his feet and strode to the desk, taking Mallory's cigarette case and lifting it to his nose, inhaling as though he might catch the very essence of her. When he turned back to me his look was shrewd, knowing, almost smug again.

"You've gotten to the center of things, haven't you, Maurice?"

He spoke my name with spite, but what he said was true; I felt it myself; I was at the place where the cogs go around. Yet somehow I felt terrible, sick, dissatisfied, filled with a restlessness I didn't understand. I put it down to being hurt. But there was more to it than that. I was starting to change.

"You've come a long way without doing a lot, if you'll forgive me for saying so."

Luis clearly didn't give a damn whether I forgave him or not; he was saying it anyway.

"You've been good at the image thing. I remember when I met you.

You'd never drunk champagne. You'd never eaten an artichoke. You were *unformed*."

Nor could I argue with him about that. Pretty much my first move on arriving in L.A. in '45 was to change my name, but the first job I had was as a publicist for the Hollywood Bowl, fixed for me by a buddy from the Air Force. I hadn't really known what I wanted to do, only that I wanted it to happen fast. Briefly I toyed with the idea of being an actor, and read for a few agents and producers. This came to nothing. Then I ran into Luis, at a concert at the Bowl, and realized I could step back into architecture. "You told me to marry money," I said. "The best advice you ever gave."

"It's true. Without Jackie you'd be . . . *nothing*." He treated me to an acid grin. "She's a very strong woman. She saw something in you, I suppose. I guess I did, too."

"Generous of you to say so, Luis. Especially since you're currently riding on my coattails."

He ignored the barb. "And Jackie doesn't mind about this absurd fling of yours?"

"We have an understanding."

"Ah, an understanding!" he said, smirking, tugging at the hair that flowed from his ear. "That's very good. But perhaps this understanding would be different if Mallory Walker was still alive."

"She isn't."

He shook his head, that smirk still spread all over his rumpled face. "She played you for a sucker, too. As a lover of the drama I can truly appreciate the situation. She's *alive*."

"The hell she is."

"She ran away from you, that's all. It's rather amusing, actually, when I think of the days I spent searching for her, all those days when she was with you, setting you up the way she did me."

"Give it up, man. She's dead. You know it as well as I do."

He reached into his jacket and pulled out his wallet, from which he extracted a newspaper clipping that he unfolded and dangled in front of my eyes. Now I did feel something, a mixture of dread and, to my surprise, excitement.

"Explain this to me, my clever and ambitious friend," Luis said, handing me the clipping. "If Mallory Walker is dead, how come she's getting married in Palm Springs on Sunday?"

PART 3

Palm Springs

24

SEPTEMBER 10–11, 1956 / PALM SPRINGS

I left that night. In Las Vegas I kept a Studebaker, the model designed by Raymond Loewy, identical to the one I drove in L.A., right down to the same lock. I was outside the El Sheik, waiting for the bellhop to bring the car around, when Joe Nelson stepped out of the door. His face was sour and in the lights that spilled out from the lobby his stiff, wiry hair looked like it was aflame.

"Where the hell are you going?"

I shrugged.

"We've got work to do, Maurice. Don't fuck this up."

The car came and I left him standing. With his threats ringing in my ears I headed south on I-15, toward Henderson and the Hoover Dam, and then out into the desert. The night was warm and windy, and, as I drove, I glimpsed a moonlit picture of rock and sand, stars and space. Everything stood out stark and clear in the silvery light. Everything, that is, except what I was doing. With a newspaper clipping in my pocket I was chasing a phantom. I knew already that I was on some crazy mission, but . . . I'd been shot. Maurice Valentine had been *shot*. I thought I was owed an explanation, even if it meant upsetting the apple cart a little.

To distract myself I stopped at a gas station and picked up a hitchhiker, a nervous guy of about my own age who wore a shabby brown suit and sat with a brand-new suitcase balanced on his knees. Maybe he was a murderer, I thought, with body parts stashed in there. You read about that sort of thing. Or an unemployed actor, or an embezzler on the run with the proceeds of a small business. At the next gas station he asked me to stop so he could get out again. Maybe he didn't like *my* character. Anyway, soon I had another passenger aboard, a gangly kid who stuck his sneakered feet on the dash and strained to read a science-fiction comic in the dim green glow from the radio until he announced suddenly that he was feeling carsick, wound down the window, and threw up with a motion I can only describe as practiced.

The kid was heading home, to his parents' place in San Bernardino, not that he thought of it as home anymore, he said. I left him where I-15 hit I-10, waiting until a truck stopped to pick him up, and rolled into Palm Springs when gold was already streaking the crimson sunrise.

We had a house in Palm Springs. Or rather, Jackie had a house in Palm Springs, bought for her by Joe and registered in her name alone. I didn't stay there. Instead I checked into the Octotillo Lodge, a new place back then. At one time, in the early 1930s, the whole of Palm Springs had been Spanish colonial; but the town had become a haven for Hollywood, for politicians, for serious power and money, for people who needed to flatter themselves by hiring architects featured in the newspapers and magazines. Architects like me. So the style of many of the buildings left even L.A. behind in terms of architectural daring and adventure, in terms of sheer outlandish flair, craziness. Thus the Octotillo Lodge: German expressionism met *Shane* in a dramatically lit and sweepingly curved lobby that was furnished with heavy wooden tables and plastic bucket chairs designed by Eames. My bungalow fronted onto a swimming pool that was shaped like a keyhole. I ordered room service and lay on the bed with the door open, trying to convince myself that I hadn't lost my mind, coming to Palm Springs like this. I waited until my watch said eight, at which time I thought it reasonable to call Jack Cody, a friend. Once upon a time Jack had worked with Le Corbusier in Europe. Now he lived in Palm Springs, wore a cowboy hat, and smoked more marijuana than Bob Mitchum. Everything with him proceeded in a leisurely way. Usually he managed to finish his houses, but not always his sentences; he was gifted with a pencil, and I guessed he'd know where to find shipping magnate Brent Walker and his daughter Mallory.

"She's getting hitched in a couple of days," Jack Cody said, and I asked if he'd ever met her.

"Never had the pleasure," he said. "This is her second time around the maypole. Her first husband was some rich oil guy. I guess they'll be plenty busy. Brent's got pretty much the whole town working around the clock. Why, when I saw him the other day . . ."

No good would come of trying to interrupt Jack, I knew; he was a man in whom stoned courtliness ran deep. Eventually, however, he got around to giving me the address.

The Walker place was in a private community that had its own golf course, and, at the gate, a security guard with a pistol swinging on his hip. The top banana from Ford had his winter spread there, and the chairman of Firestone, and Bing Crosby, and Lucille Ball and Desi Arnaz. There were more millionaires than you could swing at with a seven iron.

The guard looked the Studebaker over, taking in my dusty suit and my probably crazed expression. He listened to my story about how the Walkers were expecting me and went to make a call from inside his booth. I'm not sure if he got any answer because, after a minute or two, he came back and ushered me through with a nod and a cowboy's bored mumble: "Third on the right." To hear him say it, you'd think the house was close. Not so: the Studebaker climbed a steep hill without sidewalks for a mile and more before I came to the third estate. A high wall surrounded it, and no mailbox or sign on the tall iron gates indicated that this was the Walker residence. But the gates were open and I followed a ribbon of tarmac that swept around a brick wall and deposited me in a courtyard at the back of a sprawling, L-shaped, single-story house with a red terra-cotta roof. Arrayed around a fountain were a sleek Jaguar sports car, a new lavender Cadillac with gold trim, and an old Bentley that still looked like a million bucks. Wealthy toys, my kind of people.

A servant showed me into a large, cool living room that had a floor of polished tile, a high-beamed ceiling, and adobe walls. A white couch the size of a railway car was in front of the baronial fireplace. Silver frames glimmered atop a Steinway baby grand. A leather-bound guest book lay open to a blank page beside the current issues of *Vogue* and *Harper's Bazaar* on a table of thick oak. The telephone beside the book was hand-carved in ivory and all the woodwork was burnished to a sheen. It was a waxy room, dead and dispiriting, planned and plotted, right down to the Pulitzer Prize–winning novels, lined up like soldiers in an alcove by the fireplace, dust jackets pristine—unread, I reckoned, but arranged by year.

The servant had disappeared, so I poked about. The frames on top of the Steinway were empty—no photographs inside them. Through tall, arched windows without drapes I saw the dazzle of a swimming pool. Tall date-palms edged the pool, holding motionless their pom-poms. Off to the right, a wide and well-nurtured lawn swept down to a plateau. In the desert, water is money, and all that ostentatious green spelled a fortune. A hectic ballet was in progress on this lush, billiard-smooth swath. Several men were struggling to erect a large tent, for the upcoming nuptials, presumably. They weren't having much luck. The tent sagged badly to one side. Advising the men, bossing them, was a slender woman whose head was adorned with a scarlet-and-white polka-dotted scarf. Dark glasses shuttered her eyes, but I knew from her posture, the jerky gracelessness of her movement, that this wasn't Mallory. She seized a large wooden mallet and began to hammer at a peg. The half-erect tent wilted in front of her, a sad billow of collapsing silk. In disgust she threw the mallet aside and stalked up the hill.

A French door opened with a sudden gust of heat. "You the flowers?" she said, frazzled, a little frantic. Her skin was pale, thin, almost papery, stretched thin at the temple so a pumping vein showed through.

"No, I . . ."

"Thank God," she said, and stamped away, heels echoing across the tile and into the gloom of a hallway.

I was alone again but not for long. A man in khaki shorts and black sandals advanced around the side of the pool and burst into the room. His red shirt, unbuttoned, revealed a barrel chest.

"Did you see my wife?"

"A woman just passed through."

"That was her, the bitch," he said. His feet were flat, splayed, strong. He stood like a boxer, ready to punch. This was Brent Walker, I gathered. He had no time or need for charm. He slapped his belly and scratched at the crotch of his shorts. His hair was a wire brush, his teeth looked like they could tear a cow in half. "Who the hell are you?"

"My name is Maurice Valentine," I said. "I'm looking for your daughter."

"You fucking her?"

His eyes were on me, hard and piercing, and I tried a smile, saying, "I'm an architect."

"You're building her a house?"

It seemed safe to say: "We're talking about it."

He grunted. "She didn't tell me she's been talking to architects. But with Mallory you never know."

"She's unpredictable?"

"You'll get your dough, don't worry about that. Just send the bills to me," he said, strutting to the corner of the room, to the bar, where he began fixing a pitcher of martinis. "You must be expensive, if she chose you," he said.

"Who's expensive?" said his wife, coming back down the hallway. Her lips were freshly rouged, and a different scarf, of black silk, was knotted over the red flame of her head. The removal of the dark glasses hadn't improved her mood any. Her eyes were green like money. She helped herself to a martini from the pitcher and searched for a cigarette. "Damn!" she said. The box was empty. I offered her one, from Mallory's cigarette case, which I'd slipped into my pocket back at the El Sheik. She didn't notice it. "Thanks," she said, leaning toward the flame of the lighter.

I remembered Mallory telling me that her mother had died when she was a kid. So this was a stepmother, probably not the first. Maybe not the last, either. She looked like a handful.

"This is Maurice Valentine," Brent Walker said, scratching his bullish chest. "He's building a house for Mallory."

"We've been talking about it," I said. "It's early days yet."

"Where *is* the ravishing bride?" said Mrs. Walker, acid in her smile.

"I told you. She's playing tennis."

"That's where you're so very wrong, my darling. Freddie called. She didn't show for their game. He thought he'd swing by the dress store in case she decided to go for the fitting after all. Of course she wasn't there, either. He can't find her anywhere."

"Freddy couldn't find his dick if it was on fire."

"Let's just hope she remembers she's marrying him. The wedding's only forty-eight hours away. Not that I give a damn."

"She'll remember allright," Brent Walker said, "don't you worry about that." I wondered how long *their* marriage had lasted. A little over a year, I guessed. Long enough for him to show her the mulishness beneath the millions, and for her to reveal that, if she were a trophy, she came with a tendency to tarnish. All in all, the average arrangement of convenience. Soon, perhaps, she'd take her settlement, and he'd be in the market for next year's model. Or maybe, reckoning the grass wouldn't be greener after all, she'd stick. Then the fireworks would really begin. Their bedroom was a battlefield, I bet.

"Mallory's gonna be married," Brent Walker went on. "And you can't stand it. Because I'm gonna have grandchildren and you can forget about getting another damned penny."

"Honey," his wife said. Her nails were carmine talons. A smudgy half-moon of lipstick clung to her glass. "You are so naïve. You've got all that money and you still can't see what's in front of your eyes."

"And you, my dear, are a queen bitch in spades."

I wasn't sure whether to make my excuses and say that I'd be back later or look around for boxing gloves and start timing the rounds. But then the front door opened and, at first unobserved by Brent Walker and his wife, a young woman came in. She was tall and skinny, with her father's dark, sharp, penetrating eyes and shiny black hair that fell almost to her waist. She was like a colt, nervous and gleaming. Maybe twenty-five. Beautiful in a high-strung way. No doubt intelligent. No doubt used to being looked at and therefore indifferent to my surprised stare. She wore black satin slacks and a white shirt and she stood with her arms crossed. "Are you two at it again?" she said with weary disdain. "I wish you'd cut it out."

"Where the hell have you been, sugar?" Brent Walker said, turning toward her with a big paternal grin. So *this* was Mallory Walker. But not *my* Mallory Walker. "Freddy's been looking for you all over town."

"Lucky Freddy," said Mallory Walker. "He'll have to look a little harder. If his already overburdened brain can manage it. Which I doubt."

Brent Walker smothered a laugh. Freddie, I'd gathered, was the bridegroom, the lucky man about to marry into this perfect American family. No doubt he'd examined the less-than-blissful domestic atmosphere and balanced it against a consideration of Brent Walker's bank accounts. Freddy, whoever he was, seemed like a man after my own heart.

"And you are . . .?" Mallory Walker said, narrowing her eyes fractionally as she stepped toward me with her hand held out.

Some fancy footwork was called for. I shook her hand, said, "Maurice Valentine," and held out the cigarette case. "Care for one?"

"This is your architect, darling," Mrs. Walker said, sniffing blood. Her smile was wide as a bucket. "Surely you recognize him. Or do we have an imposter in our midst? A snake in the grass? How marvelously *thrilling*."

"What?" said Brent Walker, frowning, turning to his daughter. "You do know him, don't you?"

She wasn't looking at him, or at me. Her dark eyes were magnetized by the jewel-encrusted cigarette case, the one that Mallory, the other Mallory, had left in the cabana at the El Sheik. She studied it and almost reached out to seize it from my hand. "Of course I remember Mr. Valentine," she said. "But, Maurice—I thought we were supposed to meet at your hotel."

"It's obviously my mistake. My mind's a sieve," I said, going along with her fiction while her eyes, stony-cold, studied me. "I'm at the Octotillo."

"I'll see you there in an hour," Mallory Walker said and turned on her heel.

25

She came sooner than she'd said. Impatient, maybe, or else she wanted to take me by surprise. I'd only just got back to my room when I heard a rap at the door.

"Show me that thing," she said, anger blazing in her haughty eyes.

I handed over the cigarette case.

"Where the hell did you get this?"

"From a woman calling herself Mallory Walker."

Now it was her turn to be taken aback. She blinked; one of her dark, heavy-lidded eyes had a flaw at the corner, almost like a birthmark. She took a long breath. "Where is she?" she said, almost afraid.

"I'm sorry. She's dead."

The blood rushed from her face and for a moment I thought she was going to faint. Stricken, she sagged, gripping at my arm for support. I shut the door, led her into the room, and sat her down on the bed. "I knew it," she said. "I felt it. Something *dreadful*. What happened?"

"Her car went into Lake Mead."

"The Porsche?"

"That was yours too?"

She nodded, numb. "Poor angel," she said, and her head went down into her hands while she stifled a sob. "This isn't like me. I'm sorry. I never do this. I don't cry. I *never* cry."

But she did, her narrow shoulders heaving, still making no sound, as if she were determined to gather up all her pain and stuff it back inside so she could remember it forever.

From the bathroom I brought her a glass of water.

"Here."

She gulped it back.

I said, "You were friends?"

"Lovers," she said, looking up at me with pride and defiance. "Does that shock you?"

Being a lesbian wasn't something you owned up to in 1956, even if you were the daughter of a guy as rich as Brent Walker. Or maybe especially then, for fear of prosecution or blackmail. So I admired her bravery and confidence, understood a little better the charade she'd played out at her father's house. But somehow I wasn't shocked, not when I thought about *my* Mallory Walker. My Mallory Walker, I was starting to see, was capable of anything. The bullet that had grazed my head was only the beginning of the story.

"More?" I said, taking the glass from the real Mallory Walker's hand.

Her long fingers plucked at the blue cotton bedspread. "Got a real drink?" she said, making no attempt to wipe away the tears that ran down her cheeks.

I called room service and had them send over a bottle of Johnnie Walker with a bucket of ice and plenty of club soda. The bellhop sauntered in with a tray and departed with a five-dollar bill and a worldly smirk on his face. Little did he know.

I fixed the drinks and she drained the first like the whiskey was water, holding the glass above her head for more without bothering to look at me. With a jolt I remembered my Mallory making the same gesture the first night we'd made love—or, to be more accurate, the first time she fucked me, and I'd thrilled to her demands, the touch of her command—at the beach house. She'd finished her drink and calmly lifted the tumbler above her head, calling: "Refill."

I said, "When did you meet her?"

"I knew her vaguely from way back, at college. She was at UCLA, I was at USC—the rich kids' school. But our paths crossed. I guess you could say we noticed each other. You could say that, though to tell you the truth when she appeared in Palm Springs a few months ago I didn't recognize her. She looked so different."

"How?"

"More mature. Sadder, more guarded. But tougher, as if life had given her a whack or two. Her prettiness had turned into beauty. Funny how that can happen. She'd taken shape somehow. She stopped me in the street and said, 'You're Mallory Walker, aren't you?' She didn't think I'd remember her."

"You did?"

"Sure. The first time I saw her was after some football game. At a party. She and her friend were in a corner, wearing berets, tormenting a couple of jocks. She looked great. She had spirit and guts to spare. She wanted to be the greatest actress in the world. That's what she told me. I laughed, but she meant it. She was so serious back then, and so very ambitious. Working a little too hard at the part, if you know what I mean. The intense young actress who wanted everything now. But she had a way of pulling you into her dreams. I thought she stood a chance of making it."

"And she didn't?"

"When we met again I asked her about the acting. She said it didn't work out. Didn't seem too upset about it."

She held up her empty glass again, the same gesture. My Mallory had learned her like a book, right down to the way she gripped the glass, with her pinkie outstretched and wiggling.

"You might want to take it easy," I said.

"Why?"

"You're upset, and it's a hot day."

"Save the advice. I get plenty of that from my father. From Freddie. From everybody. As if I'm a problem they think they have to solve. As if they've got a clue what's going on with me."

She sounded angry, not bitter, defiant, not defeated, but I wondered how long she could keep up this attitude. A fake marriage, a long road of deceit and lies lay ahead of her. True love was rarely to be found, in her world, or in anybody's; she could always walk away, but that got harder as time went on—I knew.

I gave her the whiskey.

She sat on the bed with the glass in one hand and the cigarette case in the other. She bounced the case up and down on the mattress.

"A present from my father when I was twenty-one," she said. "With the instruction that I shouldn't smoke."

"Want a light?"

I stepped forward into her laughter, then stepped back again, lounging against the wall. I wanted her to have all the space she needed.

"What was her name?"

She shot me a puzzled look. "Oh, that's right. You said she was pretending to be me. Why would she do that?"

"She knew she could handle me easier if I thought she was rich."

"She played you, too?" Her smile was quick and fond. "She's something," she said, sipping at her whiskey, making the ice chink in the glass. "Her name's Beth Dyer."

"What did you say?" My mouth was dry.

"Her name is Beth Dyer. *Was* Beth Dyer, I guess I should say. It's going to take me a while to get used to that."

I was thinking of breakfast, that morning at the El Sheik: Paul Mantilini with his cup of coffee and his chair with a commanding view of the golf course. I was thinking of the guy in plaid pants bungling his putt, of Albert Kluphager with his beeping radiation gizmo, of the rail-thin pit-girl Roxie. I was thinking especially of Mallory and that spiky little exchange about Brooklyn baseball bats, of that moment when all the air had seemed to vanish from the room. "*Beth? Beth Dyer?*" Paul Mantilini had said, with pleasure in his voice, and she'd dodged the recognition, danced around it, coolly snowed us all.

"Beth Dyer?" I said.

"Are you deaf? How many times do I have to say it? Beth Dyer. That was her name."

I wasn't deaf, but I didn't want to hear.

Beth Dyer.

So she had indeed known Mantilini in some earlier version of herself. And then she'd denied it. Why? Perhaps everything had been a mere coincidence, a dreadful embarrassment for her: I'd brought her to Las Vegas, where she ran into a figure from her past she'd sooner forget. But I knew that wasn't right. She'd seen the picture of me with Mantilini in my office. She'd known. Oh shit, I thought, she'd *known*. She'd planned the whole deal. Not only had she duped me, played me for a sucker; she'd invented herself as Mallory Walker, stolen this girl's identity so that, in due course, I'd bring her close to Mantilini. Could that be true? Had that been her plan from the start?

I had a dizzy, swirling feeling. There was quicksand out here in the desert, and I was being pulled in deeper.

"Are you all right?" Mallory Walker said. "You just went white as a sheet."

I wasn't all right. The barely healed gash at the side of my head was pumping and pounding as further questions occurred to me now, questions that stung like scorpions. I screwed shut my eyes, trying once again to picture what had happened that night at the top of the hotel. There was Beth—from now on I'll call her by her true name—caked and painted in dirt. There was the snub-nosed pistol, huge at the end of her hand. I'd moved toward her. Was that right? Had I stepped into a bullet aimed at someone else—Mantilini? Had Paul Mantilini been her intended victim all along?

I knew I must take this carefully. I had to figure this out. "Tell me one more time. She showed up in Palm Springs—when?"

"About three months ago. She'd come to visit her mother. And then she bumped into me in the street. Literally—she almost knocked my purse out of my hands."

"Why was her mother here?"

"She was working in a department store. I think."

"Did you meet her?"

"Why would I?"

She was staring into her drink, pushing an ice cube with her finger.

"What happened? On the last day—how did she leave?"

"Why all the questions?"

"Just tell me," I said, and the angry rise in my voice startled her.

All the same she sipped at her drink before deciding to answer. "She asked to borrow the car. When she didn't come back that night I noticed a whole load of other stuff was missing."

Her watch, the cigarette case, some clothes.

"I couldn't exactly go to the cops, could I? What a feast they'd make of that in Palm Springs. Or to my father. He hasn't even noticed that the car's missing."

"You weren't angry?"

"I wanted to dig her green eyes out. But not as much as I wanted her back. Not as much as I wanted to hold and kiss her."

I looked down at the room's thick carpet, at the wood panels on the walls. Other questions began to jab. Frightening questions. What if, I wondered, Mallory hadn't driven her car into Lake Mead? What if Mantilini or one of his goons had caught up with her and killed her? What then, eh? What were you going to do about that, Maurice Valentine?

I poured myself another whiskey. "Want one?"

Mallory Walker had seen something in my eyes. "Did you kill her?"

"Of course not."

"But you know who did."

I said nothing for a moment. Gulping at my whiskey. "It's like I told you," I said. "She died in an accident."

She got to her feet, facing me with her hands on her hips. "I'll tell you this. Beth Dyer didn't drive her car—my car, *any* car—into any frigging lake. She drove like an expert, like she'd been around engines all her life. She drove that car fast, but she was careful. She didn't make mistakes."

I was thinking of one mistake that she'd made: she'd taken her shot at Paul Mantilini and missed. But, then, I'd crossed into her line of fire, stepped into the bullet. She couldn't have been ready for that, no matter how cool she'd been. And Mantilini's instincts were so quick and sharp that he wouldn't have given her a second chance.

"What the hell are you going to do about it?"

"You're upset, and so am I," I said. "And we're both a little drunk. Let's try and think about this calmly."

Meaning, I said to myself, let's try not to think about this at all. Because it was too damned scary.

"Excuse me a minute, will you?" I said, and went into the bathroom. Shut the door behind me, filled the sink, splashed water on my face and the back of my neck. Dried myself with a hotel towel, looking in the mirror, and found myself thinking, not of what I should do, but of the war, of the base in England where we told jokes, played cards and pranks, listened to jazz on the radio, drank all the warm Norfolk beer we could find, wrote letters, just got on with life. That was on the ground. Up in the air was a different matter. During the first few missions I wasn't scared, only sick. Being scared came later, when you learned what the chances of survival really were. Up in the air I was in the nose of the plane, exposed, but busy with a piece of machinery—the bombsight—so complicated I could never entirely figure it out. I guess I must have learned enough to get by, otherwise they wouldn't have kept me in there. I began to understand that I was just a cog in a machine. I existed only to understand the bombsight as best I could and release the bombs over the target, and man a machine gun if needed. I tried to pretend there was no danger, that I was in my own space. I tried not to think of the flak as something deadly, but as an intrusion in that space, as if I were the architect of the sky. I said to the other guys, "If something smashes the Plexiglas and lets in all that cold air, I'll be mad as hell." They laughed, telling me I was cuckoo, because if something did smash the glass, chances were that I'd be strawberry jam all over the inside of the nose. Some missions were tough, others were milk runs, and then came the time we caught hell. The target was the Messerschmitt factory in Regensburg, and the Germans came at us with everything they had. Fighters climbing from all around the clock, too many to count, rising to stop us at any cost, whole squadrons of 109s and FW190s. I had the feeling of being trapped. We *were* trapped, a fat silver pigeon surrounded by fighters so close I saw the pilots' faces. A cannon shell rocked the ship, wounding the rear turret gunner in the legs. A second shell ripped into the radio compartment and killed the radio operator. He bled to death with his chest in his lap. A third shell cut the rudder cables. A fourth took out the hydraulics, spraying fluid all over the cabin. A fifth exploded in one of the port side engines. A sixth entered the Plexiglas nose in front of me and went straight out the other side, failing to explode. All that freezing air rushed in. My space, the cocoon I'd been pretending protected me, was gone, vanished. But we made it to Regensburg, I smeared the Messerschmitt buildings with our bomb-load, and we limped back to England. I helped wind down the undercarriage by hand. My flak suit was torn to shreds, but I wasn't badly hurt—a bunch of nasty scratches, that's all. I just walked up and down, shaking and babbling and listening to the other guys babbling. We knew we were expendable, parts of a bigger plan. That's what we'd been trained for.

What is it the Bible says? Though I pass through the valley of the shadow of death I shall fear no evil. That didn't happen with me. I'd been in that valley and fear swamped me. I couldn't stand to fly anymore. I couldn't sleep, and when I did doze the station generators woke me and I imagined the sound was flak bursting through the hull and entering my throat. I choked and gagged. I sat alone and didn't say much and began to stare. Nobody blamed me. The other guys never said a word. I was shipped home, and so began my sojourn at the Menninger Clinic. Then one day I heard that the rest of my crew had bought it. The B-17 took a hit, a single hit, direct to the bomb bay in the sky over Berlin. They were dead, I was still here, and the medals began to arrive: a Purple Heart, a Distinguished Flying Cross, an oak leaf cluster to add to my Air Force Medal. I held these trinkets and couldn't understand why I was weeping like a baby. I kept seeing myself in the nose of the B-17, in control of my Plexiglas kingdom, serene in a domain of unblemished blue.

I don't want to make too much of this, or to excuse the way I felt and behaved more than twelve years later. I didn't think I was a coward, or maybe I was. I didn't care one way or the other. I suspected that Mantilini was responsible for Beth Dyer's death, but I didn't know for sure, and I didn't *want* to know. She was dead, and I was sorry, but I couldn't help her now. I'd taken all the chances I was going to take, and I had no wish to probe any deeper into the black tunnel I'd found. It was a space I couldn't control, beyond my design.

It had been a mistake, coming to Palm Springs.

Which left me with the problem of the real Mallory Walker. She was a volatile mixture of anger and tenderness. Maybe neurotic. Certainly used to having the world spin to her command. Inclined, therefore, to suspect that her lover had been snatched from her by murder, rather than reach the uncomfortable conclusion that she herself had been duped. I wasn't interested in making these judgments, only in getting her off my back, nixing the possibility that she might charge off to Las Vegas and stick her nose where it would certainly cause trouble. I figured that I needed to keep her busy only for another day or so, until her wedding, and then there'd be the month-long honeymoon in Hawaii, haven of pineapples and forgetfulness.

Returning the towel to its rack, I left the bathroom to face her.

26

Give me an hour of your time," she said from her perch on the mattress. Her eyes were bright, but no longer with tears. They looked sly. "Come on, Maurice. You're a full-grown man. A powerful architect, right? And I'm just a silly woman." She leaned forward, lowering her voice to a whisper. "A *dyke*. What possible harm could I do to you?"

Plenty, I thought, but I smiled. "Sure," I said, "whatever you want."

She was driving her father's old Bentley. It stood outside the main entrance to the Octotillo with its top down, gleaming like a gold bar. The attendant, impressed, hovered over the hood, dabbing at it lovingly with a wet chamois cloth, seeking to remove every last speck of dust. "Say hello to your father for me, Miss Walker," he said, slipping the five-dollar bill she gave him into his pocket. "And all the best for your wedding."

Mallory let out the clutch and the Bentley started to glide. As we turned out of the hotel lot a black Ford sedan pulled away from the curb behind us, and she braked to let it go by. The Ford sailed past, the guy at its wheel wearing sunglasses and a straw hat with a striped band. He didn't thank or signal or acknowledge us in any way. I thought nothing of it at the time.

Palm Springs had sprung up in the 1930s with the speed of a movie set. The wide main street was glittering and clean, with plenty of parking and branches of the ritziest New York and L.A. stores on either side. The doors of the Chi-Chi and the other nightclubs were shut, and people sat beneath umbrellas at sidewalk cafés in the heat of the early afternoon, or sped about on bicycles, lapping up that bogus charm and innocence, the sort of atmosphere that only money can buy. Passing along the main drag, we turned down a side street where brightly painted adobe bungalows lay behind white wooden fences and shrubberies of pink oleander and feathery green tamarisk trees. The neighborhood was too perfect, like a toy, and we pulled into the drive of a pretty house painted bright blue.

"I gave Beth the money to rent this place," Mallory said, pushing a key into the front door. "She lived here and I came whenever I could. Which turned out to be most of the time. I'm good at hiding myself." She added, with a shy, almost bruised pride. "Nobody ever knows where I am."

"What is it you want me to see?"

"A place where I was happy."

I wondered why she thought I gave a damn.

The air inside was stuffy, no window having been opened in a couple of weeks, but the space itself was simple, well-proportioned, lived-in, a cosy contrast to the neutered splendor of the Walker spread. I saw: a red tile floor, roughly plastered white walls, ancient leather armchairs, an oak desk to the side of a brick fireplace; no TV set but a radio and a record player; magazines, books, newspapers; an empty wine bottle with a pair of dead flies in it on the counter partitioning the kitchen from the living area. Dominating the room, however, was an enormous watercolor above the fireplace, simply framed, an abstract vision of horizon, sun, clouds, an immense and restful vision of light and space.

I was thinking of the afternoon, only eight days ago—so much had happened in so short a time—when Beth, in Mallory's Porsche, had driven me up to the Palisades, to show me the site where she said she wanted to build a house. She'd been scamming me then, of course, working me; but she'd said that she'd wanted nothing fancy, small rooms that she could feel at home in, and I wondered if she'd been thinking of this place.

Mallory unlocked a French window at the back and we went into a walled garden where red and green Japanse lanterns hung from the gnarled branches of an olive tree and a small fountain soothed with its play of water. In the shade of the tree were a table and chairs, blue paint cracked and blistered. The hot air was pungent with rosemary and lilac. A lizard ran up the wall, disappearing into a crack between two bricks with a whip of its tail. Mallory was slightly shortsighted, I noticed; she squinted at the dark space between the bricks where the lizard had gone.

"We sat out here a lot," she said. "Talked about everything. Compressed years into a night. She was married, did you know? That's what she was running from really. That's what I found out. She'd come to Palm Springs because her husband was smothering her."

"Who was the husband?" I asked.

"She wouldn't tell me. Just that she was sick of the guy."

I thought how carefully Beth had designed these different versions of herself, one for Mallory Walker, another for me. Elaborate and careful plans, fictions spun from wisps of appealing fact, cunning and convincing deceptions, all so that she could bring herself close enough to Paul Mantilini and try to kill him. If indeed that had been her plan. For me she'd played the rich bitch driven by ruthlessness and an ambition that mirrored my own; for Mallory Walker she'd been the alluring almost friend, a seductive figure from memory who unexpectedly reappeared, jaded yet unconquered, indomitable a reflection, in other words, of what Mallory herself hoped she saw when she looked in the glass. How could I not admire the art, the craft of these performances, their resilience, their singlemindedness?

"By the way, what did you study at USC?" I asked Mallory.

"Architecture," she said, and I had to stop myself smiling. It figured. "Why do you ask?" she said.

"No reason." I'd created a new identity for myself only once, and the effect had been like shedding an unwanted chrysalis, something I discarded in my slipstream as I rushed on. But with Beth, clearly, something different had been going on. Something trapped and burning.

"My father hated the idea of my working," Mallory said as we went back inside. "He wanted me to marry, have kids. His goal hasn't changed much, I guess. He's a tyrant."

"And your stepmother?"

"Oh, she's in love with plastic surgery."

I laughed.

"I know I have it lucky in lots of ways. But that doesn't mean I find my life easy," she said. "You think I'm a coward, don't you? Marrying for cover, for convenience?"

"No," I said, thinking of my own situation. "I don't."

She looked at me sadly. "She deserved better friends than us, didn't she?"

Sure, I thought; but, then, a part of Beth had been busy digging her own grave. I changed the subject. "What was your first husband like?"

"Rich. Not as smart as me but smarter than Freddie. Maybe that's why it didn't last. I need to know that I can keep a part of myself secret. Beyond eyes that are too prying or clever."

"He suspected?"

"I never let him get that close." Her reply was brisk. "I want to show you the bathroom," she said, and opened a door into the bathroom, a light room, the brightest in the house. Green and white tile marched across the floor in a parquet pattern. A large oval mirror hung above a sink that stood on spindly legs. An arch of green tile guarded the entrance to the bath and shower tub. The deco flourish of the room was unchanged since the house had been built in the 1930s.

"I need to tell you about something that happened a month ago," she said, sitting on the edge of the bath, facing me. She was tense and anxious. Her dark eyes seemed almost to swamp her face. "I had to go to San Francisco. I was supposed to be there for a couple of days, seeing some lawyer guy about my trust. I go into those meetings and a man in a suit opens his mouth and I fall asleep. Anyway—the point is this. I came back a day early. Beth wasn't expecting me. And when I came in through the front door the house was completely dark. For a minute I thought she wasn't in. But then I heard music. Coming from in here. Jazz."

Beth had dragged the record player into the bathroom and set it up on the floor, Mallory said. She found Beth naked in the tub, in the dark, with both taps running and saxophone music playing. The room was filled with steam.

"I asked her what the heck she was doing. She didn't say anything. She just stared at me like I wasn't supposed to be there. In her hand she had a block of wood. It was small, something she'd made so carefully."

Mallory held out her hand, as if to demonstrate. "Five razor blades were set into it, about a quarter-inch apart. So that when she slashed across her wrist there'd be five cuts, not one. She'd really figured it out, you see."

She shivered, staring down at the cool green tile. She pressed her hands against the sides of her black satin slacks. "It wasn't a trick or a game. She didn't think I'd be home that night. She was going to do it. Usually she was so restless—she looked at you with such intensity. But her eyes were dead. Just staring at this thing she'd made with the razors."

She described how at first she thought this was her fault. Beth must have been ashamed of what they were doing together, she thought. "That's what snapped her out of it, when I told her that," Mallory told me. "She said *she* was the one who was to blame, not me. 'I'm crazy, that's all,' she said. It was like Beth was being ripped in two. And I thought I'd found my mission in life. I'd do everything I could to protect and love her."

"What happened then?"

"We got drunk. Boy, did we get drunk!" She looked up at me with a smile. "We lugged the record player out of the bathroom and set it up in the garden and danced until dawn. To hell with the neighbors." Her voice fell away. "And two days later she was gone. I never saw or heard from her again. I failed her, didn't I?"

I wasn't a stone. I was moved by the story and I thought I understood Beth's despair. She'd devised a plan to kill Paul Mantilini by getting herself close to me. Maybe, until that moment, the plan hadn't been entirely real for her. It had been a drama she was creating in her mind, a play, another fiction. She was walking around it, contemplating its mechanism, polishing it, trying it on for size. Then the time came when she had to face leaving, and betraying, Mallory Walker, of whom she'd become fond—fonder, certainly, than she ever was of me. Had to face, too, the prospect of her own murder or death. For each time she pushed her plan a little further along, each time she moved a little closer to her goal, the tension and danger increased. Not that she'd shown any fear on the surface—but deep down, yes, I thought so. Uncertainty always exists. Only fools don't feel fear. Fear keeps you sharp and alert. It fulfills a survival function. But it can paralyze you, too, and suicide might look like a way out then, a light in the tunnel that seems to have no end. And suicide is, in its way, a great passion, like being in love. A course of action cleaner and more decisive than its alternatives. Inevitable, even, an exit from the strained necessities you've created for yourself. Beth had been troubled, and not merely driven, burdened, I was prepared to bet, by some guilt and shame I didn't know about. Hadn't I seen glimpses, hints?

I'd had my own flirtation with suicide, while at the Menninger Clinic. Over a period of weeks I kept the sleeping pills they gave me nightly. I only pretended to swallow them and took them out later, keeping them wrapped in tissue paper. I had a plan. I'd wait until I had twenty-five pills, then slip one of the orderlies a few bucks to bring me a bottle of whiskey. The booze and the pills would do the trick, I thought.

I didn't go through with it. I flushed away the pills and split the whiskey with my friend Alice, the nurse. But in some way I did die: Maurizio Viglioni found a different sort of exit—he became Maurice Valentine.

So I felt for Beth, in her moment of darkness. Though she hadn't killed herself, either. She'd become Mallory Walker and had continued on her perilous course.

I saw what Mallory Walker, the *real* Mallory Walker, was trying to do with this visit to the house and her sad story. She was inviting me to take a portion of her guilt. She was inviting me to care, to put my head on the block.

"I want to call the cops in Las Vegas," she said, and I regretted having mentioned Lake Mead, and the recovery of her Porsche. "They must have cops, even there."

"Yeah, they've got cops. Bad cops. Believe me, they won't be interested."

"It's got to be worth a shot."

"You've no idea what you're up against."

"It can't be worse than my father."

"Much worse."

"Look," she said. "A person I loved ripped me off and now she's dead. I'm owed an explanation."

"Get in line," I told her.

"You said she played you. How?"

My head throbbed and I was exhausted. "I'm not going to talk about it," I said.

She was looking at me with the expression she'd directed toward her stepmother, the look that said: To hell with you. Then her face changed subtly. "You'll do *something*, won't you?"

"I don't know what it is I *can* do."

Her eyes were bright, and that sly smile was on her lips. She had quick insight, especially for things that were going her way. "Yes, you do."

She was right. Unfortunately I'd thought of one more lead I could follow, another trace of herself that Beth had left behind. Nothing more than a hint. A wild-goose chase maybe, but still—I knew I had to give it a shot.

Mallory pulled me out of my thoughts. "You'll call me?" she said. "Tell me what you find?"

"Sure," I said.

"You know," she said with a wistful, faraway smile. She was a curious mixture of naïveté and sophistication, an awkward beauty who seemed determined not quite to outgrow her adolescence. Which might be another way of saying she was sick of the world as she found it. "I think Beth would have come back to me."

I let her live with that idea. An hour later I'd checked out of the Ocatillo and was back on the road, heading out of Palm Springs. For a minute or two, looking in the rearview mirror, I saw a black Ford following, and, at the wheel, a man in a straw hat; then the car was gone.

PART 4

The Desert

27

MARCH 6–13, 1951 / LOS ANGELES AND LAS VEGAS

$\mathcal{T}$he church basement on Hilgard Avenue smells pleasantly of wax, broken concrete, and dusty hymnals. The space is cramped, cold, ill-lit, not suited to the purposes of a drama group, but it is here that the Cocteau Modern Players, an extracurricular offshoot of the Theater Arts Department, performs *An Inspector Calls* by the British writer J. B. Priestley, one of a famous series of plays in which the author distorts and juggles time. In this production the action has been adapted, transplanted from its original setting in the north of England to a mansion in Pasadena in the 1910s. The shift works well, for the story, of a rich family whose complacency is about to be destroyed by a doom of their own creation, is tight and self-contained, and of powerful simplicity. Beth plays Sheila, the daughter of the family, a young woman who has never held down a job, never known what it's like to be desperate. Sheila discovers that she is cruelly responsible for the death of a salesgirl. For Beth, whose life has been all uncertainty, the stretch here is to get inside the security of wealth. To do this she studies the portraits of Sargent, for costume and bearing, and the stories of Henry James, to learn how such a girl might think. In the UCLA props room she discovers a long scarf of delicate pink chiffon, and from this extrapolates the careless flick with which Sheila would toss such a garment over her shoulders. She begins to catch Sheila's walk, straight-backed and confident, the product of a lifetime of riding and ballet. She imagines the daring scorn with which such a girl might view the values of her railroad baron father, and the awe she would nonetheless feel when he walks into the room. A character takes shape.

This is only the third night of the run. Despite fine reviews (the *Los Angeles Times*, indeed, singling out Beth for particular praise: "this striking and sensitive young actress gives hope of a promising career at its outset"), the audience is thin, perhaps because of the storm lashing the walls outside. Five minutes into act 1, Beth, having made her entrance and her first speech, glances out beyond the footlights and sees, sitting on the end of the third row, poised, if needs be, for a swift exit, his slick mane of gray hair almost aglow in the dark, his broad shoulders suave in the cashmere suit that she sold him, Paul Mantilini. His eyes follow her as she crosses the stage; flustered, she almost misses her next cue.

"Who *is* he?" says Margo Bosworth during intermission. "He looks like he should be president."

Margo, who shares with Beth a small four-room apartment in Westwood, has designed the costumes for the show, written the program, and sold the tickets. As friends, she and Beth present a bold attitude of experience. The tenor of the time expects young women like them to want to sleep with a man like Cary Grant, but only after they've bagged him for marriage. They just want to sleep with Cary Grant. They smoke and wear lots of black. In a few years young people like them will be called "beatniks." In 1951 nobody quite knows what to call them. They seem restless without reason in prospering America. Beth and Margo tote their copies of Camus and Sartre, and, earlier in the year, put on a revue with jazz and poems by Dylan Thomas. In the record store they head for the bin labeled "Bebop Spoken Here," disdaining the one called "Moldy Figs." With their freewheeling independence they intimidate the frat boys. To the world they present a united front, although the friendship is in many ways one of opposites. Margo has a wild streak, a garish spirit that she makes no effort to stifle. Beth's pose is already more self-conscious. She knows she's playing a role, for she is consumed by acting, thinking about it day and night, plotting how to learn, how to get better. Beth doesn't want to be a movie star. That's her mother's grand plan. She wants to win the response she's seen once before, on a blazing hot afternoon in the San Fernando Valley, in the eyes of an old man wearing a white suit. She still remembers that corny poem by Poe.

"He looks a little like Cary Grant, don't you think?" Margo goes on, leaning over Beth's shoulder in the chaos of the dressing room, dabbing at Beth's cheek with cotton wool, restoring her makeup. "He can't keep his eyes off you."

Beth rolls her eyes and Margo responds with a wag of the finger. "Naughty, naughty!" she says. "Get out there and knock him dead, kiddo."

After the show Beth strips off her costume and throws on a robe, a cigarette in her mouth while she shivers in front of the dressing room mirror, taking off the greasepaint. At the door—a rap of knuckles, and before Beth can answer, Margo pops her hand around, giggling with unrepressed excitement.

Beth, glancing in the mirror, sees the suave and smiling figure of Paul Mantilini. Her heart beats quicker, louder within the narrow walls of her chest; she knows something's about to begin. Perhaps this is it, she thinks, the adventure that will turn her into a woman, an artist. Feigning nonchalance, she returns to the job at hand, watching herself in the mirror, lobbing soiled balls of cotton wool trashwards with the poise of an expert.

"I love dressing rooms. The smell of them, the taste of them," Mantilini says, his eye searching the corners of the narrow room, seeing the hymnbooks stacked there. "I wanted to marry a singer once." Perhaps he feels the need to explain. "She was a good singer."

"What happened?" says Beth, glancing toward where her street clothes are piled on a fold-up chair.

"I was married. Still am. And the singer died," Mantilini says, his shrug neither sad nor dismissive, merely: *so it goes.*

"That's sad," says Beth, still wondering how she's going to get out of the robe and into her jeans.

Mantilini smiles, having observed her problem, but doesn't leave the room; instead he tactfully turns to face the wall. "The rain's coming down hard. It's murder outside," he says, and adds, almost like a challenge: "I have a car."

Beth sees no option but to pick up the gauntlet. "That's great," she says, changed now into Levis and a T-shirt, throwing a thrift-store peacoat over her shoulders. "You can drive me home."

He cocks an eyebrow. But his courtesy is flawless. "Where else would I take you?" he says.

Beth looks at him, again noticing his mismatched and strangely uneven eyes. Yet she feels safe with him, secure, welcomed, and his car is as she imagines, a dark cocoon smelling of wood and leather warmed by the heater. A broad-shouldered driver sits in the front, silent and anonymous. Rain hammers on the roof like shot. The windshield wipers swish aside the downpour, methodically carving clear crescents that are at once replaced by the storm's angry faces. Mantilini lodges himself in a corner, far away from her, posing no threat, legs crossed, one handmade shoe dangling at the end of an exquisite silk sock. He has oddly small and graceful feet. This man has balance, she thinks.

"I enjoyed the play," he says, and his smile carries the merest hint of mockery. "Maybe not as much as your performance the other day."

Beth is bold, self-assured, confident of her ability to handle any situation, so she takes this unmasking in stride. Her stepfather, Bill Cotterez, must have ratted her out, she thinks—the slime. "They'll let you take the stuff back if you want," she says.

"I don't want," he says, protesting. "You should definitely keep acting. You're talented. But if that doesn't work out you have a brilliant future in menswear."

She laughs, accepting the tease.

"But the acting will work out. You'll make it," he says.

"You think so?"

"I know so," he says simply, not with emphasis, not like flattery, but like giving her money to put in the bank, treasure to be socked away. "Have you ever been in love?"

Beth, watchful, wonders if this will cue a slide across the seat leather. But he makes no move.

"I've slept with boys," she says boldly, remembering the three occasions when she's let eager masculine pride go all the way. One of these times was with Margo's brother, visiting from Stanford, and Beth tried to persuade herself that something had really happened, but the minute it was over she knew it hadn't.

"That's not what I asked," he says.

"How would I know?" she says, making light, but wondering if he's seen something in her, an evasive quality. Acting isn't just a passion with her; it's an escape from pain and other involvements, a wall she puts up, a fortress.

"It's like a bomb going off in your heart," Mantilini says. "Your entire personality disintegrates. You go insane. You notice it, generally."

His tone is light, and now it's her turn to study him. She remembers how, in the store, while massing up those heaps of shirts and gloves and ties, while playing (she realizes) his own game, he had been so perfectly measured and self-contained. She doesn't see how reckless love, *amour fou*, can be a part of his wardrobe. Maybe he wishes it was, she thinks. "Tell me about the singer."

"It was a long time ago," he says, then adds, almost with longing: "In New York."

"What was she like?"

"I could never control her. She was beautiful, no doubt about that. She had skin like caramel, hair like rope. But what was inside her—that was amazing. She was a giving soul. I've not met many. She left me a son, but not her voice. Nick has *my* voice."

"Your voice isn't so bad," she says, feeling—she doesn't know why—that she must lighten his mood. "A bit growly. A bit *croaky*."

He slaps his knee and laughs. "Let me tell you, Beth," he says, the first time he's used her name. "She had sadness and swing and something else—like her voice could bring you back from the dead. But it couldn't. It was a false promise." He shakes his head, impatient with the memory: *no time for the past*. "Nick's just a couple of years older than you. He's headstrong, a little wild sometimes. But a good kid," he says, paternal pride in his voice.

Rain beats against the taut fabric of the umbrella he holds over both their heads as he walks her to the door of her apartment. Bidding her goodnight, he neither kisses her nor tries to touch her. Not then, nor when they eat dinner at the Brown Derby three nights later, nor when he sends her an airplane ticket and she arrives in Las Vegas. He meets her at the airport, takes the bag from her hand, and leads her to his car, a Cadillac convertible, all rolling curves around a nest of soft white leather. This time there's no driver. Mantilini takes the wheel himself, driving casually, with only one hand, holding the other outside to feel the wind. He wears a houndstooth sports coat and no sunglasses, even his good eye undaunted by the sparkle of the desert. The *Las Vegas Sun*, lying between them on the front seat, notes that General MacArthur has been relieved of command in the Korean War, that Senator Estes Kefauver, whose televized crime committee has been jolting a thrilled public with its hearings in various parts of the country, has announced that legalized gambling, rather than providing a solution to the problem of organized crime, has made things worse, and that an enterprising salesman has been standing outside the Desert Inn and—"for $50, just because I'm broke and need the money"—selling expensive-looking watches that are in fact seven-dollar knockoffs. Beth feels tense during this short drive from the airport, replying absentmindedly to questions, shooting sidelong glances at the older man behind the wheel, aware of the step she's taking.

In 1951, Las Vegas is a shrill and restless resort town. Cowboy clothes and old jalopies are still seen alongside the Cadillacs, and some people still ride horseback from casino to casino. But the city is changing, growing fast. The downtown Glitter Gulch is in place, and the bigger, fancier hotels are starting to spring up along the section of Highway 91 known as the Strip. Sandstorms swirl and knock out an electricity supply overtaxed by the hectic growth of this small place. Only an embryo of what it will later become, Las Vegas is nonetheless in the throes of acute prosperity, less a city than a moneymaking machine, a mecca for gamblers, divorcees, elopers, dreamers, and lamsters of all kinds.

Mantilini takes Beth to a suite at the top of the Desert Inn, the newest and grandest of the hotels. He hands her the keys and a card with his phone number, and, with an enigmatic smile, leaves, saying he'll see her later—if she likes. Beth shuts the door when he's gone, leaning against it with her back, and then bounds forward to explore the suite. Through the windows she sees distant mountains, sharply etched in the clear air; she watches the cars that move along the Strip, arriving from L.A. in seemingly endless procession; she observes the trucks, moving like giant scarabs, in and out of construction sites. She has already gathered that Mantilini is a big wheel in the town and has a hand in, indeed might be the driving force behind, these new structures. "Be careful," her stepfather Bill Cotterez advised, on hearing that she'd been invited to Las Vegas. But Beth doesn't believe Mantilini has brought her here to seduce her. Or not in the way that Cotterez supposes. For some reason that she can't discern she knows he's decided to teach her. He's hinted that her ambition outstrips her experience, and she guesses this to be true. She remembers her father's puzzlement at the succession of failures that overwhelmed him. For him the world was a labyrinth that he felt doomed never even to enter. Beth is determined that his fate won't be hers. She will make things happen. She believes that she can. She knows it. At the same time she's unclear how best to secure this golden future she's announced for herself. She needs a guide, a mentor.

Red silk adorns the walls of the suite, red is the color of the thick, heavy drapes, and dozens of red roses, odorless due to the air conditioning, stand in vases. Beth bounces on the edge of the bed. She opens her suitcase, unpacks her clothes, and sits down with her copy of *An Actor Prepares*. But her mind is restless and she can't read. She locks the room behind her, descends in the elevator, and walks through the gaming rooms, listening to the shuffle of cards, the click of the roulette wheels, the chatter of the gamblers. Eager for her education to begin.

Later, Mantilini takes her in the Cadillac and they drive along the Strip to the Flamingo, where an RKO movie, *The Las Vegas Story*, is being shot. Jane Russell plays a onetime showgirl who comes back to town and finds herself in trouble. In quick succession Mantilini introduces Beth to the amiable and amused and buxom Russell, to the male lead, the yet more buxom Victor Mature, and to the movie's producer, a gaunt, doleful man with scuffed sneakers sticking out from under his suit: Howard Hughes. Hughes mumbles a swift aside to Mantilini, and it is arranged that Beth will return to the set the next day for a walk-on; Mantilini negotiates further, and Hughes agrees to give her a line or two. Thus things work between princes, Beth observes; she retires to bed early, rising at dawn to shoot what will be her first, and only, appearance in a Hollywood film.

After a late dinner, followed by the best table at a show (the Lionel Hampton Orchestra, his pick), Beth more or less insists that she and Mantilini sleep together. The experience is businesslike and pleasurable, but Beth already realizes that although she likes this man, she will never love him. Mantilini is too shrewd and careful to give away his own feelings, and during the next two days she sees little of him, his time being occupied with two grim men in suits whom he shepherds around town and to whom he gives buckets filled with chips so they can gamble. Big-time money stuff, Beth begins to gather. Drifting among the green-baize tables, wearing the clear-glassed, heavy-framed spectacles that are part of the persona she's adopted for Mantilini, she finds herself treated with the utmost respect, even deference, by the dealers and cocktail waitresses. Almost absentmindedly, Mantilini takes time off from his negotiations to teach her backgammon and once or twice they sit at the bar in the Desert Inn, playing for nickels, while he asks her to look at what she sees and think about it, inviting her to describe the tourists, the exhausted gamblers scratching their sweat-stained shirts after twenty-four hours at the table, the fancy dressers, the fast talkers, the tough guys who wear more jewelery than a tray in Tiffany's window, the hookers, the pit-girls, the divorcees in their fabulous gowns hoping for better luck next time, the exotic showgirls from the China Dolls Revue. "Like birds of paradise!" Beth exclaims. "But they shouldn't be in cages."

"That's their role in life, sugar," says Mantilini.

"It's wrong," says Beth, and he smiles at her tolerantly, blowing on her dice before she shakes them in the leather cup.

Margo Bosworth, drunk on almost half a bottle of gin, quizzes Beth about her affair with the older man when she returns to L.A. It's the middle of the night, and the two friends have broken into the building that houses the carousel on Santa Monica Pier. They kneel on wooden boards while brightly painted horses rear above them in the darkness. In front of the two of them lies a handkerchief, spread out flat, and on the handkerchief Margo places cigarette papers and her latest contraband: marijuana. "You met Howard Hughes?" Margo says, greeting Beth's news with excitement. Having grown up in Santa Monica, being familiar with the business and machinery of Hollywood (her father is a director), Margo understands the value of such encounters: they might be the nudge that sets an entire train in motion. "Did he sign you to a contract? Did he *kidnap* you?"

"He asked if he could touch my tits," says Beth.

"No!" screeches Margo. "Did you let him?"

"I said it would be okay if he went and got Paul's permission first," says Beth, suppressing a giggle, watching while Margo sprinkles a mixture of tobacco and marijuana on the papers before proceeding to roll the joint. "Hughes looked at me like a baby, like he was about to burst into tears."

Is there something ambitious, too, in Beth's dealings with Margo? Perhaps, but then all friendships are bargains in one way or another, and, in any event, if Beth has vaguely thought that Margo's father might one day assist her career, that hope will soon vanish. Her life is about to take another turn, and his career will be destroyed by HUAC.

A match flares and the rolled cigarette papers ignite with a sizzle. The two young women lean against each other, passing the joint to and fro. Sucking the smoke down deep, Beth feels a relaxed happiness open inside her like a crocus. For some reason a story Margo tells about going with a boy to a Sophia Loren movie at the Nuart strikes Beth as hilarious. Starting to laugh, giggling, then guffawing, she realizes she can't stop. "I need air," she says, hauling herself to her feet, dizzy and swaying.

"Be my guest," Margo says. "Freeze your butt. See if I care."

Beth, staggering to the door, stops and finds herself staring at her moccasin. Hey, what's that down there? she thinks. Whoa, it's my foot! She realizes that she's stoned.

A rolling fog obscures the moon. Nor is the ocean visible, though it thunders beneath her, booming against the concrete pillars, drowning out her footsteps. Then she makes out another sound, faint at first, but growing stronger as she walks further down the pier. At first she thinks it's the deep-throated bumbling of a foghorn, distorted in her mind by the marijuana. It isn't; it's a saxophone. Someone is on the pier, in the middle of the night, playing a saxophone. In the slow progression of the notes she recognizes a song, wistful and sad, "Come Rain or Come Shine." She draws her peacoat tight around her, herself drawn ever closer to the melody, until, through the fog, a figure materializes.

A tall black man stands alone, coat hanging loose, wool cap yanked down over his ears, stooping protectively over his horn, almost seeming to sip from it as he blows the notes that float away in gorgeous clusters. His hands are strong and graceful, Beth observes, and his face is lean, with high cheekbones and vibrant eyes. His tie is knotted untidily, yet his bearing is lithe, assured, self-confident, self-contained, almost regal. His goatee is neatly trimmed. His skin gleams, slick with sweat, or maybe it's moisture from the fog. The music reaches into her, travels and explores her body, twisting around sinews, entering veins like a drug, like a caress, and she gasps. At that very moment the tempo of the melody picks up, as if it's his sax that has stolen her breath. The man turns, eyes aglow, and aims the bell of the horn straight at her, romancing a woman now, and not the sea; or so Beth imagines, in those first moments. It strikes her that he really wants an audience, needs to be told how beautiful he is.

Then it occurs to her that he really *is* beautiful, like nothing she's ever seen before, and she seems to hear something else now, rising above the saxophone and the crash of the ocean, a sound that has a kind of relentless inevitability to it, a ticking that drives the blood from her head and turns it into a fizzing fuse. Suddenly she thinks she understands what's happening. Eager, breathless, deliciously afraid, she watches. Sees his strong fingers move up and down the keys. Hears the saxophone's softness purring through the fog. Waits for the bomb that she knows is about to go off in her heart.

28

SEPTEMBER 11, 1956 / JOSHUA TREE

The Slominsky house was in the high desert, less than an hour's drive from Palm Springs. The house lay at the top of a slope in the shelter of reddish sandstone rocks. It sat on stout concrete legs, elevated, so that scorpions and snakes might find no way in, unless they were of the human variety. It was a semicircular structure, its arms hugging the swimming pool and courtyard, fashioned in concrete poured around chunks of stone that we'd hauled out of the desert. The stones were in many different shades and colors—beige, black, orange, red—giving the house a dappled effect, and the sloping roof was made from redwood. The house was a hodgepodge, but the quickest and most striking thing I'd done. The design flowed out, was down on paper in less than an hour. Yet I'd made no photographs of the structure; I'd failed to bombard the magazines with this latest evidence of Maurice Valentine's supposed genius. Because, I guess, I was ashamed of the house. As a part of the deal Joe Nelson made for me with HUAC, I'd named the Slominskys. With Konstantin Slominsky's permission, incidentally: others had already denounced him as a former Communist, so the addition of my name to the list did him no further harm, while letting me off the hook. I'd been careful, though, not to involve his wife, Vera, in the discussion. She was tough and would never have gone along with my shenanigans.

Originally the house in the desert was intended as their winter place, their winter *palace*, as I'd joked with Konstantin. But Konstantin

Slominsky's bread-and-butter work, penning scores for studio melodramas and thrillers, dried up when it became known that he'd once stood in the same room as Stalin. It made no difference that Stalin had later booted him out of the U.S.S.R. He had history, and his name was tainted. Onto the blacklist he went, and out into the desert he came, quitting the Pacific Palisades home he could no longer afford. All this I'd heard in passing, years having gone by since I'd seen the Slominskys or spoken with them. A composer with origins in the salons of St. Petersburg was perched above a primeval American wilderness, a place the Indians called "the land afire." And although I'd always been aware of my role in Konstantin's strange twentieth-century journey, only now, as I climbed out of the Studebaker, remembering how Beth Dyer had kept referring to this place, "the Slominsky house," did I realize I'd never been able to quite convince myself that I felt fine about what had happened.

I felt nervous, on the trail of something I didn't want to find; yet somehow I couldn't stop myself from looking.

It was late afternoon by then, with the sun starting to sink below the distant mountains, but a hot, dry wind still gusted through my hair, making my skin scratch and tingle. I saw a guy tending a part of the garden that had been nurtured in the shady ground beneath the house. "Hey!" I shouted, and he stopped digging and leaned against the broad handle of his hoe. He was an Indian, tall, old, wearing a cowboy hat he pushed back on his forehead. His face was tanned and gnarled like bark. He looked at me long and hard, and, unimpressed by what he saw, yanked the brim of the hat over his eyes and eased the hoe back into the dirt with a harsh scraping sound. So much for any hope of a warm greeting.

I walked up the steps to the front door, knocked, got no answer. I pushed the door to see if it was open. It was—so, knowing the house, I went in, stepping into the cool, white-painted vault of the hallway. Off to one side was Konstantin Slominsky's soundproofed workroom. If he was working, and I knew he would be, then that room would be locked. I went, therefore, in the other direction, taking three steps down into the sunken living area, a lofty space with a beamed redwood ceiling, white walls, a square white fireplace, and windows running the entire length of one side, giving a spectacular view across the flatness of the desert to the mountains beyond. The overhang of the roof protected the windows from too much glare. A shaggy white wool rug covered two-thirds of the stone floor.

Finding nobody, I went into the dining area, then toward the kitchen at the back of the house. Through the window I saw the garden, stepping down through three brick terraces before meeting a low stone wall. On the other side of the wall, in the desert proper, I saw the silver-haired head of Vera Slominsky. She had a pistol in her hand and was plunking away at a target that twitched on the fat arm of a cactus. I remembered that while Konstantin liked reading about guns in detective stories, Vera preferred the real thing. Usually she hit bull's-eyes. Opening the kitchen door, I heard the crack of another shot.

"Vera!" I shouted, and caught her attention. She looked my way, surprised, shielding her eyes with the hand that wasn't holding the gun. "I want to talk to you," I said and retreated back to the serene living room to wait.

The walls were hung with pictures, good ones, for the Slominskys had known many artists and had a fine collection. I was admiring one of them, a portrait of Vera that must have been done in the 1930s, when the subject herself hurried into the room, flushed and breathing hard from the hot climb through the gardens. The pistol was still in her hand.

"This is new," I said, nodding to the picture. "At least I've never seen it before. Maybe you had it hidden someplace."

Vera fixed me with a frosty glare. Swiftly she placed the pistol on the ledge atop the fireplace and grasped instead a pair of cruel-looking pruning shears.

"It's been a long time," I said.

"Not . . . long . . . enough," she said, aiming her words carefully, like well-placed shots, in her heavily accented English.

"I was in the neighborhood. I figured I'd drop by."

Vera didn't bother to respond to this blatant falsehood. Instead she unclipped the pruning shears and attacked the roses in a vase by the

window. Vera was in her sixties then, tall and thin and fine-boned, with
a short shock of silver hair and eyes that glittered like a frozen swimming pool. She wore blue jeans and a shirt of thin white cotton, yet the
casual attire failed to disguise her regal air. Vera had style and a poise
that she'd been spoon-fed in the cradle. She always gave the impression
that she'd been pursued by princes, and I think she probably had. In the
past I'd asked her a few times about her family history in Russia, but the
shutters had always come clattering down. Another time I asked how
she met her husband but she turned the moment into another of those
conversational duels, shooting back: "Who are you, Maurice—FBI or
KGB?" Perhaps she'd already grasped my capacity for the expedient be-
trayal. I couldn't help but admire Vera, though she'd never liked me
much, always regarding me with haughty patronage, as if to say she'd
got my number. Well: that beat the way she was looking at me now, with
a hate she didn't bother to disguise. Konstantin had told her about
HUAC, obviously.

"I was hoping to see Konstantin," I said.

Something almost resembling a smile played about her lips. *Fat
chance*, was the message. Her aristocratic fingers closed around the pruning shears. Snip!

"Only for a minute or two."

Snip! Snip!

I remembered that Vera was the gatekeeper. She, not her husband,
handled the lawyers and the movie and record companies; it was Vera
who wrote the checks, negotiated the contracts, called the plumbers and
stood over them while they fixed the john. I'd seen enough of that while
the house was under construction. She tried to shape the world, or at
least to keep it at bay. Dismissing an unwelcome visitor, unwanted history, was small beer for Vera.

"Maybe you can help me," I said.

Snip!

From my pocket I took a photograph that Mallory Walker had
handed me before I left Palm Springs. It showed Beth Dyer, but a very
different Beth Dyer from the woman I'd known. In the picture, taken in

the garden of the adobe bungalow, in the shade of the olive tree, her face was fuller, rounder somehow, and her hair was longer and much darker, chestnut in color, almost reddish, falling to her shoulders. She gazed straight into the lens, fearless, her eyes signaling both humor and haunted purpose. Or maybe that was just how I read it.

"Do you recognize her?"

Snip!

I tried to be patient. "Look, Vera. I've driven a long way. I'm hot and I'm tired and my head is hurting. Maybe you can help me and then I'll be gone. How about it?"

She gave the photograph a swift and dismissive glance. "Never . . . seen . . . her . . . before."

"Are you sure?"

With glacial hauteur she slapped down the pruning shears and gave vent to her rage. "Are you accusing me of lying, Maurice? I thought that was your department."

"I never lied to you."

"No. Perhaps not. You merely made us spend all our money on this white elephant of a house. You've made us *prisoners* out here in the desert."

"That's not fair."

"I *hate* this place," she said, with sudden, shocking passion. She banged her foot on the floor and scowled out of the window. "You see, Maurice. You've succeeded. You've made me lose my temper. You've made me *unreasonable*." A high color had risen in her cheeks and she confessed, reluctantly: "Of course, Kostya loves the house."

"I'm glad," I said.

This roused her again. "Do you think I give a damn about your feelings? After what you did? How *could* you? I want you to leave. Immediately. How dare you come here?"

We faced each other in front of the window, Vera with the pruning shears in her hand, glaring at me, neither of us prepared to budge. Maybe we'd have stood there all night, if her husband hadn't come in. I didn't hear him at all, because he was wearing slippers and his feet moved silently down the steps and into the room. I looked across and there he was, small and wiry, like a jockey, with a jockey's nimbleness and bandy legs and bony shoulders that showed through his thick blue work shirt. His mustache was so white and wispy that I only noticed it when he came closer. His eyes were pale, protuberant, milky. He had a narrow brow and a nose like an eagle's, which he thrust toward me, stretching out his wide-knuckled hand.

"Maurice," Konstantin Slominsky said, his smile revealing fine false teeth. His ears were enormous, looming out of either side of his monkeyish head almost like sculptures. "I'm very happy to see you. What brings you here?"

"Maurice was just leaving," Vera said.

"Nonsense," said Konstantin, waving his big hand. He spotted the photograph that I was still holding. "What's this?"

"It's nothing," said Vera, with a hint of carefully controlled alarm. "It's really nothing, my dear. You don't want to see it."

But Konstantin had already taken the photograph from my fingers and was busying himself with his reading glasses. Once these were set on his nose he held the picture at arm's length, and I watched him while he studied it. Recognition sparked instantly in his eyes, and something else. Pain, I thought, a hurt, and I wondered, my God, is it possible, did Beth seduce Konstantin, too? What was her relationship to these people? All this was over in an instant, then the glasses were restored to his shirt's top pocket and his bonhomie was back in place. Smiling at Vera, he handed her the photograph, the right side of his head angled toward her, as if the white hairs pouring from his ear could by some system of radar discern what she wanted him to do.

Vera was smooth, I had to give her that. She did her best. "Maurice was asking if we'd ever seen the girl in the picture and I told him that, of course, we *hadn't*," she said.

She was lying, and Konstantin, clearly, was asking himself why. He stroked the bald dome of his head, his eyebrow quizzically, almost comically, raised. The two of them, together for so long, survivors of so much, did indeed have these intuitive, nonverbal ways of communicating. They were like two animals who'd burrowed together for a lifetime.

They spoke to each other effortlessly, without words, and if Vera willed silence, and she *was* willing it, with her glance, with the nervous flutter of her hand, then Konstantin's customarily wide and eager mouth would stay shut. Especially if this were a reminder of a love affair or some other indiscretion that Maurice Valentine, the HUAC traitor, had hauled before their eyes after barging in unannounced.

"Here. Take your property," Vera said, but as she was handing me the photograph it slipped between our fingers. Now Beth Dyer was staring at me from the floor of the Slominsky's living room.

"Clumsy," said Vera, sighting me with a withering look.

"Not to worry," said Konstantin, reaching down.

"No, darling, I'll do it. Think of your back," Vera said, and the tension of the previous moments dissolved suddenly into opera buffa, for Vera's slim body darted into movement and two elderly heads collided with a mighty crack.

"I feel like I've been hit by an ax," Konstantin said with deadpan shock, and the two of them held each other, sitting on their asses on the rug. They started to giggle.

"Oh, fruitcakes!" Vera said, planting an affectionate kiss on her husband's cheek. "That was fun, wasn't it?" She sounded like a kid, girlish, filled with goofy enthusiasm, and then she remembered that I was watching. She ran her fingers through her hair. The look of tenderness that had been in her eyes, and was reserved only for her husband, became something else. Not dismissive: she couldn't quite go back to that mood, not immediately after I'd witnessed such a silly and fond moment of their marital togetherness. Another minute or so and she'd probably have gathered herself and shown me the door. But she didn't have a minute or so, she had a moment, and that moment became a hinge. She smiled. That was all. It was the smile I'd seen when she worked the room at a cocktail party, a dazzling, protective smile, a smile that meant not the opposite of what a smile usually meant, but a smile that was like a period, a smile that said: "I'm moving on now."

And I realized where I'd seen that very same smile, much more recently than any cocktail party I'd been at with Vera. Again, I was reminded, surprised, by how much had happened in just a few days. It was the second time I'd met Beth Dyer, when she came to my office. She'd been studying the photograph of Mantilini and me in front of the El Sheik and when she turned away from it, her face was wearing just that brittle brilliance, that very same guarded mask of a smile: *I'm moving on now*.

"I'll be damned," I said, because I'd realized something else.

"No doubt," said Vera, the words a wintry chime, the ice back in her voice now. But too late. Because I knew.

"She got it from you, Vera. That smile, the way she dyed her hair silver and cut it."

"What on earth are you talking about?"

I retrieved the photograph from the floor and brandished it in front of her eyes. "Her name is Beth Dyer. But she introduced herself to me as Mallory Walker. She created a character so she could get close to me. She took a part of you, Vera. And then she shot me."

I pulled back my hair, showing them the wound at the side of my forehead.

Vera studied me, and then her eyes flicked toward the fireplace. She was looking at the brick-painted mantel, at her pistol, I realized. "Maybe you deserved it," she said. "Why don't you ask her?"

"I wish I could. She's dead."

29

We sat at a long table in the kitchen. Konstantin uncorked a bottle of red wine that he positioned between himself and his wife so he could keep her glass filled. Needing to concentrate, and to stay awake, I drank tea, while outside it grew dark and the lamp above the table threw our shadows across the stone floor and into the room's dim corners.

"I taught her to shoot," said Vera, shrugging her shoulders with an air of stubborn defiance. "What else could I do? I didn't want to talk to the girl, not at first."

"When was this?"

"March 29, 1951," Vera said, and I wondered at the precision of her memory. I wanted to ask her about it, but decided to shelve the question for later. "She came here with two jazz musicians. One of them was famous. So Konstantin said. Isn't that so, *mon amour*?"

"His name was Freddy Greene," Slominsky said, nodding his monkeyish head in concurrence.

"The trumpet player?" I said. Even I, despite my limited knowledge of jazz, knew that Freddy Greene was a legend. I pictured an older man with a sweating face characteristically cut in two by a toothy grin; he'd played with Bix Beiderbecke and Louis Armstrong in Chicago, with Benny Goodman later on. He'd made hit records, and had appeared in a movie or two.

"I didn't know either of them from Adam. I've never cared for that ragamuffin music," Vera said in her haughty way. Indulgently, she squeezed her husband's hand. "With Konstantin, it's a different matter. He listens to *everything.*"

"What was she doing with these guys?" I said, trying to nudge her back toward the matter at hand. Vera on the subject of her husband and his musical mastery would turn into a lecture very fast, I knew.

"She was very much in love with the other musician," Vera said. "She'd brought them out here to meet Konstantin. She'd told them that she knew us. That was rubbish, of course. A complete and utter fabrication. But the trip was made. They arrived. They knocked at the door. Such nerve! So *die Schwarze* went with Konstantin into the music room to play. And I had to entertain the girl."

For March it had been a baking-hot day, Vera said. She had to find a straw hat for the pale-skinned Beth, and the bullets were slippery with moisture from her fingers as she slotted them into the chambers of the pistols. "I didn't want to talk to her. But she wanted to talk to *me*. She unpacked her young heart like a suitcase. She was relieved, I think. She'd more or less dragged the two men out here."

"How did that happen?"

Vera picked up her glass. She didn't sip, or gulp, but drank in a steady, determined, very Vera-like way, holding the glass to her lips until it was half-empty. "She had a romantic story. She'd fallen in love with this fellow at first sight. But he wouldn't speak to her. She followed him here and there, more or less throwing herself at him. But it was no good. Then she found out somehow that he loved Konstantin's music. It was at a birthday party, I think she said. A party for the other man, the Freddy Greene person. Someone gave him one of Konstantin's records. So she came up with the lie about knowing us."

Something troubled me. "But she knew where to come—she knew about the house?"

Vera slapped the table. "She did. And I've no idea how. Maybe you can tell me?"

I shook my head.

She threw up her hands. "Yet there they were. This slip of a young thing. And two black men, rather shy and very polite, with big grins on their faces, holding Konstantin's records like trophies, like prizes they'd won at school."

Konstantin himself had a faraway look, turning the base of his wineglass on the table, and I imagined Beth at the front door, hopefully introducing her black friends to a bemused Konstantin and a pissed-off Vera. A reckless adventure indeed.

"I started to like her, I suppose," Vera said. "I asked where she was from. She said she'd grown up in the San Fernando Valley. They'd been poor and her father had killed himself. Her mother had married again, to an oily little man. Some rough things had happened to this girl but she didn't seem to care. She had so much hope and enthusiasm. She thought nothing would harm her. She thought she was invulnerable. She was going to conquer the world. She was going to be a great actress. What else can I tell you, Maurice? Except that she was young. She had guts."

"How was her shooting?"

"Not bad," Vera said, lifting her glass to her lips. As soon as she put the glass down again, Konstantin refilled it. "Not bad at all. She was fearless. She just blazed away."

Vera herself had learned to shoot after leaving Russia in the early 1930s. Konstantin had been allowed out of the country to conduct a series of concerts of his music. In Paris the two of them slipped away. For years Vera thought Stalin would send an assassin in pursuit; so she took out a license, joined a gun club, and, wherever she went in Los Angeles, carried a pistol in her purse.

"She was a creature of instinct, then?" I said, trying to match the picture that Vera was drawing, of a devil-may-care Beth, an impulsive Beth, a lovelorn Beth, with the cool and calculating character, the actor, the manipulative performer that both Mallory Walker and I had encountered.

"Yes, indeed she *was*," said Vera, and something in the way she emphasized the word bothered me. But I was too tired to place the source of my momentary concern. "She was innocent," Vera went on sadly, suggesting that this quality could be dangerous, not only wonderful. For innocence almost begged the world to smash it, otherwise the world wasn't doing its job properly. And the world usually obliged. One of the marvelous, and extraordinary, things about Konstantin, for instance, was that his innocence had been maintained. I guess Vera knew at what price.

It was agreed that I should stay the night. Before supper Konstantin handed me a tumbler half-filled with whiskey and led me to the music room. The heavy, baize-covered steel door shut behind us with a thunk. The furnishings were much as I remembered: a sofa; a couple of chairs; a metronome; books; slender, enigmatic sculptures from Africa and Asia; a battered upright piano with children's drawings tacked to the side. It was a small, neat, comfortable room—the pacing of Konstantin's slippered feet had worn through the varnish on the blond pine floor, and a faint smell of sweat, of sustained hard work, pervaded the atmosphere.

Konstantin seized my shoulders and smothered my face with kisses, Russian-style. "And you, Maurice, how have the years treated you?" He spoke softly, with genuine affection. "Are you well?"

"Things have been good, until the last few days," I said. "I'm sorry Vera was upset."

"Ach, don't worry about it," he said, scratching one of his jug-handle ears. "Vera is tougher than me in many ways. But she expects things of people. Me, I've learned to live between the cracks. One of our children died, did you know?"

I shook my head.

"Mary. Soon after we came out here into the desert. The cancer took her quickly."

"Konstantin—I don't know what to say."

His bony, wide-knuckled hand waved above his head, as if the blows of fate were flies that must be swatted away. "It's life," he said. "Isn't that the *cliché*? Well, it *is* life. Always ready with another kick in the balls."

He looked up at me with a sad smile in his milky eyes and I made an-other adjustment in my calculation of his and Vera's marriage. She was the watcher, the guardian, the wheeler and dealer; without her Konstan-tin would be swamped; but he brought another sort of resilience to the arrangement—he was impish, a trickster, and he knew how to dodge and roll with the punches. He was pliant, and without him Vera would snap.

He fingered his wispy mustache, saying that he wanted to take another look at Beth's picture. I handed him the photograph, and he tugged at his ear again, almost cooing with sadness. "She was lovely, and she wanted to be loved. It's very sad. She was still forming herself when I met her. She would have been nineteen, I suppose. Twenty at most."

"And the musician?"

He looked at me from beneath his eyebrows. A nasty bruise was coming up on his forehead, I saw, from where he'd cracked heads with Vera. "Wardell Lane?" he said. "Early thirties, I suppose."

So, I thought, Beth's black lover has a name now—Wardell Lane. "What was his instrument?"

"Tenor sax."

"Was he good?" I said, the question coming out quickly, and with a competitive edge I hadn't intended.

"What do you understand about music, Maurice?"

I smiled, fielding the implied criticism. My first contact with the Slominskys came in the late 1940s, soon after I split from Luis Barragan. It came, like much else, through Jackie, who heard along the grapevine that an eminent Russian composer, now living in splendid exile in Pacific Palisades, wanted to build a place out in the desert. "For his lungs," Jackie had said. "So be it," I'd figured. Slominsky had the dough, it seemed, and I saw the likelihood of a splashy, prestigious commission. Only later did HUAC intrude, spreading like a virus, first into his life, then into mine. At which point Konstantin's exile ceased to be splendid. But by then I was out of there, having made my necessary accommodations, having used him, in order that I should proceed. In all our dealings—and these went on for more than a year—I'd never really spoken to Konstantin about his trade. After all, I said to myself, hadn't half the fiddlers in the known world decamped from disintegrating Europe and showed up in reinvigorating Los Angeles, world capital of identity transformation and con men posing as artists? I was wary of Konstantin's eminence, for it was genuine and solidly based. I'd tried to view him the way, in my sinews, I viewed myself: as a fake, an actor. I'd never seen him as the kind of figure a beautiful young girl might presume to impress her hip musician friends with, a living monument.

"Konstantin, I don't know a damn thing about music," I said. "You know that."

He put a finger to his lip. "Mmm. How can I explain this to you?" Clasping his hands behind his back, thrusting his chin forward like a hatchet, he began to pace, his slippered feet marching to the piano and back again. "Earlier we were talking about Freddy Greene. You've heard of him, yes?"

"Sure. Everybody has."

"He's famous, correct? A wonderful musician?"

"I guess so."

"He *is* a wonderful musician. A virtuoso, a performer. I saw Freddy play, several times. At nightclubs in New York and Los Angeles. Beautiful notes! Some like honey, some like vinegar. But Wardell Lane was something else. He was taking that horn to pieces and putting it together again. He was a composer, an *innovator*."

"That sounds forbidding."

"He wasn't like that at all. Not at *all*." This wasn't anger, but a brief, frustrated explosion of protest; he wanted me to understand. "He was a craftsman, but with another dimension."

Konstantin, I remembered, was practical rather than pretentious about his art. He thought about music the way he did his appetite. His belly was tough and he ate like a horse. For breakfast I'd seen him eat raw eggs, ham, cheese, herring, and baskets full of bread washed down with quantities of espresso and champagne. He had a taste for strong, salty, soulful things.

"Try and imagine how it was, five years ago," he said. "Vera outside with Beth, popping away at targets. Three men in here, trying to work. We talked about music at first, the composers we admired. Wardell knew about Stravinsky, Milhaud, Ravel. All well and good. That's very nice, I thought. An educated jazz musician. I suggested we play. And do you know what he did?"

"What?"

"Nothing. For thirty minutes he did nothing. He had that horn in his hands and he plodded to and fro, muttering to himself, while I pounded at the piano, working hard, Maurice, working *hard*, and Freddy blew his trumpet like it would bring down the walls of Jericho."

"Wardell was afraid?"

"That's *exactly* what I thought," Konstantin said, slamming his palms together. "I was sitting at the piano. Here." He straddled the stool in front of the upright, mimicking the pose he'd adopted five years before. "Watching him, thinking he was afraid, that big, skinny guy, filled with fear like bubbles in a bottle of fizzy soda pop, quaking inside because he couldn't really play, didn't quite have it like Freddy. You see," he said, "there's something about jazz that's like falling off a cliff every time, over and over again. The music lives in the freshness of the improvisation. It *is* terrifying."

Konstantin jumped to his feet. He scampered across the room, stopped in front of the window, and drew himself up straight, shutting his eyes and placing his hands beneath his face as if he were holding a saxophone. "He was standing here, with the sun behind him. Such drama, Maurice! I could see only his silhouette when he put that horn to his lips and began to blow. And then . . ."

He shook his head in wonder. "This wasn't just power, like Freddy. It was as if the desert floor were trembling. As if the Rocky Mountains had decided to uproot themselves and walk towards me. You're smiling, Maurice, as if you don't think art can do this. It can! I was in the room with the real deal. It doesn't happen too often, believe me."

He came back from the window on his bandy legs, crossing the room to where his record collection was racked neatly against the wall. "I'll play you something. The only record he's made. The only one I know about, anyway. I hope there'll be more."

I didn't know what to expect. In the war, like everyone else, I'd danced to Benny Goodman, Glenn Miller, and Count Basie; I'd lain on my bunk, smoking, dreaming, while Bing Crosby or Billie Holliday or Frank Sinatra sang on the radio. I understood, in a general way, that after the war a revolution had occurred in jazz, that the swing of the music had turned it-self inside out, with bop, bebop, hard bop. I knew, even, of a further devel-opment—West Coast jazz, cool jazz. Especially liking the sound of *those* concepts, I'd sped to a Hollywood music store and bought myself a cou-ple of Art Pepper records. The guy had style. He wore fine duds, was hand-some, white. He played each solo like it was a seduction. That, I could relate to. And of course jazz bands were always playing in the Vegas show rooms. I was no ignoramus on the subject, in other words; nor was I an ex-pert. But nothing had quite prepared me for what I was about to hear.

It was a quintet: the piano came in first, with bass, drums, and trumpet following behind, and I knew at once this wasn't the hard stuff, the Dizzy Gillespie kind of jazz; nor was it California cool, man. The tune was a standard, "Come Rain or Come Shine," and when Wardell Lane entered with his first solo I swear it was like being washed in the purest, freshest water I'd ever known. That horn floated with a sweet clarity that cleansed my blood and eased my bones. Okay, I was exhausted, drugged with fatigue. But I don't want to underplay the feeling of the moment. The whole room glowed, and Konstantin stood there with a huge grin.

"You see now? You understand?" he said. "Listen. He's almost on the edge, as if he were in danger of falling over."

But somehow Wardell never did. The music kept drifting, dreamily flitting.

Konstantin handed me the record sleeve, and I saw the picture of a handsome, goateed man with a long, lean, stooping frame, striding in front of a brick wall with a golden saxophone cradled in his arm. He wore a plain black T-shirt beneath the black suit that hung loosely on his frame. His face was black, coal-black, intensely black, arrogantly black, with a scar lacing the right cheek and staring dark eyes that threw out a challenge. For a black man seeking a smooth life in 1950s Amer-ica, the best way was to pretend to be white, to mimic the white man, or somehow to become invisible. Wardell Lane had rejected these options. He was proud and angry, bannering his race.

"He made the record later, but we played this tune when he was here," Konstantin said. "We played for hours, and when we finished there were puddles of sweat on the floor. It's hard work, you see, to make something that sounds this smooth and easy—and as if you'd had an interesting conversation with God."

Wardell's second solo came in, and the saxphone was indeed almost like a voice: whispery, knowing, alive, as if the notes themselves knew I was troubled and were trying to give me peace.

Head cocked to one side, Konstantin waited until the solo was done. "It makes the hairs stand up on your arms, doesn't it? When we'd finished playing, Beth came in and Wardell took her in his arms. They scarcely knew one another at that point. It seems that she'd been chasing him, like Vera said. Lucky man!" Konstantin stroked his mustache, his protuberant eyes watching me with sly pleasure and, perhaps, a hint of ironic malice. "They made love for the first time that night. She told Vera this. In the house you designed. In the room where you'll be sleeping tonight. Isn't that something, Maurice?"

30

*V*era was too forceful, too clever and shrewd to let me get away without hearing my side of the story. Over supper, on the patio, with great moths flapping their wings about the oil lamps that the gardener had lit, and with candlelight glinting in her silver hair and in the sharpness of her eyes, Vera interrogated me. "You're telling me that Beth introduced herself to you pretending to be another person?"

"She told me her name was Mallory Walker. Who exists. Who I met earlier today."

"But why?"

I shrugged.

"Was it her idea to kill you all along? Had you damaged or insulted her family in some way? Slept with her mother, maybe. I wouldn't put it past you, Maurice."

She was needling me, and I guessed I'd better put up with it.

"Bad things happen for a reason," she said.

"Do they? Don't you believe in accidents, Vera? In events that take over."

"Poppycock!" she said, reaching for her wine. She'd drunk more than a bottle already, seemingly without effect; she had a head like steel. "There's a story here and I want to hear it."

Normally I would have resisted Vera's hectoring manner. But the Slominskys had let me back into their lives and I owed them something.

Besides, my head was spinning and I realized that I wanted, needed, to confide. "She used me. To get close to a guy I work for. He owns some of the hotels in Las Vegas."

"Ah," said Vera, nodding her fine-boned face.

Again, there was something in her emphasis that I missed, and didn't think about until the next day.

"He has a name, this man?"

I hesitated. "Paul Mantilini," I said.

"Absurd. Never heard of him," Vera said, throwing herself back in her chair.

"That's good. And forget you ever did. Because I think he killed Beth. Or had her killed."

"Why?" said Konstantin, laying down his knife and fork.

"Because she tried to kill him," I said.

"And so it goes, around and around." He thrust his nose toward me across the table. "Why would she want to do that?"

"I don't know."

"Did you go to the police?"

"In Las Vegas he *is* the police. He's a very powerful man."

"But you'll do something," said Vera, a statement, not a question.

"Yes!" Konstantin said, rapping with table with a wide-knuckled hand. "Something must be done."

"I can do nothing." I've told them this much, I thought, I might as well spill the rest. "I'm going to be a senator for Nevada."

Vera looked at me, wide-eyed, almost stricken. "You're serious?"

"I'm very serious."

Konstantin exploded with laughter, his bony shoulders shaking up and down inside his jacket. His face grew red and he blew me a kiss. "Maurice is going to be a force in the land!"

"Something like that."

His laughter fell away. He coughed, holding a handkerchief to his lips while sorrow filled his milky, protuberant eyes.

I didn't want to think about what he thought; I didn't want to think about Beth anymore, and how she'd loved Wardell Lane in a way that I'd never loved or been loved. I was drunk. I was beat. I wanted to go to bed and forget for a few hours that I'd found out any of this.

That night I neither stirred nor remembered my dreams. I slept like the dead.

In the morning I made my goodbyes. This time it was Konstantin's turn to be cool. He shook my hand, wished me a safe journey, plucked mournfully at one of his huge ears, shuffled into his inner sanctum, and locked the door behind him. Six years earlier I'd named him in front of HUAC. Now I seemed to have disappointed and offended him in some more fundamental way. I was struck by the passionate and tender nature of his caring. And stung, too.

In the courtyard I was loading my stuff into the car when Vera came down from the house. She was dressed smartly in black and her silver hair was freshly combed; but she seemed tired and anxious. I don't think she'd slept much.

"Where will you go now?" she asked.

"Back to Nevada," I said.

The sun had barely cleared the mountains. The ground was still cool beneath our feet. A hawk circled overhead and the gardener was in his plot beneath the house, driving a shovel into the dirt with a booted foot, at work, or keeping an eye on Vera. Maybe both.

"This is difficult," Vera said, biting her lip. The wind lifted her hair. "There's something I must tell you. Yes, I think I must. But Konstantin is never to know. Can I trust you?"

I said that if she didn't think she could, she shouldn't tell me, whatever it was.

"I have to tell you," she said. "I can't keep this to myself, not after what I heard yesterday."

I had an odd feeling in my stomach, a tingling of apprehension. I didn't think I was going to like this. Still, I said: "I won't tell Konstantin anything. You have my word."

She put a hand against the door of the Studebaker. Her fingers were long and businesslike, ringless. "It meant a lot to Konstantin when those two musicians came. I don't pretend to know much about music, even after being around him for a lifetime. Not in the way that he does. But I know when something affects him, when he's happy, when's he's been moved. And he was. He said it was a magical time."

I said I knew what she meant. I, too, had gained some idea of how important the visit had been for him. He'd touched me, just describing it.

"Beth and Wardell said they'd come back. They promised. We even fixed a date. But they never came."

I remembered the hurt that had flashed for a second in Konstantin's face when he first saw Beth's photograph. That, now, was explained. "He says he doesn't expect anything from other people," I said. "Maybe he expects too much."

"Maybe," Vera said. "But that's not my point. I said *they* never came back."

Her sharp eyed moved away from mine, drifting toward the gardener while I absorbed the implication. "Beth was here?"

"About a month ago. She was driving a smart little sports car and we stood where you and I are standing now. She'd cut her hair and dyed it silver. Like mine, like you said. At first I didn't recognize her. She looked transformed, a little insane, actually. She said, 'It's Beth Dyer. You taught me to shoot, Vera, don't you remember?' I was . . . taken aback."

Vera, the mistress of understatement, I thought. But it was now that I remembered those strange beats in her conversation of the previous day, the hint that I'd failed to pick up when she'd spoken of how youthful and innocent Beth had been, back then. I should have guessed Vera was hiding something.

"She asked me for a gun," Vera said. "She wanted to borrow a gun."

"You gave her one?"

"I *liked* the girl," Vera said. "Besides, she was so angry, so determined. She had a plan and she wasn't going to let anything stand in her way. She was on fire with hate. Incandescent. I know that mood. I've felt it myself."

"Did she say what she wanted the gun for?"

"Indeed she did," Vera said, lowering her voice. "Understand, now, Maurice—Konstantin knows nothing of this. And he mustn't. Ever. I have his heart to think of. He's not been well."

"I won't say anything," I said. "I gave you my word."

The gardener stood motionless on his shovel while the wind whipped at Vera's hair and I waited.

"She said she was going to kill the man who killed Wardell," Vera said at last. "We didn't even know that he was dead. And Konstantin still doesn't. That's why I'm trying to be so careful."

"Oh Christ," I said, but it figured: the knowledge hit me like a nail whacked solidly into a piece of four-by-four.

"The man who killed him," Vera went on. "She must have meant . . ."

"Paul Mantilini," I said.

31

SEPTEMBER 12, 1956 / THE DESERT

I drove north through the high desert, meeting little traffic while the sun rose high and the blacktop shimmered. The inside of the car cooked like an oven, even with the air conditioning. I tried listening to the news and then to a music station, but the sound of the radio made me irritable. I didn't like the silence, either. I was in a miserable mood all around. Outside Amboy I stopped to look at a crater, gouged a half-mile long and a hundred feet deep in the desert, by a meteor, I guessed. No signs marked the crater; no tourists ogled it; no young kids scampered about its slopes, exclaiming that it was like something from a comic book. The crater was simply *there*, mysterious, frightening, dark, eerie, but as inevitable in its way as the rabbits hopping through the sage and the chameleon darting out its tongue to catch a fly. The desert was immutable, unconquerable, whatever happened; it didn't laugh at man's pain and his endeavors; it didn't complain about meteors, it merely swallowed them.

The outside of the Studebaker was hot, scalding to the touch. "Damn!" I said, and opened the door with a balled-up handkerchief in my fist. I drove on for a while but figured I needed to run my hand under cold water, otherwise it was going to blister. I stopped at a diner, a typical desert roadside place, poised behind a gas station and in front of a jumble of beige volcanic rock that glittered like treasure. Outside, the paint was discolored, wrecked by the heat; the screen on the door was dented and hanging off its frame, flapping in the wind. Inside, the

stifling air smelled of frying onions and lemon-scented floor polish. I
ordered a coffee, and attended to my first aid in the bathroom where the
sink was cracked and fat flies patrolled like fighters.

I sat by the window, nursing my hand and a cup of coffee, looking
out toward the gas station and the red flying horse on the Mobil sign. A
waitress was refilling the ketchup bottles and the sugar shakers. A
woman and her young son were eating doughnuts. The chef leaned with
his elbows on the bright-red counter, reading the newspaper. It was a
drowsy, dozy place, but the coffee was good, and I got to work with pencil and paper. I was an architect, wasn't I? I made designs, plots, and I set
about making another one, trying to piece together what I knew. I made a
rough map, tracking Beth Dyer's movements. Two months back she'd
arrived in Palm Springs, intending to seduce Mallory Walker and steal
her identity, a plan she'd already worked out with me in mind. Before
that? Was anybody's guess. But she'd left Palm Springs a little less than
a month ago, had driven to Joshua Tree, and had collected one of Vera's
nickel-plated pistols. From there she journeyed to Los Angeles, introduced herself to Luis Barragan as though she knew him, and persuaded
him to invite me to his party. She dropped Luis and attached herself
to me, her all-too-willing victim, hinting that a weekend of Las Vegas
fun might be in order, so that she could take her shot at Mantilini. But
she made a mistake, rushed her plan, and hit me instead. At which
point, I surmised, she was taken by Mantilini's people and dumped in
Lake Mead, the sad end point of this particular map.

I sketched out the time I'd spent with her. Sunday evening, the Labor
Day weekend, Luis Barragan's party—perhaps fifteen minutes in her company. Monday afternoon: her visit to my office, the subsequent trip to the
site she claimed she'd bought, the conversation in the soda fountain—
maybe two hours in all. Then a solid block of time, starting Tuesday at the
beach house, the night of hot and haunted fucking, followed by the drive
to Las Vegas and the El Sheik cabana; Wednesday morning, she leaves,
Thursday at dawn she returns—bang!

I'd spent the best part of two days in her company, hearing only lies.
And I hadn't suspected for a moment. Truly, she'd turned in a remarkable

performance. She'd come to me as Mallory and almost killed me; but it was as Beth, after she herself had died, that she threatened to overtake my life.

I couldn't afford to let that happen.

In the early spring of 1951, soon after meeting Wardell Lane, and seeking to impress him, she'd taken him to the Slominsky house, which she knew about.

How?

I wrote that word down and underlined it.

More than five years later, in the process of assuming a new identity, she ventured back to the Slominsky house to obtain the weapon of her vengeance.

Vera, when I'd asked her, had denied any knowledge of the circumstances and timing of Wardell's death.

When?

I wrote that word down, too.

Beth had sought to avenge a ghost, and it was starting to look like I was haunted by one. Again, a situation at odds with my greater plan for the advancement of Maurice Valentine. Was there any use in going up against Mantilini? None. Did I even want to? Not especially. She'd shot me and so I sought an explanation. Now that I'd gotten one, I didn't like it very much.

I didn't see the guy coming. Maybe, somewhere right at the back of my mind, I was aware of the screen door flapping, the inner door banging. But one moment I was staring at the recently filled sugar shaker and the next, before I had time to move or think, he was sitting on the other side of it, not looking sweet at all, but pale and sick with a long narrow face and sad brown eyes like a spaniel's, a man of about my own age, or maybe a few years younger, in his mid-thirties, with a straw hat pushed back from a forehead disfigured by angry pimples. I'd seen the hat before, in a black Ford, trailing me in Palm Springs.

"You're going to talk to me, mister," he said.

"Like hell," I said, and, really, he didn't look like he could persuade a duck to eat bread, but unfortunately he'd brought a friend with him, a folded newspaper, a copy of the *Oregonian*, which he laid on the table. Inside the newspaper was his hand, and at the end of his hand, turned on its side, was a Colt .45 automatic. He held that gun like a pro. Or an amateur who'd put in some practice. "I'll be happy to talk to you. You can put the gun away," I said.

"Like hell," he said. He neither smiled nor moved. Sweat meandered between the pimples on his forehead. "My name's Lou Virgiel." He sounded different now, more confident, settling into his role, easy and direct; he knew how to put himself in command. "I'm a private investigator, working out of Portland. A guy I know in northern Cal has hired me to find his wife. She skipped out on him about two months ago."

"What's that to me?" I said.

"Come on, give us both a break," he said. With one hand still on the gun he fished about in his pocket and produced a snapshot. It showed a woman sitting on a tartan picnic rug with her knees tucked under her. Her eyes squinted against the sun and the sail of a boat loomed behind her. It was Beth Dyer.

"Her name's Carol Speedwell," he said.

"Really?" I said.

"Before she was married she called herself Carol Smith, if we can believe that. And I don't know if I do. I'm open to suggestions. Start making them," said Lou Virgiel, pushing the *Oregonian* forward. I saw from the top of the paper that it was more than two weeks old. But the Colt inside it was far from defunct. The barrel was clean, slick with oil, and wide as a tunnel. You could fall into that thing forever.

PART 5

Las Vegas

32

JULY 18, 1951 / LAS VEGAS

*W*here's Wardell?" says Freddy Greene. He and Beth stand side by side, looking down from the stage on the shining tables, the booths covered in pink leather, the long sixty-foot bar, the deep-pile rose carpet, the main body of the show room. The can-can girls have left the stage, taking with them their bustling skirts and long legs sheathed in glittery stockings. It's eleven A.M., time for the Freddy Greene Orchestra to rehearse, and time is short. Everything runs on a cramped and hectic schedule, today seeing the opening of the Gai-Moulin, Las Vegas's first interracial casino, where blacks and whites will gamble together and mingle openly, where black artists will be allowed to sleep in the same building in which they're performing. A first for Nevada, and Freddy is expectant, thrilled, nervous. A little frightened, too. Not everybody welcomes this auspicious and remarkable event. The previous night, crosses were burning out in the desert.

"He'll be here," Beth says.

"When did you last see him?"

"At breakfast."

"God-*damn*," murmurs Freddy.

"He's never let you down, has he?"

Freddy mumbles under his breath, scratching anxiously at the back of his thick neck.

"Has he?" says Beth. In truth, she isn't worried. Wardell told her he

had an errand to run, some guy to see, that's all. No problem. He was a
little distracted and grumpy, eating his eggs and hash browns in the Fos-
ter's Freeze across from the Gai-Moulin. Nothing unusual in that.
Wardell always takes a while to get going in the morning. His blood, after
all, has a long way to travel from his head to his feet. Besides, he's a night
owl, Beth knows. After he's played a gig he likes to sit at a desk and write
music. Sometimes she wonders whether he'll ever come to bed at all. But
in the end he always does, lying beside her and pulling her body toward
his. After three months she still finds it amazing to wake up next to his
face. That lined, scarred face, an exquisite face, a sad face, always looking
older and wiser than the number of years it supposedly carries. She feels
almost afraid to tell him how in love and alive looking at him makes her
feel, lest she put a curse on what they have. But she tells him anyway.

"You're a worrier, Freddy," she says.

"That's true. I *am* a worrier." Freddy's teeth are yellow, strong, stumpy,
his own. "I worry because I know things can go *wrong*." He glances toward
her belly. "What about you, Beth? How are you doing?"

"I'm fine," she says, though she feels a little dizzy and nauseous.
Freddy acts on her like a steadying influence. He's stout, solid, an un-
ambiguously good man, she believes, walking evidence of humanity's
occasional ability to see things through, a jazz musician who has survived ten thousand nights on the road to prosper. A rare breed, as Wardell
has told her.

"You sure?" Freddy says, his meaty, pink-palmed hand gentle as a
butterfly on her arm. Beth recalls the first time she saw him, when she
was pursuing Wardell with no luck, when she'd gate-crashed Freddy's
birthday party. He'd looked at her with the same tenderness and concern. "Wardell treating you right?"

"He's beautiful," she says.

"You tell him yet?" Freddy says, looking toward her belly again.

"Not yet. Tonight," she says. "After the shows."

Freddy grunts. "Been on *all* our minds."

Wardell arrives five minutes later, his long, lean frame flitting between the tables, sunglasses on, black suit sharp, yanking at his dark

woollen tie as if it were strangling him. The gold cross embossed on the Bible he holds is the one bright spot in his entire ensemble. He carries no instrument case and Beth knows there's trouble.

Wardell tosses down his sunglasses, slumps into a booth, and rises again, his long foot kicking savagely at a chair.

"Hey!" says Freddy. "This is our place, remember? It's for us."

"They're fooling you, man," says Wardell, his face grim with disappointment, and something more, Beth sees—disgust. "You blind? It's just a front."

"Steady now, partner," says Freddy, hand on Wardell's sleeve, soothing the younger, more volatile man. "Tell me what's going on."

"They took my ax."

"Somebody stole your horn?"

"They *took* it. Like I was a child and it was a toy they'd decided I couldn't play with no more."

"Who?"

"A couple of white guys."

"So we go get you another one. My treat," says Freddy, showing his wide, gap-toothed grin. "Okay. No more problem. Problem gone. Problem *solved.*"

"There's more to it," Wardell says. In his eyes Beth sees anger and something she hadn't expected—shame. "I can't play. They won't let me."

Freddy's amiable face creases, while Beth slides her arm around Wardell's shoulders, kneading the tense knot she knows from experience that her fingers will find at the top of his back. She says, "What's wrong, baby?"

"Beth—this don't concern you," Wardell says, but not unkindly, as though trying to spare her.

"You're upset. Of course it concerns me."

"Go pack your stuff," he says. "We're heading back to L.A."

"You're gonna run away, is that it? Last night you were saying we have to fight the cross-burners. You're gonna quit? Let them beat you?"

"This is different," he says, looking down at his hands. "These people.

They mean it. They'll hurt me, maybe even kill me. I hate it, baby, believe me, I do. But sometimes you have to know when not to fight."

Beth's eyes appeal to Freddy, but Freddy shakes his head—no help coming from that quarter.

"I'm leaving you in a jam," Wardell says to Freddy. "You'll need a tenor man. There's Lenny Schiff. He can probably make it out from L.A. in time."

"I'll get on the horn," says Freddy.

Beth, who has been watching the two men, turning from one to the other in mounting disbelief, explodes. She seizes both of them, a jazz guy in either hand. "Hold your horses, people! Would someone tell me what the hell's going on here?"

Wardell looks up at her, unable to stop his smile. Every love affair has its own system, its own economy, and an understood part of the bond between them is that Beth is practical, a fixer, a doer. This is a burden she's happily assumed, believing that with her verve and drive she can make anything happen. Didn't she take him to meet the Slominskys? When he was sick with pneumonia, didn't she nurse him through the fever? When the checks started bouncing, didn't she go butter up the bank manager and sort everything out? When he was blinded with migraine, didn't she sit beside him in a dimly lit hotel room, pressing an ice pack to his head and reading him poetry and passages from the Bible?

"Let's go. There's nothing you can do here, honey," Wardell says, standing, taking her in his arms, and planting a kiss on her cheek.

"Try me," she says, pushing him away. "Try telling me, for instance, who you mean by *these people*? Who?"

Wardell and Freddy exchange a look.

"Are they demons? Are they ghosts? Are they *devils*?"

"They're the guys who run the town," Wardell says, with a quiet simplicity he takes to be definitive. Incomprehension, and a flash of anger, move across his narrow, goateed face when Beth starts to laugh. "What?"

"Give me the keys to the car," she says. "Hand them over, mister. I mean it. And tell me everything. I want to know the names of these people. I want to know what they look like and what cars they drive."

"They wore Old Spice," Wardell says. "Is that gonna help us any?"

Ignoring the rebuff, raising herself on tiptoe, she grazes her lips against his. "Tell me what's going on, baby."

Outside, a tropical wind from Mexico travels through the Las Vegas valley and the air swoons, heavy with thunder. In Wardell's ancient Mercury coupe Beth starts to sweat as she goes searching for Paul Mantilini. First, she tries the Desert Inn, but he's not there, nor at the Flamingo. Hearing he might be at the Thunderbird, she drives along the Strip, pulls into the lot, and hurries inside to find the pit boss.

"Who shall I say's looking for him?" the guy says, offhand, cool, alert, promising nothing.

"A friend. My name's Beth Dyer."

She waits, pacing among the aisles of slot machines. An athletic woman in a gray suit hits a jackpot and whoops, collecting the gushing silver in a plastic bucket that is soon filled to overflowing. Beth empties her mind, preparing to face Mantilini. The last few months of her life have been spent with Wardell, traveling with Wardell, caring for Wardell, loving Wardell. But she hasn't quit on her ambition to act; she still studies, reads, performs her exercises. She knows that a performance is what's called for right now, though she doesn't know what the nature of her performance will be. That will depend, naturally, on the mood of Paul Mantilini when she finds him. She hasn't spoken with him since she met Wardell; she wrote him a letter, thanking him for the times in Las Vegas, hoping that he'd understand—the bomb had gone off in her heart, she said. With Wardell she has discussed neither Mantilini nor any of her other boyfriends. Why would she? She and Wardell have begun life together with a clean slate, no questions asked, like grown-ups. That's understood.

"He'll see you now, Miss Dyer," the pit boss says, with a changed look in his eye. He seems brisk and (dare she hope?) impressed, leading her to the back of the casino, through a locked door, a man standing guard outside, and into a low-ceilinged room with a floor of shiny black linoleum and one-way glass that looks over the gambling pit. The room, almost devoid of furniture, is punishingly lit by bare, fizzing bulbs. Two men wearing visors sit on stools behind a high glass table, tips of orange rubber on their forefingers, counting money, banding the bills before stacking them neatly into piles of different denominations. A fat satchel of money lies, ignored, beside a half-empty bottle of Coke at the feet of Paul Mantilini, who sits on a sofa, eating peanuts in his shirtsleeves. On either side of him is a beefy, younger man in a black suit; they look anonymous yet threatening, like twins, like Odin's ravens, she thinks, the birds her father used to tell her about, who brought news from afar and whispered in the ear of the god.

"Hello, Beth," Mantilini says, not standing, his face a mask, brushing salt from his palms before wiping his hands with a napkin and taking a swig of Coke. "What can I do for you?"

In the brusqueness of his voice she hears a hint of disapproval, of disppointment. He seems tired, tense somehow, but filled with an energy, or anger, that he's waiting to unleash. The thought touches a flutter of panic in her belly, but she reassures herself: Whatever's going on with him, she thinks, whatever campaign he's about to launch and win in his world, has nothing to do with me.

"Listen, you probably think I've got a nerve coming to you like this," she says, keeping her voice calm, reasonable. "I've got a problem."

"We've all got problems," he says, no emotion in his voice, his face deadpan, although one of the ravens sitting beside him almost laughs, a smothered croak echoed by his partner on the other side.

"I need your help," she says. "I can't offer anything in return. I need a favor."

He screws up the napkin in his hand, lobbing it onto the spotless floor.

"*Please*," says Beth, struck by a dizziness, wobbling on her feet, pleading, not quite sure herself whether this desperation is part of the performance or the true Beth, the real Beth, whoever she may be, begging that her idyll with Wardell not be shattered.

"Are you okay?" Mantilini says, on his feet now, taking her arm.

"Come on, sit down. You guys," he says, motioning to the ravens, "get out of here, will you? The counters too. Leave us alone for a minute."

Beth sits, taking the Coke bottle that Mantilini hands her, the same one he's been drinking from. The sweet, ice-cold liquid burns and fizzes in her throat and the sudden faintness passes.

"Tell me about it," Mantilini says, when the other men are gone and the door is shut behind them.

"I have a friend," she says. "A special friend. He's a musician."

"I know."

"He's playing at the opening of the Gai-Moulin."

"I heard that, too."

"This morning two guys took away his horn. They threatened to break his fingers and kill him because he wouldn't sell their drugs."

Mantilini raises his chin, scratches the underside of his throat. "What were they trying to make him sell? Weed?"

"Heroin," she says.

His teeth shut with a click. His right eye seems dead and flat, as usual, and there's a cold fury in the usually bright left one, which Beth has never seen before. The look on Paul Mantilini's face at that moment could turn a man to stone.

"That's not possible," he says.

"All the same. It's true."

"Had your friend met these guys before?"

"Five years ago. In Los Angeles. He used to be an addict."

"He sold for them, then?"

"I think so," Beth says, hesitating, this being the part of the story Wardell had found toughest to tell. His addiction, its repercussions, had cost him his marriage, and almost his life. But she knows, after all this, that she'd better be straight with Mantilini. "He did, yes. He sold for them. But he's clean now. Has been for more than two years."

"Dammit!" says Mantilini, on his feet, his hand coming out of his pocket, shooting to the top of his head, and then slowing down, caressing the gray hair at his temples with an almost unearthly self-control.

Every story I've heard about this man, Beth thinks, and I've heard a few, every wild rumor about the things he's done, and what he's capable of—it's all true. Nausea squirms inside her again.

"Wait here," he says, and before she can protest, Mantilini, too, is gone from the counting room, leaving her with the money satchel on the floor, and all that money on the table, more money than she's ever seen or ever will again. She walks around the room, resting her fingers on the money, her nostrils filling with the smell of the money, almost afraid of the money and what it will cause to be done once sent back out into the world.

Mantilini comes back into the room a few minutes later, grinning and bearing a tray like a waiter, giving his own performance now, sweeping the money aside and setting down the tray with a courtly flourish.

"You remember Nick, my son?"

Beth nods—*of course.*

"I've sent him over to the Gai-Moulin. He'll ask your friend to accept my apologies and assure him that everybody in Las Vegas is waiting to hear him play tonight. Does that sound good?" Mantilini says, handing Beth a bowl of chips and a fresh Coke with a twirly red straw bobbing in the neck of the bottle. "We'll have the saxophone within an hour, and I've asked Nick to bring it here. I guessed that you wanted to give it to your man yourself."

Beth smiles, blushing: Is she really so easy to read? For this, of course, is the exact scenario that she's envisioned: sweeping back into the Gai-Moulin, instrument case in her arms, laying the horn in Wardell's lap and watching the pleasure light his stoic face—another miracle performed.

"I think I owe *you* an apology, too," Mantilini says. "I was rude. I'm sorry, Beth. What can I say? I've got something big going on—business, you know. I've been distracted."

In this remarkable confession Beth hears something she hadn't expected, not a boast, not really an apology, either—he's not *sorry*; he cares for her.

"That bomb," he says, regarding her with a fond, almost paternal, smile. "It really happened, didn't it?"

33

SEPTEMBER 12, 1956 / LAS VEGAS

*S*enator Walton "Boss" Booth was a small man, sleek and well-groomed, vain as a rooster, his years of climbing long behind him, his time of power dwindling but not yet exhausted. All smiles, in his element, he stood on the steps of City Hall, speaking to Will Rothschild of the *Las Vegas Press*. "Naturally I'm delighted to accept the nomination of my party," Boss Booth said smoothly, without bluster. "And I believe the good people of this wonderful state of ours will find it in their hearts to elect me to one more term. My fifth Senate term." He raised a fist and shook it belligerently. "There's still some fight in this old bird!"

Rothschild inquired about the Boss's health.

"That's a good question, Will," Boss said. "And one that deserves a straight answer." His tough eyes twinkled, and his voice lowered a notch, picking up in sincerity what it lost in enthusiasm. "I'll tell you this. The people of Nevada know me, they *know* Boss Booth. It's true that I've had some problems. But I wouldn't be standing here unless I could get the job done. Now would I?"

The customary platitudes, backed up in force by the Boss's almost raffish manner. I'm an old warhorse, he seemed to say, but I'm still a winner. And isn't that what this is all about?

"You're concerned about the future," he went on. "And so you should be. Let me tell you something." He rubbed his chin, the slow and careful gesture of an actor playing a wise old man, playing Abraham Lincoln, and his voice changed gears yet again. "I love this great state of ours too much not to have given some thought, some *careful* thought, to that issue. Why, this very day I've been talking to a young man, a fine and promising young man, a man who has served his country with valor, an architect who's helping build Nevada, Maurice Valentine, a *dear* friend of mine . . ."

The Boss and I, it should go without saying, had met for the first and only time about thirty minutes before.

"Maurice and I have our differences, of course. But we see eye to eye about lots of things, too. And we agree about this—that the future of Nevada is not in doubt. It's a lock. This great state of ours will grow, and prosper."

It was the tail end of a burning-hot afternoon, the same day I got back from Joshua Tree, and I was trying not to sweat, standing five steps down from where Boss held forth. Jackie stood on one side of me, the kids on the other, Joe Nelson and Paul Mantilini close at hand. And when Boss's interview was done, when his blessing had been secured, Will Rothschild turned to me. I kept my speech short. Holding Jackie's hand, hugging Ches and Bobby close so that they were in clear view of the camera, I spoke about continuity and fresh starts and the splendid career of Boss Booth.

When it was over, Boss came up to me, hugged me close, and whispered softly in my ear, "You miserable little shitheel." Then we all climbed into limousines and were taken back to the El Sheik, where a buffet had been laid on in the dining room. Boss Booth and Joe Nelson stood in one corner, tumblers of bourbon in their hands, plates piled with beef and potato salad lying ignored on the table beside them, hissing at each other like snakes, smiling all the while. I put myself to work, in the next ten minutes meeting the lieutenant governor, a congressman, three justices of the Nevada Supreme Court, and a bunch of union guys, each of whom seemed to be attached to a showgirl. I pressed the flesh until my fingers were sore.

"This is going all right," Jackie said, leaning her head against my shoulder.

"I guess," I said.

"Senator Valentine," she said, brushing her mouth against my ear.

"Not any time soon."

"Soon enough," she said. She squeezed my butt. "Let's go to the cabana, *Senator*."

"We'll be missed."

"Not for fifteen minutes."

"What about the kids?"

"Paul gave them each a bucket filled with chips. They're going crazy at the slot machines."

"Is that such a good idea?"

Jackie's eyebrow shot skywards. She was wearing a new Balmain and looked like dynamite. "Do you care?"

It took more than fifteen minutes. An hour later we were back at the party, Jackie trailing her fingers through my palm and going off to find her father. I saw Boss Booth at the other side of the room, florid in the face, drunk probably, with something wild in his eye. He, too, was now surrounded by showgirls—he was showing them a magic trick with a deck of cards—and I found that Paul Mantilini was at my side. He was dressed in a dark suit, but he wore no tie, and the collar of his white silk shirt spilled over the neck of his jacket.

"Charming old man, isn't he?" he said, looking in the direction of Boss Booth.

"Like a bloated rattlesnake," I said.

"He gave you the nod."

"How did you manage it?"

"He wanted something. Everybody wants something, Maurice. It's the secret to power. You just have to find out what it is."

"He hates me."

"You're the future. That's why. Does it matter?"

"I guess not. But can you trust him?"

Ultimately, it seemed to me, Boss's warm endorsement might prove worthless. What was to stop him, a year from now, announcing that he'd changed his mind? Or simply deciding to throw his weight behind somebody else?

"You think Boss will try to double-cross us? Maybe he will," Mantilini said with a vague, enigmatic smile. "He's a devious bastard. But he's staying in town for a couple of days. I think we'll find that he's done enough, the old Boss." His tone was intimate, soft, conversational. He turned my way: "How was Palm Springs? I was worried you might not be back in time."

So he's found out, I thought with a tingle of apprehension, of danger. Mantilini was like a great chess player; he didn't try to see too far ahead but looked deeply into the moves close at hand. What he needed to solve he did, and what he couldn't solve, he didn't worry about.

"Palm Springs? It was dull. Not my kind of town," I said. managing to keep the shock out of my face, just about. "You had me followed?"

He broke out laughing. "Why would I do that?" he said. I couldn't help finding something threatening in his unforced amusement. He glanced across the room toward where Luis Barragan sat at one of the tables, drunk already, with a huge cigar in his mouth, almost sliding off the side of his chair. "He's a great architect—a blabbermouth, too. He told me you were going to a wedding. Mallory Walker's wedding. That seemed kind of remarkable to me."

Fucking Luis, I thought, and, as if I'd aimed the thought like an arrow, directly into Luis's brain, he jerked himself straight, shot me a look of belligerent defiance, removed the cigar from his mouth, and raised his glass in a toast. Ironic, no doubt.

"Mallory Walker was getting married, that's true," I said, picking my words carefully. "Not *my* Mallory Walker. Luis sent me on a wild-goose chase. My Mallory's dead."

"You doubted it?" Mantilini said, jiggling the coins in his pocket, watching me carefully.

I felt chill and sour, standing there beside him. The man who controlled my destiny was a murderer. Not in some abstract way, but the murderer of a woman whose touch I remembered, whose history I was coming to understand almost better than my own, and of a man whose music had reached into me with such a delicate hand. Mantilini had eradicated these two souls. Wardell Lane was where? Out in the desert probably, resting place for unwanted properties going back to the Jurassic age. And Beth was in the morgue.

Should I go to the cops? Futile, as I'd explained to the Slominskys. Should I plot to expose Mantilini after I was elected, *if and when* I was elected, somehow get Joe Nelson in on the deal? Mantilini pretty much owned Nevada, while I would be the state's cardboard senator merely. And Joe was clearly beholden to him in some way. What then? Mantilini has power and power owns justice. This was scarcely news. Moreover, for years I'd been telling myself that it was a proposition I was in favor of. I'd better be, I thought, otherwise I was against it, outside in the cruel desert with the rest of the herd, and that was a sad situation to contemplate.

Back at the roadside diner I'd told that private eye, Lou Virgiel, that the woman he was looking for was dead. That, yes, I'd known her, spent time with her, slept with her. I told him that she'd run away from his client, her husband, with some warped idea of gaining revenge for the murder of a lover from an earlier part of her life. "Believe me," I'd said. "You don't want to dig too deep into this. You'll probably wind up getting hurt. Or dead, like her." I'd told him to head back to northern California and inform his client that a terrible tragedy had occurred—his wife had been killed in an automobile accident. "Say how sorry you are. Don't tell him his whole life with her was most likely a sham. Spare him that. Tell him she was a great kid and everybody loved her. Give him a routine. You'll be doing him a favor." And I thought I'd done Lou Virgiel one. But now, facing Mantilini, seeing again the smooth burnish of his power and authority, I felt pissed, pricked by guilt. Emotions that Maurice Valentine didn't allow near the drawing board. I wanted to be senator, but I also wanted to find out what had happened to Beth and Wardell, and make Mantilini pay somehow. What I wanted was impossible, of course.

"No, I guess I never did. But it turns out her name wasn't Mallory after all," I said to Mantilini.

He was watchful, the coins still rubbing and jostling in his pockets, the way they often did when he thought things through. "So—who *was* she?"

I should have backed off; but I found myself incapable of following the good advice I'd given to Lou Virgiel. "I don't know," I said. "I'm working on it."

"If you find out, let me know, will you?"

"Maybe I will," I said, wanting to challenge Mantilini, at least let him know that I had his number; stupid ego stuff. "And maybe I won't."

Now he looked at me sharply. His good eye narrowed.

"A snap of the two of you together?" said Will Rothschild, materializing in front of us.

Mantilini and I stood arm in arm while his leveled his Leica, the shutter clicked, and the explosion of the flashgun drowned us in light.

34

 $\mathcal{T}$ he ballroom at the Desert Inn was packed, the dance floor was crowded, the house band was playing a version of "Oh, Lady, Be Good!" This wasn't quite nightclub Vegas at the height of its glamour and power—that came a few years later, with the Rat Pack and Jack Kennedy, who made himself at home in the town, or was made to feel that way, drinking and schmoozing in the lounges, fucking the mob guys' mistresses, picking up hundreds of thousands of dollars in campaign money, in leather satchels, in cash. All the same, I felt the energy the minute I walked in. The atmosphere buzzed. Everyone was beautifully, expensively—but not *self-consciously*—dressed, inhibitions having been left at the city limits. I saw middle-aged couples dancing, middle-aged guys dancing with young girls, and younger couples, too. A dusting of famous faces, celebrities, like the sparkle on top of a cake. Candles, immaculate white tablecloths. One young couple dancing passionately, almost violently. A drunk scattered twenty-dollar bills as a pair of bouncers rushed him out. "You don't understand," he was shouting. "I've got the dough. I can pay." Nobody deigned to pick up the money. The maître d', Pancho, moved around the room, patrolling the bar, weaving between the tables, watchful as a hawk.

"Mr. Valentine," he said, swooping down in a mist of perfumed hair oil, leading me to a choice table, snapping his fingers for a leggy waitress. "A bottle of champagne here, please. A bottle of the best."

The champagne wouldn't be *absolutely* the best; that was reserved for the likes of Mantilini, or the five guys who sat in a row on a banquette, saying nothing, silently eating their steaks, two of them wearing sunglasses though it was after midnight. All the same, I knew that my own stature was growing in Vegas. I saw it in Pancho's look, felt it in the way his hand lingered on my sleeve.

"When's Freddy Greene coming on?" I said.

Pancho shot back a cuff and glanced at his watch. "About twenty minutes. I'll have them bring another bottle before the show starts," he said, his attention drawn suddenly to the bar, where a young woman in black was shouting and slapping a guy's face. Pancho didn't flinch or adjust his smile but said, "Excuse me," and moved swiftly over.

I settled back to wait. It was soon after leaving the Slominsky house, but before my confrontation with Lou Virgiel, that I remembered Nick Mantilini talking to Beth, telling her about the various shows in town. I remembered, too, seeing Freddy Greene's name on an advertisement in the *Las Vegas Press*: "Wilbur Clark's Desert Inn presents the Las Vegas PREMIERE of the FABULOUS singing star EARTHA KITT, with special guest FREDDY GREENE, Sept. 7 thru 14." The ad had scarcely registered at the time; no reason why it should have; but now I put it together that Freddy was already in Las Vegas when I'd arrived in town with Beth.

I was thinking about what Virgiel had told me. "This client of mine, see—he's not rich or important. He's just a regular guy. Runs the electrical appliances department in a store," he'd said. "She came to him needing a job, more than four years ago. Some time towards the back end of 1952. They hit it off just fine, dated for a while, got hitched—just the way it's supposed to work. They were trying to have a baby."

For Beth, aka Carol Smith, aka Carol Speedwell, there'd been order, a haven—which she abandoned. Why now? I wondered. What had been the trigger? She'd been living in Crescent City for more than three years—why give that up? Maybe she'd found her anger lingering, festering, flaring once more, twisting her inside, and she'd been unable, therefore, to accept her secure new life. Or maybe fate had aimed something at her, pricked her with one of its nasty little arrows, prompting her to act and seek revenge.

These were questions I hoped Freddy Greene might help me with.

The lights in the ballroom dimmed, and without fuss or fanfare Freddy Greene ran onstage and bowed, a solid man with a round, grinning face, clad in a dashing white double-breasted suit and a wide silk tie that shimmered like a peacock's tail. The sticks flew in the drummer's hands, the bass settled into a beat, and the horn that Freddy raised to his pursed lips with a flourish glinted in the twirling lights. He grinned, a look of powerful, almost hideous rapture on his face, like a priest contemplating the beginning of a sacred rite; then his cheeks puffed out like a hamster's and a cascade of notes poured forth, each in place and tied to the next. He played two swing numbers with something that resembled a controlled fury, the sound coming in waves, one close after the other, until all the air in the room began to dance; then a fast stomp, then a slow blues, his battered lips and banana-sized fingers coaxing tender jewels from the bell of his horn. He stopped, raised his arms high to acknowledge the applause, then plucked a towel from the top of the piano and mopped his face and, smiling with the quiet assurance of a magician about to pull off one of his most impressive tricks, said: "Thank you, folks. And now I'd like to introduce an old, dear friend of mine!" Eartha Kitt stepped onto the stage, *pranced* onto the stage, a sleek panther of a woman—long legs, eyes flashing and wet. Her personality, like Greene's, was massive in that room, and, as if scrupling not to overwhelm us, she sang "The Man I Love" with the sweet yearning of a nineteen-year-old, backed by Greene's softly wailing horn.

That's how it was in Las Vegas back then: you'd go to see one world-class entertainer—the headliner—and get another thrown in, no extra charge. The money was outrageous and everyone came through. I'd seen Noël Coward play one of the supper rooms, and Marlene Dietrich in a dress that looked like she was nude. But what struck me that night was something completely different. Like most Americans of my class, I opposed racial prejudice in principle, an easy posture since I had little contact with blacks. I didn't meet them through work. Not too many blacks were commissioning houses from snazzy architects like me in those days. At the country club, if I ever saw them at all, they were the boys who

cleaned the pool or washed the dishes. In Vegas the unions kept them off
the construction sites. They lived on the other side of Bonanza Road and
ventured onto the Strip only to shine shoes or labor—invisibly—in the
kitchens. Then they went home. Even when noted black entertainers like
Greene and Kitt were in town, playing the Desert Inn, or the Flamingo,
or the El Sheik, they didn't stay in the hotels or fraternize with the gamblers they entertained but rode in their cars or cabs back to the hotels
and boardinghouses in the ghetto. I was hip enough to know that this
was all wrong but I never had to *do* anything about it, and I thought how
brave, how reckless, and maybe self-dramatizing, too, Beth Dyer had been
to enter this other, black, world, to penetrate it deeply. At what? The age
of nineteen? Twenty? I thought of the photograph of Wardell Lane on
the record sleeve I'd seen in the Slominsky house, the daunting, defensive
arrogance of his gaze. He'd not been a welcoming, grinning trickster like
Freddy Greene, but a spikier package altogether. And thus, I guess, to
Beth, more attractive; she'd really wanted to prove something; falling in
love with him had been a gauntlet thrown down to convention. But then
I'm supposing she had some choice in the matter; maybe she really *had*
been struck by one of those thunderbolts that had never hit me. Was this
a grand tragic love? Vera Slominsky had thought so, but for me it was
tough to say, having nothing in my experience to compare it to. Ambition had always kept my passions in check.

In his dressing room Freddy Greene had taken off his suit and his
shirt, and sat on a chair in his undershorts. He was a slab-sided man with
shoulders big as a bridge. His bare torso was thick, packed. Maybe that's
why he could blow so hard and long. He probably had lungs like a bull.
His feet were huge on the floor and his trumpet lay in its open case on
the dressing table; taped to the plush interior of the case was the photograph of a middle-aged woman in a stylish red hat—his wife, I supposed.
On one side of the trumpet was a typewriter with a sheet of paper rolled
into it; on the other, a bottle of scotch, a couple of fat reefers, and a telephone that was pale blue, the color of airmail paper. In a corner was a tall
screen of green silk with Freddy's clothes hanging on it.

Freddy was staring at the floor and a moment or two went by before he noticed that I'd come in. His startled expression soon turned to the familiar, dazzling grin, as though he were slipping into a crisp, clean shirt; the act of putting on that grin seemed automatic to him, and although the warmth of the smile was genuine, I gained two immediate impressions: first, of a life lived in hotels and boardinghouses, on the road, on buses, trains, and planes, of a life not exactly lonely, but one in which company was a welcome diversion, almost a necessity; second, contradicting the first, but lying beneath it at this moment, that he was scared—he had something to hide.

"Greetings!" he said, his voice a deep, bass rumble, and he rose majestically, sliding his feet into worn leather slippers and padding toward me across the butt-littered floor. The grip of his hand was crushing. "Whiskey?"

Without waiting he grasped the bottle, those enormous fingers enclosing it as though it were no wider than a straw, and splashed hefty measures into a pair of paper cups.

"You don't know me, but I'm a big fan," I said. "My name's Maurice Valentine. I'm an architect."

He beamed, as though this were the best possible news. "What can I do for you, Mr. Valentine?"

I took things slow and easy. I'd figured out my plan of attack while watching the show. "Some friends of yours and mine asked me to send their best. The Slominskys."

His grin grew wide again. His eyes bulged in their sockets. "You know those folks?"

"I designed their house."

"You did?" His delight bubbled like the champagne I'd been drinking. "That Konstantin Slominsky, man, that old Russian cat, mmm— but he's *good*. The best, man."

"He told me you played together once. A happy afternoon, he said."

"Hot dog! That *was* a time."

"He asked about a friend of yours. Wardell Lane was the name, I think. He wanted to know if Wardell ever made any more records. Konstantin said he had just the one."

Some of the fizz went out of Freddy, but he was still smiling. "I ain't seen Wardell in a long time," he said, ambling across the dressing room to the green silk screen and reaching for a shirt that was on a hanger. "He only made the one record."

"How come?"

"I don't rightly know," Freddy said, looking down, his enormous fingers deftly buttoning the shirt.

"Did he die?"

Freddy's look was sharp, wary.

I shrugged. "I'm just asking. I didn't mean to upset you. Konstantin and Vera—they're worried about him."

"Someone told them Wardell was dead?"

"Only Vera—Konstantin doesn't know. He's still wondering why Wardell never came back to see him."

"Circumstances," said Freddy, almost under his breath. He pulled on a pair of pants.

"Was he murdered?"

He slapped a tie around his throat, his fingers working the knot like a magician. "Who are you, mister? Why you askin' these questions?"

"Like I said, I'm an architect. I had another friend you knew. Beth Dyer."

Those big fingers stopped. Freddy was motionless, the wary look in his eyes replaced by a flicker of something else: terror. Then the fear was gone, and he reached for his jacket, thrusting his arms inside. Quickly he snapped shut the trumpet case. "Sure, I remember Beth," he said. "How is she?"

"She's dead, too."

Freddy blinked. "I'm sorry to hear that," he said. "I want to hear all about it. Maybe we can go get a drink. Someplace we can talk, you know what I'm saying?"

"Sure," I said.

"That's good. We'll do that. I'll tell you whatever you want to know. Will you excuse me for a moment?" He reached for the pale-blue phone on the dressing table and showed his short, stumpy teeth in another of those huge grins. "I need to call someone. A *lady*, you understand. Tell her I'll be a little late."

I waited for a minute or so outside the dressing room door, listening to the deep, reassuring rasp of Freddy's voice. I was thinking about where we could go, Freddy and I, someplace where we wouldn't be noticed. Not one of the big hotels, obviously. I remembered that dingy bar on Fremont Street, the place where Beth had walked out on me. It would do. Maybe Freddy would see some poetic justice in my taking him there.

Freddy's voice rumbled on, paused briefly, as if he were listening, and then began again. I must have waited a couple more minutes before suspicion began to nag. Wasn't this taking too long? I knocked on the door, calling: "Freddy?" No answer.

The room was empty but still filled with the fruity sound of Freddy's voice. The spools of a tape recorder were spinning in a drawer that had been pulled open in the dressing table. The Chinese silk screen in one corner had been pushed aside, revealing another door.

Clever Freddy.

I rushed through the door, into a dim, narrow corridor stacked with crates and beer kegs. The corridor ran for twenty yards or more before another door led back into the racket and bustle of the show room. I made a quick scan of the tables, seeing no sign of him, and walked briskly to the front of the casino. I didn't run. Anyone running in a Vegas casino was likely to find himself embraced by strong, unsympathetic arms. I hurried with a forced smile on my face.

Outside, a hot wind gusted the hair back from my face and a line of cabs stood waiting. Freddy was nowhere to be seen but on the other side of the Strip was a black Ford, an older model, its faded paintwork shining with a dull gleam beneath the neon, a man in a straw hat at the wheel: Lou Virgiel, not returned home after all, but here in Las Vegas, trailing Freddy Greene, presumably. He'd ignored my good advice; people rarely heed good advice, I've noticed. I jumped in a cab and ordered the driver to follow him and make it snappy. But we lost Virgiel, too, the Ford merging into the late night rush on Fremont Street, making a right turn, gone when we got there.

35

On arriving at the El Sheik, in the afternoon, Jackie had insisted on moving me and the entire Valentine crew to a different cabana, a larger space on the other side of the pool. "Away from the love nest, darling," she said, once the boys had changed into their swimming gear and scampered outside. "At least you haven't been fucking some young thing in this one." And then, with an acid smile, she added: "As far as I know."

It was two-thirty in the morning when I went in and the boys were asleep, snuggled in sleeping bags on the foldout sofa. I stopped to look at them, the way I did that night after I first met Beth Dyer. A thousand years ago, it seemed; less than two weeks in reality; almost an infinity in my own lifetime's terms. I felt tired and afraid, but seeing Ches and Bobby did me good. Bobby had his mouth wide open and was snoring like an ox. Ches, as usual, slept with his arms rigid by his side, like a tin soldier. They were side by side on the foldout sofa, safe in a structure that I'd built, human proof of how far I'd come since the war, evidence of a stability that seemed under threat. The hot desert wind rattled the windows as I locked the door and went through into the bedroom.

Jackie was alert and awake, dressed in black silk pajamas, leaning on one elbow with smoke rising from the cigarette burning in the corner of the ashtray beside her. The gold crucifix dangling from her neck grazed the pages of the book she was reading and she didn't look up. "You went to a show?"

"Eartha Kitt."

"How was Eartha?"

"Leonine," I said.

"You might have bothered to invite me," she said, but sounding chipper and buoyant, not angry. "I spent the whole night with Dad, and he's in a lousy mood. You know how he hates Las Vegas."

"He's staying?"

"For tomorrow's test. He wants to see the big bang."

That's right, I thought, they're letting off another bomb at the proving ground. Another of my swiftly designed, army-executed, and therefore painstakingly built, mock-suburban streets would turn to ashes. "I didn't think Joe gave a damn about what actually happens. Only who controls it, and who makes money out of it."

"Cynic," she said with an appreciative smile.

I kicked off my shoes and unbuttoned my shirt, unable to forget the fear, the momentary terror I'd seen in Freddy Greene's eyes. Why? What scared him so?

"This is going to sound like a weird question," I said to Jackie, "but what was I like when I met you?"

Jackie looked away from her book and sat up straight, plumping a pillow behind her. "You're right," she said, drawing on her cigarette. "It *is* a weird question."

"All the same, if you wouldn't mind."

"Is this a game?"

"I'm interested."

"Okay, I'll play for a minute," she said, raising her chin and blowing smoke at the ceiling before stabbing out the cigarette. "We met at a party, didn't we? You were standing on the other side of the room, about the only guy there not in uniform. But I knew you'd been in the war."

"How?"

"From your eyes. You were talking to a woman but you weren't paying attention. It made you attractive."

"Who was the woman?" I said, searching my memory, remembering no such person.

"Darling, I haven't a clue. I'd flown in from Hawaii that morning and I had a terrific tan and I wanted to get very drunk. You made me change my mind. I decided I wanted to get *laid*."

What I remembered myself about the party was that I'd been *too* careful. I'd just changed my name and was devising a future for myself. Jackie—young, attractive, and obviously well-bred, rich—had swum into my vision like a godsend, like providence itself. I'd felt at once that I needed to impress her, not a single false step. I'd talked big, about my plans, about forgetting the war. "There was nothing inside me. I was trying to tell myself that I wasn't afraid anymore. But I was."

"You didn't look it. You had ice in your eyes."

"I'm afraid now," I said. "It can all come crashing down. What if I *want* it to?"

She was amused. She'd seen my moments of self-dramatizing doubt, from time to time, and she didn't know this was different. As far as she was concerned, I was playing a character she understood and I wanted her to bring me into line, the way she had a score of times before. "Something's gotten into you, honey," she said, flapping her hand and reaching for her pack of filtered Camels. "You're talking like a guy in a French novel."

"I don't read French novels."

"But I do. And, believe me, the main guy always doubts himself. He's always scratching about, picking at the scab, searching for that pesky lint in his navel. Don't do it, darling. It's not worth it. Don't be a bore." She held out her cigarette, and I struck the match. "We know where we're going. All the way to Washington, and no regrets."

"I guess."

"I *know*."

I told her that I'd been out in the desert. "I saw the Slominskys. They're living in that house like prisoners. One of their daughters died. She had cancer."

"Life's cruel," Jackie said, not glib, not gloating, but with sympathy, the certainty of one who has been presented with evidence. Jackie had been young when I met her, scarcely in her twenties, but she'd already honed her skill at undercutting emotion. She'd always seemed tough beyond her years, not hard-boiled, but unreachable in some way. It was something I'd liked about her.

"That was nice, earlier," I said. "The fucking. Making love. We hadn't done that in a while."

"Do it with me more often. You don't have to travel. The spark's still here. For me, anyway."

I seized her hand. "Let's take the kids and buy a house someplace. London. Hawaii." It seemed plausible, somehow, right then, a path away from the mechanism and its champing jaws. "Just start again."

"Maurice!" she said, feigning the impatience that I knew would soon become real. "*Washington*, remember?"

"Right. Washington."

The lamp on the bedside table rocked a little in a draft, wobbling the shadows in the corner of the room. Glancing toward the closet, I half-expected to see Beth's dress, and her clean laundry hanging in its bag on the door, the way it had been in the other cabana. What happened to that stuff? I wondered with a stab of sadness. Taken by one of the maids, most likely.

I said softly, surprised by my own voice: "He's a murderer."

"What's that, darling? You're not making any sense."

"The woman who shot me—her name wasn't Mallory Walker. It was Beth Dyer. And she wasn't shooting at me. She was trying to kill Paul Mantilini."

Jackie's hand left mine and flew to the golden cross at the base of her throat. "That's the craziest thing I ever heard."

"He killed her boyfriend. A jazz player. And now he's killed her, too."

"Cut it out, Maurice."

"It's not pretty, even from a distance. And when you're up close, it's not pretty at all."

"I'm not hearing this," she said, and clamped her hands over her ears, a habit of defiance she'd retained from childhood, when she'd discovered it reduced her sister to tears.

"But it's true."

"I'm not listening."

"Most likely he didn't kill them himself. His goons did it. That's the way it works."

In her fury, which was genuine, she flung out her arm, and the diamond in her engagement ring struck and cut my lip. "Why say these things, Maurice? What do you expect to achieve?"

I told her I didn't know.

"Then stop. Don't ruin everything."

I took a blanket from the bottom of the closet, shut the bedroom door behind me, and threw myself down on the floor beside the kids. But I couldn't sleep. My mind *wouldn't stop*. I kept thinking about the look on Freddy Greene's face. What was he hiding?

36

$\mathcal{I}$t was the hottest September day in Las Vegas in recorded history, a long and dusty day, a brutal day. For me it began innocently enough, even if I guessed that it couldn't continue like that, swimming and horsing around with Ches and Bobby in the pool, and then back to the cabana. Jackie was already through with breakfast. We hadn't spoken, for fear, perhaps, that one of us might announce that the line had been drawn through our marriage; and then it would have been. Jackie gulped another cup of coffee, fortifying herself for something, kissed the boys, stopped in front of a mirror to fix her lipstick again, and said to me: "I'm running a few errands."

Fine, I thought, I've got a few errands of my own.

I went to see Will Rothschild. The *Las Vegas Press* had its offices, and Rothschild kept an apartment, downtown, crouched between City Hall and the bus and train depots, almost as if Rothschild realized that his grab for a slice of Las Vegas stood a chance of being knocked aside and had determined at the outset to hedge his bets, maximize his exits. The *Press* building was functional, a nondescript box sheathed in beige stucco, and when I swung the Studebaker into the parking lot, a Santa Fe freight train rumbled behind, the bright orange cars clacking, snaking.

"Air conditioning's on the blink, dear heart. Be prepared to cook," Rothschild said.

With an offer of his limp hand and a flash of his mean, rodent-like

teeth, he led me through a half-glass door marked PUBLISHER, EDITOR, RESI-
DENT GENIUS and threw himself in a swivel chair that tilted back alarm-
ingly, threatening to dump his lanky frame on the floor as he thrust out
his legs and pushed his feet through the forests of paper on his desk. Black
steel ballot boxes were stacked in the corner of the room, ready for the upcoming election—the boxes would be sent out to the polling stations and
then brought back here for the votes to be counted, Nevada's testament to
the independence and integrity—or convenient corruptibility—of the *Press*.

"How did you enjoy Boss Booth, dear heart?"

"Not much."

"He's spitting about you. 'Ambitious asshole. Creepy little bootlicker.
Jumped-up son of a no-good two-timing whore.' These were some of his
kinder words, I believe. Such vivid language, these old Nevada types.
Positively Shakespearean." He clasped his hands behind his head.
"Now—what can I do you for?"

I told him I needed to speak to Freddy Greene.

"The trumpet player?"

"That's the guy."

"Nothing simpler." Without taking his feet off the desk, and without looking, either, he reached behind him for one of his many phones,
which he then settled in his lap. "We'll get his manager on the blower.
Only take a tick."

I told him I didn't want to do that; I wanted to know where Freddy
Greene was staying.

"Ah." He returned the phone to its original place. "In Spooktown, in
Ghosttown. But you knew that."

"Sure," I said with a nod. "I need the precise address."

A tough curiosity glittered in Rothschild's eyes. The wary newsman
in him had been aroused. "You're a civilized fellow. Why on earth would
you want to go there, mingling with the darkies?"

"Does it matter?"

"Actually, probably, yes. Probably rather a lot actually."

He clasped his hands behind his head, smiling, waiting, and I decided to take a chance.

I said, "Let me tell you a story."

"Goody gumdrops. Will likes a story."

"A hypothetical story."

"Better yet. Is anything more enticing than imagination at play?"

"In this story a black musician comes to town. Let's say his name is Wardell. Let's say he's a saxophone player. And let's say he has an older friend, a trumpet player, sort of a father figure. A mentor, if you like."

"Like Freddy Greene?"

"Hypothetically."

"Oh, of course, dear heart. *Very* hypothetically."

"Now, this Wardell, sadly, he's a hothead. Brash, full of piss and vinegar. He gets into trouble. Somehow. He winds up dead. In the story."

"I see," said Rothschild, his dark eyes steady. "It's a murder mystery."

"I guess. And in the story the black saxophone player has a girlfriend, a young white girl. She loves him very much."

"It's *Romeo and Juliet* now, my favorite." Rothschild frowned. "Or do I mean *Othello*?"

"In my story the white girl harbors a grudge. And one day she decides to do something about it. She comes back to town and tries to kill the man who killed her friend. But she gets it wrong, and hits someone else instead. In the story. And so she gets murdered herself."

The swivel chair creaked, and Rothschild lurched slowly forward. "Would this story, I wonder, have anything to do with a man who's planning a crack at the Senate? With a man who, very carelessly, gets shot in the head?"

"Maybe."

"You interest me strangely, old bird." He walked over to the door, opened it a crack, shut it, closed his fingers around a key, which he then turned with a click. "This reminds me of a story I once heard myself. Wouldn't it be rather amusing if our two stories were connected? Were, in fact, a part of the same story?"

I said it would be a riot.

"*My* story takes place about five years ago."

"In 1951?"

"Spot on, dear heart. And it happens in a town not unlike this one. A frontier town where pretty much anything goes. Perfect setting for a chap like me. A town that is run by certain people with certain connections who constantly deny they have those connections. It's a little game they play, although they're awfully serious about it. They're like the fellows who come to do the windows—very concerned with keeping everything clean."

Rothschild was in his chair again, the hinges creaking as he stretched his hands back behind his head. "Five years ago. A lifetime in terms of this frontier town. Almost an epoch. Back then, in my *extremely* hypothetical story, there was a bit of a struggle for power. Isn't there always? Causes such a lot of trouble, doesn't it, power? Makes you wonder why people are so very interested in it."

He smiled, nothing more than the briefest flash of his ferrety teeth. Of course, he seemed to say, you and I, Maurice, men of the world, we *know* why everybody wants power. It makes things go. Power, not goodwill, not democracy, not love. Especially not that.

"One of the chaps who's in charge of some of these other connected chaps, one of the big chiefs, has an idea. It concerns the growth of our notional town. He wants it to happen fast. He has grand plans. Lots more casinos. Big new hotels. 'Oh,' say his friends, the other big chiefs, maybe beginning to get the idea that our man fancies himself the biggest chief of all. 'And where's the money coming from for all this?' 'Well, I have an idea about that,' he tells them."

Hearing some disturbance outside the office door, Rothschild rose to check. Satisfied that there was nothing, he returned to his perch, sticking out his long legs and big feet. "Our man has a particular friend or two, high-ups, big-wigs in a very powerful trade union. These other people, well, they have lots of *trucks*—very useful for getting about the place. And a large pension fund, very large indeed, *gratifyingly* large. Enormous, indeed. Untold millions of smackeroos."

"The Teamsters?"

"*Sssshh!*" Rothschild pressed a languid finger to his lips. "But, yes, in our story, hypothetically, this one big white chief, the man who wants to be the biggest chief of all, makes a deal with these union-leader persons. A very private deal. It's all very delicate, strictly on the q.t., extremely hush-hush. *Comprenez-vous?* They will divert large amounts of the pension money to our frontier town for the building of swanky new hotels designed by fancy young architects—like yourself, Maurice, if I may be so bold. In exchange, our great leader agrees to let his friends handle distribution of certain specific substances through several states. Narcotics. Heroin, actually. They can use those thousands of trucks at their disposal, you see. Very handy indeed. In our *story*."

Restless, he stood once more, crossing to the watercooler, where he filled a Dixie cup and drank, then crushed the cup into a ball, which he tossed in the direction of the steel ballot boxes. His voice came from far back in his throat and he had a wistful, almost dreamy look in his dark, small eyes. "There was one place, however, that the trucker people were *not* allowed to bring their skag-bearing vehicles: the frontier town that our big chief sought to control, the dear, young place where only such clean and lively fun as gambling and whoring was permitted. That was another clear part of the deal, and our friend assured his friends that, naturally, nobody would be selling said substance on his turf. Marijuana, weed, fine. Keep the natives happy. Heroin, no. Why? Because he wouldn't allow it. So everything seemed very clear and tickety-boo, didn't it, dear heart?"

"Until something went wrong," I ventured.

"Indeed, something *did* go wrong. Not a big thing, but an irritating thing, and at a dangerous time. While all this delicate negotiation was going on about very many *millions* of dollars and positively *hundreds* of trucks bulging with dope, our leader discovers that the very thing his friends promised him would never, under any circumstances, happen, is indeed going on. Heroin is shooting around like billy-o, right under his nose, he discovers, in his paradise of a frontier town. It's *awfully* embarrassing."

"He has to do something about it."

"In the *story*. In the story the chaps who've gone against his express edict are dealt with in some stupendously nasty and violent way. Very,

very much *pour encourager les autres*. A principle that our man very, very much believes in. A black musician, a saxophone player, has somehow got himself tangled up in all this. Naturally, he's gone. *Pfft!* His girl-friend, too."

"What happened to them?"

"Not sure, dear heart. Nothing good. Well, it was a story all right, wasn't it? Not one that the boys in blue were interested in. Nor this boy at the *Las Vegas Press*, for that matter. I mean, I was interested, I am a *reporter*, but I couldn't print anything, now could I? Of course not. Quite out of the question. Something more important came up that week. Maybe Mickey Rooney was in town. I think that must have been it. Yes, dear old Mickey."

He stood at the watercooler, his long fingers drumming against the plastic. He was frowning, but he still looked supercilious, aloof, an art-ful dodger. "But here's where our stories don't quite match. Because in my story the girl, the young innocent, she was killed, too. Shot twice in the head, if I'm not mistaken. Which I find tends to dampen the im-pulse for vengeance, don't you agree?"

I crossed the room and stood beside him at the cooler, helping my-self to a cup. "Where did you hear all this?"

"My story? Here and there. A little bird who flew in from San Quentin dropped some of these crumbs in my lap. As if I wanted them. But stories do have a way of sticking around, don't they? And making one thirsty, it seems." A bubble rose from the depths of the cooler and burst, rippling across the surface of the water and wobbling the plastic sides. "Anyway, it's just a story, and we're not *talking*, are we, dear heart? Not talking at all, not having a proper conversation. Just gossiping and rabbiting on, the way Johnson did with his young friend Boswell. Only *chatting*."

Rothschild's smile was self-amused. He wore an eau de cologne that smelled tartly of lemon. His cheeks were pink from the heat, and he was sweating, but I saw how this languid and theatrical Englishman might stand up well under pressure. He was an adventurer who watched his back and made sure he knew the rules. He knew *which* casino he was playing in, and at *what* tables, and he had no intention of using most of the information he collected. He knew he couldn't, not if he wished to keep his English head attached to his English neck. Maybe he planned to write his memoirs one day, from the safety of some Cotswold retreat. Meanwhile he watched and gathered, plotting his own advancement, living by his wits and playing the fool.

"Do you still want that address?" he said. "There are a few places where these chaps usually stay. I can dig up the details. If you still insist."

"Please," I said.

"What's your interest here, dear heart? If I may ask."

"Like I said, I want to talk to Freddy Greene. I think he can fill in some more of this hypothetical story."

He unlocked a filing cabinet, his long fingers flicking through a row of buff folders before he pulled one out. "I'd watch my step, if I were you, Maurice," he said, uncapping a fountain pen and writing on an index card in an elegant, flowing hand. "People love a good story, don't they? But try to make sure this one has a happy ending."

37

*I*t's your mother's birthday, Nickie," Paul Mantilini says, sitting down to breakfast in his suite at the El Sheik. A gray silk dressing gown decorated with silver dragons, an ostentatious garment, is sashed about his waist. His barber, who also delivered breakfast, part of the daily ritual, departed a few minutes ago, and his cheeks tingle from the shave. His mane of silver hair is slick, groomed. He smears butter on a bread roll. "I don't know how old she'd have been, because she lied about her age. I could never get the truth out of her. Like it mattered. But she always hated it, that she was born on the thirteenth."

"You never told me that," Nick says, pulling a chair across the rug, sitting down.

"I didn't?"

"Nope," says Nick, pouring himself a coffee, spilling a little, and licking the hot liquid from the back of his hand. "Damn that jug," he says.

"It's from England. Eighteenth-century, Georgian."

"Damn thing never pours right," Nick says. "For *your* birthday I'm making a trip to the appliance store."

"I *like* this jug. And I was talking about your mother. She hated to walk on cracks in the sidewalks. And in Manhattan there are a lot of sidewalks. You know what I'm saying? She skipped about like a kangaroo."

Mantilini sizes up a fly that has strayed into the room and is beating against the window. Drawing himself up straight, silently, he shoots out one of his big, scarred hands. He shakes his fist next to his ear and opens his fingers, not watching while the fly crawls across his palm and onto his outstretched pinkie. The fly buzzes away. "She had magic numbers. Everything had to be a five or a seven. She liked gray and green. Those were her favorite colors, her lucky colors. She gave me this dressing gown. That was one of *her* birthday presents."

Mantilini wipes his hands on a napkin, working the linen between each finger. From a blue-and-white china saucer he selects a wedge of lemon and squeezes the juice over a plate of smoked salmon; he pauses a moment, savoring the comingled odors of citrus and ocean, then forks the pink flesh into his mouth. "She said a show would always go well on a Tuesday. She thought if she'd been on the *Titanic* it never would have hit that iceberg. She believed in charts and astrologers, and old women who took her dough and stared into her hand."

"She was weak," Nick says, his blue eyes restless, his knee bouncing, his muscular frame tense in the chair that seems too small for him. He touches the tip of his nose.

Nick lacks poise, Mantilini thinks, he has no patience. Mantilini has watched his headstrong son learn a lot, come on well in these last years. But there's still a way to go. There are certain instincts that Nick lacks, and others with which he is too richly endowed.

"She was an artist. She had her own special point of view," Mantilini says. "But, yeah, she was a little crazy."

Nick laughs his blunt, locker-room laugh.

Is this what you get, Mantilini thinks, when you send your kid to one of those fancy eastern colleges? In his son his own qualities of subtlety and patience seem markedly diluted. Or maybe they're waiting to grow to full strength, he thinks. Nick always wants the big effect, the quick result, Mantilini tells himself. But, then, who was he to talk, with his dream of a whole new city in the desert?

"Never laugh about your mother, Nickie," Mantilini says, realizing that he invited the laughter. "She was a remarkable woman. Bless her."

He takes another roll, ripping it with a swift twist of the hands.

Popping the warm bread into his mouth, he observes the fly that he let go; dazed, it beats against the glass. "She'd be proud to see you now. I mean it," he says.

Beneath the table Nick's knee goes on bouncing, sending vibrations through Mantilini's chair and into his spine.

"Here's to her, Nickie. On her birthday," he says, raising his coffee cup and waiting until Nick follows suit. Whereupon father and son chink cups. "Okay," says Mantilini, setting down his coffee, dusting crumbs off his hands. "Down to business. How did it go with Senator Booth last night."

Nick snaps to attention, makes his report. "Boss ate a big dinner. Then he gambled. He made seven straight passes before he crapped out. We let him take the five thousand anyway. He took a couple of girls with him to his suite." Nick regards his father with a sly, happy smile. "Pops, I think he went to bed a happy and satisfied man."

Mantilini, leaning back, drums his fingers on the arms of his chair. "Did he eat breakfast yet?"

Nick checks his watch. "He called the kitchen thirty-two minutes ago. Ordered a pot of coffee, no milk, a glass of orange juice, and two soft-boiled eggs. The Boss seems to be worried about his weight. And I guess the girls have gone."

"Or Boss is starving 'em," Mantilini says, buttering himself another piece of roll. He observes the fly, battering against the windowpane. His hand snakes out with a napkin, crushing the insect. "He's a mean old man, don't let's forget that." He sips at his coffee. "I'm having lunch with him, right?"

"Then he's meeting with the mayor."

For a moment Mantilini regards one of the silver dragons on his dressing gown. Almost as if taking counsel, it seems. He steeples his fingers and presses them to his mouth.

"He'll be back from the mayor's office by four. He'll make some calls. He'll maybe nap a while. He'll probably want a massage. See that the bell captain is warned and a masseur is ready. A guy, Nickie, not a girl."

"Got it."

"I don't want Boss shooting his wad too early, spoiling his fun. The phone calls, the massage—that takes us to six, maybe six-thirty. He'll probably want to hit the tables. Make sure he wins again."

"Got it, Pops. And then on to the Colonial House and the whores who make Boss so happy."

"I don't want you in the car with him, Nickie."

"I know, Pops. We went over this already."

Mantilini pushes back his chair and stands up, drawing tight the sash on his dressing gown. "We'll go over it again, just to be sure." Leaning over the table, Mantilini pours himself another cup of coffee. The fly, imprisoned within the napkin on the table, buzzes once more, its dying spasm. "Kluphager goes with Boss Booth in the car to the Colonial House. You meet with your attorney, drink a couple of martinis, get some dinner."

Nick rolls his shoulders, rubs at the stiffness in his neck. "While you fly to L.A. I've got the ticket here in my pocket. We discussed it a dozen times."

He's easily bored, always has been, Mantilini thinks, it's a weakness and we'll have to work on it.

"I know, Nickie. We did. Probably more than a dozen times," he says. "But something just came up that I need your help with. Maybe it's gonna change things. I don't know."

Nick joins his father at the window and together they look out over the Strip and the desert, their empire, where twisted trees and cacti rise from the rock-littered floor of the scrub. Real badlands, bleak, flat, menacing. A green thicket of trees in the distance marks the only visible watering hole. The Joshua trees have their arms flung out like drunken hitchhikers.

"It's Valentine," Mantilini says. "His wife just came to see me. Let's see if I can put this gently. She was *upset*. You've probably never seen Jackie that way—she's got a helluva temper."

"What's Valentine done now?" says Nick, who's never liked the architect. Nick almost wishes he could get over it, but he still gets a kick out of his father's trust, his father's belief in the guy's talent.

"He told Jackie I murdered his friend. The girl who shot him. And her name wasn't Mallory Walker. It really *was* Beth Dyer."

"What?"

"Her boyfriend was killed and she was out for revenge. Used Valentine, got close, but hit him instead of me. That's what Valentine's saying."

"He's such a jerk."

"Maybe. But he's a *useful* jerk," Mantilini says. "I was right. I *did* recognize her. But you said she was dead. You were so sure. How come? We need to talk about that."

"It was Cohen and Wallace," Nick says with his usual confidence.

"Beth called them 'the Ravens.' She thought they looked like evil birds or something."

"Is that so?" Nick says. "They were behind the drug thing. I told them to clean up their own mess—fast. Then I dealt with them."

"And Wardell was a part of their mess. Is that it?"

"Must have been."

"You told me you sorted this out, Nickie."

"I did, Pops."

"They *killed* him, for chrissakes. That wasn't on the agenda. And she was in the way—so they killed *her*, too?"

"That's how it was, I guess."

"You *guess*? Except obviously they failed. They didn't even do that right, Cohen and Wallace. The Ravens. And now we have another situation, just like five years ago, just when we don't need one. *Shit!*"

Mantilini's hand sweeps upward, a gesture unusual in its suddenness, and Nick steps back, fearing a blow. Once, when he was a kid, he saw his father batter and stomp a man to pulp, and now he braces himself, waiting for the hurricane. But Mantilini smooths his hair, scratches his jaw, letting his anger subside. In a way, Nick finds this unearthly self-control even more frightening. Usually it signals trouble ahead, for somebody.

"I'm sorry, Dad." Nick catches himself, realizing he's used the giveaway, the word of his insecure childhood. "I screwed up."

Nick sees the storm flicker across his father's face. But Mantilini says, "You did okay, Nickie, don't worry about it." He reaches out and touches his son gently on the cheek. "Besides, what are kids for? I guess I didn't give you enough fire trucks when you were a kid or something."

Nick tries a smile, looks down at his shoes. "What are we going to do, Pops?"

"Take care of this my way," Mantilini says. "Carefully. And make sure Valentine doesn't hurt himself. That's the last thing we need right now."

38

I'd never been to the Westside before. You could spend a white life-time in Vegas without needing to venture there. And I never did figure out why they called it the Westside. It was north of the downtown Fremont area, and it was east of the Strip; it didn't seem to be west of anywhere, except west of everywhere you might want to be. This was the other side of glitzy, anything-goes Vegas, a sore, unlooked-at appendage, a shantytown, a ramshackle ghetto of unpaved roads and honky-tonks and shacks without plumbing, alongside such recent additions as tract-style bungalows, a school, and a golf course—some of the advantages, for better or worse, of suburban middle-class America, some of the bland, shallow amenities of that prosperous decade, the 1950s: *Life* living. You reached this area by passing through an unlit concrete tunnel; you went, literally, to the other side of the railroad tracks.

Rothschild had given me three addresses. The first was in a neighborhood of old frame houses with sunken roofs, blistered shutters, and dusty yards that were fenced against the desert; my destination was a sagging bungalow with a dog-pen at the side. As soon as I got out of the Studebaker, a one-eyed German shepherd started barking. The dog wasn't inside the pen; nor was it on a leash. It growled, showing its yellowed teeth.

A tall skinny black man came out of the house while I stood with my hand on the chain-link gate. He was gaunt, perspiring, in his twenties, with shaved hair that was already peppered with gray. The dog licked his hand. "What you want?"

"I'm looking for Freddy Greene."

"You know Freddy?"

"Sure. Is he here?"

"Wouldn't tell you if he was," he said, and spat in the dirt.

"Hell of a day," I said. "This heat's murder."

No response.

"Do you know where I can find him?"

Nothing.

I asked the guy how long he'd lived in Las Vegas—maybe he'd worked for Basic Magnesium in Henderson during the war, making the fiery materials we dropped over Germany?

"The fuck you know about it?" he said, rebuffing my clumsy attempt at small talk. I guess I was being given a lesson in campaigning. "Git off my land," he said, and loped back inside, banging shut the door behind him.

The dog looked at me in a lopsided way, daring me to try.

I called out: "I'll only take a minute of your time."

The skinny guy's face looked around the door. With his slow, stooping, long-strided walk, he came back down the path, and I caught the tobacco and stale-onion reek of his breath as he said: "You stupid or something?"

Clearly this wasn't going to be easy.

I struck out, again, at the second place on Rothschild's list, one of the newer hotels; the clerk said he'd heard of Freddy Greene but hadn't seen him in more than a year, and I was turning away from the desk when I saw Nick Mantilini coming toward me across the lobby, a swaggering figure dressed in tan slacks and a sports shirt of bright blue silk. His hair was thick and glossy as fur. He wore sunglasses and sweat beaded his tanned jawline. This was no chance meeting, I knew, and my heart skipped a beat.

"A little premature to be out chasing votes, wouldn't you say?" he said, cracking his gum, taking off his sunglasses to reveal those nervy and unnerving eyes. "You don't have to work this hard to get elected in

Nevada. In your case, Maurice, you won't have to work at all. We'll take care of everything. So what are you doing here? In the Wild West?"

Nick's smile was as cocky and self-satisfied as always, but behind the nonchalant act I sensed something else, a tense concentration. "My father knows what you think," he said.

"Oh really," I was aware that I was blinking. "About what?"

"About what happened to Mallory Walker. Or Beth Dyer. Or whatever the hell her name was. Dad knows you think he killed her and her boyfriend."

My heart did more than pause. It hit my boots. That bastard Will Rothschild, I thought—he must have picked up the phone the minute I left his office.

I was wrong about that, as it turned out, but how was I to suspect that my own wife would have taken it into her head to inform the great man of my suspicions?

Nick went on: "Dad had nothing to do with it. He wants me to tell you that. He also wants to talk to you. Shall we go?"

"You've come to take me in, is that it? By force, if need be?" I said. "Got the cuffs yourself, Nick, or do you have a couple of goons outside?"

"You're dumb," Nick said, shaking his head. "I don't know what my father sees in you."

"A lot of money, Nickie. One of the girls at the Sheik told me you've got a dick like a broken pretzel. It's still got to be twice the size of your brain if you don't recognize that what your father sees in me is a dollar sign."

Nick showed his movie-star teeth in a smile of unexpected pleasure. Nor was this the only surprise he had in store. "I guess you're not coming with me," he said.

"Not unless you insist."

"Which I'm not going to do," he said, grinning, staring at me with those icy-blue eyes of his.

"Is that it?"

"That's it," he said, donning his sunglasses. "We're not butchers. You've got some funny ideas, Maurice, you know? Take care."

From the hotel door I watched Nick stride across the parking lot, vault into his Cadillac, a convertible the same brilliant blue as his shirt, and pull out with a spray of gravel and a screech of whitewalled tires. I must have waited ten minutes, leaning against the glass of the door, expecting him to come back, but he didn't. What was *that* all about, I wondered. I sat in the hotel diner for the next thirty minutes, trying to figure it out. Nick's smooth manners had unsettled me. I was both relieved and spooked. What if Nick was telling the truth, I thought. What if Mantilini had nothing to do with Wardell's murder? Or Beth's? Had I jumped in haste to the wrong conclusion? Had I seen him in that role because a part of me was secretly kicking against his plans for me in politics? Had I incorrectly identified the area of my mistrust? It occurred to me that, for some reason, the Mantilinis were allowing me to go on, perhaps *wanted* me to continue my investigation.

From my pocket I took Rothschild's notecard and scored a line through the two places that I'd visited; one address still remained. I finished my coffee, went to the Studebaker, and drove through the Westside to a wide street and a three-story red brick hotel, an older building, close by the railroad tracks and across the street from a funeral home that had a lofty white billboard and an immaculate square lawn, the best-watered patch of green in the whole neighborhood. A gang of kids played in the street, using a wad of newspaper bound up in tape for a ball, shouting and running, oblivious to the heat that sapped my energy and nagged like a headache. I parked, slipped one of the kids a buck to watch the car, and, with my tie loosened and my jacket over my shoulder, walked up the broad stone steps, cracked and sparkling with mica, that led to the hotel doors.

Inside the lobby a fan creaked on the ceiling, chopping the heat. Bedraggled palms rose out of cracked pots. Spittoons of pitted and blackened brass sent a clear message: Don't look inside me. Seeing no elevator, I realized the structure was older than I'd presumed: at one time it had been the railway hotel, I gathered, and dated from the 1890s or early 1900s—classical antiquity in Vegas terms. The site of brawls and gunfights, no doubt. A giant of a man, dressed only in white undershorts, hung over the stair rail. He studied me hard through bloodshot eyes before turning away.

The desk clerk wore owlish, horn-rimmed spectacles and a vest of green brocade. "I'm here to see a guest," I said, giving the guy my best smile. "Freddy Greene. Is he in?"

"I'll check," he said, showing me his vest's satin back while he hunched over a phone. With a surprised, slightly alarmed smile he turned, stood to attention, and said, "Third floor. Fremont Suite."

Upstairs the place was a maze, a fire-trap, a warren of stairs and pinched, high corridors to which the stench of urine and disinfectant clung more tenaciously that did the faded, threadbare carpets; these seemed to shift and crumble underfoot, as if given spring by decades of packed-down dirt and crumbs. On the third floor a radio blared jazz, some old Count Basie number with stomp and swing. The Fremont Suite was down on the left, facing the hotel front. The white-painted door had peeling letters in gilt. I knocked, got no answer, then tried the door.

The room was square, crowned with heavy mahogany furniture that seemed too big and chunky. A chandelier dangled from the center of the ceiling. In the mirror above the fireplace my face looked bright and falsely hopeful, as if I had every right to march on in.

"Freddy?"

I was trying to figure out how to make my pitch. He was scared, as the previous night had proved. But he had a story to tell, secrets to disclose, if only I could unlock them.

His trumpet case was on a rolltop desk alongside the typewriter with a sheet of paper twisted in at an angle.

Good, I thought, he hasn't skipped town yet.

A door led to a small kitchen with gray cupboards and a groaning refrigerator. A pack of Cheerios had spilled on the floor. On the carving board stood a half-loaf of bread, a melting butter pat, and an opened jar of raspberry jam with a fly buzzing inside. I touched my fingers against the aluminium coffee pot—still warm.

I went back into the main room. In one corner was a tall, high-backed chair, its cushions sprouting horsehair. A book lay on the chair, open, and Freddy, or someone, had underlined a passage: "And remember you don't have to be a complete fool in order to succeed. Play the game, but don't believe in it—that much you owe yourself. Even if it lands you in a strait-jacket or a padded cell. Play the game, but play it your own way—part of the time at least. Play the game, but raise the ante, my boy. Learn how it operates, learn how *you* operate."

In the bedroom the drapes were open and the rumpled bed was unmade. The closet, its door open, revealed a neat array of suits and shirts; shoes buffed to a high polish were on parade beneath them. On the dresser was a hairbrush set of ornate silver. A robe lay on the floor. A few seconds went by before I located the source of a *tick-ticking*, a gold watch lying facedown on the bedside table. A brown medicine bottle had been knocked over; its cap was off and through its open neck pink goo dripped to the carpet.

The bathroom door swung open and I faced him. He was squashed, doubled up in the bath, chin on his chest, legs hanging over the side of the porcelain in their shabby pants. Blood caked the bashed-in side of his head, mixed with flecks of white bone. Blood had congealed in a shiny crimson pool at the cleft of his clean-shaven, boyish chin. His staring eyes were filled with red, as if yet more blood were leaking out. A baseball bat with blood and hair sticking to it was wedged in his lap. I bent down and felt for his artery but found no pulse.

It was Lou Virgiel, the private eye; he was dead.

Gagging, I lurched toward the sink, turned the tap, swilled my mouth, and splashed my face. Water ran down the back of my neck in a cool trickle. Poor bastard, I thought.

A voice said: "Find what you're looking for?"

He was leaning against the door, a stout, stocky guy with a boozy face, sweating heavily inside a sports coat that was several years old and a size or two too small. His open-necked shirt showed reddish hair and freckles at the top of his chest, and a gun bulged beneath his jacket. Everything about him said cop—Irish, Vegas, corrupt cop.

"Who the hell are you?" I said.

He pushed himself off the door with an evil look, but then his partner appeared, balding, fingering his mustache, with his badge hanging over the breast pocket of his shirt, and a bored look in his racoon eyes. It was the cop who'd shown me the wreck of the Porsche. He quickly whispered in the other's ear.

"You're Maurice Valentine?" said the Irish cop, leaning against the door again.

I said that was right.

"You're some kind of a politician."

This, too, I confirmed: *some kind of a politician*. He probably knew better than me.

"You work for Paul Mantilini?"

Ah, he had it now: the holy trinity. He didn't like it, but he was going to have to let me walk.

"I guess you don't know about this guy," he said, motioning toward the corpse. "You never saw him before."

I was thinking of what Lou Virgiel had told me that morning back in Amboy. His mild appearance had been deceptive. He'd been an infantryman in the war, was wounded in Italy, won medals out the wazoo. When I asked how he became a private eye he'd smiled, pleased that I was interested. "When I got home, guys with thirty missions over Tokyo were working as busboys. I tried to be a cop for a while. It didn't take. So here I am." He'd been stubborn and reckless, no sap, but a regretful optimist, a man who'd seen the very worst in people and wished he didn't continue to hope for the best. I'd liked him, on that brief acquaintance.

I said, "His name was Lou Virgiel. He was a private eye. But I guess you know that already."

"Get out of my sight," the cop said.

I wasn't prepared to do that. "Where's Freddy Greene?"

"We're trying to do you a favor, Mr. Valentine," the cop said. "May I politely suggest that you get the fuck out of here?"

"Did you arrest him?"

It was the one with the racoon eyes who said: "We're *questioning* him."

"He didn't do this. The guy plays trumpet, not baseball."

"That's what he says," the first cop said. "Maybe we know better."

"I sincerely doubt that," I said with a smile. "I want to see him."

The cop didn't like it, not even a little. But what was he going to do? I was some kind of a politician, and I worked for Paul Mantilini.

39

They had Freddy in a holding tank, with his fists cuffed and his ankles chained—for his own safety, they said—though no charge had been filed. A uniformed deputy worked the key and opened the gate, letting me into a narrow space where Freddy sat on a woollen blanket on a bench on one side; the steel john was in a corner on the other. The walls were streaked with dried excrement. A powerful disinfectant fought a losing battle against the stench. The concrete floor was scratched and cracked, and flies circled around the meshed bulb on the ceiling. The air was fetid, oppressive, bringing the bile back to my throat. It must have been over a hundred degrees in that cell.

"I'm getting you out of here."

"How the hell are you going to do that?" Freddy said, his round face filled with anger and dismay. "They won't let me make no phone call."

"So I heard," I said. "I made a couple myself."

I sat beside him, making no attempt to talk until the deputy came back, unchained Freddy's feet, and unlocked the cuffs. Freddy hunched forward, rubbing his wrists, working the circulation back into those famous hands, glancing toward the open cell door with disbelief, like someone who'd been in this situation before and knew better than to hope.

The Irish cop was at the front desk, filling out the paperwork. The loose bags of his boozer's face reddened a little. "You're a lucky guy,

Freddy. Your friend's got juice." Reluctantly, he offered me his hand. "Mr. Valentine, sir—it was a pleasure."

"Thanks for your help, Detective," I said, not wishing to crow, asking myself what the attorney I'd called had said to this guy; whatever, it had worked a treat, almost uncannily well. I wondered, then, if the cop had taken it into his own head to contact Mantilini, but didn't dwell on the thought. I had Freddy to worry about, and he was turning into truculent freight.

"Don't give me no bullshit about how I owe you now," Freddy said, stony and mad, in the passenger seat of the Studebaker. In the rush of his relief, whatever fear he'd felt in the lockup had turned to anger, and that anger was directed at me. "I don't owe you dick."

I had to sit it out. Freddy would come around. I hoped.

"You hungry? You want to get something to eat. A steak, maybe." This was a cheap shot, I knew, but I could almost hear Freddy's plumbing begin to gurgle. "A couple of baked potatoes with butter and sour cream. Some greens. A few beers."

"You don't play fair, mister. I want to eat, all right, but I sure as hell don't want to eat with *you*."

"I think I need to get out of Vegas for an hour or so," I said. "What'd you think?"

"Let me out of the goddamned car."

I booted down hard on the gas, taking us out toward Indian Springs, to a diner I knew, a family joint, not much more than a shack, but clean and well lit, with wooden booths and an air-conditioning unit that sat like a tank in one wall and seemed actually to work. In silence, sipping at a glass of water, I watched Freddy go through one steak and then another, chewing deliberately and with occasional grunts, heaping mustard and ketchup and spinach and potato onto his fork along with the meat, washing them down with Tecate beer so cold the condensation trickled down the brown glass of the bottles and puddled on the table. From time to time he cocked an ear toward the jukebox, hearing some new tune, or something different in an old one, leaning his head to one side, ignoring his food for a moment, listening with the wonder of someone who was still a fan, with the wide-awake concentration of an expert.

Freddy was starting to regain his footing. For a while, back there in the cell, he'd thought the bottom was dropping out of his world. I knew the feeling.

"I still ain't talking to you," he said.

A black sergeant from the Signal Corps came up with a camera, asking Freddy for a picture and an autograph. With a broad, stumpy-toothed smile, Freddy threw an arm around the sergeant's shoulder, handed me the camera, and demanded that I do the honors. They talked about Billie Holliday, Adlai Stevenson, and Jackie Robinson's retirement. When the soldier was gone, Freddy selected a piece of bread, mopped the gravy from his plate, finished his beer, plunked down the bottle, and belched contentedly.

"I'm ready," he said.

"That was quite a trick you pulled last night in your dressing room," I said. "You're a regular Houdini. What are you so afraid of?"

"Take me back."

I made no mention of the strings I'd pulled. Nor did I plan to let Freddy off the hook. We left the diner and I drove us further out into the desert. I pulled off the road, guiding the Studebaker to the top of a rise. Freddy sat rigid and unbending, staring through the windshield at the scrub, the broiling sand, the Joshua trees, the shadows of the distant mountains. He looked at that desert as if he hated it. Or me, more likely. Circumstances bring unintended friends and enemies in this life. I didn't imagine that Freddy would admire or thank me for what I was trying to do. But I was set on my course.

"The dead guy in your bathtub was a private eye, working out of Oregon. His name was Lou Virgiel. Did you know that?"

Freddy's face was a mask, impassive.

"He was looking for a woman married to a friend of his. She disappeared a few months back. Upped and left without a word." I pictured Lou Virgiel, telling me all this, snapping a toothpick, sipping at his coffee, brushing the hair out of his eyes; he'd been busy as a lizard. And I wondered again, what *caused* that departure, what was the trigger? I thought of the scrapbooks that Luis Barragan had found, the files of material about me. "Her married name was Speedwell. You and I know her as Beth Dyer."

Freddy couldn't stop himself: he turned his head a fraction, then snapped it back, straight ahead.

"That's news to you, isn't it? The part about Beth having been married. When did you last see her?"

He didn't say a word.

"Did Virgiel speak to you?"

"Damned fool was looking for me all over town," Freddy burst out. "Came to see me in my dressing room, the way you did. Wasn't as smooth as you. I kicked him out right away. Then, this morning—I eat my breakfast, go to church, and the sucker's lying dead in my bathroom when I get back."

"What time was this?"

"Eleven-fifteen, eleven-thirty, something like that. Then the cops show up. Man, those boys licked their lips. Thought they'd got me but *good*. They was gettin' ready to throw away the key."

"Who killed him?"

"I ain't got a clue."

"You didn't see anybody? Hear something."

"Nuthin'."

I had my own ideas, of course. Having learned that I suspected him of murder, Mantilini had tracked my footsteps, guessed my moves, and some of his people had gotten to Freddy Greene's hotel suite before me. But why kill Virgiel?

"What had Lou found out? What was worth beating him to death for?"

"The hell should I know?" Freddy said, but his eyes wobbled and flickered like crazy searchlights.

"You're a lousy liar, Freddy."

"The fuck do I care? You ain't hearing anything from me."

"Tell me about Wardell, then." With a reluctant Freddy starting to open up a little, I was anxious to leave no pause, to keep the conversation going. "How did you guys meet?"

"I ain't talkin' about him."

"Give me *something*."

I was hot, tired, drained, angry. The desperation in my voice was real and took Freddy by surprise. He turned toward me.

"Talk to me about your friend," I said. "*Remember* him—the way he'd want to be remembered. That's the least we can hope for, isn't it? Or maybe it's a big thing, after all. To be thought of with kindness when we're dead."

"I met him in Oklahoma City, before the war," Freddy said. His eyes were no longer hard, seemed almost relieved to show the sorrow, the sadness, the warmth of memory, too, that lay beneath the anger. "He was this skinny kid trying to blow on a horn held together with rubber bands. He was maybe sixteen then. I didn't think he'd amount to nuthin'."

"You were wrong?"

"Man—was I ever." His smile was wistful. "Next time I saw him was in the war, in France, winter of '44. That winter was colder than a motherfucker. I was flying around in a plane with Marlene Dietrich. Can you credit it? Me and a German lady with legs you'd want to pray to. She was okay, that German lady. Had a mouth on her like a sailor. Smart, too. Couldn't get the best of the kraut. No way."

I nudged him back on track. "You were talking about Wardell Lane."

"I was *getting* to that part," Freddy said, affronted, as if I'd yanked his trumpet from his mouth. He wiped his lips, and I gave him a beer I'd slipped into my jacket pocket when we'd left the diner. "Thanks," he said, popping the top in the glove compartment door and lifting the bottle to his mouth for a hefty swig. "One of our stops, we played for a bunch of guys from Patton's army. They had their own band going, a jazz band, I mean, a six-piece, real music. And there he was, the skinny little runt from Oklahoma City. And, boy, could he blow. He'd learned the music. He was *living* the music."

"You met him again?"

"We hooked up after the war. Los Angeles, 1946. He was playing different then, the new style. I never reckoned much to it. I've always seen myself as an entertainer, but Wardell thought of himself different. He was trying to get away from that. Finding his way. Shooting up, too, like most of the young guys. That wrecked his marriage, and nearly killed him. But he kicked that shit. Found God, found his God. Got *deeper* into the music."

I told him I'd heard the record, at the Slominskys' house.

"He was just *startin'*. Wardell, he had the whole game. Jackie Robinson and Joe DiMaggio, all rolled into one and coming out of his horn like the sweetest beam of sound anybody dreamed of. There's no tellin' what he might have done. He'd already turned himself into one of the best I ever heard. And, I tell you, mister, I've heard plenty."

His voice was soft, a sad, growling mumble; he coughed, pressed the back of his hand against his scarred lips, drank some more.

He asked if I'd ever seen one of those British movies. "You know, the ones with the planes and shit, the RAF, with the squadron-leader guy who's sitting in the radio room, twirling his mustache and keeping up the English stiff upper lip while he hears about his guys who ain't coming back? That's what it's been like for me, man. More dead than survivors. A lot of fine players who ain't never comin' back."

"Wardell is dead, then."

Freddy's glance was angry for a moment, as if I'd caught him out, tricked him, but we had a mood going by then, and he responded with a swift, sad, duck of the head.

"What about her?"

His look was sharp again, and I thought he hadn't understood the question.

"What was Beth like?" I said.

"A student, an actress, a climber," he said, but his dismissal was too hasty. He sounded like he was trying to convince himself. Taking out a handkerchief, he mopped at his face. Then more beer, a couple of quick gulps. He nursed the bottle between his legs.

"She was clever. And brave," I said.

"Yeah, she had guts. That was the thing about Beth. She wouldn't give up." He sounded not hasty or dismissive now but angry again. "Not even when it was the smart move."

"How did she get her hooks into him?"

"Ain't you got *ears*?" His rage mounted a notch. "She was a kid, but she was a force, a whirlwind. Driven by something. You couldn't stand in her way. Sooner or later she swept you along."

That, I understood. After all, I'd been another of her targets. In Wardell's case the motive had been love, passion, headlong and uncontrollable infatuation. Whereas I'd been her mark, her tool. The one relationship was a function of the other, the love she'd felt for him being, almost by definition, the love that I could never have known.

"She scammed us. That was how I first met her," Freddy said. "She went to Wardell's place. She'd seen him on the pier, I guess. And a coupla days later she showed up at his apartment. Somehow she found out where it was. He didn't ask her or nuthin'. He just walked up the stairs, opened the door, and she was there."

"How did she get in?"

"Picked the lock," said Freddy, lifting the bottle to his lips. "Wardell was coming to my birthday party, and he didn't have no car. Rather, he *had* one—but he got busted and they took away his license. So she drove. He had a gift for me, all wrapped up with a ribbon and everything, real nice. *Symphony for Dead Angels* by Konstantin Slominsky. And when I open it, Beth says, 'I know that old guy.' We're like, 'Yeah, sure, baby.' And she says, 'Are you guys calling me a liar?' Next day she takes me and Wardell out into the desert. Marches us right up to the front door. But she didn't know him. She was playin' it by the seat of her pants."

"She knew the house, though?"

"Yeah, she did at that." He remembered something: "Last night you told me you built the place."

"That's right," I said, still unable to figure how Beth might have known about it.

"She was the kinda girl, you ask her to go steal a car, she'd say, 'What do you want, Chevy or Ford?' and then she'd bring you both, and probably a Cadillac besides. She thought she could fly. And sometimes she almost did."

I caught the edge of anger in his voice again.

"You blame her for his death."

He flinched. "I blame myself. They were my friends and I failed them. I let them down."

"How? Tell me what happened."

He glared, refusing to answer. His round face seemed all jowl suddenly, sagging and wet.

"What's going on, Freddy? Tell me the rest of the story," I said, my mind reaching for the secret he was hiding, the secret Lou Virgiel had somehow discovered and maybe died rather than reveal. Already I thought I knew. And didn't know. Didn't want to know.

40

*I*t's after midnight. Already the opening of the Gai-Moulin is a triumph, complete and still ongoing. Since the doors opened during the afternoon the place has been packed with patrons of every color. Within just a few hours the take at the roulette and crap tables—almost $500,000—is without precedent. The slot machines chatter like relentless machine guns. In the show room, the excited social center of all this hubbub, the Freddy Greene Quintet prepares to take the stage for the third time. Scores of white entertainers, their own shows already over on the Strip, have turned out to show their support and dig the scene. Frank Sinatra holds court at a table in one corner, posing for a photo with Zsa-Zsa Gabor. Dean Martin lurches about, drunk, or maybe only pretending. The comedian Joe E. Lewis jauntily grasps the hand of the boxer Joe Louis. The mirror behind the bar reflects sequins, silks, and teams of faces; the vibrations came up through your shoes, into your legs, spreading upward. It was like being in a power station when the turbines have started to spin.

The house lights dim, conversation subsides into a smattering of applause, and a spotlight hits the stage. Wire brushes sizzle across the skins of the drums. Ernie Klavans, the tall and rangy bass player, plucks the strings, sending forth a rolling, effortless beat. Freddy Greene, his big fingers poised on the pistons of his trumpet, gives the slightest of nods and the piano comes in like a whisper, followed by Freddy himself, blowing clear, bell-like notes, each one true, and sustained. The first number is a slow blues, a ballad, fit for the late-night mood, "Come Rain or Come Shine." Wardell waits, not with his back to the audience but standing sideways, thin as a shadow, his goatee trimmed and oiled, immaculate in the suit of charcoal-gray that Beth picked out for him.

He looks the part, Beth thinks, sitting alone at a table near the stage. A cigarette burns in the ashtray in front of her. A drink, Jack Daniels and club soda on the rocks, sits ignored. My man looks sharp, she thinks, somber yet soulful, and she recalls Wardell describing how he once saw Charlie Parker. "When the rest of the band went on stage, Bird was still finishing his dinner," Wardell said. "Took his time about it, too, and everybody out front, in the audience, was getting real impatient. Then we heard him start to blow, coming in off the beat. And he was still in the dressing room. Then his horn started blowing louder, and we knew he was on his way out. He blew past the bar. He blew his way to the bandstand, weaving among the tables and through the aisles. Like the Pied Piper. He *had* us, man. That cat had us eating out of his hand even before he stepped on stage."

Such flamboyance, Beth knows, isn't Wardell's bag. But he has his own way of making an entrance, and when he turns to the audience, ready for his solo, the moment has its own quiet drama, an intensity, like a prophet about to bring down the news from the mountain. He lifts his horn—the horn she retrieved and delivered back to him that morning, a French Selmer, handcrafted, with pearl buttons on the keys and a swift, sure action—and on his face she sees joy, tranquility, peace. He blows, sliding over the notes, emphasizing the sadness of the beat by eluding it, and it seems to Beth that the whole room shivers.

This is the moment when, night after night, he invents, when he balances light and dark in the heart of the listener, when she has to share him; but she feels that, tonight of all nights, he plays for her alone. She knows it, from the way his eyes, looking out from over his horn, never leave hers. "Miracle girl," he said, when she swept back into the Gai-Moulin, swinging the Selmer in its reinforced case. "How did you *do* that? You're something else. *Wonder* girl." They'd gone to their room,

made love, listened to Rachmaninoff, Ravel, Slominsky, lounging on
the bed, loafing. They'd ordered room service. She'd eaten an English
muffin, using his taut belly for a table. She'd spread jam on his penis,
licking it erect again. Then there'd been a repeat performance. The future? It wasn't up for discussion. In general, Wardell thinks only a few
days ahead at any one time: the next gig, the next recording date, the
next prayer meeting, the next afternoon lying on the floor with a bunch
of records, the next practice session. Beth knows she'd like to get back to
acting, but that can wait. She's got all the time in the world, she believes,
time for everything—even laundry. After the sticky jam episode she
washed his shirt. "Don't do that, honey. Send it out," he said, but she
was determined. She scrubbed the shirt in the bathroom sink, wrung it
out, ironed it dry, and feels pleasure now that the cotton worked by her
fingers sits tight against the heat of his back.

Beth fingers her belly, wondering how what she's carrying inside her
belly will fit in with this topsy-turvy life, this ecstatic adventure, this
journey to a land of voluptuous calm and pleasure. She still hasn't told
Wardell, but that's another thing for which there's surely time. Wardell's
been saying that he wants to travel, to play in Paris and Stockholm,
where he's heard they treat black jazz musicians like princes, America's
true aristocracy. So we go to Europe, Beth thinks. And maybe the baby
will be born there. On a train, rattling through the night. In a field, surrounded by sunflowers. Who can say? Anything's possible.

Lights catch the curved surfaces of the Selmer, throwing off reflections that spangle the corners of the room. One of these beams shoots
straight into her eye and she blinks, dazzled, her heart a lake of peace il-
lumined by this radiance. She's completely happy, she realizes. She has
no qualms or longings; if this moment could endure forever, unbroken
until the end of time, she could ask no more; she'd be in paradise.

But that's not how our world works. Already, although Beth
doesn't realize it, discord—a cacophony of hums, squawks, shrieks—
begins to intrude on the song that she and Wardell have been making.
Sitting at a little round table in the Gai-Moulin, her eyes narrow against
the smoke that drifts from the ashtray, Beth senses something: a change

in the atmosphere, a chill on that hot night, a threat, unknown but tangible, a flapping of fate's wings. Shivering, she hugs her shoulders and takes a drag on the cigarette, sucking the warm smoke into her lungs. But still she feels a coldness at the center of her back, as if someone is drilling a hole there. At the bar she sees two men, two black-suited backs seated next to each other on stools—four blank eyes regarding her in the mirror. The men who were in the counting room when she went to see Mantilini, she realizes. The Ravens.

What the hell are they doing here, she wonders, averting her eyes. On stage Freddy Greene, mopping at his forehead with a huge handkerchief, is introducing a new number, but Beth finds herself falling into the tunnel of one of her worst memories: she remembers her father, dressed in his only suit, hanging on the noose he fashioned for himself in that house in the San Fernando Valley. A wild fear sweeps through her, as if the whole of her being has been thrown into shadow. "Snap out of it, girl," she says to herself. "You're being stupid." She concentrates on the calm of Wardell's face as he readies himself for his next solo, willing the bliss of a few moments before to return. But instead she feels that drilling cold in the small of her back, and she knows without needing to look that two pairs of malevolent eyes watch her slightest move. Refusing to be daunted, she turns and gives one of the Ravens a dose of his own treatment. The guy's face is small and white and his thin-lipped smile never reaches his eyes.

"Doesn't mean a damned thing. Those guys are creeps. That's all," she says, trying to swagger it off, fixing her attention on the stage, where Wardell, horn leaping in his hands, surges into his solo on "April in Paris."

Since she was a child Beth has believed in the strength, the almost magical power of her own will: her will has gained her success at school and in auditions; her will has suppressed every grief and disappointment, kicked aside her fears and lame anxieties; her will has kept the unwanted advances of her stepfather at bay; her will has won her Wardell. And the next time she turns around, she *wills* that the two men should not be looking at her in the mirror. And, indeed, it proves to be so. The men are gone, nowhere to be seen. She taps a fingernail on the table, signaling her satisfaction and relief, and when "April in Paris" winds down and the set is over, she doesn't wait until Wardell comes offstage, but jumps up the three steps and flies into his arms.

"You see," she says, forcing him to look into the sea of ecstatic faces to acknowledge his applause. "America ain't so bad."

"Praise the Lord," he says with a wry smile.

Within a few moments Wardell is surrounded by well-wishers, admirers, back-slappers, hand-shakers, shoulder-tuggers, some of them merely hangers-on, some of them women, black women, staring at Beth with cold envy and dislike. Making music, Beth knows, is attractive to certain types of women. She numbers herself among them, but she knows she's different: she's no groupie. She'll stick with Wardell always, through whatever, through poverty, through failure, through abuse, through success, too, if that comes.

"You gonna take him home?" Freddy says, taking her hand and squeezing it. His flesh is thick, hot, comforting. "He played so good tonight, some of these motherfuckers watching want to go and *kill* themselves. Instead, they have to grin and tell him how great he was. And he *was* beautiful."

Freddy grins, showing his stumpy teeth. Blinking, he looks down the dress of a passing showgirl. "What we have tonight is gold. Pure gold. This is the best, you dig? Moments like this don't come along too often in the kind of life we lead, Wardell and me. Let him stay awhile."

"He hates it."

"I know," Freddy says. "Make him stay awhile. Make him *savor* it. He'll thank you later."

Beth sees his point, and the Gai-Moulin is fun that night, the whole of Las Vegas, streaming in, whooping and hollering, throwing bills like confetti, as if determined to report later, "Yes, I was there, the night they opened the Gai-Moulin. That was *something*." So Beth and Wardell do stay, talking, laughing, dancing a little.

Beth doesn't notice them at first. And when she does, she realizes they must have been there awhile, leaning against the bar, not drinking, watching: the Ravens. "I'm Ollie," one of them says, the small-faced guy with the thin lips. "And this is my friend, Stan."

Oh sure, Beth thinks. Phony names—these guys are acting, badly, though their intentions are real enough, and no good.

"Hello, little girl," says the one who hasn't spoken before—Stan. He's wearing too much aftershave, she notices, and his breath stinks. But that's the least of it. In his left hand he's got Wardell's Selmer, swinging it idly like a bat. "We're taking this."

"The hell you are," Beth says, grabbing for the horn. Stan, smiling, lofts it out of reach.

"What's the idea?" says Wardell, who's come over. Beth sees the anger twitching in his cheek.

"There isn't any idea," Stan says. "No idea at all."

"Give me my horn," Wardell says. "Right now."

"Fuck you, nigger," says Ollie. He smiles, almost thoughtfully, fingering his lip, when Beth slaps his face. "Thanks. I'll remember that."

"Your boss is going to hear about this," says Beth, hands on her hips, fingers stinging from where she gave the slap.

"Oh yeah?" Ollie says. "Talk to him yourself. Our boss is waiting in the car."

Beth is silent for several moments, staring into the guy's eyes. "I don't believe you," she says.

"What's the matter?" His voice gloats; it's almost a croak. "Afraid you don't know him as well as you think, little girl?"

It's that word: *afraid*. She draws herself up, Beth Dyer, unafraid, undaunted by anything, and says: "Let's go. You're gonna be sorry, you *schmuck*."

41

I said to Freddy Greene: "You were talking about the Gai-Moulin. Beth and Wardell left that night with the two guys. They were going to speak to Mantilini. What happened next?"

"I don't know. And I'm *damned* glad I don't."

We were in the Studebaker, driving back to Vegas, heading away from Indian Springs and a setting sun that turned the blacktop into a ribbon of bronze. I already had the headlights on because a wind was gusting and sand was starting to hover above the desert floor; the sand looked like fog, creeping toward the edge of the road.

"I never saw either of them again," Freddy said.

"That was it?"

"I called the cops. They didn't want to know."

This, I believed. "He was killed?"

"I try not to think about it."

"Killed by Mantilini?" I said, marveling at how cunning and deceitful Paul had been, sending Beth back, happy, with the sax, and then dispatching his soldiers. He was a cold piece of work. "What about her?"

"I don't know, man."

"How did she get away?"

"I've said enough, you dig? I've said *too much.*"

"You didn't hear from her. She never contacted you again?"

"You going deaf on me again, Valentine? I thought I made myself clear. I don't want to talk about this no more. Take me to the airport—if you please."

"You don't want to go back to the hotel?"

His snort was explosive. "Shit, I ain't going back to no hotel. All I'll find there is cops and a bum rap."

"What about your horn?" I said, thinking of his trumpet in its case on the desk.

"I'll call a buddy. He'll pick it up."

"I'll get your stuff," I said. "Only take a minute."

"Don't put yourself to no trouble."

"It's no trouble."

"Just drive me to the airport, okay?" Freddy slapped the dash, impatient, infuriated by my meddling. "I want out of this town, man. It's like I always say—Vegas, it's fine for a short visit. After that, it *palls*. You dig?"

"The airport it is," I said, and pressed on with my questioning, gently but insistently. I figured that, since Freddy would be my captive for only a brief while longer, I'd better try and get more answers. "The guys that Mantilini sent—the Ravens, she called them—had you seen them before?"

Freddy's eyes were angry headlights. After he hit me with them for a while he turned away, heaved his shoulders, and peered out of the car window. His sigh was mighty and determined. He made a show of looking for landmarks, no doubt calculating the distance to the airport.

"Were they using Wardell to sell drugs?" I said, remembering some of what Will Rothschild had told me, his very hypothetical story.

Freddy, unable to restrain himself gave me a sharp look that I took to mean: *How'd you know that?* It had been a good guess, although I didn't piece together most of this part of the story until later.

I thought of something else Rothschild had said; namely, believing that his money deal with the Teamsters was on the line, Mantilini had wished to stamp out the sale of heroin in Vegas. How did that figure? Maybe he'd only wanted to *appear* as though he were stamping it out. In which case Wardell would have been a handy fall guy.

I didn't quite know it then, but I was nosing around an important truth, a key to what had happened, and what *would* happen. Mantilini always thought in terms of the big picture. His eye had been on the future, the prize; the human wastage of the present had been unfortunate, to be sure, but not, in the end, a worry, not enough to cause him unease. You can't make an omelette, and so forth. Mantilini looked like a man on better terms with other people's broken eggs than his own bad dreams; but, then, I'd heard he didn't sleep all that much.

I was thinking of Beth's bravery, standing up to those two hoods, marching out of the Gai-Moulin with head high and anger in her stride, expecting to straighten things out and proceed with her life. It was moving: her determination not to be daunted. I asked: "How did she survive? How did she make it? Did she make a deal with Mantilini? Did she betray Wardell?"

"She didn't make no deal," Freddy said quickly, his bass voice rising as if in response to an insult.

"What, then? You know, don't you? Tell me, Freddy."

I'd pushed him too far. He started talking, but not about Beth and Wardell. Instead Freddy spoke of what came easily into his mind: his early life in New Orleans. The words came fast, almost tripping over each other. It was like a solo, a cascade, and I marveled at Freddy's lung capacity. Years of blowing all night long meant he had plenty of breath to spare. And right now he was afraid of what he might be pressed to say if he allowed another silence. Therefore he remembered the dance halls he'd played in—the San Jacinto, the Pythian Temple Roof Garden, the Sans Souci Hall, the Winter Garden, Pete Lala's Cabaret in Storyville. He remembered the street characters he'd known: Black Benny, Yellow Lugene, Roughhouse Willie Logan, Cocaine Buddy, Ikey Smooth, Lips the Camel, Big Vi Green, Steel Arm Lil. He remembered his father, "Dirty" Dick Greene, who'd been a prizefighter and, when in the money, had all his white teeth crowned with gold. He remembered his first marriage, to a hooker who drank, and cursed, and one night after a brawl in their railroad apartment bit his face and ran at him with a bread knife.

"I almost lost my goddamned *ear*," Freddy said.

He gave me a guided tour of his youth, some episodes heightened and mythologized, no doubt. I should have been taking notes. I could have made a book out of Freddy's tales. Instead I kept trying to interrupt; but Freddy, in a groove, kept talking, about guys he'd played with, promoters who'd robbed him, women he'd kissed. The monologue went on all the way to the airport.

"Leave me here," he said, when the Studebaker pulled up at the curb, but I insisted on going inside with him. I stood at the newsstand, flicking through a magazine, while he bought his ticket. Then he came back to me, determined, splay-footed, disheveled and smelling of the day. "Plane leaves in five," he said, and thrust out his hand. "You saved my ass, Mr. Valentine. Thanks. And goodbye."

"I wish you'd tell me, Freddy. I know there's more."

He ducked his head, straightened his shoulders, hitched his pants, and threw up his hands as if he were pushing a wall, a sudden and definitive gesture. "I'll go now, Mr. Valentine, if you don't mind."

Showing me his back, he marched to the gate and handed over his ticket, a small but big man, solid, grizzled, with spiky hair and his shirt sticking to his back.

Ten minutes later the plane was in the air.

Driving back into Las Vegas, I felt low, frustrated; it seemed like I'd come to a dead end. But then I pulled the Studebaker off the highway and killed the lights. I reached for the radio, flicked it on, flicked it off again. Wind peppered the car with sand and grit. I tapped the steering wheel. I waited for maybe fifteen minutes before a taxi sped by, heading for town, splashed by light from a car heading the other way. Silhouetted in the back I saw a strong, round head, the huge bridge of his shoulders—Freddy Greene.

Maybe Freddy's nervous belligerence had tipped me off. This cloak-and-dagger stuff wasn't his style. Nor mine, either, but I followed the taxi's glowing red taillights, keeping about fifty yards back as we headed for the glow of Vegas, shimmering above the desert. We moved through the dazzle of Fremont Street and into darkness, passing the railroad station before the road swooped down, speeding us through the dismal tunnel that led into the Westside.

The taxi cruised by the hotel where Freddy had been staying but didn't stop, heading instead for the poorer, unpaved section of the neighborhood, pulling up in front of a bungalow where no lights showed. Black smoke rose from trash burning in an oil barrel in the yard, and the walls of the house were smeared with soot and shadows. Only when a dog started barking did I lean over the steering wheel, looking more closely; in the dimness at the side of the house I saw a pen made of chicken wire and I realized that I'd been here before. This had been the first place on Rothschild's list, the house guarded by a one-eyed German shepherd and a lanky and less than welcoming resident.

Freddy paid off his driver and hurried up the path toward the sagging stoop. A screen door opened, admitting him, and banged shut. The taxi pulled away, and once again I was waiting. But not for long: within minutes the tall man I'd met loped out, a sawn-off shotgun slung over his shoulder. Freddy was behind him and the two men climbed into an ancient pickup. The starter let out three piercing shrieks before the motor grumbled into life. The pickup rattled and clanked away, no lights showing.

I put the Studebaker in gear and rolled in pursuit, keeping further back this time, my own lights dimmed, tracking them for three miles through the Westside slums, all the way to Bonanza Road, where they drove between two stone gateposts, the entrance to the empty parking lot of the Gai-Moulin, sad as an abandoned showgirl. Yet the Gai-Moulin, when it opened back in 1951, had been as striking and luxurious as any building in town, a long, low-level structure, modernist and boxy in its outlines, with streamlined detailing and splashy deco colors. Although the place had been billed as the first Vegas casino where blacks and whites could gamble together, eat together, drink together, piss next to each other in the same restroom, almost as an experiment in race relations, the owners had harbored no such altruistic intentions. They were lily-white associates of Paul Mantilini, interested only in the bottom line, the cash that flowed into the drop boxes. And the Gai-Moulin was successful for a while, maybe too successful, pulling money away from the Desert Inn, the Sands, and the other swanky joints on the

Strip. But then the Moulin folded almost overnight; or, rather, was closed, shut down—abruptly. Nobody got to the bottom of what really happened. Someone with pull, someone with lots of juice, wanted the Moulin gone. Maybe Paul Mantilini himself. Who knows? History gets written by the winners and in this case the winners weren't interested in keeping a record. Isn't that often the way with history, and winners? The furnishings, the gaming tables and so on, had been left in place, ready for the day when the Moulin would open again. That day had been a long time coming. Recently I'd been asked if I thought the property could be converted into an office building—the Atomic Energy Commission was giving the matter some thought. So much for desegregation in Nevada.

Freddy and his friend climbed down from the pickup and headed for the entrance. I left the Studebaker a block away and followed on foot. It was a hot night, the air filled with the odors of jasmine and burning rubber. Dusty, crackling dry tumbleweed whipped at my ankles. A sudden gust of wind lifted my hair and threw dust into my eyes. All the same I hurried, eager to keep up, filled with excitement and expectation. An empty tin can swirled across Bonanza Road. A rattling chain-link fence surrounded the abandoned fountain in the middle of the parking lot. Maybe I was a little afraid, too.

The doors of the Gai-Moulin were unshuttered and unlocked. In the lobby I waited, letting my eyes get used to the dark. Silence hummed in my ears, and my skin tingled after the wind outside. I'd been in the Gai-Moulin only once before it shut down. Reception was off to the left, as I recalled, with gambling tables in front of it and slot machines running around the walls; the show room, the theater, was at the back, and steps took you down into the main well of the casino. Forearmed with this memory of the floor plan, I took a pace forward and promptly fell, missing a step, stifling a yelp and clinging to a rail until the pain went away. Then I tried again, edging my way blindly down the remainder of the steps.

The air was dry and hot, a fug, chalky, stale, and so thick it was like pushing against a solid substance. The darkness seemed almost a living thing, pinching at my throat and playing tricks with my eyes. I thought I'd gone blind again. It was a suffocating darkness like a fallen tent, and malevolent somehow. I knocked into a table, my fingers trailing the smooth wooden edge, the leather trim, the soft nap of the baize. My hand brushed a roulette wheel and the wheel began to spin on its coasters. I felt as though I'd entered a cave from my nightmares. I was following two men into a dark and empty place. One of them didn't like me and the other was armed with a shotgun. How smart is *that*, I thought, and decided to get out.

Then I heard the voices, muffled at first, growing louder as I inched forward.

They seemed to be arguing.

Now I knew I had to stay. I found the aisle at the side of the casino and with my hand trailing along the cool steel of dozens of slot machines made my way forward.

I still couldn't distinguish the voices, or make out their words.

In the darkness ahead I espied a crack of light, glowing at the bottom of a door. With my arms outstretched I stepped toward it, and then I heard, quite distinct, Freddy Greene's *basso profundo*. "It's no good," he was saying, an urgent plea in his voice. "You gotta listen to me. No good's gonna come of this. You dig?"

I took further steps, more confident of my footing, until I was in front of the door. With my outstretched palm I gently touched the surface of the door: a soft fabric, baize, I guessed, covered something hard beneath—steel. It was like the soundproof door I'd installed in Konstantin Slominsky's music room, a door that said, *You're not welcome, don't come in.*

I pushed.

42

*T*hey didn't notice me at first. Freddy Greene had his back to the door, his hands at his sides. His friend, the tall, lanky guy, was rubbing his chin, leaning against a counter in front of a sheet of darkened plate glass, a one-way mirror. He had a scarred face that you could light a match on.

We were in the casino counting room, I realized. The shotgun lay on the table where the drop boxes had once been emptied; the gun's twin barrels shone in the flickering of an oil lamp, the only light source. The floor was painted black, as always in such rooms, the easier to spot any paper money. There was no paper money. What I saw was a magazine, a paperback, an ashtray, a steel bucket, clothes folded in a neat pile. What I heard was Freddy, issuing orders, seemingly, but making them sound like a plea: "We're leaving for L.A. We're getting in Ray's pickup and driving through the night. That's all there is to it. It's what we're gonna do."

Freddy moved to one side, throwing up his hands in frustration, and I saw, sitting in a quilted sleeping bag, with her knees drawn up, her black T-shirt hanging loose around her neck, her pale gray-green eyes gazing straight at me, Beth Dyer.

I gasped, but the strange thing was, I wasn't surprised, or only at first. So here we are, I thought, and this is Freddy's secret: she's alive after all. And I realized that her presence had an inevitability, was the natural end of my quest, an outcome both longed-for and dreaded, for it posed the question—what do you do now, Maurice Valentine? Whose side are you on? I'd spent these last days tracing the footsteps of Beth Dyer, digging into Beth Dyer's past, starting to obsess about Beth Dyer, and now, it seemed in those first moments, I'd summoned her up. It wasn't really so, of course, and I was kidding myself, too, if I thought my will and character had a fraction of the force, the damaged intensity, of hers. The subject of Maurice Valentine, I was to learn, had scarcely ruffled her thoughts. Certainly his presence didn't seem to worry her any. She held my eyes for a few seconds, then looked away. She didn't smile; she didn't frown; she didn't acknowledge my presence in any way. It was left to Freddy Greene to react.

"Holy *shit*," Freddy said, almost jumping out of his skin.

The other fellow, Ray, eased himself away from the counter and calmly extended a hand, taking hold of the shotgun.

"No need for that," I said, raising my hands.

"Is that right?" said Ray, aiming the barrels at me anyway, an almost-smile appearing on his scarred face. "Who's with you?"

"I'm alone."

"The hell you are," Freddy said. "I don't trust you, Valentine. How'd you find me anyway?"

"I followed you, Freddy. Trust me, it wasn't so hard."

"Don't move, sucker," said Ray, keeping the gun on me while he went to the door and poked his head out. He loped back to his previous position lounging against the counter, the shotgun trained with equal casualness in the direction of my midriff. "All quiet," he said. "Maybe he is alone."

"What do you want?" said Freddy, stepping toward me, his small, solid frame quivering with belligerence.

"To talk with Beth."

"Ain't gonna happen," Freddy said, eyes flaring. "She's coming with us. Somewhere safe."

"I'm going nowhere," Beth said. To my ears her voice seemed tired, but firm, determined; it also sounded strange, filtered through the knowledge of all that I'd learned about her since I last heard it; it sounded older, wiser, stronger than I'd remembered, all in that one short sentence—*I'm going nowhere*. It was as if she wasn't talking to us at all, but to someone who wasn't in that bleak little room, to Wardell's ghost. She was going nowhere; she was staying with him. Always.

"See?" I said to Freddy Greene. "She *wants* to talk to me."

"The hell I do," she said.

At last: a *reaction*, I thought.

"You shot me," I said.

"I didn't shoot you," she snapped back. "You were in the way."

Like I was to blame.

"Used me, then."

"Yeah? So?"

"Ever hear of a guy named Lou Virgiel?" I said, firing a shot of my own.

"No."

"He was a private eye. Your husband hired him."

I let this sink in for a moment.

"That's right—the guy who works in the store and thought he'd found himself a wife to love forever. Try telling me you never heard of him either."

She ducked her head, clutching her knees, rocking to and fro, her eyes far away.

"I met Mallory Walker. The real Mallory Walker. That's quite a trail you've left. One broken heart in Crescent City. Another down in Palm Springs. And Lou Virgiel, no longer a private eye. Dead in a bathtub."

This got to her. Her body shivered as if a shock had passed through it.

"You're a one-woman hurricane. I guess I got off lucky. Just a flesh wound."

She wouldn't look at me. She went on rocking, staring at the flickering light of the oil lamp. "Who killed the private eye?"

"I'm not sure."

"Mantilini?"

"Maybe."

Now her eyes hit me. "Your boss," she said with a cool scorn.

"He's not my boss."

"Sure he is," she said, and started to cough, a low, dry, hacking sound that shook her whole frame. The coughing didn't stop.

"You're sick," I said, moving closer to her. She flinched but didn't stop me touching her forehead. Her skin was burning. By the light from the lamp I noticed the red sore that blistered the corner of her mouth, and when I drew my hand away it was sticky and a tuft of her silvery hair was glued to it. "You need a doctor," I said. And then to Freddy: "We've got to get her to a doctor."

"That's what I've been tellin' her," Freddy said. "I've told her that a hundred times."

She was coughing again, holding her chest, racked with pain; Ray put down the shotgun on the counting table and stepped forward with a cup of water.

"How long she's been like this?" I said.

"A week."

"She's been here a week? *Jesus*."

"Just today at the Moulin," Freddy said, quick to defend himself. "Before that she was at Ray's place. Beth wanted to move last night. When she heard you and the eye was pokin' around."

I said to Beth: "Freddy's been looking after you?"

"He's a friend," she said with proud finality, leaving me to draw my own conclusions about my place in her scheme of things.

"But you still won't listen to a goddamned word I say." Freddy turned to me. "She won't see a doctor. She won't leave town."

"That's one thing you've got right," she said, and I didn't need to ask what she meant. She was sticking around, waiting until she got well enough to try to kill Mantilini again. It was crazy and sad, and I thought back to that afternoon when she'd been scamming me about the house she wanted to build. I'd told her that a home needed shelter. Now I saw that *she* needed shelter, something to pull her out of the ruin she seemed determined to inhabit.

"This is what I've been dealin' with," Freddy said. "I've had a week of it. And it's still no good."

Was there a chance, right then, that she might have come with us?

Probably not. Things might have gone differently, though any hope of that was extinguished by what happened next. I saw it first in her eyes. They changed; the life went out of them and they turned dull, frozen. She wasn't looking at me, or Freddy, or Ray. She was staring at the door, where Paul Mantilini had slipped in, silent as fate.

"May I join you?" Mantilini said, his nonchalance real, as casual as if he were visiting some high roller's table at the El Sheik. A sumptuous overcoat of canary yellow cashmere was slung over his shoulders despite the heat of the night. His head was bare and his slicked-back pompadour gleamed. His face was in shadow but his teeth showed in a smile that might have meant anything. His good eye was trained on Beth but he was aware of all movement in the room, each tremor, each little shifting of a limb. "Don't," he said to Ray, even before Ray began reaching for the shotgun. But Ray's impulse was there, and Mantilini felt it, and Ray hesitated in the face of the other's authority, whereupon one of Mantilini's guys stepped from behind his boss, pushed Ray back, and collected the weapon. Another man appeared, shining a flashlight, and brandishing a Colt the size of Lou Virgiel's. He covered Beth and me while the goon who took the shotgun returned to his position at the door. All this happened in a blink—we were trapped.

I tried to tell Beth I knew nothing of this. "They must have followed me. I'm sorry."

She spat in my face. Fair enough: she probably had good reason to suspect that I'd betrayed her.

"Everybody out," Mantilini said. "I want to talk to Beth."

"I ain't leavin'," said Freddy Greene, feet planted wide apart for balance, his position of maximum strength, leaning back a little on his elephantine legs, the way he did when getting ready for a solo. He was ready to make a stand, no doubt about it.

"Don't hurt Freddy or Ray," Beth said. I noticed that she left me out of this equation. "They're not involved in this."

"Sure they are. They're in it up to their necks," Mantilini said, brushing a speck of dust from his coat, smiling with almost lupine contempt. "But am I going to hurt them? Why would I?"

"I ain't movin'," Freddy said, although he *did* move, taking a step closer to Beth, and I realized that he'd die for her. It sounds dramatic, but I know it was true. People don't always act out of self-interest; people can be fond and foolish at the same time as they're being noble. Freddy was putting himself out on a limb although the branch was starting to crack.

"Let them go," Beth said, looking at Mantilini with the same hatred, but appealing to him in a way that suggested intimacy, the awful past they shared. Whatever was going on, they were bound up in it together. This is *our* show, she was saying, not theirs.

"You have my word," Mantilini said. "They won't be hurt."

Beth studied him. She was still in the sleeping bag, rocking to and fro, and she was pale, her eyes bright with fever. No fear showed in her face. There was the determination to match Mantilini's smart wariness with her own. She was bringing her will to bear, as if she could control the situation. "It's okay, Freddy. Do what he says."

Freddy scowled; the old trumpet player didn't like it.

She reached up from the sleeping bag for his hand. "You've done enough," she said. "I love you."

The words, simply said, were offered in the spirit of a sister, and Freddy's face creased. "Don't ask me to do this," he said, voice catching. "I want to stay."

"Very touching," Mantilini said. "Now do the smart thing, Freddy. Go make us happy with your trumpet."

Freddy bridled.

"Please," Beth said. "It's okay. I promise."

Freddy was stubborn, and he was hurting. Beth was doing her best to save him and no doubt he wanted to be saved, but it drove him crazy that he was powerless and could do nothing to help her. At the same time he was a pragmatist and saw the futility of making a move against Mantilini and his guys. His big eyes blinked. He didn't know where to put his hands. He wanted to stay, but Beth won this battle of wills, as she did so many. Before leaving, Freddy took his solo, however. He turned to Mantilini and wagged a banana-like finger in his face, saying, "You think you're a slick customer, don't you? I'm telling you this and you'd better listen. If you hurt a single hair on this girl's head I'll get even with you and yours and I don't care if I have to come back from my grave to do it. I will come back. They teach us about that where I come from."

"I'll bear it in mind," said Mantilini with the hint of smile, not condescending, not unfriendly, *unruffled.* "What about you, Maurice?"

I was the one under Mantilini's scrutiny now.

"I'm staying."

"Suit yourself," he said.

Then the three of us were alone: me, Beth, Mantilini. Shadows wobbled on the walls in the lamp's sputtering flame. Mantilini ran his hand along the counting table, trailing his fingers; there was something tentative in the gesture. His mood had changed now that the others were gone. He was shy, I realized. "Hello, Beth," he said. "I knew it was you, that moment in the Desert Inn. When you stood up for Roxie. I said to myself, 'That's Beth Dyer—just the ballsy kind of thing she'd do and say.' But then you snowed me. You were good. You were slick. You ran rings around me."

"I didn't kill you, though, did I?" Beth stood up, wobbling a little on her feet. She was dizzy. Her jeans were faded and frayed at the bottom and her feet were bare. "And this is where you try to kill me." Her eye moved to the door, figuring her chances. "Again."

Mantilini shrugged, and his overcoat fell from his shoulders. The gesture was menacing in its carelessness, its almost sublime neglect. He pulled something from his pocket—a knife with a handle of worn white bone. "This belonged to a friend, to a man who died a long time ago," he said, opening the blade, which was long and thin, with a cruel curved edge. "He was an architect. Like you, Maurice. Actually, a better architect. And he was killed with this knife. But I didn't kill him. Everybody has this idea about me. That I go around killing people. It isn't so."

He smiled, inviting our disbelief, it seemed. His eyes were dark and hard. "I remember the first time I met you," he said to Beth, inspecting the edge of the blade against the light. "You sold me about a hundred pairs of gloves. I remember it well."

His voice was lulling, hypnotic, and he moved toward her.

"You had a lot of nerve. Then and now," he said. "I've still got those gloves in a box somewhere. I never wanted you to be hurt. You should understand that. I always liked you."

"Sure, you liked me. So your Ravens killed the guy I loved. And then they raped me. While you watched."

"Bad things, terrible things," he said. "I know that, and I'm sorry."

"Sure you are," she said, and then she drew her head back like a snake and spat. The gob flew through the air and hit his shoulder, *smack*.

"I know it's hard for you to believe. I didn't kill your friend. And I didn't have him killed," he said, in the same voice, soothing and calm.

He was poised, like a plane before touchdown, the knife comfortable in his hand, and I had a sudden picture of him as a much younger man, slicing flesh in brawls, in alleys, never showing his fear or losing his cool, brushing the other guy's strokes aside, always on his feet, while his foe bled in the gutter. That's who Paul Mantilini was. He was almost cooing at Beth, hypnotizing her, and I knew that in a moment he would spring forward, twist the blade, and that would be the end.

Blood throbbed in my ears. I thought that if I threw myself forward I might just be able to grab Mantilini's arm and send the blade flying away.

"I'll give you more than words. And this is how you'll know my word is good," he said, spinning around and splaying his fingers on the counting table. He held the knife above his outstretched hand for a moment and then pressed down with the steel's razor edge, severing the top of his pinkie while blood feathered the table's smooth glass surface.

Beth's gasp entered my mind simultaneous with the crunch of splintering bone.

Quickly Mantilini wrapped a handkerchief around his mutilated hand. Then, as if it were a trophy, he picked up the severed portion of the finger and offered it to her. "This has to be over now. Do you understand? It's finished," he said, not wincing, ignoring the pain, but the blood gone from his cheeks. "Whatever happened, it's *done*."

His gesture was absurd, breathtaking, barbaric. I felt like I was witnessing some ritual I didn't understand, an act of drama and self-sacrifice wholly outside my ken. I could imagine neither Mantilini's state of mind nor the extent of his self-control. If he'd been dealing with me the gesture would have worked, he'd have won the game hands down. The problem was that Beth's will was as monstrous as his own. Neither her head nor her body moved. Then she scratched her neck, her gray-green eyes flicking from the offered flesh, quivering in his hand, to the knife where it lay in blood on the counting table. Suddenly she made a dive, plucked up the knife, and darted forward. She lunged hard but her thrust struck bone and the knife jerked from her hand, clattering to the floor.

"Bitch!" Mantilini said, red showing through the slash in the weave of his sports shirt.

"Damn right, and who's to blame?" Beth said. In a moment she found where the knife lay on the floor. But by the time she picked it up again Mantilini was gone. Without a word, without hurrying, he staggered out of the counting room and into the dark, leaving his overcoat where he'd dropped it, the luxurious yellow fabric speckled with blood. Beth ran after him and was halfway across the counting room when her legs gave way and she clutched at the table. Her sickness had weakened her. No doubt the events of the last few minutes had also taken their toll.

"Work!" she said, punching her thigh, cursing her body, but her legs managed only a couple more steps before she was forced to reach for the table again. "Fuck!" Her hate-filled face, needing somewhere to go, turned on me. "You still here?" Her voice was like a wire, like a garotte, and the knife was still in her hand. "What the fuck do you *want*?"

PART 6

The End

43

*M*antilini sits in the emergency room, perched on the edge of a gurney. Having refused to lie down, he jokes while the youthful doctor numbs his chest with a hypodermic, and turns his head to observe a nurse making ready with needle and thread for the stitches.

"Careful with that stuff," Mantilini says, but he could scarcely be more urbane and affable.

Somebody just tried to kill him and he looks like he's at some goddamned party, Nick says to himself.

"I don't want to end up looking like Frankenstein's monster. I met him once, did I ever tell you, Nickie? Karloff, I mean. Not a bad guy. He was kind and he wasn't tall. But put an ax in his hand and he looked menacing as hell. Bad Boris!"

"Pops, quit horsing around," Nick says, still gathering his breath after rushing here from the Desert Inn, where he'd been dining, as arranged, with his attorney. Someone had burst in and broken the news: "He's been stabbed! Your dad, he's been stabbed!" Nick watches his father's eyes, unblinking, while another needle goes in and the stitching begins.

"What news of Boss Booth?" Mantilini says.

"Nothing yet," said Nick, and his father's glance flicks toward the clock on the wall. Shit, the old man's cool, Nick thinks. Where do you learn that? "Who did this, Pops? What happened?"

"She's got a temper on her, that girl."

"Who?"

"Beth Dyer."

Nick swallows carefully, pushing down the panic that flutters in his belly. *Beth Dyer*—he's been haunted by that name all day. "That's impossible. She's in the morgue. They fished her out of Lake Mead."

Mantilini smiles merrily. "Nickie, let me tell you. Plenty of strange things have happened to me. I've led a pretty full life. But I've yet to be stabbed by a ghost."

"She tried to kill you?"

"For the second time. See what a lucky guy I am?"

Hot anger spurts through Nick's blood. Keep calm, he says to himself, watch your father, learn from him, be cool. "Where is she?"

"At the Gai-Moulin."

At least that part figures, Nick thinks. A couple of hours back he'd heard from the guy who was trailing Valentine that he'd parked outside the Gai-Moulin. Nick hadn't made anything of it. He knew that Valentine was following Freddy Greene, Freddy's release from the slammer having been engineered so Valentine could continue to do precisely that. And the blacks were always checking out the Moulin, reminiscing about the place, or dreaming of opening it again. Nick had relayed the information to his father, who'd seemed unmoved. Nick hadn't dreamed he'd go down there.

"You see, Nickie," Mantilini says. "When Jackie came to me this morning, telling me what her husband was doing, I figured, 'Something's up.' I figured Beth might be alive."

"You didn't say anything," Nick says, trying to keep the whiny edge out of his voice, trying not to sound aggrieved.

"I wasn't sure," Mantilini says. "It was a hunch, that's all. A feeling in my gut. I didn't want you thinking I was acting crazy like Valentine."

"Did you talk to her?"

"Didn't get much of a chance. I apologized, the Italian way." Mantilini holds up his bandaged hand. "She didn't buy it. Came right at me with my own knife. Women! I tell you, Nicky, that girl's got more balls than any guy I ever knew. You'd better go and check on Valentine."

"He's still at the Moulin?"

"Yeah. Or he was. She won't move, and he'll most likely stay with her. She'll be waiting for me to come back. She's still got the knife, so watch out. Calm them both down. See that everything's okay," Mantilini says. "And let me know as soon as we hear about Boss Booth."

Leaving the hospital, striding along the bright-lit corridors, catching sight of his reflection in the darkened windows, his mirror image stalking him, Nick, despite his panic and rage, is clear about what he has to do. He reasons like this: if Beth Dyer is alive, and if she sees his father again, then sooner or later she's going to start wondering if another Mantilini, not Paul, was behind what happened to her and her boyfriend on that night five years ago. And then his father would have some questions of his own, questions that Nick could not, will not, answer.

Fuck, Nick thinks. Don't panic. Stay calm.

With the windows down, his elbow resting on the door, the wind hot in his face, Nick guides the Cadillac down the Strip, his foot weighing down on the gas, the car doing ninety for the three miles of desert between the Sands and the approaching glow of the El Sheik. In the lobby he encounters the nervy, buoyant figure of Albert Kluphager, bubbling with news that Nick says he'll convey to his father. From his room, he collects a gun, a nickel-plated Colt, which he slips into his pocket. Then, back in his car, heading downtown toward the Westside, he stops at a gas station, forcing himself to concentrate, trying not to allow the past to take over his mind the way it was threatening to take over his present.

He'd planned it all so neat. Wallace and Cohen, the Ravens, handled the jazz player and his girlfriend, and then he and Sandy Berman snuffed Wallace and Cohen, surprising them after they'd taken turns raping the girl, Nick leading the way. Sandy Berman had excluded himself from that part. She didn't have a name, not in Nick's mind, not then. Afterwards he'd noticed that she was still alive, crawling around in the dirt. Nick had drawn back his shoe and booted her in the belly. He'd felt pretty much like a god at that point, dizzy with the moment of joy and power. So he'd taken another portion, giving it to her up the ass, his belt in his hand, whipping her and gouging her back with the point of the buckle. Then he'd kicked her again, almost straining his ankle he went in so hard. *Who's gonna help you now, bitch, crawling on your hands and knees, thick blood gushing from your nose? Not my father. Not anybody.*

Afterwards, leaning against the hood of the car, he watched Sandy Berman stand over her and put two bullets in her head. He'd seen the muzzle flashes.

It had been a bloodbath, Nick's self-scripted initiation, proving to himself that he was his father's son after all, and *loyal*. Wallace and Cohen had pulled him into their drug deals, made him a lot of money, actually, before revealing their true interest: they were after him to set up the old man, and he'd gone along with the idea for a while. Heck, he'd been tempted. The people behind them had promised him the moon, saying his father was over the hill, delusional, crazy with his dreams for what could be achieved in Nevada. And his father, at that time, had been keeping him at a distance from the business, treating him like a kid. But then suddenly the old man had said, "Nickie, I got this problem with the drug thing. I need your help." That was all it took. Nick's heart had *glowed*. There'd been just the one snag: *he* was the problem, or a large part of it.

Hence the gunshots in the desert, Sandy Berman, a guy who knew how to keep his mouth shut, called in to help with the wrongdoers who were breaking Paul Mantilini's rules and plotting against him.

It must have been Berman, Nick realizes—he couldn't bring himself to finish the girl.

And where's Berman now? In San Quentin, he recalls, writing odes and sonnets for the prison newspaper, a clever Jew with a head for figures and a mastery of backgammon. Or did he get out already? Doesn't matter, Nick thinks, or only insofar as he must now complete the work that Berman had no belly for.

Once upon a time, Nick thinks, I considered betraying my father, I plotted his *death*. The memory, and the thought that his father might find out, make him writhe and sweat with shame.

Nick sees Valentine's car, parked fifty yards back from the entrance to the Gai-Moulin. Nick cuts the Cadillac's headlights, kills the engine, and rolls into the parking lot. From the trunk he retrieves a flashlight and the gallon-canister he topped off at the gas station.

Back at the hospital his father told him that Valentine and Beth were at the back of the casino, in the counting room. *See that everything's okay.*

Nick's plan involves a little more.

To Valentine the line will be: "This is what my father wanted, and you'd better like it."

And for his father? "She tried to kill Valentine, Pops. What could I do?"

Something like that.

Nick enters the Gai-Moulin quietly, using the flashlight only for a second or two while he takes his bearings. He uncorks the canister and splashes gas onto the carpet and fittings. Then he lights a match and jumps back, eyebrows singed as the gas goes up with a satisfying *whoomph*.

44

*H*e'll be back," Beth was saying. "And when he comes I'll be ready."

She seemed set on killing herself. This is madness, I thought. As Mantilini had said of Freddy Greene, I was in this up to my neck, a neck I'd sooner save than not, if possible. But I wanted to save her neck, too. "I'm taking you to a doctor," I said.

"You want to help, get me a gun." Her eyes blazed. "Otherwise, get out of my sight."

The knife was nowhere to be seen. She'd put it away somewhere. Close to hand, no doubt, maybe in her jeans pocket, or beside her in the sleeping bag. Her hands were smeared with blood that she hadn't bothered to wash off; she wore it like a badge. The tang of her body filled the air; she smelled unwashed and unwell. Her face was drawn and thin, not haggard, but sculpted by her hunger for revenge. Her frozen eyes stared at a point halfway up one of the counting table legs. The wavering light of the oil lamp threw half of her face into shadow and I wondered how the rest of her life—her childhood in the San Fernando Valley, her ambitions, her months with Wardell—looked to her from where she was sitting. Like something that no longer belonged to her, I guessed, like time that had been stolen. I'd sought to obliterate my own past; hers had been ripped away and tainted.

"Cigarette?" I said.

She didn't reply; maybe she didn't even hear.

"I gave the lighter back to Mallory Walker. I liked her."

Something, an animation, not quite a smile, broke out now in her face. "Yeah, Mallory's okay," she said.

"She said she'd studied architecture. I guess that's where you got the idea of how you could come after me."

"Must we talk?" she said, retreating into her anger.

"I figure we might as well pass the time."

"I don't want your help. I don't need you. I want you to go," she said. Her voice was tired but emphatic. "That's pretty clear, isn't it?"

"Very clear."

"So why are you staying?"

Why *did* I stay? It wasn't in my best interests; it certainly wasn't because she made charming company. I told myself it was because I was curious. I told myself that if I could make her talk, loosen up, then, maybe, she'd be prepared to leave with me. We could go find that doctor.

"I saw the Slominskys," I said. "It's funny. I'd almost forgotten about that house until you mentioned it. I'd blocked it from my mind, I guess. I was ashamed of the place. Because I made a deal with HUAC. Named the Slominskys' names."

This brought a look.

"You didn't know that?"

An almost imperceptible shake of the head.

"The way you played me about that house, I was guessing you did."

Her pale eyes were watchful, inscrutable, but not quite shut down. I took that as a sign to go on. I'd been planning to anyway. "Konstantin played Wardell's music for me. He explained to me why it was so good," I said, remembering that recent evening in the Slominsky music room, the record sleeve with its picture of a gaunt black dude striding in front of a brick wall. Konstantin responded to Wardell's technique; Beth had, no doubt, heard a love song; I'd seen a purity. That's a statement as much about me as him, of course. I pictured Wardell Lane as a guy who'd been passionate about his craft for its own sake, not as a means to an end. His credo had been artistic, almost religious, not worldly. Even Freddy

Greene was a cynic by comparison. But maybe I was making him into something that he wasn't, investing him with qualities I'd discarded, or, if I'm going to be honest, had never possessed.

"I've always been trying to juggle too many things. To make an impression. To please the client. Getting publicity, so the next gig comes through. Always thinking on my feet, thinking about the next step up the ladder," I said. "Wardell wasn't interested in any of that, was he?"

"I won't talk about him."

"He meant that much?"

She looked at me and yet she wasn't looking at me, at least she wasn't searching for anything in my face; she didn't want anything from me.

"My life stopped when I met him. There *was* no before," she said. "And then there was no after."

"He wouldn't want you to die."

"No," she said, shy suddenly, her fingers picking at the quilt of the sleeping bag. "He wouldn't."

"Come on, then," I said, and held out my hand.

From the sleeping bag, in the wavering light of the oil lamp, she looked up. She studied my hand for a long time, brooding. And then she laughed.

"You're weak," I said, angry.

"I'm strong enough."

"You think he's going to walk back in here, rip open his shirt, and say, 'Here. Take another stab at it.' Grow up, Beth, be *smart.*"

"I don't want to be smart. I want to kill Paul Mantilini."

She put her hand on her chest, took a deep, wheezing breath, and began to cough again. Her eyes seemed to sink inside her head, and she was shivering. Within a few moments she was retching in the bucket and I had my hand on her back, rubbing between her shoulder blades gently. It was a crazy situation. I was stuck in a room with a woman who held me in contempt and seemed halfway delirious, a woman in a fugue state, and I was expecting that at any moment men would come through the door to kill her, and probably me, too. I should have left. My instinct for survival told me to get out of there. But I couldn't do it. My hand felt the racing of her heart through her rib cage. I sat down on the floor, stretching out my legs and leaning back against the wall. I forced my body to relax in the hope that she'd begin to relax, too. In a minute or so she was through with her puking. I gave her a cup of water from the plastic container on the floor.

"I'm sorry," she said.

"What for?"

"You're right. I'm *not* sorry," she said, but her voice was softer. "Not for anything I've done to you."

"You wanted revenge. I understand. But vengeance isn't real. It won't keep you warm at night. It won't make you happy. It'll wither you away. You'll be dust inside."

"You sound like a priest," she said, not with scorn exactly, but as though she hated lectures, authority, orders. Was there religion in her background? I had no idea. I knew both so much and so little about her.

"I'll be the happiest woman alive," she said, and she seemed to be-lieve herself.

"What makes you think you'll *be* alive?"

"Who gives a damn?"

"I do," I said.

"Why? What's it to you, Maurice? Are you expecting to make love to me? Look, I'm a wreck."

The thought hadn't crossed my mind until then. But suddenly I did want her. Desire can be an ugly bear.

She had her head turned sideways, watching the door, listening.

"What?" I said.

"*Sssh!*"

There was nothing.

"Was he your lover? Mantilini, I mean."

"For a while," she said. "That was some mistake."

I wanted to point out that this mistake had saved her life, if briefly, had most likely been behind Mantilini's attempt to make amends, a state of mind I doubted had survived her stabbing him in the chest.

"What started it? I know what started it. But why *now*?"

With a wan smile she said: "It's your own fault."

I had my hand on her back again. I was rubbing between her shoulder blades and she didn't tell me to stop.

"At first I felt guilty and ashamed. Filthy, defiled. As if everything had been my own fault," she said. "I went to my mother for a while. She took me in. But she didn't want to hear about what happened. She wouldn't let me discuss it. She just put her hands over her ears. I'm not kidding."

The suggestion of a wry smile, my specialty, must have crossed my face, not that I was laughing at her, but because I was thinking of Jackie and how she'd refused to listen when I tried to tell her about Mantilini. "Some people tell themselves if they don't have to look at a horror then maybe it doesn't exist. It's a way of evading emotion and responsibility," I said, sounding very high and mighty. "But I want to ask you something. Back up a minute. Why didn't they kill you, too, in the desert?"

My hand felt the shiver that went through her.

"I don't really know. After, after . . ."

"It's okay," I said. "Don't talk about it if you don't want."

She gathered herself. "I heard shots. Some were close. I didn't know what I was doing. I was just crawling," she said. "I crawled in the dirt and sand. After a while everything was quiet and I got to my feet and went to the side of the road. A trucker gave me a ride all the way to L.A. I was lucky, I guess, if you can call it that.

"I wanted to find a hole and hide in it," she went on. "And I guess that's what I did. After I left my mother I hit the road. I went to towns I'd never heard of and I changed my name. I met a guy. Not a bad guy. I married him. Tell me—was that so terrible?"

"You did what you had to do."

"I *survived*. I held on. One time, one of the women up there in Crescent City, she wondered if I was interested in trying out for some show they were putting together. She asked if I was interested in amateur theatricals. Amateur theatricals! I said I wasn't hip to acting or anything like that. I was just a dull old housewife with no interests outside my marriage and my part-time job. I was working as a secretary to bring in some extra money.

"More than three years I lived there. Sometimes I got angry with myself. 'Who the hell are you, Beth Dyer? How can you go on living? Why haven't you slit your wrists?' Then I saw your picture in the newspaper. And I realized why I hadn't slit my wrists. All that while I'd been waiting. Getting myself ready."

I didn't need to ask her which picture she meant. It had been in the press earlier in the year, around April, at the time of the opening of the El Sheik. Me and Mantilini. I had a copy of that very same photograph framed in my office and I remembered the way her mood had changed when she'd studied it.

"I saw it and I hated you, Maurice. I saw you standing next to him, and I hated you. I hated your suit and your million-dollar smile. But it was like I could smell the way you were through the newsprint. I understood you. Yeah, I thought, I see how I could get to that guy. I see how I could *use* him. You gave me a plan. A way to proceed."

"Don't mention it," I said in a murmur. I remembered very well the morning when the photograph was taken: a spring morning with no chill in the air, the Nevada mountains clear and sharp in the distance. A morning on which great things were presaged, it had seemed. I'd stood beside the fountain outside the El Sheik and Mantilini had clasped one of my hands in both of his as the photographer's flash failed to go off. We'd waited, Mantilini and me, our hands glued awkwardly together, while the photographer screwed in another bulb and behind us soared the flamboyant outlines of the El Sheik, my ticket to the sort of future I had in mind, a future promising wealth and power, and maybe fame, too. I'd seen that moment as an endorsement of all the decisions I'd made since the end of the war, of the whole *idea* of Maurice Valentine.

"I knew if I got close to you, you'd take me to him," she said. "The plan wasn't to shoot him at the party. The plan was to impress him, make him like me. Get him alone and then do it. I wanted him to look into my eyes when I killed him."

The coldness in her voice, its desperate calm, sent chills down my spine. Beside her on the floor, I watched her face with sympathy and a wary fascination, the way you watch a beautiful animal that might turn on you at any moment.

"It didn't work out, did it? I lost my temper and he looked across the table and said, 'Beth? Beth Dyer?' It had been five years and I'd disguised myself so well. I didn't look like the same woman. I *wasn't* the same woman. He saw through me in about five minutes."

She'd been betrayed by her own outraged decency, her impulse to stand up for the pit-girl who was on the carpet for theft. "You recovered yourself," I said.

"I was spinning. I didn't know what I was going to do. Just that I had to do it fast."

She was nodding to herself as she talked, affirming her own words. During these last few minutes, I said to myself: She's come back from somewhere, I've made a connection with her. She seemed more relaxed and human, I thought. But then her expression became intent, she was listening again, and this time there *was* something. The silence was punctured by distant creaks and pops, like dried twigs snapping. And the counting room seemed brighter, as if lights were burning out in the main body of the casino. That was impossible, I realized; the juice had been off for years. I got to my feet and went to the door. Orange light splashed against the wall at the far end of the passage, beyond which the slot machines were lined up like gleaming soldiers. Advancing, I felt the shock of the air, a wall of heat pushing against my face. Flames licked forward from the casino entrance, enveloping a roulette table. The baize and tinder-dry wood crackled and smoked before they, too, ignited. Beneath the mirrored bar a bottle went off like a grenade. The fire, as if alive and angry, enraged by my presence, flickered at the feet of another gaming table before rushing up to consume it. More bottles exploded and breaking glass shot across the room. A deck of cards, left all these years on one of the tables, burned swiftly, shriveling into glowing embers before a draft picked them up and whirled them in the air like butterflies. The Gai-Moulin was ablaze.

45

*P*ut this over your mouth. And give one to her, too," said Nick, brandishing a pair of handkerchiefs. Somehow he'd found us in the smoke and was helping us escape. He slipped his arm about Beth's waist, almost carrying her. "Come on. Let's get you folks out of here."

Outside the service entrance to the Gai-Moulin a car was waiting. The doors were open and the engine was running. It was the same light-blue Cadillac convertible I'd seen earlier in the day but this time the top was up. "Get in, quick," Nick said. "My father's on the rampage. He'll be here any minute. It's been years since I've seen him like this." His manner seemed kind, concerned, brisk. He avoided eye contact. He wanted to get going. "Hurry," he said. "Lie down on the back seat. Both of you."

"Where are you taking us?"

"There's no time to talk about that," he said. "Get in."

And so we went along with it. I lay down on the soft leather of the back seat, holding Beth in my arms, and Nick threw a blanket over us. The back door slammed, the front door shut, too, and the engine revved as the car sped forward, crunching at first on grit and sand, then whispering over tarmac. Beth and I were snuggled together like spoons, her back against my chest, her head nestling beneath my chin. She didn't like it much and tried to keep me at a distance with her elbows. Even so, I felt her fever, the tension in her body.

"You people keep your head down, you hear?" Nick said. "It looks like we're being followed. Yeah, I can see the headlights now. Hold on, I'll see if I can lose them."

My body pressed even closer to Beth's while the Cadillac made a violent turn and rubber screamed. It was dark, almost suffocatingly hot beneath that scratchy woollen blanket. "Beth," I said. "Are you okay?"

No reply.

"That's good," Nick said. "I think we lost them. But keep your heads down. I want to be sure."

"Where are we going?" I said.

"I've got a cabin. Up in the foothills. You'll be safe there."

"We're heading into the desert?" I said, picturing the route. We'd be headed out on 95, I guessed, toward Beatty and beyond, and it occurred to me that we stood a chance. More than a chance, now. We were getting away, escaping.

"Into the desert," Nick confirmed, and I felt Beth's body grow tense again beside me.

"Beth?" I said, but she wouldn't talk. She was panting and a catch in her breath made her sound like an animal in distress, choking. "Beth?"

. . . that earlier drive, the blindfold itching at her eyes, the rope burning her wrists, her mouth fighting uselessly against the gag in her mouth, screaming into it to no avail, the suited men, the Ravens, laughing each time the car goes over a bump and Wardell yells out from where they've stuffed him in the trunk as they head deeper into the desert night . . .

"My father's not a bad man," Nick was saying. "But he's made his own world and he lives by his own rules. Break 'em and you'd better watch out."

"Why are you doing this?" I asked. He was taking an awful chance.

There was a silence before Nick answered. "Enough damage's been done," he said.

"Your old man—he'll be mad."

"Don't worry. I'll handle my father."

I wondered whether he had the brass.

"He'll forgive me."

Sure he will, I thought. Well, now wasn't the time to worry about that. We'd be in Nick's cabin, and I'd make my peace with Mantilini after I'd gotten Beth to a doctor and away from all this, when she was safe. The air beneath the blanket grew sourer by the minute and I could feel and hear her distressed breathing.

> *. . . the car door opens, and she's thrown out, landing in the desert, scraping her side on a rock; still blindfolded, she blunders through the dark before a hand catches her and her body jerks as her dress is ripped off. Wardell cries out, wailing in pain and frustration. She tries to say, "It's all right, baby, it's all right," but the words won't come out because of the gag. A fist smashes into her face. She's in the dirt; then, with her nose caved in and the taste of blood in her mouth . . .*

Nick turned on the radio, but I heard his voice over the muted sound of jazz. "It's my mother's birthday today," he was saying. "I never really knew her. She was a singer. I heard one time that she killed herself, but I don't believe that. She wore herself out, that's all. So Pops brought me out here to be with him. I'm a bastard, I guess. When I was a kid I was afraid he didn't trust me. But then he started giving me jobs. I'd do *anything* for my old man."

Nick seemed nervous, proud, anxious, justifying himself maybe, perhaps wondering, I thought, if he'd done the right thing after all, in taking us away from the Gai-Moulin, out of the city. I was thinking: Just keep your foot down on the gas, baby.

He said: "When I was a kid he tossed me in the pool. That was how he taught me to swim. Said, 'Keep your head above water.' Once, at school, I learned the name of every state. He said, 'What about the state capitals?' We had kidnap drills. 'If some guys you don't know ask if you're Paul Mantilini's son, you say, "NO!" and run like hell.' He told me I'd be the first Mantilini to go to college, and he was right."

I wasn't really listening anymore. I heard the steady rush of the tires over the blacktop, the murmur of the radio, Beth's labored breathing. I was thinking of our conversation in the counting room. I'd trotted out some of the old platitudes and warned her against revenge, but I understood why she wanted it, thirsted for it, especially now that I knew more of the story, and it was ironic to me that the violent, compulsive flood of her need had been released by that one minor event: seeing a picture in the newspaper. I still didn't know how she knew about the Slominsky house; but for now we were getting out of Vegas and that was enough. I brought up my hand and touched her back; the T-shirt was damp with sweat. She was sick and in the dark, heading out into the desert. I'm not the most imaginative guy, but I knew where her thoughts must be tending.

. . . the first gunshot, and Wardell's howl of agony, bring her back to her feet. For a moment she escapes her captors and, guided by some inner radar, rushes across the sand and throws herself on top of his body, pressing her bloodied cheek against his, nuzzling, rooting desperately. Hands seize her, throw her down in the dirt again. Then comes another shot and she knows they've delivered the coup de grâce. Wardell is dead. Head thrown back, mouth biting against the gag, she shrieks, a long and terrible scream that they hear only, if at all, as a shapeless moan . . .

"He has this way, Pops does, he never tells you what he's thinking. Not until he's decided exactly what to do," Nick was saying. "Then, boom! It's done. When I was a kid I never understood that. It was frustrating, kind of. I used to say to myself, 'You old bastard. I'll never be good enough, will I?' But that's not what was going on with him at all. He'd lived so much of his life in a state of war, it was impossible for him to say what he felt. Even about his own son."

. . . Beth is on her hands and knees, crawling, shaking her head like a dog, trying to toss away her vision of what has happened. He's gone, she knows he's gone, and she wants to die, too. But she fights nonetheless, kicking and bucking when hands grab her again. Fights free, plunging ahead, blind, running pell-mell, but then her feet are gone, swept from under her by a well-aimed kick. A shoe stomps down on her face and her mouth shovels up sand. Cruel arms splay her, and again her cries fight the gag.

But, again, not a soul to witness them, only enemies delighting in her fear and agony. A belt unsnakes from a pair of pants with a leathery hiss. Pain sears her bowels, like a hot sword . . .

My legs were stiff and my back was starting to ache. I figured, surely, that it would be okay for us to get out from under the blanket. At last. But Nick said, "Wait a while longer. Better safe than sorry," and went on talking about his father. I wasn't listening at all by that point. I'd blanked him out. I was hoping that this cabin, wherever it was, would have a phone, so that when the doctor came, and Nick had returned to Las Vegas, I could call for a cab, blow a hundred bucks on a ride all the way to L.A. I was grateful to Nick for what he was doing, but the way he kept talking about Mantilini worried me. Something seemed off.

The rush of the tires became a rumble as the Cadillac slowed, turning onto a rougher road, and then we were bouncing along. The car spun about, almost throwing us off the seat, and stopped. A door opened quickly.

"All clear, folks," said Nick, his voice loud and a bit grim, I thought.

"We're here already?"

"This is the end of the line," he said.

I was closest to the door, so I got out first, and then helped Beth Her eyes were bright with fever. Her shoulder was hot to the touch. She stood in the sand and stretched her back, keeping her eye on Nick. His movements were slow, a little exaggerated. He was grinning and his startling blue eyes wouldn't keep still. "You guys go first," he said. "I need to get something from the trunk. The cabin's up ahead."

"I don't see it," I said.

"Just over there."

My eyes followed the direction of his arm, staring beyond the creamy fans that the headlights scooped from the desert.

"I still don't see it."

"Go on," he said, pushing me in the center of my back with his powerful hand. I almost fell, his shove was so hard and impatient, but I recovered myself, spinning around, furiously, beginning to curse him. As I did, Beth stepped clear and turned back toward Nick. Her hand flashed and I almost didn't believe what I saw.

Nick was gasping, groaning, clutching at the delicate, exposed part of his throat as blood spurted through his fingers.

Beth stabbed again. It happened that quick. She lunged, brought herself up straight, and twisted her arm, this time leaving the knife in. Then she stood back, her eyes wild, her cropped silver hair agitated in the desert wind.

The bone handle of the knife stuck out of the side of Nick's throat, the same knife that his father had used to slice off part of his own finger just an hour before. He took a step toward her, his gargled words drowned out by the blood spraying from his mouth. The blood hit Beth full in the face, like surf, and she didn't blink. Nick's hand clawed uselessly at the bone handle and he fell, onto his knees, slumping on his side like a bag of dropped cement. Feet writhing, kicking in the sand, he arched his back and worked himself, crabwise, across the desert floor. But she followed, stepping slowly, deliberately, not bothering to wipe his blood from her face, talking all the while. The wind drowned out her words. I saw her yank out the knife and wipe it clean on his shirt, still talking, but inaudibly. Then she kicked him once, viciously, on the side of the head.

Nick no longer moved. He'd shit his pants and even in the wind I caught the stench. She kept her face only a few inches from his, watching, gloating while he died.

46

$\mathcal{I}$ didn't know what to do. I was in shock. I fetched the blanket from the back of the car and threw it over Nick's body. Beth took it off again, draping it around her own shoulders. To my daze and dismay add fear: at that moment I was more than a little scared of her.

"Look at him," she said, prodding at the corpse with the toe of her sneaker. "Now Mantilini will know how it feels to lose a child."

I was staring at her.

"I was pregnant when they raped me," she said. "They messed me up inside. I'll never have a baby."

They'd murdered that, too. I wanted to hold her, I wanted to scream at her. She was crazy and driven and sad and I was sure she'd killed the wrong man—without hesitation or regret. I saw how clearly Mantilini had designed and plotted what she'd become. He was the architect of her flawed vengeance. And she wasn't done yet.

"Drive me back to Las Vegas," she said. "I'm going to kill him."

"You need a doctor," I said, trying. "We'll find a motel."

I was standing by the driver's door of the Cadillac and she tried to shove me aside. "Out of my way," she said, but I didn't budge.

"You want to leave me in the desert, with him, in the middle of the night, in the middle of a sandstorm. Is that the idea?"

"It's up to you," she said, showing me, tucked in the waistband of her jeans, the pistol she'd taken from Nick's body. "Either way, I'm leaving."

I reached inside the car and palmed the keys. "Not without these," I said. "Now what? You planning to shoot me?"

I'd surprised her. The night wind cut at her hair, lifting it away from her narrow face; she spun, kicking angrily at the sand. "No, Maurice, I'm not going to shoot you. Give me the keys."

"I can't do that."

An exasperated sigh, almost a hiss, escaped her lips. She seemed to be yearning to hit me. "You're such a sucker, Maurice. All these years, and you're still in the dark. Don't you get it? Mantilini doesn't just own you. He *made* you." A look of sorrow passed across her face and she added softly: "You're like me. You're his creation."

"I think you'd better hand me a dictionary. Because I don't understand a word you're saying."

In exchange for my sarcasm she shot me a tough look. *Have it your own way*, her expression seemed to be saying, *but you won't like it.*

"Let's get in the car," she said.

"No tricks. I'm not giving up these keys."

"I'm not asking for the keys, Maurice. I'm going to tell you something, if you think you can handle it."

"After this"—I nodded toward where Nick's corpse lay in the sand, still leaking blood—"you think you can shock me?"

"I know I can."

I smiled, but the cool firmness in her voice spooked me. "What's the game?" I said.

"No game," she said, sure of herself, like a poker player after the hand has already been won.

"Do your worst," I said, stepping into the car on the passenger's side, but keeping the keys. Beth positioned herself in the driver's seat.

"Well?" I said.

"When I was fifteen I stole a motorcycle. I wanted to get on that thing and get away so far, so fast, that nobody would ever catch up with me. My stepfather pulled some strings to keep me out of reform school."

"This is your shocking secret?"

"No," she said, her gray-green eyes flashing. "I'm just letting you know—I could hot-wire this thing if I wanted."

"You could *try*. Maybe it's not so easy with a late-model Cadillac."

"Maybe not," she agreed. "Your eldest son—what's his name?"

"What's he got to do with this?"

"Just tell me, will you?"

"Ches, short for Chester."

"He's not actually your son, is he?"

Wait a minute, I wanted to say, but she saw from my face that she'd hit home. How could she have known that?

"He's Mantilini's," she said, looking me right in the eye. "Ches, short for Chester, is another of Paul Mantilini's bastards."

My hand flew out and slapped her. I couldn't stop myself. I didn't want to.

"Let's go ask your wife," she said, her cheek slowly reddening with the print of my fingers. "Let's go do it now."

"You're sick," I said, although I was the one with the feeling of something sour starting to curdle in my stomach.

"You wanted to know how I knew about the Slominsky house? I went there with Mantilini."

This was news. Why had Mantilini never told me that he'd seen the house?

"And he knew about it because your wife told him, begged him to take a look at it."

"Say what you like. I don't believe a goddamned word."

"Or maybe you can put your hands over your ears. Become one of those people. The people we were talking about, the ones who think they can't get shit on their shoes because they've always got somebody to wipe it off. You want to hear the rest of this story or not?"

My throat had gone dry. My hands looked ghostly in the light from the dash. Outside, the wind had picked up and threw grit against the doors. In the fans of light made by the headlamps I saw Nick Mantilini's body, with one knee still drawn up, the way it had been when he died, pant's leg fluttering.

"This was before I met Wardell," she said, not waiting for a reply. "I was in Las Vegas with Paul and one afternoon a woman shows up. He didn't bother to introduce us. He let us look each other over, as if we were prize specimens in his zoo. Your wife didn't go for that. 'I'm Jackie Valentine,' she said, not like she expected me to bow or anything. Pretty nice, really. Paul asked if I'd mind giving the two of them a minute. 'Sure,' I said. And when they went into the bedroom I sneaked in the bathroom to listen. That was bad of me, wasn't it?"

I didn't answer. I was thinking of Jackie and Mantilini, and the way they always seemed awkward with each other, the way Jackie would pick up the phone and go tense if it was him on the other end of the line. This triggered other memories, of Mantilini looking at Ches, not wistfully, but maybe staring at him for a heartbeat too long. No, I said to myself, you're imagining this.

"She was after him to give you work. She said you were ambitious and eager and quite talented and she told him to go look at a house you'd built in the desert. Then the room went quiet. They were kissing. For about three seconds I was angry. She showed me that I was the latest in a long line. And I was okay with that, when I thought about it, because I didn't love him and he'd never pretended any different. Funny thing, she was jealous of me. Later on she asked me if Paul had bought me any fancy clothes yet. I said I'd never let him do that. She showed me the label on her coat. Givenchy, Paris. Like it made her better than me."

Yes, that sounds like Jackie, I thought.

"Then she said something. 'Enjoy it while you can, darling. And be careful—otherwise you'll find yourself with a baby you don't want.'"

She did Jackie perfectly. I heard in her imitation my wife's offhand, witty voice, a mixture of the competitive and the coolly cynical.

"Paul heard what she said and he looked at her. It was the way he looked at her that told me what was going on. A quick, sharp look, like he was warning her, like this was a tender area for him. And he's not an easy guy to hurt, as I've found out. That's when I thought—she's talking about her own baby, *his* baby."

Her cool eyes never left my face; she watched to see how I took this, knifing me as surely as she had Paul Mantilini. Playing me, yet again. She'd killed a man only a few minutes before, and yet she could still do this. In her drive for revenge she was implacable. At the same time, I didn't doubt her. Feeling like I'd been kicked in the gut, I believed.

Oh God.

What was it Jackie had said, back in 1946? This was on our third or fourth date—we hadn't even made love yet. We were sitting in front of the fire in the lounge at the Beverly Hills Hotel, a storm going like mad outside, rain thundering against the pink stucco walls and hammering off the marble slabs of the patio. With a mink stole around her pale, freckled shoulders, she'd leaned forward for me to light her cigarette. Her exquisite perfume smelled to me of money, of class, of my future.

I'd had no idea how right I was.

"I'm going to have a baby," she said. "I don't know who the father is. And I don't care. Do you?"

I knew, by then, that she was Catholic, Irish-Catholic by heritage; abortion, therefore, was out of the question.

"Does that bother you, darling?"

I smiled, the smooth Maurice Valentine smile that in those days came more and more easily to my lips. I reached for the martini pitcher.

"Not a bit."

"Good," she said. "Shall we get a room?"

No mention of Mantilini, of course, then or after, no hint that she'd known him previously when I met him at last. The assumption was that it was me who introduced her to him. Proudly. As in: "Here's the guy I told you about, sweetheart, the guy I'm building the hotel for." They'd played it beautifully, looking each other over as if for the first time. He: calm and affable in his negligent, magisterial manner. She: pleased but grand, the daughter of power and the wife of the coming man, eager to please and assist her husband whenever and by whatever means.

That ridiculous game Mantilini played all those years, never quite refusing to let me know how he'd heard of my architecture, but never telling me, either. I'd put that down to him being a nut for control.

I'd fallen for it utterly.

Blindly.

Beth was still studying me, not gloating, perhaps even with sympathy, knowing that she'd exploded everything I knew.

47

SEPTEMBER 14, 1956 / THE DESERT—1:00 A.M.

$\mathcal{I}$ found a motel outside Beatty. The red neon sign had most of the letters missing. The letters B and N fizzed in the darkness above the manager's office. Beth waited in the car while I checked in and collected the key. Our room was on the ground floor, beyond a kidney-shaped swimming pool into which the wind had pitched various items of garden furniture. Two tables and several chairs were down there, wavering in the misty green of the underwater lights.

I'd taken Nick's pistol from Beth, saying that from now on we did things my way. Her fever was high and she was in no position to protest. In the bathroom I turned on the shower and tested the water until it was warm. I helped her undress and got her under the spray before phoning a doctor—a number I'd gotten at the reception desk. The guy was touchy, not thrilled about being disturbed so late at night, but he agreed to come.

Beth emerged from the bathroom wearing a white cotton robe that flopped around her ankles. She was rubbing at the back of her head and I saw silver strands sticking to the rough fabric of the towel and falling onto the shag carpet like filaments.

I'd turned back the covers on the bed and I was about to tell her to climb in but she started up again, replaying the conversation we'd had in the car: "So you'll do it?"

"Go to hell," I said.

"But you'll do it?"

"I said I'd do it. Now leave me alone."

She was standing in front of a tall closet. The furnishings and de-sign of the room were almost completely anonymous: a couple of chairs, a queen-size bed with a floral cover, a lamp on a table—late period *noth-ing*. The privacy, the purity of her martyrdom had been transformed by her own wiles and drive; the picture was different, and she had trouble accepting it.

"I'll come with you."

"No, you won't. You're sick. And they wouldn't let you beyond the door."

Her pale green eyes assessed me. Was I to be trusted? Did I have the resolve?

As for myself, I thought I'd recovered from the initial shock. Part of the attraction of hot revenge, I told myself, was the position of cold rec-titude from which you launched it. The epigram, of course, was merely a Band-Aid on a wound that was still raw and bleeding. I was devastated. I'd known all along that my marriage wasn't a love match, that it was a mutual understanding from which unexpected and considerable gifts had sprung. I'd known that Ches wasn't mine, that I'd entered into a deal. But that deal had become a part of my scheme of things—I loved the kid—and I'd never dreamed of this. My whole life was a lie.

"He made you his stooge," Beth said, watching me from where she stood at the closet.

I'd been the blind actor in a play that Mantilini had devised and was continuing to plot. Jackie and Joe Nelson were in it, too, but he was the impresario, the puppet-master. All these years I'd been proud of what I'd become, seeing myself as the architect, if not exactly the hero, of my own story. I told myself that I'd cheated my original destiny and conjured up another. What a clown.

"He set you up."

I hefted the weighty Colt from my pocket. I checked the magazine, thumbed off the safety, racked the receiver.

"You know how to handle that thing?"

"Haven't held one since I left the Air Force," I said, sighting down the barrel toward the lamp on the table. Pow! The hopes, the achievements of the last ten years had vanished. Maurice Valentine had been blown away like cardboard on a windy night. Maurizio Viglioni, surveying the void, allowed it to be filled with anger. A future removed, a past obliterated, was hatred and purpose given.

I checked the magazine again. "I guess some things you don't forget."

"I wrecked your life, didn't I?"

I looked into her eyes. Did I see shame, sympathy, sorrow? Maybe. But matter-of-factness, too. This, her look seemed to say, is what happens: people are drawn, oblivious, into the machinery of other people's worlds and plans, there to be destroyed. She knew because it had happened to her, too. The wisdom wasn't world-weary so much as world-terrorized.

I couldn't go along with the proposition entirely. I wanted to stand up for my own part in my downfall. I'd gulled myself, been the victim of my vanity and ambition as much as her will.

But I did say to her: "You use people. You're good at it."

"I wasn't always this way," she said, averting her eyes. "The wonder girl, that's what Wardell called me. The girl who was going to do great things. Everybody thought so." Her voice dwindled, falling away. "I remember when I was a kid. I walked through a cemetery one time. I said to myself, 'I'll never end up here. I'm going to *do* something.' I wanted so much to be special."

I crossed that dingy little room and held her. Beneath the cotton robe her shoulders were trembling. Her hair was damp and smelled of cheap shampoo. Patches of her scalp were almost bald, and scores of little red pimples stood out.

There's no way to blow on someone and make them well; but that's what I wanted to do.

"Tell me about Wardell," I asked, for the second time that night. "What was he like?"

This time she spoke. "He was tall," he said.

"That's it? That's the best you can come up with?"

She laughed, sniffing back her tears. "He was tall and he was skinny and we had trouble getting pants to fit him. He had a temper. He could sulk and go all day without talking. He loved to dance, but, boy, it was tough to get him to do it. 'Hell, no, I ain't dancin'. This is one nigger don't dance for nobody.' Then he'd lift me in his arms and sweep me onto the floor. His dad had been in the Marine Corps, a violent guy. But Wardell was so gentle. One time he reached up and caught a butterfly without hurting it. He gave it to me. Its wings quivered in my hand."

"You're young," I said. "There's plenty of time. You can make a life."

"Why would I want to?"

Someone was knocking on the door. "I'll get that," I said, and let in the doctor, a tall guy with dark, reddish hair. He entered, swinging his black leather bag and stooping to disguise his height. He was young, in his late twenties, I'd say, and alert, more cheerful than he'd been on the phone. By the time I shut the door he'd already gotten Beth sitting on the bed and he was looming over her like a protective bird. The light from the lamp picked out the fiery color of his hair. With a snap he opened his bag, took her pulse, checked her blood pressure, slid a thermometer between her lips, and clucked disapprovingly.

"You've been feeling tired, lethargic?" His voice was calm, kindly, confident, independent, a voice of the West, of the frontier not long forgotten.

"Sometimes," Beth said.

"Vomiting?"

"A little."

"But you *have* been eating?"

"A friend made sure I did," she said, and I guessed she meant Freddy Greene. It was clear that she hated to assume the role of patient. She tried to stand up but the doctor gently made her sit.

"Let me take a guess," he said. "At dawn, a little over a week ago, you were in Nevada and you were outside. Driving a car, maybe."

Her look was suspicious. "How could you know that?

"What you've got is what we call around here the 'ghost disease,' " he said. "It comes, it goes, and nobody wants to admit that anybody might have it. Especially the guys in the government—they *very much* don't want to have to admit it."

She said she didn't follow.

"You're suffering from radiation sickness," he said. "It killed people in Hiroshima. Now it's killing them in Nevada. If we'd looked at your bones the day after the blast we'd probably have been able to light up a room with them."

"You're telling me I'm going to die?"

Her face was neutral, the delivery of her question direct and unfazed. I couldn't tell whether she was delighted or horrified.

"Oh, gee, I hope it won't come to that," he said. His smile was undaunted. "Was the car a ragtop?"

A nod from Beth.

"Up or down?"

"Up."

"Good girl!" he said with such enthusiasm that she smiled, too. "From my experience I'd say this'll pass." Touching the side of her head, he inspected the two of three strands of hair that came away in his fingers. "We'll see, won't we?"

We were more naïve and trusting about what we were told in those days, especially what we were told about the nuclear world, and the government wasn't in the habit of advertising what happened if the wind blew the wrong way when one of those explosions rocked the desert. And sometimes the wind did blow the wrong way. On escaping from the El Sheik, the morning she shot me, she'd headed north on I-15 toward St. George, driving beneath a dark and glowering sky, until she noticed that something was falling on the windshield. Only it wasn't raining. When she turned on the wipers they swept smeary semicircles, and she remembered something that one of Wardell's friends had told her, about black prisoners being bussed up from one of the southern states and chained to cages within the test zone so that the effects of a blast on human beings could be examined. It was another crazy story, to be filed with those suggesting that test-site victims, and aliens who survived UFO crashes, were being kept in federal-built caves in Nevada. But, then, Beth knew that some very weird things were indeed going on. Hadn't I shown her the model streets I designed so that they could be destroyed? Hadn't I told her about the herds of pigs that were dressed in military uniforms and released within the drop zone? So, when making her escape, and seeing the black rain settling against the windshield of the Porsche, she decided she'd best turn around, even if it meant going back to Las Vegas. It was almost as if the bomb was sending her back, giving her a message: *Do your job, Beth, it's not finished yet.* Therefore she came up with the next phase of her plan. She'd dump the Porsche in Lake Mead, contact Freddy, and plot some new way to kill Mantilini.

"Are you her husband?" the doctor said, taking me aside.

"No."

"Her father?"

I let that one pass. "Will she be okay?"

"She needs to rest. To eat. But she should be okay. For now."

He was a soothing, attractive presence, and I asked if he'd mind sitting with her for a few hours. "I have to go somewhere," I said.

"Now? But it's the middle of the night."

I sensed his disapproval, but what could I do? I had things to take care of before I headed back to Vegas and looked for Mantilini. And it would've taken a book to explain who Beth and I were and how we'd got there. I let him live with his presumption that I was selfish and had wronged her or let her down in some final way.

"I'd be grateful," I said. "You'll be well compensated for your trouble."

Then I turned to Beth, the Colt heavy in my pocket, sitting beside her on the bed. "The doc's looking after you," I said. "I'll be back as soon as I can."

She said nothing.

"Goodbye, then," I said.

She called me back from the door.

"What?"

If I was looking for some further expression of softness, of caring, of tender feeling, I'd dialed the wrong number. Her eyes were cool again, her face flinty, still eager for victory and wild justice. And in that moment, sick though she was, she was more commanding than ever.

"Do this right," she said.

48

The car was where I'd left it, standing in the motel forecourt. Climbing in, I turned the key in the ignition, and as the motor purred to life, a thought occurred to me. So instead of heading back to the El Sheik at once, I swung the Cadillac the other way, back toward where Nick's body lay in the desert. I was resolute. I would return to Las Vegas and kill Paul Mantilini. But there was something else I had to do first.

49

I stepped out of the elevator into the Thousand Suns Lounge, my plan clear in mind. I'd tell Mantilini that I needed him urgently, that Beth was downstairs and refusing to come up, that she was ready to make peace, that she, like him, wanted this to be over. I figured I'd have his attention. The idea was to kill him in the elevator. I'd never tried to shoot anybody up close, but at that moment my veins ran with a cold and furious anger. I owed it to Beth, and to the ten years of my life in which I'd been living Mantilini's fiction. I planned to get away with it, too, to take back control of my family, and my life. I was going to tell the world that Nick had done it, had killed his own father and then vanished into the night. The deed would be done with his gun, after all.

It went haywire from the start. First, I'd forgotten that the lounge would be so crowded. It was bedlam, with maybe three hundred people jammed between the tables and more up on the balcony, all of them abuzz with excitement about the coming blast, most of them milling between me and where I spotted Mantilini, standing on the far side of the room, in front of the wall-length window, in his tuxedo, chatting with a woman, his gray hair coiffed, his eyes steely, the color returned to his cheeks, the only sign of anything untoward being the bandaged hand that hung at his side.

"Darling, where have you *been?*" said Jackie, rushing to my side, looping her arm through mine.

You lying *bitch*, I thought. She'd never looked lovelier, in a black dress that showed her freckled shoulders. Her eyes shone like diamonds.

"I've been worried sick," she said. "You've heard the news, of course."

"News? No, I don't believe so."

"Boss Booth croaked," Joe Nelson said, appearing at my other side. His snaggletoothed smile was gleeful, merciless. "The old fucker died. In the arms of a whore—which seems only appropriate, wouldn't you agree?"

Joe's stiff, gingery hair crackled with static as he ran a hand over it.

"It's true, darling," Jackie said. "Six weeks from now you'll be in the Senate. Maurice Valentine—the junior senator from Nevada. My husband."

"I'll say this—the timing couldn't have been better," Joe said. He swilled back the rest of his martini. I'd rarely seen him drink, so I knew this must be big. In his excitement I thought he was going to chew the glass. "Right after he gave you that endorsement. It's perfect! I've already spoken to everybody. You'll step in and accept the nomination. It's on a plate, Maurice."

"No more plotting, darling. No more scheming," Jackie said. "We're *there*."

I wanted to point out that there was always the election, but I knew Joe would say that Mantilini was going to take care of that. And now I was going to take care of him. For a moment I looked into Jackie's face.

"What?" she said. "What, darling?"

I bit back my words. I'd talk to her later about Ches. "I'm looking for Paul," I said, and started fighting my way across the room. By the time I got over to the window my back was sore from being stroked and thumped. People were already looking at me in a different way. It would be only the very best champagne from now on.

Mantilini turned to greet me with a smile. "The old Moulin burned to the ground." His voice purred like the engine in Nick's Cadillac; it was steady and soft. "I was afraid you might have gone up with it."

At the very moment I'd been compelled to examine life's seriousness it seemed that I was being forced to play in a farce. But I planned to change that.

"That was a crazy scene," he said. "I sent Nick to get you."

What's this? I thought. *You* sent Nick?

"I didn't want you being hurt, tonight of all nights. I didn't figure you'd start playing with matches," he said. "Where is Nick, by the way? He come with you?"

"I don't know where he is."

Mantilini frowned. "I need to talk to him. I spoke to an old friend of mine a couple of hours ago. Fellow named Sandy Berman, he just got out of San Quentin. Turns out Nick's been holding out on me. My own son—can you believe it?"

His voice was without rancor, but I read something in Mantilini's eyes, a sadness, a defiance, a denial, a hint of some guilt he would never express.

"I need to talk to him, straighten a few things out," he continued. "Nickie's a good boy."

For a moment there was anguish in his tone, and I gathered the truth—which, it seemed, he had only just learned himself. "It was Nick, wasn't it?" I felt dizzy, a little faint. "Nick was the one. He killed Wardell and raped Beth."

Mantilini's look was sharp, bad-tempered. "What's it to you?"

"It's something, Paul. It's *something* to me. Answer the question. Was it Nick, or was it you?"

"People blame me for plenty, and I can take it. Anyway, it's all done now."

All done now? Oh *fuck*, I thought. Suddenly I was back in the nose of the B-17 and shards of glass were flying around. I was trying to make sense of it all. Nick had been planning to kill her once we got out there in the desert. The business about the cabin, the rescue—that was a blind. I wondered what his plans for me had been? Probably he thought I'd go along with it. I was his father's man, wasn't I? And Beth had gotten what she wanted without even realizing. What is it they say about revenge? It's the arrow that flies in the dark and tends to hit the wrong target. She'd hit the right one and not been aware. She'd looked into his eyes, gloating, while Wardell's killer squirmed in the sand. She'd killed Paul

Mantilini's son and I'd witnessed it. This, I knew, Paul would never forgive.

"Where is she, anyway?"

My throat was dry. I felt the sweat trickle down the inside of my palms. At the moment Mantilini suspected nothing but he was looking deep into my eyes, and that could change any second. I had to come up with a story, quick, and it better hold water.

"I don't know," I said. "The place was going up like a torch when Nick showed up. He got us out of there."

"Who started the fire?"

I shook my head. It had been Nick, obviously. "No idea. Nick dropped us at the Desert Inn. She refused to come to the El Sheik. She ran out on me as soon as Nick left."

"She's got a habit of doing that, doesn't she?"

"I tried to find her. No luck. She's looking for you, probably. Maybe she'll show up in a minute or two with a gun again. What can I tell you? She's nuts."

Was he buying this?

"But I guess she has a reason," I said.

"She got in the way and I'm sorry," he said, looking out the window with his good eye, the dead one staring at me as if it could see into my soul. "But it's like I said—this has to be over."

Albert Kluphager, the pit boss, was standing on a chair and calling for quiet. That metal box, the Scintillator, dangled from his neck, and his terrible wig was on straight for once. "One minute to go, folks," he said, looking toward Mantilini, expecting the usual speech, but this time Paul was unforthcoming. He shook his head, no. It was left to Kluphager to lead the way, to crack a joke and tell people to help them-selves to dark glasses from the trays at the bar.

"Or turn your head away. I hear it's gonna be a big one, the biggest yet. And we don't want to see anybody with their eyes on their cheeks," Kluphager said.

The familiar atmosphere of tense, excited expectation descended upon the room. People donned the dark glasses, or turned their backs, whispering, gulping their drinks. The pianist played a trilling chord and then slammed shut his instrument. In the silence a pair of dice banged against the side of a craps layout.

"Nine . . . eight . . . seven," said Kluphager, feeling for his wig.

Mantilini wasn't bothering with dark glasses. He wasn't looking at the window. He was studying me, searching me, reading me.

"Four . . . three . . ."

Kluphager's timing was on the money. With the conclusion of his countdown—a beat after his calling out "ZERO!"—a piercing flash transformed the dawn. Beside me, for a moment, Mantilini became a skeleton, aglow with nuclear light. Then I watched his body come back, in negative at first, and then gradually reassuming the form of solid flesh. Outside, the mushroom was rising slowly from the desert floor, possessed of an animal vitality, writhing and raging, emitting fierce flashes of red, purple, green, and lapis lazuli. It loomed over the desert like a predator.

I thought of the last time I'd been standing here. I'd gloated, reveling in the manic terror, the weird thrill of liberation that the threat of nuclear extinction had released. It had seemed to give me license to do anything. That had been moments before Beth shot me and turned my life inside out. Everything had changed, and this latest A-bomb seemed like a part of the trap that was closing around my future.

"Maurice, I'm going to ask you one more time," Mantilini said. "Do you know where Nick is?"

I said nothing, knowing that Nick was dust, vaporized where I'd dumped him, in Survival Town. A perfect body-disposal plan, courtesy of the AEC and the U.S. government. All that was left of Nick was a shadow. No evidence of him would ever be found. He'd fall as rain someplace.

I had to live with this secret forever, otherwise Beth's life wasn't worth a dime. I didn't much care about myself. Mantilini wanted me in the Senate? So be it. And Beth, too, would vanish, disappear into another life. That would be *my* revenge.

What was it the book in Freddy Greene's room had said? Learn how the game operates, learn how *you* operate. The game was cruel, but I was catching on.

Paul's instincts were sharp. He knew something was up. He stood close to me, sniffing me almost, concentration emblazoned on that hard face of his. But he had me figured as a particular kind of guy. That was to my advantage.

"I heard about Boss Booth. Useful for us," I said.

"Yeah, that worked out," Mantilini agreed.

"Very convenient, the Boss dying like that."

"Yeah, you could say that," he said, not trying to stop the smile that played about his lips. "Convenient. A good word. You have a way with words, Maurice."

That part of his evening had been a triumph. The carefully orchestrated death of Senator Walton C. "Boss" Booth, expired in the arms of a high-class Nevada hooker—and speeded up the stairway to heaven (I have no doubt) by a pillow held over his face at Mantilini's bidding—meant that in less than two months' time, Maurice Valentine, the rubber-stamp boy, would be on his way to Washington. Mantilini could start drawing up plans for his new city in the desert. This was power at work. But some part of power is always blind, and only now was Paul beginning to sense that, somehow, even he was caught in the machine. He wasn't just running the juggernaut; he, too, had become its victim. He'd known sorrow in his life, and there would be more.

"You really don't know where Nick is?" he said.

The pistol dragged in my pocket. I'd have to get rid of that thing fast.

"Paul," I said, "I'm tired and I don't have a clue."

Outside, the sky continued to boil. The aftershock hit, belting the El Sheik, but once again the hotel swayed serenely on its foundations, per the design, and stood firm.

50

I met Beth Dyer one more time. This was weeks later, in Malibu, on another of those fiercely hot days when the devil's wind blew, turning the surf back on itself, and the sunlight had a cruel glitter. Being outside in that weather was like punishment, but I'd agreed to take the boys diving. They'd been after me about it ever since an Air Force B-29, a Superfortress, en route from Hawaii, pancaked a hundred yards off Point Dume and sank in only thirty feet of water.

"Did people die? Will there be monsters?" Bobby said, looking at me from beneath his mop of unwashed blond hair. We stood on the jetty amid all our gear, suiting up, and Bobby was joking about monsters because he feared there might actually *be* monsters. It was his way of protecting himself.

"Don't be stupid, Bob," said Ches, waiting patiently while I checked the tanks. "Dad wouldn't be taking us out to the wreck if anybody had died on it. Would you, Dad?"

"That's right," I said. I didn't tell them that I'd swum out to the wreck once already, to check that it was safe. They wanted the experience to seem freshly minted.

"Squid. Octopus. Eels," Bobby said, springing up and down, waving his arms with antic glee. He mimed the attack of a conger, jaws gaping. "Sharks. Two-thousand-pound great whites. Creatures of the deep."

"*Dad*," Ches said, slipping his tanks over his shoulders, moving with the poised solemnity of the big man he'd probably become, exasperated by his brother, appealing to the court of last resort: me.

"Okay, Bobby, calm down. Let's concentrate on what we're doing. This could be dangerous."

Bobby liked the sound of that. He cocked an eyebrow, looking just like his mother.

"We snorkel out to the buoy. Then we start using the tanks. A line goes down from the buoy to the airplane. We take hold of that line and follow it down. We stay close. We never lose sight of each other. What do we do?"

"We stay close. We never lose sight of each other," said Ches. I'd been quietly studying him for anything he might have inherited from Mantilini. I'd found little: the squarish shape of his head, the sturdy chin, and maybe this—the fact that he was so clear and decided about everything. For sure, he hadn't inherited *that* from me.

"Bobby?" I said.

"I got it," he said, a tough little guy who would rather die than admit he was afraid or sad. I touched his head.

"I need to know where you are every second."

We snorkeled through cool water and a gentle swell. A pelican, long-beaked and ungainly, observed our approach and took flight from the buoy, dipping its wings and skimming between the waves. Grasping the line that was hooked to the buoy, I signaled to Ches and Bobby to start using their tanks, and we went down.

The airplane looked long and gleaming as a skyscraper, lying flat on the bottom. Wrecks get covered in weeds and shells pretty fast, but this hadn't happened yet. There was only a fuzz of moss that didn't hide the bright silver paint. Finning down past the mighty cliff face of the tail, we circled the B-29 twice, stopping in front of the turrets, the mascot painted on the nose—a sultry brunette in a bikini—and the seat where the bombardier had hunkered, surrounded by Perspex, exposed yet protected, waiting for his world to be shattered. A sound, an insect humming, a crackling, eating sound, seemed to emanate from inside the plane, and I wondered if some part of the electrics hadn't shut down yet.

This seemed unlikely. So maybe the noise came from unsalvaged cargo, or was a device placed by the Coast Guard to warn away sharks. Either way, it was weird, like being too close to a power cable, to a mindless energy that could surprise you.

The wreck, like all wrecks, spooked as well as thrilled me. A wreck, any wreck, is a disappointed hope, a venture that failed. Perhaps it's also what we secretly want to happen. That's the scary part. And it can happen, at any moment. Everything's so fragile.

I was relieved, I guess, when we got back to the jetty. The adventure had gone well—that is to say, safely—and the boys bubbled with excitment. They couldn't wait to tell their mother about it. I had a towel in my hand and the wet suit off my shoulders when I saw her, not Jackie, but a slender woman with a lean face, standing at the end of the jetty. She wore jeans and a blue UCLA sweatshirt that was faded. Some of her hair had grown in again and it was dyed black now. But it was her. Beth Dyer.

"Wait here," I said to the boys. "I'll be right back."

I walked toward her, feeling an almost dreamy calm.

"I know I shouldn't be doing this," she said. "But I had to see you."

After my confrontation with Mantilini at the El Sheik I'd gone to a pay phone and called the motel where she was holed up with the doctor. At first she thought I was trying to trick her. She yelled into the phone. I was gutless, worthless, a prick, a weasel, a coward, a traitor, she said. She called me all the names under the sun before I managed to convince her of the truth. "It was Nick?" she said. "And I didn't even know?" She sounded flat, cheated. "You mean it's finished?" I said it was very far from finished if Mantilini got to the bottom of what had happened. She had to disappear, back into her Crescent City life, maybe. Somewhere, anyway, but somewhere I didn't know about. That way I wouldn't be able to tell Mantilini when he put the pressure on.

And now here she was.

"Are you okay?" I asked.

"I'm not going to die anytime soon," she said. "That's what they tell me. But who knows?"

There was candor in those gray-green eyes, a reasonableness, an acceptance, as well as the usual courage. I wanted to ask if she was with somebody, but that couldn't be part of the deal. The less I knew the better.

"How do you feel?"

"Do I feel guilty, is that what you mean? Sure. A little. Guilt, but no remorse, I guess. You won your election," she said. "I read it in the paper."

"It was harder than I expected."

"You'll go to Washington?"

"That's what everybody wants. It's a part of this, isn't it? Besides, I'd like to surprise them. Maybe I won't be such a rubber stamp after all. They might get more than they bargained for."

She studied me. She was, all at once, concerned. "That could be dangerous."

"You've given me a taste for it."

I was being flip, acting cool, but in truth she'd changed me. It was as if, during those two weeks in September, I'd gone over my life with an eraser. Now, when I started filling in the blanks, the design would be different. I'd found something. I'd been given an education.

She asked about Mantilini. Did he suspect?

"Sure," I said. He'd had the cops out, and his own people, searching, for weeks. They were still searching. But they kept coming back with the same report: Nick had vanished; no trace of him was to be found. I'm sure a part of Mantilini was frantic. But I'd seen no sign of that. His iron self-control was unshakable. Casually, or so it seemed—in other words, not casually at all—he'd asked me a few times to go over again what happened that night when Nick came to find Beth and me at the Gai-Moulin. I'd stuck to my original story. It wasn't Mantilini's nature to interrogate; it was his nature to act. He went on watching me, studying me, and one day I'd be called to answer. But for the moment he was in the dark and I was important to him. He needed me. Perhaps he recognized that blunt justice had been done, an eye for an eye, and so forth, though I doubted it. Nick had been his son, and like most powerful men Mantilini took a utilitarian approach to scriptural and moral edicts. He liked them when they were clubs to beat the other guy with.

"If it ever comes to it, I'll tell him I killed Nick, by accident, or in self-defense, and then panicked and got rid of the body," I said.

"He won't buy it."

"Maybe not."

"So why do it?"

"It's a commitment I've made."

She took my hand, grabbing my fingers so fiercely I thought they'd break in half like twigs; I shivered, but in an almost voluptuous way. It's the sun, I said to myself, warming my skin after the water. But I knew that wasn't it. Something shifted inside me, like tumblers clicking, or the final piece of a design falling into place, or a fever announcing itself. I was hopelessly in love with her.

Holding my hand, she studied me, without any special tenderness, or suggestion of romantic surrender. We know each other, you and I, she seemed to say, we found something at the center of ourselves together. "I'm going to Europe," she said. "I wanted to say goodbye."

There it is, I thought, some sort of an ending. I felt a wave of sickness, of sadness, though I knew I couldn't go anyplace with her, or with what I felt. I couldn't even tell her about it. I couldn't say to her—to hell with everything, let's run away to Mexico and wait until he sends someone for us. Because I wanted her to live, to have a second chance.

"Do you need money?"

"That's not why I'm here," she said, stern and glowering for a moment. But then she smiled, with a hint of her wit, her impudence. "Those your kids?" She looked over my shoulder down the jetty, where Bobby was slapping at Ches with a rubber fin. "They look like a handful. Which is Ches?"

"The tall one not losing his temper."

"Beautiful kids," she said, and I remembered that she'd never have children of her own. They'd never heal, some of her wounds, and new ones had been added. But at least she was no longer a prisoner of her past, not in the same way. "Did you say anything to your wife?"

"I told her that I knew. And that Ches is *my* son, always has been, always will be. I told her to tell Mantilini if she wanted."

"How did she take it?"

"Oh, she was surprised. It *penetrated*. She raised her eyebrow like I'd won a hand at cards," I said. "Where in Europe?"

"I'm not sure. Italy, maybe."

"You'll like it."

Her smile was bright. "You think so?"

Standing on tiptoe, she brushed her lips against my cheek. She whispered something, a few words, but a sixteen-wheeler thundered by on Coast Highway and I couldn't make them out. Did she say: *I love you, too*? I sincerely doubt that, but what are dreams for?

Her fingers left mine and she walked at a brisk clip across the sand toward the road, alert and agile, head down, shoulders hunched a little, as if pushing against a wind she was determined to beat. Beautiful woman, you'd say, if you saw her, unusual woman, a woman to die for.

She'd dropped something, I saw, a piece of folded notepaper. I called out after her, "Hey, you lost this!"

It was no use: she was gone, so I opened the notepaper. It had nothing on it. I was looking at a blank.

"Who was that?" said Ches.

"Nobody," I said. "She was looking for the way to Santa Barbara. But she seemed to know where she was going."

I never saw her again.

ACKNOWLEDGMENTS

*A*ndy Dowdy, owner of Other Times Books in L.A., first told me about the tenor sax player Wardell Gray, whose death suggested the mystery at the heart of this book. Gray's recordings, and there aren't many, were located for me by Digelius, a great jazz shop located in Helsinki. Where else? The reporting of the *Las Vegas Sun,* the *Las Vegas Review-Journal,* and *The New Yorker* provided invaluable detail and background for a wild period in the history of America's most bizarre city. The writings of David Thomson on Nevada and on film were inspiring, likewise those on film noir by my old friend Guillermo Cabrera Infante. Behind all this, somewhere, is the thrill I felt as a teenager, listening to Charlie Parker records and reading Ross Russell's *Bird Lives!* American innocence, it seems, always burns brightest before it is destroyed. Many thanks to all at HarperCollins, and especially to Dan Conaway, who is not only the most talented editor of fiction it's my privilege to know and work with—but who also knows when to apply a judicious kick in the seat of the pants when needed. Thanks, Dan, yet again. You're the best.